Praise for

With or Without You

"Matthews is a master of compelling stories about women and men at crossroads in their lives, and her latest is a winner in every way."
—*Booklist*

"A lover's infidelity prompts a homebody toward big adventures and new priorities in Brit Matthews's entertaining romantic comedy. Matthews throws a few wrenches into Lyssa's voyage of self-(re)-discovery, but never leaves any doubt that happiness is around the bend."
—*Publishers Weekly*

"Through her journey, she finally is at peace with herself. Told in the author's fun, sharp style (especially the exhilarating sections in Nepal), *With or Without You* is a terrific summer read that will have you smiling while speed-dialing your travel agent."
—*Bookreporter.com*

"Matthews is one of the few writers who can rival Marian Keyes' gift for telling heart-warming tales with buckets of charm and laughs—this is definitely one of the summer's must-reads."
—*Glasgow Daily Record*

"Carole Matthews is adept at putting a fresh spin on each and every one of her chick lit tales... Pick up *With or Without You* today, and see why Carole Matthews is blazing her way to the bestseller lists!"
—*Romance Reviews Today*

Praise for

CAROLE MATTHEWS

"A big five points for humor."
—Kelly Ripa, *Live with Regis and Kelly*

"She entertains her readers with serendipitous trysts and near misses."
—*Publishers Weekly*

"British author Matthews...will charm Bridget Jones fans on both sides of the Atlantic."
—*Library Journal*

"A best-selling romp with a great sense of fun."
—*Kirkus Reviews*

"Her humorous storytelling resurrects the power of romance to conquer all."
—*Booklist*

CAROLE MATTHEWS

With or Without You

If you purchased this book without a cover you should be aware that this book is stolen property. It was reported as "unsold and destroyed" to the publisher, and neither the author nor the publisher has received any payment for this "stripped book."

WITH OR WITHOUT YOU

A Red Dress Ink novel

ISBN-13: 978-0-373-89593-9
ISBN-10: 0-373-89593-3

© 2004 by Carole Matthews

First U.S. edition August 2005

All rights reserved. The reproduction, transmission or utilization of this work in whole or in part in any form by any electronic, mechanical or other means, now known or hereafter invented, including xerography, photocopying and recording, or in any information storage or retrieval system, is forbidden without written permission. For permission please contact Red Dress Ink, Editorial Office, 225 Duncan Mill Road, Don Mills, Ontario, Canada M3B 3K9.

All characters in this book have no existence outside the imagination of the author and have no relation whatsoever to anyone bearing the same name or names. They are not even distantly inspired by any individual known or unknown to the author, and all incidents are pure invention. Any resemblance to actual persons, living or dead, is entirely coincidental.

® and TM are trademarks. Trademarks indicated with ® are registered in the United States Patent and Trademark Office, the Canadian Trade Marks Office and/or other countries.

www.RedDressInk.com

Printed in U.S.A.

To everyone who made my visit
to Nepal so memorable:

The beautiful, humble people of Nepal.
Our charming guide Sanjiv Thakuri and his team of
Sherpas—Captain Dendi, Tek, Dorge, Jangbu,
Nawang (the cross dresser) and
Mr. Bom the chief cook.

Plus all the wonderful porters
who made our lives so easy.

To my easy-going travelling companions, especially
Jacqueline, Rosemary, Gail and the white-water rafting
team, Peter and Val, Peter II and Kev's Dad, John.

And to Lovely Kev for carrying my rucksack
and letting me have most of the sleeping bag.

Namaste!

Chapter One

'This isn't working, is it?'

For one mad moment I thought Jake was talking about the toaster. It had been on the blink for a while. But then so had we.

Two perfect golden-brown slices of wholemeal toast pop up with a cheerful ping and my heart sags a little.

I glance up from my own bowl of dubiously named 'luxury' muesli and try to look as if every dry, claggy, *unluxurious* spoonful isn't choking me.

Jake grabs his toast, wincing as it burns his fingers. He tosses it onto a plate before he returns my gaze. 'You know what I'm talking about, Lyssa.'

Yes. I do. Our fourth and most gruelling attempt at IVF has just ended in a watery red blob in the toilet bowl and misery. My misery. Our misery. I give up with my spoon. 'Of course I do.' I'm trying not to cry and I guess I should go over to comfort him, but I haven't got enough emotional energy for myself let alone any to spare. I force a rigid smile. 'But we can try again.'

Jake hasn't made any attempt to butter his toast and it must be getting cold. In a pan on the cooker, two eggs are knocking around in our only All-Clad pan, the bubbling water tossing them to and fro. My boyfriend, or whatever we're supposed to call them these days, sounds irritable. 'Not the IVF.'

I mentally trawl through a list of all our other domestic appliances that might be dodgy.

'Us,' he says starkly. 'Us. *We're* not working.'

I nearly laugh. I was just wondering if he meant the fridge—which frosts up far too quickly for my liking. I'm sure it never used to—but then you really never pay that much attention to your fridge, do you? Or your partner in life, it seems. And then I realise that Jake is deadly serious. The skin round his eyes is more drawn than I've ever seen it before and his mouth is pulled down at the corners.

'It's a difficult time for us,' I say calmly when I really want to scream, You're not the one that's bleeding here, Jake! Instead, I turn to him and quietly say, 'All couples have them. We'll get through it.'

Jake comes and sits down. He takes my hand and turns it over, examining it as if he's never seen it before. 'And what if I don't want to get through it? What if I've suddenly woken up to the fact that there's more to life than getting through it?'

I open my mouth to answer with some platitude about how life can't always be a bed of roses, but he rushes on before I can speak. 'What if I don't want a baby? What if I don't want to spend any more time alone in cold cubicles with crumpled wank mags?'

My eyes widen. I thought that was the bit he liked best. Sometimes he specifically chose his own porny material to take with him.

'What if I don't want our sex life littered with charts and thermometers and injections?'

'I...'

'When did we last go wild and have a purely recreational shag?'

'I...'

'When?' he says with the triumphant note of the just in his voice.

'What are you saying? I don't mark notches on the headboard, like some old Lothario.' I do, however, mark notches on my heart after every failed coupling. Failed in the sense that it didn't produce a pink, bouncing baby at the end of it. 'I thought you enjoyed our sex life.'

'Then you are truly delusional,' Jake says.

I'm stunned. I had hoped that in the face of another disappointment, another thwarted dream, he'd take me in his arms, shush my tears—even though that isn't politically correct these days—and tell me that it would all be fine, we would find another wad of our hard-earned cash to blow on hormones for Jake to inject into my bum, and that next time Sammy Sperm would get it together with Esme Egg and we would no longer be the complete failures we are with our inability to succeed in the most basic of human tasks.

How difficult can it be to make a baby? These days our teenagers are popping them out all the time. Britain has the highest rate of child mothers in Europe. Aren't a mobile phone and a baby at the top of the 'must have' list for every schoolgirl? Go anywhere near Miss Sixty in any high street, on any Saturday and it's like a teen mums' convention. Okay, so I'm a little past the acne stage, but at thirty-four it does seem a bit unfair that all my eggs, like the ones in Jake's unattended saucepan, appear to be turning hard-boiled.

'I need space,' Jake says into my self-pity.

'You're not an astronaut,' I say. 'You don't need space.'

Jake looks unconvinced, whereas I remain resolute. Only astronauts and Sigourney Weaver need space to function in. The rest of mankind have to operate in confined quarters—offices, homes, relationships—that's what it's all about. No man is an island. And no man whose sperm has been called 'sluggish' has a right to lay all this at my feet.

'I need time to myself,' he continues.

This is a man who every weekend plays some sort of sport—football and cricket in the appropriate seasons, golf and squash when he can fit them in. This is a man who I think has plenty of time to himself, and before we used to argue about our lack of babies, we used to argue about how much time he had to himself. I wonder why all this is going round in my head, but none of it is coming out of my mouth.

Jake takes a deep breath. He puts my hand down. Right into some milk I hadn't realised I'd spilled on the kitchen table. 'I think we should have a trial separation,' he says. 'For a few days. A few weeks.'

'Have you met someone else?'

'No.' He looks at me as if I'm insane to even entertain the thought. 'This isn't about anyone else. It's about me—and you. And your obsession.'

'Wanting a baby is not an obsession. It's a…'

Jake waits.

'…a preoccupation.' That sometimes borders on slightly obsessive. Very slightly. 'I just want a baby. Is that too much to ask?'

Jake stands up. Patently, it is. 'I've packed a few things. I'm going to Pip's place for a couple of days. I need to get my head round this. I need to decide what I want.'

'And what *I* want doesn't come into it anymore?'

Jake looks very tired of me. 'Suppose we can never have a baby, Lyssa? What then? How long would it be until you stopped hoping that one day modern science will no longer be baffled by our inability to conceive?'

'I don't know.' I shrug lightly. 'Three weeks? Four?' This fails to add levity to our desperate situation.

'I'll phone you tonight,' Jake says. 'To make sure you're all right.'

I won't be all right, I want to say. I'm not all right now. I may never be all right again. 'You can't just go.'

'I'll phone you.'

'Jake. Don't go. Not like this.' I can feel panic rising in me. Begging words are rushing up to my throat, but I won't let them out. I can't let them out. Why is he doing this? He can't be thinking straight. I'm the one who's supposed to have raging hormones and mood swings. He never behaves like this. We've been together for years. How many years? Four. That's twice my usual quota for long-term relationships. He is The One. My heart's desire. I thought I was his. We are joint owners of this rather nice terraced house in a rather desirable area of deepest, darkest St Albans, a pleasantly leafy city on the outskirts of London. Although we haven't actually tied the knot, we've discussed marriage on several occasions. Usually after a couple of bottles of vino blanco, admittedly. We're trying to have a baby together. You don't just leave someone at eight o'clock on a Friday morning before you go to work, do you? You wait until Friday night or the weekend or Christmas or their birthday—a catastrophic date they'll always remember. Friday morning is such an insignificant time to do something so momentous. He's nearly at the door. Anxiously, I cast a look at the bubbling pan. 'Your eggs. They're drying up.'

He looks as if he's about to say something and then changes his mind. 'They'll be too tough now.'

Like mine. 'What will I do?'

'You'll be fine,' he says, and it seems he's already managed to convince himself that I will. But I'm not sure how I'll cope at all.

My lover, my life, the father of my as-yet-unfertilised foetus, is walking, *strolling,* out of my life. He picks up his holdall at the front door, the one I thought contained his squash gear. He gives me a distant little smile—one that doesn't even begin to reflect what he's doing to me. And with that he closes the door behind him.

Chapter two

I *can't* go into work. I *have* to go into work. I am blessed with great colleagues who will be hugely sympathetic and will call Jake all manner of obscene names including 'fuckwit'. That will make me feel heaps better. They won't mind that I'll be horribly late and will spend the entire day crying into cups of manky machine coffee.

Boiled eggs and toast strips are supposed to be comfort food, but somehow it's just not happening. I bash in the top of Jake's abandoned eggs with the back of my spoon, using rather more force than is necessary, and stare at their rubbery white skins and dried-up yolks without enthusiasm and with a stomach that's decided eating isn't on the agenda. The toast has gone all floppy and wouldn't even make a dent on them anyway—you can draw your own metaphorical conclusions on that one.

Jake is in advertising. I don't really know what he does other than wear sharp suits and make up slogans. His latest project is to convince a sceptical general public that eggs are good for you again. Now they're no longer stuffed full of salmonella and they're a safe and wholesome foodstuff once again. So Jake says. One of the very few benefits of this is that we've been getting free eggs. But it's not the type of egg donation that's any use to me.

Work for me is as an assistant editor at Global Magazine Publishing—a bit of a misnomer because none of our magazines ever venture out of the British Isles. This sounds very glamorous to people until I say that our main magazines are called *My Baby* and *My Divorce*. I can never decide whether these are extremely dull titles or marketing masterpieces. Certainly the circulation is steadily climbing—well, of *My Divorce* anyway.

After an uneventful schooling, I thought very seriously about becoming a teacher with a view to watching my eager charges blossom under my tender tutelage in the manner of Miss Jean Brodie. But after one terrifying work-experience stint at a North London comprehensive, I decided that it was far too hideous and desperately underpaid. And that even the formidable Ms Brodie would have cracked under the strain of trying to control a room full of shaven-headed, pierced twelve-year-olds. So, instead, I joined the world of publishing, which, several years later, I still now inhabit—marginally less hideous, but still desperately underpaid. Plus all the shaven-headed and pierced people are over thirty.

My day consists mainly of compiling the letters page for *My Baby*—which means I'm constantly knee deep in tearful epistles from cooing mothers or tirades from childless harpies, not unlike myself, who feel that the world has dealt them a lousy hand. I also commission and edit articles that are given whizzy titles by Monica, my editor, such as—'Make Your Fallopian Tubes Your Friends', 'The Greatest-Ever Guide to Baby Poo', 'Feeling the Strain—All You Ever Need to Know about Constipation and Pregnancy'. There are also far too many titled 'Great Expectations!' Occasionally, when there's no one else available and my desk isn't swamped under a deluge of urgent copy, I'm allowed out with my trusty Dictaphone to interview 'C' list celebrities about their joyful, and often alternative, birth experience or their long and painful struggle with polycystic ovaries or similar.

Jake has, on one or two occasions, voiced the opinion that my current employment is doing little to quell my 'obsession' with babies. I just feel that when the time comes I'll be fully equipped—

mainly with toddler-type freebies—and confident in my knowledge of the wonderful adventure that is pregnancy.

I do admit that every now and again I tear up or toss a letter from some whining, sleep-deprived mother who is writing in saying she's permanently tired from disturbed nights. Some women don't know how lucky they are. I'm permanently tired from disturbed nights trying to bloody conceive!

I give the eggs another whack for good luck and toss the spoon onto the table. With my loved one gone, it looks as if that's going to be a thing of the past.

Chapter three

Monica and Charlotte are smokers. I can see them as I stomp up the road from the Tube, scarf wound around my neck in an effort to keep warm. It's only November and the temperature is barely above freezing already, but that doesn't deter them from pursuing their chosen vice. I join them in their shivering huddle outside the front door of our offices.

'Afternoon,' Monica says. It's not even eleven o'clock yet. Sometimes I wish I smoked and then I could join the select band of lepers who come out here on the hour, every hour, to damage their lungs despite what the elements can throw at them. Sometimes I come out just for the hell of it because I'm sure they gossip about the rest of us when we aren't there. But we all know that cigarettes lower the birth weight of babies so I've resisted temptation. Next they'll be telling us that trying to conceive by having sex is bad for unborn babies and we'll all be in a dreadful mess.

'Nice of you to join us,' she adds, but I'm not sure that she's being sincere. Monica is a relocated Liverpudlian and I've always found that they tend towards aggression when riled. In theory, Monica is my boss, but she very rarely chooses to exert any authority over me and is generally one of the girls—albeit a rather short-tempered one.

'You look dreadful,' Charlotte says through her low-tar lungful. 'Are you okay?'

I move away so that I won't be damaged by inadvertent, passive inhalation. I shake my head. 'Jake's gone,' I say.

'Gone!' they chorus in unison. 'Jake?'

'The latest IVF's ended in a big fat zip,' I explain with a wobbly lip. 'I don't think he could take it. He's gone to stay with Pip for a few days.'

'I wouldn't mind a few days with Pip,' Charlotte confides.

'Get in the queue.' I'm never quite sure what women see in Pip, but a lot of them do see it. 'I don't know what to do.'

'Come on.' My friends have one last hefty drag on their cigarettes and then stub them out on the pavement—recklessly risking a fifty-quid fine. Charlotte takes my arm. 'Let's get you some of that vile brew they call coffee and you can tell us all about it.'

The offices of *My Baby* and *My Divorce* are wonderful. We're housed on the eleventh floor of a huge chrome-and-glass monolith on the South Bank, overlooking the murky expanse of the Thames. For all my lowly position, I've managed to bag myself a desk right near the vast window and can spend hours watching the river rippling by. Nothing on this earth would persuade me to give up this coveted space. In the summer I fry, but we have so few hot days, who cares? Today the low, reluctant winter sun is playing hide-and-seek behind the white iron skeleton of the London Eye and encouraging the water to look grey and glum. I'd like to think it's coming out in sympathy with me.

'So.' Monica plonks a plastic cup in front of me. She and Charlotte sit on my desk. 'Tell all.'

And I recount my story while casting occasional wistful looks out over the Embankment. Even as I'm filling in the gory details and slagging off my partner in life with much gusto, I know that in my heart when I get home tonight Jake will be there. He'll have realised that it was all a terrible mistake and will be waiting for me full of remorse, hopefully clutching a bunch of suitably expensive and nicely arranged flowers and wearing a mortified expression. In all, he will have come to his senses the minute he realised what he was about to lose.

'Well.' Monica scratches her chin as I finish. She and Charlotte exchange a worried look. 'It's not good, is it?'

'He'll be back,' I say as confidently as I can manage. 'I'm sure he will. You know what men are like.'

'You are a bit obsessed with this baby thing,' Monica suggests.

I'm not sure I like how many times 'obsessed' is being linked with the word 'baby' in conversations about me.

'I'm not obsessed,' I insist. 'I'm focused.' I think there's a difference. 'I'm going through an IVF programme. It's costing us a lot of money. And it's flipping time-consuming.'

Charlotte lays a hand on my arm, but she looks over my head at Monica, who grimaces in return. Charlotte pats. 'It's not surprising that your relationship is under strain.'

Monica sighs. 'Perhaps Jake has had enough of it all.'

'He wants a baby just as much as I do.' I take a sip of my coffee and push it away. Perhaps this is why I'm not with child—it's like drinking a cocktail of toxic chemicals. I'm sure the plastic cup's melting. 'Well, he did until this morning.'

Charlotte and Monica exchange another nervous glance. Monica gives a small nod and Charlotte takes a deep breath before she speaks. 'You do talk about babies an awful lot, Lyssa.'

'I work at a bloody baby magazine! My entire day is spent talking, writing and thinking about babies!'

'Do you think that's healthy, given your situation?' Monica offers.

'I can't get knocked up,' I cry. 'I'm not psychotic.' Although at the moment I do sound a bit borderline.

'It must be very hard for Jake.'

I close my eyes, blocking out the view, blocking out my friends and blocking out the flashback of Jake closing the door with a decisive little click. 'It's hard for both of us.'

'He did look a bit put out at the office party when you were talking about his sluggish sperm over the Christmas pudding.' To avoid the Christmas rush our company decided to be innovative and hold the annual festive bash in July. Go figure, as our American friends would say.

Charlotte chews her lip. 'He dragged you off to dance to Shakin' Stevens's "Merry Christmas Everyone". That's always a sign of desperation.'

'If anyone knows about desperation it's me,' I point out.

'Why don't you give this whole baby business a rest?' Monica again.

'Oh, that's a good idea. I'll forget all about it—right this minute.' I give them a vacant stare. As if I wouldn't if I could. No one in their right mind would go through the gruelling process of artificial insemination if they could avoid it. I've taken so many damn forms of hormones—I've popped them, I've sniffed them and I've shoved them in my bum—that I'm a walking mass of puberty, PMS and menopause. I've been counselled about my 'Inexplicable Infertility' until I'm blue in the face and aching in the heart. I've had my fill of sitting in bleak waiting rooms in clinics stuffed with tearful women who avoid eye-contact in case talking might mean addressing their worst fears. I'm sick of reading in the daily press that, despite the emotional and physical trauma that women like me endure in their quest to satisfy their maternal urges, the majority of IVF attempts just don't work. I can't bear to think that I'm one of the statistics in the box marked 'Failed'. Who would put themselves through this torture if a pet poodle were an adequate substitute?

How can I explain that my cocktail of hormones is making me feel as if there's some madwoman locked inside of me? My progesterone is in deadly combat with my oestrogen. My body is screaming at me to get pregnant! I have taken to looking at babies in prams and being tempted to take them out and give them a cuddle. I'll swear that some days my breasts leak milk, but I think it's wishful thinking. If I don't get up the duff soon, I'll become like some sad old bitch—the canine variety—moping around with a phantom pregnancy.

'You need to get things right between you and Jake.'

'You think this is all my fault, don't you?'

They do that how-do-we-tell-this-crazy-woman-the-truth? look again.

Charlotte clears her throat and puts on an understanding face. 'Perhaps Jake thinks that having a baby is more important to you than he is.'

I don't know what to think. Is it? What if I could have a baby and not Jake—or Jake but not a baby? Which would I choose?

Monica is losing interest. She glances over at the clock. It's getting towards time for the sandwich run, and her growling stomach is starting to take precedence over my life falling apart.'Maybe you should just try to give yourselves a break. Get this back into perspective.'

'Yes,' I say. Is this what Jake thinks too? Is that why he's gone to Pip's? 'You're right. Maybe I should.'

Maybe I should try to stop seeing babies everywhere. Maybe I should romp round the bedroom with Jake, exhibiting gay abandon and not consulting my charts to see whether it would be a waste of effort. Maybe I should try not to view my monthly period as if I were being afflicted by some deadly disease. Maybe I should think more positively.

But how can I, when everyone else in the world is pregnant except me?

Chapter Four

Jake was in the boardroom, preparing for his presentation. It was possibly the very last thing on earth that he wanted to be doing. He wasn't the slightest bit interested in portraying Mr Egg—'The Good Egg'—as the most creative advertising campaign of all time. He was sick to death of eggs—chicken, human and any other kind there might be. The presentation was due to start in half an hour. It was a multi-million-pound promotion, and the importance of it was steadfastly refusing to stay in his mind.

At the moment his PowerPoint wasn't playing ball either. He punched a few keys on his laptop. There were some impressive whirring noises, but nothing—absolutely nothing—appeared on the projector screen. Jake felt his slender grip on his patience slipping away. 'Oh, bollocks.'

His friend and fellow Dunston & Bradley inmate, Pip Henshall, crossed his feet, which were up on the highly polished, yew boardroom table. 'Take five minutes to calm down, Jake,' he advised. 'It'll be all right on the night.'

Jake tossed down the laser pointer and threw himself into the seat opposite Pip. He blew the air out of his lungs in a steady stream.

'That bad?' Pip asked.

'Worse,' Jake said. He looked rather sheepishly at his friend. 'I've told Lyssa I'm staying with you.'

'Oh, thanks. Involve me in your sordid little schemes.'

'This isn't sordid.'

'Office flings always are.'

Jake shook his head. 'This isn't a fling. Not for me.'

'And what does Lyssa think?'

'She doesn't know,' Jake admitted.

Pip made a steeple with his hands. 'Marvellous.'

'I could hardly tell her that I was moving in with Neve, could I?' Jake raked his hair. 'Walking out while she's in the middle of her latest baby quest is bad enough. I can't tell her that I'm going to shack up with a nubile twenty-five-year-old with legs like Lara Croft whose urge to go through the motions of procreation is very much in evidence. It would crush her.'

'I didn't realise you were so sensitive.'

'What would you do in my situation?'

'I'd like to think that I possessed more sense than to get myself in your situation.'

'I feel terrible about leaving Lyssa,' Jake said. 'Terrible.'

'But not terrible enough to stay?'

'I'd stopped being a boyfriend and become a baby-producing machine.' He shook his head in dismay. 'We've been at it every night for months.'

'I thought that's exactly what you were looking forward to with Neve?'

'Yes, but the intention is very different. With Neve it's for pure eroticism and mutual pleasure. With Lyssa it's for years of sleepless nights, family-sized transport and hideous expense.'

'Call me perceptive, but do I detect that becoming a father has lost some of its attraction?'

Jake rubbed his hands over his face. 'I didn't think it would be so hard.'

'Isn't this supposed to be the fun bit?'

'I think it probably is when Mother Nature deigns to take her intended course. It's when you have to get a bunch of doctors involved in the process that it all goes a bit cock-eyed.' Jake could feel himself getting a headache—which was ironic because it was something he'd tried to feign several times over the last few weeks. 'It's so horribly mechanical. It's all injections and hormones and specimen jars. If I'd known it was going to be like this, I'd never have agreed to it in the first place. It completely undermines all you believe about manhood.'

'Is it trouble with…?' Pip jerked his head.

'With what?'

Pip glanced round the room furtively, before saying: 'Getting it up.'

'Good grief, no. Do you think "Nymphomaniac Neve" would give me the time of day if that was an issue?' It seemed strange to be using the derogatory office nickname now that it referred to his girlfriend rather than just a work colleague, and he wasn't sure that he was comfortable with it even though he'd never overly concerned himself with office sexism before.

Pip shrugged. 'I suppose not.'

'That's the problem, mate. To the casual observer the whole thing functions perfectly well. It's just when you come down to the nuts and bolts of it, there's a slight difficulty.'

'Are your sperm still sluggish?'

'Sluggish sperm,' Jake sighed. 'What does that say about me?'

'How the hell do they get sluggish? They can't start out like that.'

'I don't know. I did eat a lot of curry at college,' Jake confessed. Maybe that was what had taken the sting out of their tails. 'You know, I have this vision of them sitting around in a comfy chair with their feet up, doing the *Daily Telegraph* crossword when they should be out there swimming for England. Still, you can't blame them. Every time they've popped out over the last year, their performance has been criticised for being sub-standard by some suit in horn-rimmed specs. I just don't think they can get motivated anymore.'

'Sounds like one of our creative meetings.'

'Yeah.' Pip and he had worked together at the Dunston &

Bradley Advertising Agency for the last five years. In theory Pip was senior to him, but Jake had no intention of letting it stay like that for too much longer. Out of the two of them, Jake was the more obviously mean and hungry. Pip gave the impression of being laid-back, but behind the foppish exterior of velvet chalk-stripe suits and purple shirts there lurked a superbly twisted and razor-sharp brain capable of the most obscure lateral thinking and resulting brilliant marketing campaigns. Everyone assumed Pip was heavily reliant on cocaine for his inspiration, but his particular vices were nothing more serious than the occasional six-pack of John Smith's beer and licking the coating off Pringles.

'Whichever way you look at it, it's a very messy business,' Jake complained.

Pip nodded sagely. 'And it's going to get messier.'

His friend was probably right. That was the most annoying thing about Pip, he usually was. Jake wasn't sure how this whole thing with Neve had started—actually, that was a complete lie, he *was* sure. The fact was, the whole of the male contingent of the office thought she was totally horny, and he'd been ridiculously flattered that he was the one she'd shown attention to. 'Shown attention to' in that at a fabulously trendy launch-party at the Soho nightclub Snappers, she'd pressed her finger to his lips and silently led him into the ladies' toilets where, less silently, she'd had sex with him standing up in a cramped cubicle. He could get an erection just thinking about it. And their dangerous liaison had sort of progressed since then. Dangerous because if either Lyssa or their bosses at work found out about it they'd both be for the chop—and Lyssa's version of it would be a lot more painful and would make fatherhood an even more difficult concept in the future. But then wasn't the fear of discovery part of the attraction of these things? Heaven knows, he was the last person to think about analysing the reasons—all of his life was spent focused on his nether regions for one reason or another at the moment. At least in this situation there wasn't a bunch of doctors overseeing him and telling him he wasn't good enough. Neve seemed to think he was perfectly adequate.

The work issue was a worry though. He loved his job and was damn good at it, but fraternising between colleagues—other than a sociable Vodka Absolut—was considered a sackable offence. Gross misconduct his contract said. And some of the things that he and Neve had done could certainly be considered gross misconduct.

The only consolation was that in these days of supposed equality, Neve would probably carry the can. She was a more junior member of staff, a woman and, therefore, despite employment legislation, considerably more dispensable than he was. The truth of the matter was there would always be a queue of tall, leggy and beautiful graduates ready to take her place.

Pip peeled his tall frame out of the Philippe Starck boardroom chair and stretched. 'Come on, Mr Swift. Time to stop dwelling on your tortured love life and turn to the rather mundane, but infinitely more pressing matter of work. Time to put your corporate underpants on outside of your suit and transform yourself into a superhuman advertising executive.'

Jake dragged himself up. 'I can't get fired up about this one. Eggs are a bit of a turnoff for me at the moment. I need something more meaty to get my teeth into.'

'We've got a pitch for a New Zealand–lamb promotion coming up,' Pip said with a smile.

'You know what I mean. I need something sexy, something glammy. My testosterone is in turmoil, I need to channel it,' Jake said. 'Whatever happened to the Blow aftershave contract? We got that one, didn't we?'

'Yeah,' Pip mumbled.

And if Jake hadn't been quite so preoccupied with his own problems, he would have noticed that his friend had suddenly become rather shifty.

Chapter Five

I can't believe how long it took to get to five o'clock. I deliberately didn't ring Jake all day, but you would not believe the amount of effort it cost me. It was only the fact that I know he hates personal calls at work that kept my fingers away from the phone.

The house is still in darkness when I arrive home. I can't bear this time of the year when the nights start to draw in and the mornings are pitch-black too. I hate going to work and coming home in the dark. On top of everything else, I'm sure I get that Seasonal Affective Disorder—SAD. Although at the moment it's been rather surpassed by UBM—Utter Bloody Misery.

I'm going to make a fab dinner for Jake this evening. Instead of working this afternoon, I took the opportunity to pick some stale crumbs out of my keyboard and had a long think about what the girls said. I have to admit that I was a bit shocked that their sympathy leaned more towards Jake's plight than my apparent abandonment. But, on reflection, they could well be right. I probably have been neglecting us as a couple and focusing instead on why we aren't a threesome. All that is going to change. Tonight, I'm going to woo him with my culinary skills instead of talking about my ovaries.

I drop my bag on the table and shake off my coat before I head upstairs to the bathroom. A long, hot soak is needed to restore me to the human race. We've been in this house for just over three years. Jake and I had a bit of a whirlwind courtship—if that's not too unhip a word. We bought the house and moved in with each other within six months of meeting, which is not generally how things tend to go these days. People seem so determined to remain fiercely independent that we've got friends who are married but still live in different houses. How weird is that? After the initial whirlwind, things have calmed down to a gentle breeze. Now that we've taken one tentative step towards entwining our lives, we've put the brakes on galloping onto the next stage. Jake still sees marriage as more of a 'commitment'. I'm not sure how he reconciles the addition of a couple of kids in the middle. My mother is truly horrified by the whole thing. She's of the generation who can't understand why I'd 'risk' getting pregnant by a man who won't marry me.

I met Jake at a local nightclub. It was supposed to be a posh and happening place, but to me it seemed to be populated by forty-five-year-old divorced men looking for a semi-clad, nineteen-year-old girlfriend. Quite frankly, in all the Saturday evenings I spent there, Jake was the only man I met who could actually string a sentence together. The fact that he's a tall, blue-eyed blond bombshell helped too. I'd never gone for blue-eyed blonds before, but Mr Perfect never comes in the shape or often the size you'd imagined. I usually go for swarthy types, but when Jake asked me out, I said yes at once without even considering my preferences. And I'm so glad that I did. I'd like to say that he completes me, but he doesn't—not quite.

The bathroom is at the top of the stairs on the way to the bedroom, so I take a detour and turn on the taps, then start stripping off as I head down the landing. This is a small, Victorian terraced house and I've spent an inordinate number of hours sanding off layers of paint to reveal original pine doors and skirting boards. My knowledge of paint stripper is second-to-none. The house used to be in the shadow of the old gasworks and at one time you couldn't give properties away in this street. Now the gasworks has gone and even the scruffy parts of St Albans have been spruced up. So, of course, the houses carry a hideous premium because they're within walking distance of the mainline railway station and the city is slap-bang in the middle of a prime commuter belt. Even J.K. Rowling, with all her dosh, would quake at some of the prices round here, believe me. Still, it's a very cosy place and not just because of its neat proportions. I've decorated it all in shades of rich cream and gold and sumptuous burgundy, and everything glows warmly. I love coming home in the evenings to my little love nest. I don't think Jake is that mad on it though. He's more of your minimalist type of guy. My boyfriend hankers after one of those trendy loft-conversions overlooking St Catherine's dock or somewhere complete with steel staircase, slate floor, state-of-the-art mood lighting and a wall-to-wall sound system. I like paintings that look like things—sunsets, landscapes, animals. Jake favours red splotches on plain white canvas, preferably three metres square. Maybe he'll mellow when we have the baby. Perhaps then he'll concede that steel staircases and toddlers are an unhealthy mix. Not that we have steel-staircase money, anyway. We are currently IVF paupers and I think I ought to address that with Jake too. It's about time that our stretched finances were turned towards something more hedonistic. I'll suggest that we have a nice, romantic holiday somewhere hot and glamorous—the Caribbean springs to mind—before we embark on our next drugs frenzy. It may be our last chance to get away by ourselves for a while. People often say that if you relax and stop thinking about having babies, then quite frequently you get pregnant naturally—actually, they say it to me far too often. I could tell you two dozen different stories about people teetering on the edge of adopting a Chinese orphan or buying a border collie only to find that miraculously and without surgical intervention they were knocked up. Wouldn't that be great, to come back from the Bahamas with a home-made baby and a suntan? I would be a fabulous, glowing pregnant woman!

Our bedroom is very lacy. I've tried to keep it traditional-looking with a wrought-iron bed and a white cutwork duvet cover—which is an utter pig to iron—and a traditional Victorian wash-stand which we bought at an inflated price from one of the three thousand antique shops that we now seem to have in St Albans. I keep a photograph of Jake and me on top of it in an old marquetry frame. Picking it up, I mimic Jake's wobbly smile and trace my finger over his ruffled hair. Even after four years when the first flush of lust has died down, I still love him to bits. He's handsome and generally very dependable and he works so hard at the agency—he's going to go a long way some day. My mother wouldn't trust him as far as she could throw him—she says he has dangerous eyes. And I know what she means. He has a dark twinkle in them somewhere that says I'm a man with secrets—but I don't think he is. Not really.

Putting the photograph back in its place, I peel off the last of my clothes and, taking the phone handset with me in case Jake rings, pad through to the bathroom enjoying the roughness of the Sisal flooring on my tired feet.

I love our bathroom. I take so much care over making it look nice. There are shell-shaped dishes of little soaps on the windowsill, church candles in white ceramic holders and matching towels. I could happily spend my life in here. The bath is overfull and too hot—I'm very particular about water temperature. I don't want broken veins by the time I'm forty, so I never stew myself—well, not often. Occasionally it's very therapeutic to boil your own bum, but not tonight. So I plunge my hand in and pull out the plug to let a bit of water out so I can add some more cold. Then I pour in some bath oil—lavender and something or other—to soothe my weary bones.

I hate it when Jake and I fall out. It doesn't happen very often—no more so than with most couples—but it still unsettles me. Catching sight of myself in the mirror, I give my body a critical scan. I have a good figure—slim, lithe—almost athletic in a minuscule way—which must be down to genetics rather than hard work in the gym, because much as I like to kid myself I don't really do anywhere near enough exercise. I run my hands over my belly—which is flat. Enviably flat I would think. It does sometimes seem like madness that I can't wait for it to be swollen with our child. I stick my tummy out, but no matter how far I force it, I really can't make myself look remotely pregnant. Perhaps once I am, we can put all this unpleasantness and petty bickering behind us and become a couple again. I'm sure when all technicalities are done, Jake will be thrilled to be a father. I pat my tummy—not long now, I hope.

I lower myself into the steaming, scented bubbles, and the wondrous, healing power of plain old water never ceases to amaze me. We have one of these long, claw-foot baths that is the perfect shape for lounging. I can feel the stress floating away and lie back, submerging myself as deeply as I can. I close my eyes and drift off.

As I do, the phone rings and I pick up the handset.

'Hi.' It's Jake. On his mobile. I can feel my face soften and I smile down the phone at him.

'Hi.' I wriggle up a bit in the bath, so that I don't dunk the phone. It wouldn't be the first time. 'Are you feeling okay now?'

Jake doesn't answer.

'Look, I'm sorry about this morning,' I continue. 'It's tough. Tough on both of us. We need to take time out. I've got some fizz in the fridge. I'll make us a nice supper. We can cuddle up and watch some crap on telly.'

I hear Jake sigh. He's clearly still mad.

'Where are you?' I realise I can't hear the noise of the train clattering in the background, so he's not on his way home yet. He's been working late on Friday night for weeks and I'd sort of hoped tonight would be different. 'When will you be home?'

'Lyssa…' Jake sounds a long way away. 'I'm not coming home. I told you.'

The bathwater suddenly seems a lot colder. 'I know…but I thought…I thought you might have changed your mind.'

'Why? Why did you think that?'

'Well…things are different. I know how you feel. I wanted to call you all day. I understand. And we can have a break from the IVF. Six months. More, if you like…'

'Lyssa, don't you think it's a bit late for that?'

'No.' I don't. 'You only told me about your feelings this morning, Jake. At least give me the chance to talk it through with you.'

'What else is there to say?'

My knuckles are white where I'm gripping the phone. 'We can't just end like this.'

'It may be for the best.'

'For who? Not for me.'

'You'll be fine, Lyssa.'

'I'm not fine. I'm dreadful. I want you to come home. Where are you?'

I can sense a hesitation. 'I'm at Pip's. I told you.'

'You said you needed a few days.' That urgent note of hysteria is creeping back into my voice and I try to stop it. If I want Jake to come back I have to be calm, I have to be collected. 'Stay until Sunday. I'll ring you.'

'I don't think that's a good idea, do you?'

'Yes,' I say. 'Otherwise, I wouldn't have suggested it.'

'I have to go,' Jake says firmly.

'Why? Why? What else do you have to do?'

'This isn't doing either of us any good, Lyssa.'

'Then why are you doing it?'

'Because I have to,' Jake insists and he hangs up. Just like that. He has cut me off. Cut me out of his life. Cut my heart out.

I put the phone down before I drop it in the bath. The water's chilly now, all the soothing warmth gone from it, and I should get out, but for some reason I seem unable to move. Jake really has gone.

'Jake's gone.' Even saying it out loud doesn't make it register fully. And I know that, in theory, he went this morning, but on one level I didn't think that he actually meant it. I thought that he'd spend the day sulking at work, that Pip would give him a good talking-to and after a few fortifying beers in the local pub, he'd come home, tail between his legs, and that would be the end of it. But no. Jake really has gone.

Reaching out, I turn on the hot tap. I like the water to be scalding when it comes out and we have the boiler on all the time. I put my hand under the flow, but I can't feel it burning me at all. The water level rises steadily. It's almost at the top of the bath. I've never filled it this full before. I turn on the cold tap too. The bath fills more and more quickly. The layer of white, bubbly foam from the bath oil is higher than the rim of the bath. It looks like clouds suspended in space. The bubbles are tickling at my chin, like grandmas do to babies. The water eases itself, slowly, slowly, painfully slowly over the curved sides. It runs down the bath and onto the floor. If I don't turn the taps off straight away, the water will run through the floorboards and into the kitchen ceiling below—and what will I do then? Perhaps when Jake knows that we have a domestic emergency, he'll come rushing home. I know him. He won't let me cope alone. I can't cope alone. Jake will come straight home and sort it all out. He's like that. He's good in emergencies. He'll sort it all out. And then we'll be fine. We'll be fine again. Everything will be fine again. I lie back in the bath and stare at the ceiling, listening to the lapping of the water.

Chapter Six

'Make yourself at home,' Neve said as she shrugged out of her coat.

'Thanks.' For some reason, Jake felt very awkward. He'd been to Neve's place loads of times over the past few months of their affair, but only for fleeting visits, a few snatched, illicit hours; never before with a view to becoming a permanent resident. This felt different and very, very weird.

'Drink?'

'Yeah.' He put his bag down by the front door.

Neve carried the Chinese takeaway over to the kitchen area. 'Sorry about the takeaway,' she said over her shoulder. 'I've never got any food in.'

He thought about the fridge in the kitchen in Roland Street and how it was always stuffed to the gills with his favourite treats. Some things were bound to be different now. Neve was a completely different type of woman to Lyssa. But that was good. Different was good. He could live with different. It was what he wanted.

'I've always got plenty of this though!' She waved a bottle of champagne at him and pouted. 'Bubbly?'

'Why not?' Jake slipped off his jacket and then didn't quite know what to do with it. Everything here was so beautifully placed that he didn't want to spoil it and he didn't know what Neve had done with hers. As a stopgap he arranged it as aesthetically as he could over one of the white leather chairs. This was the sort of place he'd envisaged himself living in around ten years hence, when he'd achieved the sort of salary that would be able to support it. And now he was here. This was going to be his home for the foreseeable future.

'This really is a fabulous place,' he said to Neve as she poured the champagne.

'Yah,' she agreed. 'Daddy's an architect. He bought this place as a little project.'

Neve had told him this before. Daddy's 'little project' was a four-storey derelict pub just off the Fulham Road. He'd converted the ramshackle building—with no expense spared—into three spacious, open-plan, hideously tasteful and hideously expensive apartments. They all had oak floors, rough exposed brickwork and all the pipework in visible galvanized-steel ducts. The ceilings must have been twenty-feet high and the entire back wall of the place had been knocked out and replaced by glass panes, giving an unhindered view of the stark, Japanese-style garden beyond—the epitome of trendy conversions. Neve, by virtue of being Daddy's only daughter, had been given one as a twenty-first birthday present. Jake seemed to recall getting a camera from his parents—very useful in its own way, but not quite as memorable.

'Bring the food, sweetie,' Neve said. 'We'll eat downstairs.'

Obediently, Jake collected the tray piled with foil dishes, plates and chopsticks. 'Downstairs' was reached by an open oak staircase and featured a dining-room table that would probably seat more than a dozen people. To the right-hand side of the huge floorspace was a snug, more intimate area with a cast-iron log-burning stove in front of which were two perfectly placed, classic tan leather chairs adorned with oriental, beaded cushions.

Neve took the tray from Jake and put it on the table. She flicked a Zippo lighter over a pleasing group of gothic candlesticks before she handed a plate to him and they sat down opposite each other.

'Cheers.' Neve lifted her glass to clink against his.

'Cheers.' They let their fingers touch, caressing each other. 'You are okay about this?' Jake said.

'Thrilled,' Neve said.

'Me too.' In fact, he was so thrilled he still couldn't believe it. Out of all the guys in the office—and there were quite a few of them who would be eager to take his place—Neve Chandler had chosen him. And she was fabulous—not tiny and waiflike as Lyssa was, but statuesque, tall and imposing. Her limbs were long and lean and she rather liked showing them off. Even at the office her skirts barely graced her thighs. She had feline features, not the least of which were green, slanting eyes. Her hair was black like a raven's feathers and, not that he knew much about hairstyles, it was cut in one of those razored affairs favoured by trendy Radio One DJs. The sort of hairdo that made lesser mortals look as if they'd just fallen out of bed. On Neve it was perfect. And she was ferociously rich and well connected, which—if Jake were being honest—he found very attractive too. He wondered if Daddy had any idea that his only daughter also preferred raunchy and rather risky sex.

'The food will be getting cold,' Neve said as she spooned some fried rice out of the metal containers.

Jake's mobile phone rang and he pulled it from his pocket. 'Damn.' He glanced at the display in dismay. 'It's Lyssa.'

'Ignore it,' Neve instructed.

'Yeah,' he said, though it was harder to do than he'd imagined. Perhaps it was guilt brought on by the opulence of his surroundings and the fact he was sitting here with a beautiful woman who Lyssa knew nothing about, toasting his rather hasty departure with a decent-vintage champagne. His phone continued to ring before the voicemail kicked in.

Neve clinked her glass against his once more. Her eyes fixed on his. 'You're here with me now, darling,' she said.

He smiled, but he could feel an uneasy tightness at the corners of his mouth. Being here was going to take rather more adjusting to than he'd previously envisaged.

Chapter seven

What a fucking stupid idea that was. Truly fucking stupid. I look at the sodden kitchen floor. It's definitely an insurance job. There's water dripping from the light fitting and I daren't turn on the electricity or I might blow up the whole damn place. I hold my hands to my eyes and try to block out the damage. Jeepers—what was I thinking of? Jake—that's what. In the cold light of day it seems like an extraordinarily daft thing to do.

I tried Jake's mobile a dozen times last night at the height of the kitchen-waterfall scenario, but it kept going straight to voicemail. Probably just as well. He might not have seen me as the helpless victim in this, but as a stark raving loony. When I'd eventually convinced my brain to shut off the bath taps, I nearly got in the car and drove round to Pip's but that would have seemed too, too desperate even though I was. Instead, I just left the whole, dripping mess as it was and crawled into bed and sobbed.

I try Jake's number again, but he is still determined to be unavailable. I feel like hurling the thing at the wall, but I've probably done enough damage for one day. Instead, I flick through the Yellow Pages, dialling a dozen different numbers until I find an electrician who is actually willing to come out on a Saturday morning. Then I go upstairs to the airing cupboard and dig out as many old towels as possible and start the ignoble business of mopping up. I can't even make a cup of tea first to gird my loins—I'd have to paddle to the flaming kettle.

The electrician eventually turns up and tuts a lot. His overalls say SPARKY on the rather grubby breast-pocket, but he doesn't seem very sparky to me. Nor is he the gorgeous, toned electrician with come-to-bed eyes of my dreams. He is a crusty old bugger with a bald head and wire-wool hair coming out of his ears. Monica had her wooden floor fitted by a man who could have been a reincarnation of Adonis, and Charlotte says the man who fixes her washing machine looks like Heath Ledger. All my domestic engineers fall woefully below the mark.

'Where's your fuse box?'

'Er…' Fuse-changing has always been Jake's department. Isn't that how it is in most households?

He rolls his eyes in despair and I refrain from asking him does his wife know where their fuse box is—but then I hope she had the sense to leave him years ago and isn't still saddled with a husband as miserable as this.

Sparky wanders out of the kitchen and I trail behind him until he finds the elusive fuse box—which is in the cupboard under the stairs. Who'd have thought it. My surly saviour turns off the electricity. He tuts a lot more at the kitchen light fitting and then unscrews it, grunting and puffing as he does. 'It's wet,' he says profoundly.

'Really.' I seem to remember giving him that expert diagnosis on the phone.

'Needs to dry out.'

'I expect so.'

'Could take a few days.'

'A few days?'

My electrician shrugs. 'You could stand on a chair with a hairdryer at it.'

This sounds like a deeply dangerous thing to do. I'd probably set the house on fire, knowing my luck. 'I don't think I'll risk that.'

He shrugs again. 'Try it tomorrow. It might be dry by then. All you'll do is blow a fuse.'

'Right.'

He looks at me with disdain. 'You do know how to change a fuse?'

'Er…' We trail back to the fuse box and he makes a great performance of showing me how to pull out one little thing and plug in another. How hard can that be? If I'd known it was so easy, I'd have taken charge of the fuse-changing years ago.

Easy or not, Sparky charges me one hundred and fifty quid for services rendered and I'm too shocked to quibble about it and simply pay up in stunned silence. This is an expensive lesson in how not to be a pathetic prat. At least I have the sense to give him a cheque and not cash, so that he'll have to put it through his books instead of diddling the Inland Revenue. Ha! Not quite so stupid as I look. Although I admit it's marginal.

A disgruntled Sparky hands me a receipt. 'Phone me again if you can't manage,' he tosses behind him as he departs.

'I can manage,' I say. And I can manage. From now on, it looks as if I'll have to.

Chapter eight

Neve sat straddled across Jake's lap as he lay in bed. It was not quite seven o'clock and Jake fought to open his eyes against the light that was streaming into the bedroom. Neve leaned down and kissed him full on the lips. 'See you later,' she said.

Jake was suddenly awake. 'Later?'

'I'm going to the gym, sweetie.'

'Gym?' This was news. 'Do you have to?'

'I'm training for my trek to Everest base camp. I can't afford to miss a session.'

'Oh.' This was also news. 'And when's all this taking place?'

'Soon,' Neve said, and bent down to kiss him again. 'After I've been to the gym I'm seeing a couple of girlfriends for lunch.'

'Lunch?'

Neve swung off the bed. She was already fully dressed in one of those stylish fruit-coloured tracksuits favoured by Madonna and Britney Spears. 'Have you got any plans for today?'

'Plans?' His brain was reeling and seemed incapable of making sentences. 'Er…no.'

'I'm out tonight too. Clubbing.'

Despite his sleepy state, Jake was aware that he felt vaguely put out. 'Clubbing? I like clubbing.' Although he could only remember once in living memory that he'd been to a club and that had been the start of all this business. He didn't think he was too enamoured with the idea of Neve going to a club on her own—not now that he knew exactly the sort of thing she was likely to get up to. 'Can't I come too?'

'Saturday is girls' night.' Neve pouted. 'We always go to Blackout.'

Jake propped himself up in her bed. 'This wasn't quite how I'd imagined our first weekend.' He took her hand and tried to pull her back towards him. 'I thought we'd have a romantic dinner for two.' He gave her his most appealing smile. 'Somewhere special.'

Neve wriggled away from him. 'Then you should have given me more notice,' she said. 'I've already arranged it.'

She blew him a kiss across the room.

'What am I going to do?'

'I don't know.' Neve grinned. 'Phone Pip. I can't organise your life for you. You're a big boy.'

Jake rolled over. 'Flattery will get you everywhere.'

'Not now or I'll be late,' she said, and with that she left.

Jake watched her go with an empty feeling inside. He heard the familiar purr of her BMW as it started and a screech of tyres as she shot off down the road. He rolled over again, but he was awake now and there was no way he was going to be able to get back to sleep without some sexual relief. And there was no way he was going to do it for himself—that held too many bitter memories.

'Bloody hell,' Jake muttered to himself. 'I didn't even get a cup of coffee.'

He forced himself out of bed and wrapped a towel round his waist. What could he do when he hadn't got any of his stuff here? He didn't even have a dressing-gown, let alone his squash gear. At some point soon, he was going to have to go back and face Lyssa to collect some of his clothes and a few essential items.

He padded across from the bedroom into the kitchen. The units were all brushed steel and the absence of fingerprints suggested that Neve must have a cleaner to keep the place like this, as it was already clear she wasn't the most dedicated of homemakers. Jake opened all the cupboards until he found a container marked *coffee.* There was a dirty mug in the sink, which he rinsed out before filling the kettle and flicking it on. He risked a look in the fridge, but there was no milk, seemingly no butter and an apparent lack of anything resembling jam. Another search of the cupboards failed to produce any other foodstuffs—no cereal, no bread, no freshly baked *pain au chocolat* or croissants. He'd have to go to one of the little posh cafés down the road for breakfast—which would be nice. It wasn't a problem. He tried not to think about Lyssa bringing him coffee and the newspaper in bed every weekend morning. Tending to his every whim. He couldn't help wondering what she would be doing now. This was a very strange feeling. Rather than worrying about having two women to contend with, he appeared to be without one at all for the time being.

The high-tech kettle beeped that it had boiled. Still, at least he could drink his coffee black. He found a spoon and opened the coffee container—but like the cupboards, it too was bare. The gym, it appeared, took precedence over Sainsbury's too.

He felt very small in the vast emptiness of the apartment. There was no way he could kick round here all day on his own. He'd have to ring Pip and see what his old mate was up to. Hopefully it was something he could tag along with. At the moment, his first day as a single man didn't seem to be shaping up to much.

His phone rang again. It was Lyssa. There was no way he could answer it. What could he say to her? The temptation to go round there was unbelievably strong. He hoped that she was okay alone. As an answer to his indecision, the phone stopped. It was a bit of a quandary that Lyssa apparently needed him so much when Neve didn't appear to need him around at all.

Jake poured himself a glass of water and sat at the breakfast bar, slightly chilly in nothing but his towel, forlornly staring into space. As he hadn't been given a tour of the place, he had no idea where the central-heating controls might be—there didn't even seem to be any radiators—and this was an enormous, cold space to warm through. He wished Neve were here, not only to turn up the thermostat, but as he didn't really want to be left to his own devices. She didn't seem to understand that this was going to be quite a transition for him. But then, the trouble with independent, feisty women, he decided, was they were prone to act independently and feistily.

Chapter nine

I don't know when Britain's weather pattern changed, but I'm sure that we never used to have these awful high winds that we have now. It is blowing an absolute hurricane out there. The sky is black and ominous—which is a bit of a shame because I can't put the power back on downstairs yet, and having to do everything in the gathering gloom is more than depressing.

Outside in our tiny back garden the terracotta pots are blowing all over the place. There are leaves and plastic bags whipping across the top of the fence. I go upstairs and switch on our little portable telly in the bedroom—at least I still have power up here. I click it to *BBC News 24* and am plunged further into depression. Gales lash Britain. No trains are running. All the airports are shut. Ninety-mile-an-hour winds predicted. Don't go out unless it's essential. Oh good. This could yet prove to be the longest day of my life.

I flick through the rest of the channels hoping to find something more cheery, but there's nothing. I'm not a big telly fan, anyway, but Saturday-morning TV is clearly intended for no one over the age of twelve. I've mopped up all the water in the kitchen and although everything smells a bit wet, I'm sure it will be fine in a day or two. There are some bubbles appearing on the ceiling and

I guess that will have to be redecorated. I wonder what the hell Jake will say when he comes home, and then the thought occurs to me that he might not come home. Ever. I wonder what will happen to the house. I wonder what will happen to me.

I can't lie here for much longer, I'm seizing up. Mentally and physically. I switch off the television and then sit in some sort of suspended animation. The bizarre thing is, I don't know how to entertain myself anymore. It's exactly one day since Jake announced he was leaving and I'm already dreading spending time alone. I used to look forward to having a day to myself without Jake under my feet. I'd fill it with shopping and girl things. Now I'm looking at the prospect of endless days to myself, I've no idea how I'll fill them. I'm sure it's worse because I'm trapped here today, unable to go out and with no light. It's so bad I even think about doing some work, but dismiss it as the first sign of madness. There's only one thing I can think of that I want to do and that's eat. The wind is howling round the house making ghastly and ghostly noises. Thunking sounds are coming from the loft—when I can't imagine what there is up there to thunk—and the letterbox has taken to knocking all by itself. There's only one thing for it.

Balancing on a chair, waving a hairdryer at a light socket isn't my first choice of a fun way to spend half an hour, but needs must. I feel very precariously placed and my arms are aching already, and I remind myself to do some more work on my biceps when I next see fit to grace the gym. I've set up some candles downstairs, but whilst candlelight is great for creating atmosphere and mood, it isn't actually much use for providing essential lighting. We just get so used to the convenience of modern living—I'm the type of person who reaches straight for the light switch to search for candles on the rare occasion when we have a power cut.

There's an almighty crash from outside and, in the back garden, the pergola has fallen headfirst into the flower bed like some Saturday-night drunk. It's going to have to stay there. I don't know any of my neighbours well enough to go and ask them to pick it up with me. The way things are going it would just blow over again, anyway. I watch as the last of the crisp, golden autumn leaves are tugged from the trees and sent careening down the garden. I've had enough of the hairdryer—both of my arms are about to drop off. The socket should be dry by now, surely? I get down from the chair and I can feel myself getting tearful. I want Jake here. I *need* Jake here. We'd be having a laugh about this. We'd have battened down the hatches and be snuggled down together. Maybe we wouldn't have got out of bed at all. I could kill him for leaving me alone on the coldest, windiest day of the year.

Wincing, I flick on the light switch and, after a momentary flicker, there's a horrible popping noise and all the lights go out again. I could just lie down on the wet kitchen floor and die. I really could. This day simply cannot get any worse. Except it can. Thanks to Sparky, the world's most miserable electrician, I know where the fuse box is, but I don't know if we've got any spare fuses or where we keep them. While I ponder this new addition to the equation, there's a loud, grating noise that I can't identify. I stand frozen to the spot, holding my Vidal Sassoon Maximum Hair Hydration System like a Magnum 45. At the very least my roof sounds as if it's parting company with the rest of the house. Then there's a splintering noise and a loud thud from near the front door. I rush to the window and look outside. A selection of roof tiles have detached themselves and are now sprinkled like slate confetti across the tiny patch of green we laughingly call the front garden. But more importantly, one roof tile is wedged, pointy end down, right in the middle of the bonnet of my previously unblemished and lovely little car, which has done nothing to deserve this ignominy. This is the last straw. It's more than I can take. I need tea and sympathy and a large piece of chocolate cake and I'm going to get none of these shivering and shaking at home alone in the dark. There is only one place I can retreat to. One place where I will be welcomed with open arms. Friends may let you down. Fickle boyfriends may desert you. But a sister is a sister for life.

Chapter ten

What can I say about my younger and only sister, Edie? Similarities—we share the same mother. Sometimes we are pleased about this. We share the same hair colour—blond. We both have it cut into a classic bob. I go to a top-of-the-range hairdresser every four weeks and pay eighty-four pounds to get it trimmed back into shape. Edie goes to the hairdresser at the end of her road once a year if she can find the time and has her hair hacked back into shape with Black & Decker hedge-trimmers by a woman with a blue rinse called Marjorie for five quid. I spend hours blow-drying and straightening mine—when I'm not using my hairdryer on my domestic appliances, of course. I'm not even sure that Edie possesses a hairdryer. I like to consider myself immaculately groomed. My toenails have not been their natural colour since I was fifteen. I wear make-up every day—even Sunday. And even if I'm only going to wash the car. Edie gave up her battle with cosmetics years ago. The last time my sister wore make-up was when she stole my No 17 Glitter Stick to wear to the school disco. No, I tell a lie. She did wear make-up at her wedding, but only because I forced her to by telling her I wouldn't be seen dead as her bridesmaid if she didn't. I don't think she's ever had a close encounter with anything as glamorous as nail varnish. The sickening thing about Edie is that she is still extraordinarily good-looking without having to try—which is just as well because she doesn't. But there are very good reasons why at the tender age of twenty-nine Edie doesn't have time for the vanities of the flesh. Six of them. Yes, in this age of falling birth rates and increasing infertility, my sister and her husband have somehow managed to buck the trend and produce six children. Her family nickname is Rabbit.

I park my poor battered car outside her house and, clutching my overnight bag, fight through the increasingly strong gusts of wind to the front door. Edie lives just across town from me in a house that's far too small for eight people. Despite that, they'll still find a space for me—even if I have to sleep on the dining-room table. I haven't phoned to tell her I'm coming, but it doesn't matter because she never goes out. I can hear shouting as I ring the doorbell. Edie opens the door. As usual she is *sans* make-up and with wild hair. She sighs heavily and kisses me on the cheek. 'Welcome to the madhouse.'

I follow her inside and am greeted by the sight of a tear-stained niece—Kelly, fourteen. Kelly is clearly in possession of one of those things that twists your hair into tight strands, as all her hair has been twisted by it. She's very red in the face.

'I hate you!' she screams at Edie, before turning to me and calmly saying, 'Hi, Aunty Lyssa.'

'Hi.'

'I hate you all! I hate living in this house!' she continues at full volume. 'I'm going to leave as soon as I can!'

'Good,' Edie says. 'It looks like Aunty Lyssa needs your bedroom.' She eyes my overnight bag.

Kelly stomps upstairs.

I follow Edie into the kitchen. 'Where are the others?'

'Archie's asleep. And we've managed to fob the rest of them off on other more gullible parents for the afternoon. They'll be back soon.' She casts a glance at the mountain of potatoes in a pan on the hob and a towering heap of chicken pieces marinating in an unnaturally coloured sauce. At every mealtime Edie has to produce enough food to feed a battalion. The kitchen is run with all the efficiency of an army manoeuvre. My sister would have no idea how to cook for two. There are no salmon fillets and asparagus tips in this house. Food is fuel and every meal is designed to fill its recipient up to the gills as quickly and as economically as possible.

'Let's take advantage of this rare moment of calm, shall we? Tea or wine?' she offers.

'Wine.' I plonk myself down at the table.

'She's rebelling,' Edie informs me as she wanders over to her gargantuan, American-size refrigerator, which has mostly been obliterated by a host of yellow Post-it Notes on which are scribbled shopping lists, the time of various dental appointments and dancing lessons and other reminders to get her through her life. 'I told her she can't have a leopard tattooed on her boob.' My sister roots in the depths of her fridge. 'She hasn't quite worked out that if she was really a rebel, she wouldn't have asked me in the first place.'

'Oh bless.'

'She'll thank me when she's sixty and her tits are round her knees.' Edie pulls out a bottle and finds some mugs to go with it.

'And I suppose you mentioned this to her?'

'Of course I did. I'm a mother.'

My sister's kitchen can only be described as a work in progress. As is the rest of the house. I don't think there's one room that has its full quota of wallpaper. There's always a pile of wood somewhere that's in the process of being constructed. I read somewhere that children cause one thousand, five hundred pounds' worth of damage to a home during their first five years of life. If you multiply that by six then it's no wonder that Edie's is always a bit of a building site. Her husband also has an unhealthy addiction to Do-It-Yourself. I think he just likes hitting things with a hammer. My sister cares not a jot for all this. She can happily lie on the sofa eating chocolates and watching *Heartbeat*, unconcerned by the fact that her cornices have been covered by nothing but B&Q own-brand undercoat for the last two years.

'Cheap crap,' Edie says as she puts a mug of something white in front of me. 'Sorry. At least it's cold.'

'I'd probably drink bleach if that was all you had.'

'That bad?'

I nod.

'Jake's left,' she says flatly.

I'm shocked. 'How do you know?'

'Why else would you be here on a Saturday afternoon looking like your world had ended and carrying a fully laden overnight bag?'

I take a swig of the wine. She's right. The wine and my life are both awful. Its saving grace is that the plonk is mind-numbingly cold and my mind could certainly do with a bit of numbing. I shudder as the acidic cut of the wine hits my stomach and shrivels my taste buds, but then I think everything would taste bitter to me at the moment. 'He went yesterday,' I admit. 'One day on my own and I can't cope.'

'Has he got someone else?'

'No.' I pull a face. 'He needs space. He's had enough of the IVF programme. He's had enough of me.'

'Do you really believe there's no one else?'

'Yes.'

'Men don't usually leave cosy relationships unless they've found someone who wears ridiculously short skirts and stockings.'

'Grief, Edie, he never has time for that. He spends every hour God sends at the office. And when he's not at the office he's knocking some sort of ball around or filling pots at the fertility clinic. Jake doesn't have any spare time for another woman.' I drink the wine quickly so that it tastes better. Edie kindly refills my mug. 'It's only for a few days. While he thinks. He said he'd be back. Maybe tomorrow.'

Edie snorts doubtfully and I must admit that I'm not entirely convinced either.

'Don't tell Mum,' I beg.

'What am I? Mad?' Edie says.

Edie and I spend a lot of our time not telling Mum things. Our mother has had a very difficult life and we try to protect her from as much unpleasantness as possible. This is mainly because she can rant for England. My father, when he was around, was a serial philanderer—her term, not mine. Throughout their marriage, he worked his way through a succession of neighbours until he found one young enough and compliant enough to agree to run away with him. My mother, Cecilia, has never recovered. She was left alone to bring up my sister and me. More often than not, she took to her bed with an attack of the vapours or a migraine and left me, a rather world-weary nine-year-old, to bring up Edie, a beautiful, confused four-year-old with a penchant for climbing trees and, subsequently, falling out of them. In the twenty-several years that have passed, my mother has grown ever more bitter and twisted. There are hundreds of taboo subjects—babies, money, lawyers, divorcées, newlyweds or anyone too obviously happy. She detests Posh and Becks, simply because they are phenomenally wealthy and look as if they idolise each other to boot. Though there was never the slightest hint of a custody battle over us children, even now both Edie and I dread *Kramer vs Kramer* coming on the telly at Christmas. The smallest thing can start her off. And Jake expressing his discontent by buggering off for a few days would be like applying jump leads to a long-dead battery.

Up until now, I've given my mother relatively little cause for concern. I've been an ideal daughter—if you overlook my inability to produce grandchildren for her. But then, with my sister's brood she has more than enough to keep her occupied. It's only due to the fact that all of my sister's children are unspeakably adorable, with the possible exception of a teenage tantrum every now and then, that my mother has forgiven Edie for not being an ideal daughter.

Every family survey undertaken now seems to take great delight in stating that the children of single parents will go on to have underage sex, form unsuitable attachments, achieve less at school and turn into juvenile delinquents. There weren't heaps of condemning statistics back then, but unfortunately my sister and I weren't the exceptions that proved the rule and Edie obliged by becoming pregnant at fifteen and leaving school before she sat any of her exams. She also stole sweets from the corner shop, but to this day we've managed to keep that from my mum. Edie's pregnancy, however, was rather more difficult to conceal.

Don't get me wrong, Edie wasn't jumping into bed with all and sundry. She was, at least, 'suitably attached'. Edie has been with the same bloke since she was fourteen and, as far as I know, he's the only man she's ever slept with. On cue, the lovely Lee comes into the kitchen. He's always in the throes of some DIY project and, as such, is splotched with paint.

He kisses me on the cheek. 'Hi, sis.'

Lee is the most wonderful, dependable man on the planet and I'm only pissed off that my sister got to him first.

'Jake's left her.'

'Oh man.' Lee nudges my bottom out of the way and slides onto the seat next to me.

'He's fed up,' I explain. 'We both are. The latest IVF frenzy has failed.'

He leans against me and gives me a comforting nudge.

'For goodness' sake, Lee,' my sister says, 'can't you just take her upstairs and get her pregnant?'

'I don't mind.' Lee shrugs. 'It won't take long.'

'He's right,' my sister says. 'Five minutes and it will all be over'

Lee grins. 'I have to rush before you fall asleep,' he counter-accuses my sister—who responds with a frown that says there might be a modicum of truth in there somewhere.

My brother-in-law wriggles his bottom against mine and gives me a friendly smile. 'I'm up for it if you are.'

'It's very tempting,' I say, and I think I'm joking. It's not the worst offer I've ever had and it would certainly be a lot cheaper than IVF.

'Aren't there some religions where you can marry your wife's sister?' he adds.

I lean against him. 'I don't know, but it might solve some of my problems.'

'I'll go and wash out my paintbrushes,' Lee says. 'Then I'll be ready.' He pushes away from the table and gives my shoulders a squeeze. 'Love you.'

'Yeah.' I feel choked. 'Love you too.'

Lee kisses Edie on the nose and ambles out towards the garden shed, which, like for most men, seems to be his only place of sanctuary.

I sigh. 'You're so lucky that you're still in love after all these years.'

'We're not in love,' Edie tuts. 'We're just too exhausted to leave each other.'

Kelly, grim-faced, marches into the kitchen and yanks open the mega-fridge. It is stacked with cheese, yoghurt, fruit and all manner of goodies and tempting treats. 'There's never anything to eat in this house,' she says, slamming the door.

'Give me one of your children,' I suggest. 'You've got kids coming out of your ears. I bet you wouldn't even notice one less.'

'You can take that one with pleasure,' Edie says, unperturbed. She turns to Kelly. 'You wouldn't mind if Aunty Lyssa adopted you?'

'It'd be better than living here,' my niece spits and bounces out again.

'Told you,' Edie says.

'I don't want a big, grumpy one. I want a small, cute and cuddly pink one.'

'They all start out cute and pink and end up big and grumpy like that.'

'Have another baby,' I beg, 'and give it to me.' I think it's the wine talking.

'No. You have a very unrealistic vision of life as a mother,' my sister informs me. 'Black cashmere and milky sick don't make a great statement. You'd hate it.'

'You must think I'm very shallow.'

'I think you're very idealistic,' she says. 'And slightly obsessed with the *idea* of having a baby. The reality of it is generally very sticky and expensive.'

She can tell that I'm not convinced.

'If you really think you want children, take all of them—for just twenty-four hours. And the husband too. It'll be doing me a great favour. You'd bring them back begging for mercy and rush straight out to have your tubes tied.'

'I would not!'

'Your life's fantastic compared to mine. Why ruin it?'

'I wouldn't go through all this emotional trauma if I wasn't absolutely serious.' I sound indignant.

'Your life and your figure are perfect,' Edie insists. 'You have fabulous holidays—plural. You go to the cinema, the theatre, out to dinner. You know what happens at cocktail parties. You're all glossy and gorgeous. You never have a hair out of place.' Edie pulls at a strand of her own wayward locks. 'And yet you want to be me. Haggard and harassed.' She looks suitably amazed. 'It's very overrated, Lyssa. Raising children is crushingly boring. Believe me.'

'Yes, but you keep doing it. You're so lucky. Six kids and I can't have a measly one. Grief, you must be at it like rabbits. Can't you watch more telly?'

'There's nothing on worth watching,' Edie says. 'And we've no money to go out. You have to do something to make the long winter evenings pass.'

'So the BBC is responsible for your contribution to the St Albans population explosion?'

'Yes.' Edie is adamant. 'And for the fact that I have a vagina with all the sensitivity and size of a galvanised steel bucket.'

We both laugh.

'A hundred quid for a TV licence proved to be a false economy.' Edie gestures around. 'Is this what you want for yourself?'

'No.' The wine is making me giggle and some of the knots of tension are creaking out of my neck. 'I just want one baby. Or maybe two. At the most. A matching pair would be nice. I don't want a shed full or the entire lineup of *American Idol*. You're a freak of nature, Edie. No one has six children these days—unless they've had IVF and it's a multiple birth.'

'Still, this is an end to it,' she assures me. 'We've got this contraception thing sorted out now.'

I'll believe that when I see it. I'm not sure whether my sister is very stupid or very accident-prone. I think it swings from one to the other. She had unprotected sex at fourteen, which was asking for trouble. And trouble she got. Big trouble when my mum found out. If that wasn't enough she had another contraceptive catastrophe at eighteen. A cock-up, you might call it. Edie failed to realise that the Pill didn't work if you had a stomach upset. That stomach upset turned into Anna, who's now eleven. A split condom at twenty—on their honeymoon—produced Mark, nine. Deciding three was enough to keep them impoverished for the foreseeable future, they forked out for a vasectomy that failed spectacularly in the form of Liam. Too much to drink at Edie's twenty-fifth birthday party resulted in Daisy now four—mind you, it was a very good party. My sister finally bit the bullet and booked a sterilisation to put her baby days behind her—the day before she was due to have it done she found out she was pregnant with Archie, a smiley eighteen-month-old bundle of fun. I glance up at my sister with a look of utter disbelief.

'We have,' she insists. 'I'm back on the Pill, I've got a diaphragm fitted the size of a dinner-plate and Lee wears two condoms.'

We both giggle into our mugs.

'I bet one of those little bastards will still get through,' she mumbles. 'Every time Lee sneezes I get pregnant.'

'I must sit down and have a talk with you one day,' I offer. 'I don't think that's what causes it.'

My sister takes my hand and squeezes it. 'You'll be all right,' she says. My eyes start to fill with tears. 'Some people pop them out like shelling peas,' she adds. 'With others…well…it takes a bit more effort.'

'Things have never been right since they told Jake his sperm was sluggish,' I sniff.

Edie laughs.

'It isn't funny.'

'It wasn't then, but it is now. The arrogant bastard probably thought his ought to win an Olympic gold medal at medley swimming.'

And despite my misery I too laugh. I wonder where Jake is now and I hope that he's as desperately unhappy as I am.

Chapter eLeVen

'Wow!' Pip looked round in admiration. 'This is some gaff.' He takes off his motorbike helmet and then stands awkwardly, not knowing what to do with it. Eventually, he handed it to Jake—who wasn't sure where to put it either.

'Yeah,' Jake said. 'And all paid for by Daddy.'

'Wow. Has Neve got a sister?'

'No. Only child.'

'Spoiled,' Pip observed. They both nodded. 'Still,' his friend said as he took off the rest of his motorbike gear, 'at least you get the benefit too. She could never afford this as a junior exec at Dunston & Bradley.' It was implicit in his friend's sentence that neither could Jake.

Pip looked round. 'Although I doubt the lovely, thrusting Ms Chandler will stay junior for long.'

It seemed weird to hear Pip talk about Neve like that now they were officially a couple. They'd still have to keep it quiet in the office, but a few select people were now in the know. Lyssa, unfortunately, wasn't yet one of them.

'So where's Neve gone?' his friend asked.

'Dunno, mate,' Jake admitted, trying not to sound too morose.

'Clubbing somewhere. She went off with a gaggle of giggling girls in a taxi and told me not to expect her back until late.'

'Mmm,' Pip said. 'And she's been out all day?'

'Yeah.' Jake shrugged it off. 'She already had plans. And she's doing this Everest-trek thing soon, so she's spending hours in the gym.'

'She was telling the guys in the office about it a few weeks ago.'

Jake felt piqued as he wondered why she hadn't told him as it seemed to be common knowledge.

'You wouldn't catch me hauling my arse up to Base Camp. It must be freezing up there,' Pip continued with a mock shiver. 'What's the point?'

'I suppose she's doing it for the challenge.' Though he couldn't quite see the attraction in it himself, Jake felt more than a bit put out that she hadn't asked him to go with her.

'Sounds insane.'

'That's today's women for you,' Jake said sagely.

'But not quite the romantic start you'd imagined?'

'No. Not really.'

'Well, you didn't want clingy anymore. You didn't want dependent.'

'I'm not complaining,' Jake insisted a little too defiantly even to his own ears. He had some serious nagging thoughts at the back of his mind that wanted to know just how much solo training this trip would involve. 'It's just going to take some getting used to. Lyssa and I have always been so…coupley.'

'And what "coupley" things would you have been doing tonight?'

Jake thought. 'Staying in with a pizza and watching telly.'

'I can cope with that. You can play couples with Uncle Pip instead.' Pip settled himself on the sofa. 'Mine's a Hawaiian with extra cheese.'

'Already ordered,' Jake said and joined him. He felt pathetic that he couldn't even entertain himself for one evening. 'Thanks for coming over, mate.'

'No worries. You're a sad and lonely guy who's been given the elbow by his new girl on their first weekend together. I'm glad I can be here for you. Besides, I was at a loose end myself.'

'I take it you're not seeing sexy Stephanie with the fishnet stockings anymore?'

'No,' Pip said. 'Oh no. She dumped me, cruel woman. Said I didn't listen to her.' Pip winked at Jake. 'At least I think that's what she said.'

'Have you never thought of settling down?'

'Me?' Pip said. 'No one would have me. I have too many disgusting habits. Too many brains cells that cry "Freedom!"'

'Married men are the new sex symbols. You only have to look in the tabloids—David Beckham, Brad Pitt, Sting. All married men and the sexier for it. Even in this day and age women like all that stuff. Homes and babies.'

'Yeah,' his friend said. 'And look where it got Lyssa.'

Jake shifted uncomfortably. 'I was just thinking, it would be a great pitch for the new Blow aftershave.'

'Yeah, well don't worry your pretty little head about that. You've got enough on your plate.' Pip fidgeted on the hard leather. 'It feels weird being here rather than in your old place.'

That was something Jake could empathise with. After he'd been out to get some essential supplies, he'd spent all day kicking his heels, watching sport on Sky and generally feeling as if he didn't belong here at all. Neve's apartment was fantastic, it was his dream home—but now that he was here it all felt very stylised and manufactured. His old house had been homely and cosy—at the time he'd hated it, but at least he'd felt comfortable putting his feet up on the sofa. Maybe when he'd been here a bit longer he'd settle in and feel able to treat it like home, instead of feeling he'd been accidentally dropped into a *Loft Living* photo shoot.

He'd phoned Pip out of desperation and thankfully, despite all the severe weather warnings that advised otherwise, his mate had agreed to hotfoot it over. Pip had a flat in Islington which he shared with a hairdresser called Simon. Jake had always found this a bit suspect. Pip was very flamboyant, but he was sure he wasn't gay—there were too many women passing through his life on a regular basis for that to be in doubt. Simon, however, was undoubtedly a homosexual. It was a bit like sharing a house with Harvey Fierstein. Neve's apartment was a bit of a schlep across town, but Pip had recently become a born-again biker and didn't need much excuse to get out on his Yamaha whatever-it-was.

'Do you think it's going to work out with Neve?'

'Oh yeah,' Jake said more confidently than he felt. 'Yeah. Yeah.'

'There are a lot of guys waiting to take your place.'

'Well, let them try. I think Neve's happy to be in a committed relationship.'

'I hope you're right, bud. You've given up a lot to be here. Lyssa is a pretty fantastic woman.'

Was a pretty fantastic woman, Jake thought. In the days before she started to incorporate the word 'baby' into every sentence.

Pip looked around him. 'What am I saying? You lucky bastard! You've dumped Lyssa and landed lightly on your feet. You're like a cat with nine lives.' Pip shook his head. 'Neve's fabulous too. She's got a brain the size of a planet, she's stacked and she's loaded. Even if she blows you out, you'll have great fun while it lasts.'

'She's not going to blow me out.' Jake could hear the edge in his voice.

'So what's the catch?'

'There isn't one.'

'Mate.' Pip patted his arm. 'With someone as gorgeous as Neve, there's always going to be a catch.'

Chapter twelve

I'm woken by sticky, milky fingers prising my eyelids open and the weight of my four-year-old niece, Daisy, sitting on my chest.

'Hello, Aunty Lytha.'

Daisy has blond curls, cornflower-blue eyes and a pronounced lisp. She sprays my face with the esses.

'Are you awake?' She gives my eyeball an exploratory prod, making me recoil into my pillow.

'I am now.'

Edie follows her in, bearing a welcome cup of coffee. 'Aunty Lyssa eats small children for breakfast,' she says.

I grab my niece and tickle her under the arms as I growl menacingly. It has the desired effect and she runs screaming hysterically from the room.

'Is that really the time?' I ask, peering at the clock with my unpoked eye. The little hand has not yet reached nine and I very rarely see this time of the day on Sunday. This is normally our designated day of rest. A break from the bind of commuting and household chores. As a treat Jake and I have a long, late, lazy breakfast in bed with the newspapers—even though the ink gets all over the white duvet. Then we make love for hours...

'Mum's downstairs,' Edie tells me with a grimace.

This stops my reverie in its tracks. I shrink back into my duvet. 'Don't let her know that I'm here,' I beg.

'Your car's outside, lamebrain. She saw it at some ungodly hour this morning when she was on her way to church.' My sister and I both direct our eyes heavenwards.

My mother is the least religious person I know. She doesn't go to church because she believes in God, but because other people believe she's a good, saintly woman and she likes to keep up appearances. My mother goes to church for the gossip, the free tea and biscuits, and because the neighbours do and she wouldn't want them to get one over on her. She also likes to wear a hat and doesn't get much occasion to these days. In reality, she thinks the vicar is a child-abusing faggot and a liberal because he'll remarry divorcées in church, and my mother says so in a very loud voice at every possible opportunity.

'She "dropped in" to find out what you were doing here.'

'You didn't tell her?'

My sister chews her lip. 'I might have unintentionally mentioned that Jake had left you.'

'Cheers. You're a pal.'

'Come on. Face the music. She won't go home until she's seen you.'

'Are my eyes still red and puffy?'

She shakes her head vehemently. 'Well, yes,' she says. 'Yes, they are.'

'Don't send her up here,' I plead. 'At least let me put some slap on first.'

'Get a move on then or I might have to make the children tie her to the chair.'

Edie leaves and I take a grateful sip of my coffee. My sister makes coffee so strong that you can stand your spoon up in it. Even the smell is enough to make my eyeballs rotate. I can feel it vibrating my veins into life as it works its way into my system. So much of me is aching that I feel as if I'm coming down with flu. But none of it aches as much as my heart. I didn't sleep at all—

apart from the hour before my niece very kindly woke me up, of course. I just lay awake tossing and turning, wondering how I could have got this all so wrong. It's very strange sleeping in a single bed after so long sharing a double. I didn't know what to do with my legs and spent all night thrashing them about as if I was on a bike. Jake's constant complaint that I hogged all the space in the bed could well have had some foundation. And it occurs to me that all of these small dissatisfactions could have been building up for some time. My first instinct is to ring him. He might have had a miserable night too and be feeling more convivial towards me. But if he isn't, I might cry again and I couldn't face my mother with the threat of tears close by.

With a heartfelt sigh, I haul myself out of bed, regretting that my ritual Sunday-morning soak in the bath isn't going to happen in this house. You can't even have five minutes to go to the loo in peace here. My sister has perfected the art of the six-second shower. She rushes in and out so quickly that I'm surprised she even has time to get wet.

Deciding that I don't even have the energy for any ablutions beyond a quick scrape at my teeth, I opt for a 'French wash' instead—a squirt of Daisy's Flower Fairy perfume under each arm. I have a quick rub round with some foundation, pull on yesterday's crumpled clothes—because that's exactly how I'm feeling—and reluctantly plod downstairs to face my mother's verdict on the proceedings.

Grandma Cecilia is sitting on a kitchen chair while Daisy—bless her—is kneeling on the kitchen table putting pink, spiky rollers in her hair. Edie is fluttering her eyelids angelically at my mother's back. My mother has her tolerant face on. Daisy is tugging at her hair with a Glitter Girl comb. If there were a TV programme called *Hairdressers from Hell*, then my niece would surely appear on it. So this is how my sister managed to keep her quiet. I can't help but smile.

'I would have thought you'd got very little to laugh at,' my beloved mother observes, instantly wiping the grin off my face. 'He's got someone else, you know. They always have.'

Because this is based on years of bitter experience with my father, I resist the urge to point out that not all men can be tarred with the same brush.

'I never liked him,' my mother continues. 'His eyes are far too close together.'

Not that I'm defending him, but for the record, Jake has perfectly spaced eyes. 'He's taking a few days to think about things.'

'Men don't think,' my mother states. 'They are genetically incapable of logical thought.'

Is it any wonder that she hasn't tripped down the aisle again? My mother is tall, but still managed to produce two fairly petite daughters—we must be genetic throwbacks, or as Mum insists, all our worst traits come from my father's side. She's slender and is still a looker. Today she's wearing a pale grey cashmere fitted dress that matches her eyes, and I bet she managed to turn a few heads in church—and not just because she mutters darkly through most of the service. The reason she has chosen not to re-enter the unholy state of matrimony is that she harbours a deep suspicion of all things male that borders on the wrong side of hatred.

'Come home to Mummy,' she says, addressing me as if I'm younger than Daisy. She takes my hand and pats it.

Quite honestly, I can't think of anything worse. 'I'm fine,' I insist, even though I'm feeling very touchy. 'I just didn't fancy staying in an empty house last night.'

I don't add that it has also been flooded and has no power—that would involve too much further interrogation.

'You'll have to get used to it.' She shakes her head. 'I have. It's no fun living alone, believe me.'

It would be less fun living with my mother. I've been away from home now for over ten years. If ever I moved back, my mother and I would kill each other within days and I'm not sure I'd like to risk a fiver on who'd strike the first blow.

My mum eyes me critically. 'You're looking thin.'

'He left last night, Mum. It has made no significant impression on my weight yet.'

'It will,' she says in a voice that sounds like the Prophet of Doom.

'You're done, Grandma,' Daisy announces. 'Now you have to go under the dryer.' You can tell what standard of hairdressing establishment my sister frequents with her daughter.

'Thank you, sweetheart,' Grandma says. It's a good job there's not a mirror in sight.

'Come with me, madam,' Daisy says in her best posh voice. I hope that 'going under the dryer' involves putting Grandma's head in the oven. Preferably for a long time. But no—Daisy simply leads my mother to another chair and makes a hairdryer-type sound that seems to involve spraying her with a lot of spit. My mother suffers in silence, which is not her normal *modus operandi*.

'Stay for lunch, Mum,' my insane sibling suggests.

I do my very best demonic glare. My sister shrugs as if to say, 'What else am I supposed to do?'

'I can't, darling.' We both sag with relief. Our troublesome parent gives a flick of her rollers. 'I'm going to see Mildred. She's having trouble with Oliver. He's becoming incontinent.' And no, we're not talking about a dribbly old dog. This is some woman's poor husband we're discussing. Quite how having my mother to lunch will help the situation, I have no idea.

'You'd better comb me out now,' she instructs Daisy.

'But you're not cooked yet, Grandma,' my niece wails.

'I have to go, sweetheart.'

'I don't want you to,' she says, and promptly bursts into tears.

At least my mother has some devoted fans. Daisy is inconsolable and has to be cuddled on Edie's lap, leaving me the task of unravelling the pink rollers. Daisy has wound the hair every which way and my mother is hair-sore. My victim, sorry, client, oohs and aahs as I try my best to pick my way through the tangle.

'I want you to be happy,' my mother says through gritted teeth.

As that would involve having both Jake back and a baby, I'm not sure it's going to be possible.

'This is a temporary glitch,' I insist as I pull a little bit harder. 'We'll be fine.'

'I wouldn't be so sure about that,' my mother gasps, her eyes watering.

I really hate her when I know she's absolutely right.

Chapter thirteen

'She doesn't get any better, does she?' my sister observes.

'You've only just realised?'

After my mother's departure to interfere in her friends' marital and urinary problems, Edie cooked a fabulous roast lunch that involved several chickens and enough carrots to keep a family of bunnies happy for a year. We're now sitting in her lounge letting it slowly add inches to our waistlines.

After yesterday's gales, it's now pouring down with grey, relentless rain, which means the kids can't go outside—not that kids seem to go outside anymore. All they ever want to do is watch television and play at killing people on the computer. Edie is making a token effort of trying to restrict the number of people that her boys can slaughter. As a result, I have two squabbling nephews hanging round my neck and a sleepy baby on my lap. Daisy is on the floor using a pretend iron to press her doll's clothes and I'm amazed that my sister hasn't seized on this talent and taught her to use the real thing on real clothes. She is listening to *Bob the Builder* on the CD player and Anna is lying across the rug watching *The O.C.* on the television at a volume that suggests she is hard of hearing. It's like trying to have a conversation in the middle of a premier-division football match. And I know you're not supposed to have adult-type chats in front of the children, but this lot never listen to a word we say. Really they don't.

'The terrifying thing is,' my sister continues, 'we're getting more and more like her every year.'

'Speak for yourself.'

'Mark my words, one day you'll be getting ready to go out, thinking you're looking very funky, and staring back at you in the mirror will be Cecilia.' Edie swigs her wine. 'A short version of Cecilia.'

'Is that really all the future holds for me?' If I wasn't depressed before, I am now.

'Then you'll find yourself saying the same things she does.'

'Never.'

'You wait until you have kids of your own…'

Tears threaten my eyes.

'Oh bugger,' Edie says. 'I didn't mean that. What a silly-arse thing to say.'

'You're my sister,' I offer. 'I'd expect nothing less.'

I find a crumpled tissue in my pocket and blow into it. Then I lower my voice, which is sort of pointless because then Edie can't hear me. 'Do you think she's right about Jake?'

'What? Turn that down!'

No one turns anything down.

I increase my volume accordingly. 'Do you think she's right about Jake?'

'No,' Edie says. 'His eyes are perfectly spaced.'

'Not that. Do you think he's got someone else?'

'Yes.'

'You could have thought about it for a nanosecond.'

'Men don't leave if they haven't got someone new to go to.'

'This is not making me feel better.'

'Face it, Lyssa. It's not in their natures.'

'Now you do sound like Mum.'

'Would you rather I lied to you?'

My nephews disembark and start a fight behind the sofa. If I ever manage to have children I vow that they'll be better behaved than Edie's lot. They'll like reading encyclopaedias and listening to classical music and will play instruments to concert standard and excel at art. I think my sister lost the upper hand after number four.

Sinking back into the chair, I let out a sigh. 'No.' My brain feels as if it is twice as big as my skull and with every beat of my heart it throbs. 'What am I going to do?'

'Why don't you just drop the baby thing for a while?'

'Why is everyone telling me to do that?' I punch one of Edie's cushions, making all the kids jump.

'I think it's become your main focus,' Edie suggests in as kind a voice as she can manage—which is clearly meant to indicate that I'm self-centred and obsessive. 'I'm not surprised Jake is fed up.'

I think packing your bag and leaving speaks of more than being 'fed up' but I say nothing.

'Men don't like competition,' she continues, taking my silence as consent to further annihilate my life. 'Particularly from small, pink people.'

'How can you say that? You've got six children. Lee doesn't see them as competition.'

'And where is he now?'

He's actually in his shed, where he always is.

'You'd be surprised. He did at first. We had a lot of fights in the first few years. He's worn down now,' my sister says brightly. 'With nowhere to run.' She chuckles slightly maniacally. 'What woman in her right mind would take on a bloke with six rugrats in tow? He's stuck with us.'

'And I adore you all,' Lee says, sticking his head round the door with impeccable timing.

'There is that too,' Edie admits.

'Where do you want this shelf?'

'As if I care, Lee.'

'Well don't complain that it's in the wrong place when I've finished.' He ducks out of the door again.

'Damn! He can put shelves up too? How unfair is that. Great sperm *and* handy with a hammer.'

'Look, Lyssa,' my sister says, and she has her serious voice on so I'd better take note.'You've been pretty hard on Jake these last few months.'

I open my mouth to deny it, but her look silences me.

'Men don't like to have their virility questioned and I bet even your hairdresser knows what Jake's sperm count is.'

'Er…' I hate to admit this, but she does actually. Only because she asked.

'Give him a break, Lyssa. If you really want him back, be nice to him. He must have been feeling very pressurised.'

And I'm not!

'Perhaps some space is a good idea.'

'I've been awful, haven't I?'

'Not awful.' My sister slides onto my seat and cuddles me.'Just a bit desperate.'

She rocks me backwards and forwards, like she does to Archie. And I know that things must be bad. This is a very unusual situation because all of my life I have been more like a mother to her than a sister. There's only a few years between us in age, but sometimes it feels like twenty-five. Motherhood is the one thing my sister excels at.

Edie smooths my hair from my forehead. 'You okay now?'

I nod. Not really, but I don't want to make this into a bigger deal than it already is.

My sister untangles herself.'I'd better go and see where my dear husband is putting this shelf.'

I reluctantly ease the dead weight of Archie from my lap, kissing his soft, warm baby head, and lower him into my sister's arms. I could be good at this, really I could, but I'm not going to go there now.

'I think I'll head for home.'

'Stay,' Edie says.'I don't want you to be alone.'

'Jake might have come back.' He might have. And I want to be there waiting in case he does.'I'll push off. I'd better check if my electrics have dried out.'

'What if he's not there?'

'I don't know,' I say with a heavy heart. 'I might go round to Pip's and try to talk to him.'

'Are you sure that's the right thing to do?'

'No, I'm not sure at all,' I admit. But I'm going to do it any-way.

Chapter Fourteen

I brace myself as I flick the light switch. And, lo, there isn't a hideous exploding sound, there is light where light should be. A little bit of my gloom lifts—at least one of my problems has been solved. Instant electricity is another one of those things we take for granted—like boyfriends. It would be nice if I could flick another switch and miraculously make Jake come home and love me again. But there isn't such a switch and he isn't at home.

The house seems so empty without him—especially after coming straight back from Edie's chaotic abode. I dump my overnight bag and try his mobile phone again, but Jake seems determined not to answer my calls and it goes straight to voicemail. I don't even bother leaving a message this time. So what do I do? I could sit here feeling sorry for myself, watching crap Sunday-night TV—that always features some weepy drama about a pregnant woman—and wondering what Jake is really thinking. Or I can go and find him and try to sort it out. If I'm going to beg, I'd rather do it face-to-face.

So I spruce myself up—applying another layer of foundation to hide my unnatural pallor and putting on some less crumpled clothes. I don't want to dress up, because the word 'desperate' has entered too many of my conversations in the last two days, but I don't want to look as if I've fallen off the back of a lorry either. Deciding on jeans, teamed with a silk sweater, I jump back in my dented car and head off towards North London and Pip's house. I've got far too much time to think on the journey, but I can't put the radio on because every damn station is playing something about love gone wrong and all the CDs in the glove compartment are abandoned-women-type songs. I'm finding this difficult enough—I don't want to get there looking and sounding like a tearful wreck. I concentrate on the clack-clacking of the windscreen wipers and try not to go into a trance.

It's ages since I've been to Pip's house. We all used to go out together quite frequently about a year ago, but we seemed to have drifted apart as friends as Jake and I haven't seen him socially for months now. I think this is mainly down to Pip's inability to keep a girlfriend for longer than it takes a pot of yoghurt to go off. I got to the point where I stopped trying to remember their names. I have a feeling Pip did too.

I circle the house, but as is typical in this part of North London, it's absolutely impossible to find a parking space anywhere in his street. I'd hate to be paying all this money for a flat and still have a half-mile schlep every time I needed to get to my car. Finally, I find somewhere to squeeze my Peugeot into that's still in the South of England—just about. My umbrella is black and has a huge orange-and-yellow-striped Tigger on the side—Jake bought it for me for my birthday. I can't keep gloves or umbrellas or sunglasses. They mysteriously vanish from about my person when I'm not looking. I'm single-handedly responsible for most of Accessorize's business. I huddle under the brolly while I lock the car and then brave the rain, rushing along the pavement, trying to dodge the puddles.

Pip has the ground floor of an old Georgian townhouse—which sounds slightly more salubrious than it is. In reality the door could do with a lick of paint and there are always piles of black bin bags in the street. Some of the houses have been renovated and are inhabited by advertising executives and magazine editors. Some look as if they're inhabited by students or dossers and have grubby lace curtains with holes in. I rap at the door, shivering in the cold. No matter how many clothes I wear, I can never seem to get warm enough when I'm outside. I think I should have been born in Southern California or Italy to suit my ambient blood temperature. There's no answer. It's not looking promising. I can't see a light on through the main window or through the frosted glass in the front door, even though I push my nose right up against it. I don't know what to do. If I'd managed to park right outside I could sit in the car and wait, but as it's miles away I won't be able to see when Jake comes back. I could just go home and chalk it down to bad luck, but I want to know where he is, I want to talk to him and I've driven too far to give up on my quest now. Indecision knocks around my skull. Why is it when you're suddenly alone, even the most basic of mental processes becomes a Herculean task? The sky is almost black and obviously still has plenty more rain to disgorge on us poor unfortunates below. I crouch on Pip's doorstep while I think. There is one dry patch in the corner where the bouncing rain has missed and I claim it as mine. I pull the Tigger umbrella close over me, cuddle into a ball and try to pretend that this will stop me from freezing to death.

A headlight flashes across the front of the house in a lazy arc like a searchlight, and a motorbike slowly mounts the pavement, pulling up by the wrought-iron railings. The rider dismounts and chains his bike to the bars. I assume it's Pip as I heard from Jake that he'd got a new mode of transport. He tugs his helmet off and heads towards the door—and me.

'Hi,' I say and Pip nearly jumps out of his leathers.

'Good grief,' he says. 'Lyssa! What are you doing here? You're soaked through. How long have you been waiting?'

The truth is I don't know how long I've been sitting here. Long enough to have made my legs go numb and for the rain to have gone straight through my coat. Why hadn't I noticed that before?

'Come on,' he says. 'Let's get you inside.'

'You'll have to give me a tug.' Pip takes my hand in his big, hard leather gauntlet and heaves me up. My knees creak into action.

Pip tuts at me. 'You'll catch your death of cold,' he says and I have to smile because he sounds like someone's mum. My mum, if I'm not mistaken.

He fiddles about with the key in the lock and then ushers me inside. I follow him through to the kitchen and he throws me a small hand-towel as he starts to peel off his gear. I rub the towel over my hair, which is plastered firmly to my head despite Tigger's best efforts.

The inside of Pip's flat is much more spruce than the outside. It has a black slate floor in all of the rooms and stream-lined leather furniture in lollipop colours. There are original movie posters on the walls—*Casablanca, Brief Encounter, From Here to Eternity*. All the ones that make you cry. The kitchen is all steel and boysy.

Pip tugs off his boots and socks and pads round in his bare feet, keeping busy doing nothing. Eventually, he looks back at me. 'Better?'

'Yeah.' I give up with the towel.

He eyes his pile of wet clothes making a nice dark pool on the kitchen floor. 'It's not the night to be riding a bike,' he admits. 'Or to be squatting on someone's doorstep.'

'I'm waiting for Jake,' I say, and can't believe how lame I sound.

'Jake?' Pip's eyebrows shoot up in surprise.

I sink onto one of the kitchen chairs. 'Do you know when he'll be back?'

'Er…'

'I've tried calling him, but he never answers his phone.' My voice sounds so tired and old and weary. 'Any idea where he is?'

I stop rubbing with the towel and look up at Pip. He's taken off his wet jacket and is looking vaguely stricken.

'Er…' he says again.

And then from a very great height a very large penny drops. 'He's not here, is he?'

Pip scratches an imaginary itch.

'Not just now,' I say. 'He's not here at all. He told me he'd moved in with you. And he hasn't.'

Pip sighs heavily. 'No.'

'So where the hell is he?'

'I'm going to make some great coffee,' Pip says. 'That'll perk us both up.' Pip has one of these all-singing, all-dancing stainless-steel coffee-makers that come with an instruction manual the size of a phone book and can do frothy milk all by itself. It gives him a great excuse to fiddle with things without looking at me.

'Where is he?'

'This is very difficult for me, Lyssa.'

'It's not that great for me either.'

'I'm his friend.'

'A very good one, if you'll lie for him,' I point out. 'I thought you were my friend too.'

'I am,' Pip says as he tips coffee beans into a grinder. 'I just don't have to work with you.'

The grinder rattles and vibrates and I feel the noise twinge all of my fillings.

'There's someone else, isn't there?'

Pip tips the ground coffee into a filter and clicks it into the machine. The rich, thick scent makes me feel nauseous.

'She must be a work colleague. He doesn't go anywhere else to meet anyone.' Unless he's having it off with one of the nurses from the fertility clinic and that would just be too ironic for words. Pip puts two stunning little stainless-steel cups in a specially designed place on the coffee-maker.

'Speak to me, Pip.'

He flicks a switch and the machine jumps into life. Whirring and gurgling like a robotic baby. 'Don't do this to me.'

'I need to know.'

'Then speak to Jake.'

'I would if I knew where he was!'

Pip comes and sits down next to me. He takes my hand in a rather tender manner, which I view as a bad sign. His fingers are soft and warm like freshly baked bread. Mine are cold and hard, like ice cubes. I can see words passing through his mind as he takes his time to select them to form a sentence. 'You're right,' he says eventually. 'He's seeing someone from work. He's at her place.'

'Where?' I say. 'Tell me where.'

Pip holds my hand tighter. 'It won't last, Lyssa. It's a fling. She'll get fed up with him,' Jake's friend tells me. And I notice that he doesn't say that my boyfriend will get fed up with her. 'She's young. She's not into commitment. Well, I'd be very surprised if she was. I'd put money on it.'

'So why has Jake decided to chuck everything in for her?'

'She's gorgeous,' Pip tells me flatly. And I think this may be too, too much information. 'All the guys at work are crazy about her.' Now I'm sure it is. 'She's pursued Jake for months. He's flattered.'

'And you think now she's got him, the attraction will wane?'

'Hey,' Pip says. 'I'm the worst person in the world to ask about relationships. I'm getting to the point where "long-term" means seeing the same woman for two weeks running. But for what it's worth, my guess is that it will all be over in a few months.'

'And he'll come home, wagging his tail behind him?'

'Jake's stupid, but I don't think he's stupid enough to blow it completely.'

'Maybe he already has.'

'I don't think you'd have been sitting out there in the rain for hours, if you'd given him up as a lost cause.'

Pip turns his attention back to the coffee machine. Reluctantly, he lets go of my hands and goes back to attend to it. He pours the coffee, presses a few more levers and perfect white froth spurts out into a jug, which Pip then adds to the coffee, finishing it off with a flourish of cocoa powder.

'You're quite domesticated, really,' I say with a smile as he puts it down in front of me.

'If only I could find an unattached woman of your quality to appreciate my more subtle charms.'

'I might be unattached from now on,' I point out. Then my smile fades. 'Where have I gone wrong?'

'What makes you think this is your fault?' Pip asks.

'Low self-esteem, deep insecurity.'

'Vulnerability,' Pip adds softly. 'You've both been under a lot of pressure. Jake gets it from both sides at work and at home…' His voice tails off.

'Thanks.'

'Shit. I didn't mean that, Lyssa.'

'No. You're right. You're not the first person to have said it either.' I taste the coffee and it's smooth, black-velvety and comforting. 'I feel like I've pushed him away.'

'Don't be so hard on yourself. He's a big boy. And a bloody idiot, if you ask me.' Pip dips the tip of his finger into his coffee froth and scoops some into his mouth. 'He's the one who's chosen to run in the opposite direction.'

'And you think that all I need to do is sit and wait for him to come back?'

'That depends whether you think he's worth waiting for.'

Until this last revelation, I would have said so. But now I'm not so sure. I stare into my cup wondering whether you can read the future in coffee grounds like you supposedly can in tea leaves.

'I'm sure you've got plenty to keep you entertained,' Pip says

Have I? I'm not so sure at all. And perhaps this is where I admit to myself that everything has been focused on having a baby over the last year and I don't know where the time has gone, but I can't think that I've done anything else of great note. I couldn't even amuse myself for a day. What am I going to do if Jake takes months to come to his senses or get dumped?

Pip gulps down his coffee and then slowly spoons the last remnants of froth from his cup. 'What do women do while they wait for their loved ones to return?'

'In Jake's case, I think I should sharpen knives.'

'Didn't they used to sit in rocking chairs and knit?'

'I haven't got a rocking chair and I can't knit.'

'There must be a modern equivalent.'

'They go to the gym. Learn to scuba dive…'

'Take a lover,' Pip suggests.

That makes me laugh. 'Are you volunteering?'

'Absolutely. It would certainly rattle a few cages.'

It might increase my chances of getting pregnant too, I think before being horrified at myself for even letting it cross my mind.

'I'll sleep with you if you tell me where Jake is and with who.'

'If I thought that was a serious offer,' Pip says, 'I might very well be tempted.'

'As it is, you're not going to tell me anything else.'

'No.' Pip is very firm. 'And I'd be grateful if you didn't tell Jake that you've been here. I do have to work with him, Lyssa. This…this…*fling* is causing me enough grief as it is.'

'It's causing me quite a bit too.'

'If I can do anything…' he says. 'Anything.'

I flutter my eyelashes at him even though it feels as though I'm blinking over sandpaper.

'Apart from completely grass up a mate,' he adds when he sees my look.

'I'd better be going,' I say. 'I feel incredibly foolish.' I push myself from the table and suddenly am overcome by weariness again. 'I love him very much.'

Pip comes over and kisses me on the cheek.

'Then Jake's the one who's very foolish,' he says and he pulls me to him in a bear hug. At which point I break down and really, really sob.

Chapter Fifteen

So. If I'm not going to drop Pip in the deep brown smelly stuff then there's only one thing for it. I have to catch Jake at it. Not too much at it. I don't want to see bottoms going up and down. Just a little bit at it will do.

As I seemed to have developed insomnia in the last few days, I've had plenty of time to lie awake scheming and plotting. My original plan had been to wait outside Jake's office from the crack of dawn to see who he arrived with. Job sorted. However, my insomnia was cured round about 7.00 a.m. this morning and I fell into the deepest, soundest sleep I've ever had, which continued long past the alarm clock and then I had to scramble and rush into the office. Which is where I am now, pretending that I care about work.

'I need to talk to you about this,' Monica says as she puts some copy on my desk.

It's fast approaching lunchtime. 'I have to go,' I tell her.

'You've only just arrived.'

'This is important.'

'And earning your salary isn't?'

'This is catching Jake with new girlfriend type of important.'

'Ooo.' Monica's eyes and mouth widen slightly. 'We haven't had this instalment yet.'

'That's why I've got insomnia.'

'You said you overslept.'

'That was after the insomnia.'

Monica puts her hands on her hips in a very authoritative manner.

'I'll buy some doughnuts for afternoon tea,' I promise in my best grovelly voice. 'Cover for me.'

'I'm your boss,' Monica points out. 'I'm the one who shouldn't catch you skiving off.'

'Don't give me a hard time, Mon,' I plead. 'My lips are one cross word away from a full-on wobble.'

'Go on,' Monica sighs. '"Nappy and You Know It" will have to wait.'

I pick up my handbag. 'Thank you. Thank you. I love you. You're like a…friend to me.'

'How long are you going to be?'

'As long as it takes,' I shout over my shoulder. And hope against hope that it isn't very long at all.

It's a fabulous day. The rain has finally conceded defeat. The sky is bright blue, mockingly so, and dotted with billowing white clouds that grow, spread and drift like the wax bubbles in a lava lamp. The air is cold and, for London, relatively clear. I take a cab to Jake's office and get the driver to drop me off just round the corner from the glass tower of Dunston & Bradley so that I can take up my spying position unseen. The only good thing about there being so many detective shows on TV these days is that you can get loads of information for mounting covert operations. I hadn't previously considered this a plus point. Funny how your perspective on all sorts of things changes when you find yourself a wronged woman.

Jake has lunch every day. He's very particular about it. He says he becomes all light-headed by three o'clock if he doesn't get out for some air and a sandwich. I know which sandwich bar he uses and it's only a few hundred yards from the office. Opposite Dunston & Bradley there's a tiny garden, not big enough to be classed as a park. It's surrounded by a low brick wall and has a few stoic cherry trees—bare and spindly at this time of year—plus a couple of trendy steel benches that look like the cutting foils from Remington shavers folded over. I take up my position on one of the benches, as yet unoccupied, which is obscured by a few hardy shrubs and a bit of the wall. I make myself comfortable—well, as comfortable as I can—and train my gaze on the revolving front door of Jake's office. I wish I owned a pair of binoculars. My eyesight has never been that great and I won't wear glasses because they make me look exactly like my mother. After about thirty seconds, I'm already getting bored, when a tramp comes and sits down next to me. He's wearing several overcoats tied round the middle with string. He has a hat on with no top and plastic bags tied over his shoes. I think he's possibly the smelliest person in the whole world.

'Spare change for a cup of tea, love?'

I hate being accosted by tramps. Especially when they ask for a cup of tea. If they really wanted a cup of tea, I'd have no problem in stumping up. But I always have that sneaking suspicion that they want to spend it on meths or crack cocaine and then I'm very reluctant to feed their habit.

'Spare change for a cup of tea, love?'

I turn downwind a little. 'No, sorry.'

I have lots of change and this makes me feel awful. The tramp opens a carrier bag and gets out a can of Strongbow cider. I edge further along the bench.

'Do you want a drink, love?'

Now how dreadful do I feel? I couldn't be charitable enough to give him fifty pence and he's still willing to share his last tinny with me. 'No. No, thanks.'

'Waiting for your boyfriend?'

'Yes.' In a manner of speaking.

If he keeps on, I'm going to have to move, yet this is my best spot. Why does nothing ever go to plan in my life?

Suddenly, there's a commotion across the street. The revolving doors of Dunston & Bradley spin on their axis and a group of happy, giggling people push out onto the pavement. And she's there right in the centre. Call it woman's intuition, call it gut instinct, call it insanity, but I'd know her anywhere. Even from the few brief details Pip gave me about her I just know—I just know that she's the one sleeping with my boyfriend. And Pip was accurate too, she is beautiful, but not quite in the way I expected. I thought she'd be small and girly and look young and gullible. But she's not. Oh no. No way is this one gullible. Or small. Or girly. She's tall, uncommonly so.'Statuesque' would be a kind word. But I'm not feeling kind, so I think she looks like a rugby prop forward. Action Man with boobs. She's got short, black hair, all chopped about, and is wearing a tight, unutterably cool black business suit with a skirt that wouldn't look out of place on a streetwalker. And that's not being unkind, that's being truthful. This woman is fully loaded with weapons of mass distraction. The group surrounding her are all guys and they're hanging on her every word and she's quite clearly mistress of all she purveys. They gradually peel themselves away from her, dispersing in little clusters down the street until she's left standing there alone. No. Not quite alone. Lurking behind her is Jake. He sidles closer to her and they both scan the street and the office behind them furtively. Furtive, in that they are making sure that none of their colleagues catch sight of their intimacy, but not furtive in that they think Jake's ex-girlfriend might be watching them from across the street. Jake reaches up and touches her hair and then kisses her softly on the lips. I touch my own hair. Did Jake ever do that to me? Was he ever mesmerised by my hair? I can't remember. I feel as if someone has reached into my chest and pulled out my heart. They part and it takes me by surprise that they walk off in opposite directions and, just for a moment, I don't know who to follow. Should I chase after Jake and confront him? Or should I arm myself with a few more facts first? I'm in such a quandary that I very nearly ask the wino for advice. And then as the woman strides out, I break cover and decide to follow her.

She's wearing very clippy-cloppy heels and I have on sturdy, sensible boots—bought when I was imagining being in the advanced stages of pregnancy at this time of the year. I sprint across the road, dodging between the traffic, and have caught up with her in no time at all. Pip said she was young, but she doesn't look young. She's so confident and self-assured that I'm sure she's much older than me if not in actual years then surely in mental age. He has, however, left me for someone whose bottom is bigger than mine and I'm not sure whether that makes me feel better or worse.

She swings into Bite Me!—the sandwich bar that is Jake's favoured haunt, and joins the lunchtime queue. And I follow, slipping in behind her. We shuffle forward and I watch as she scans the menu board on the wall. I'm so close to her, taking in her hair, her eyes, the shape of her nose, her suit, her heels, the size of her comely bottom, her expensive watch, and yet she has no idea. She has no idea that I'm picking her apart, bit by bit. No idea that I'm watching her. No idea that she is bound to me. That she is part of my life.

'I'll have brie and cranberry with salad on granary,' she says. She looks like a brie and cranberry type of woman. Her voice is cool and confident. And I notice that she doesn't say please. Perhaps she's used to other people saying please to her.

'Yes, darling?'

I blink myself back into the real world when I realise the woman in the white hairnet behind the counter is talking to me.

'What would you like?'

'Er…'

I haven't had time to study the menu. I can't see it properly from here.

'Er…' I have to hurry.

'We've got some nice poached salmon today.'

'Ham,' I say. 'I'll have ham.'

'Tomato? Pickle? Salad?'

'Yes.'

'All of them?'

'Tomato.' It's great to be so decisive. 'And salad. Please.'

My lover's lover is already collecting her sandwich, paying her money, smiling a broad, insincere smile. Turning away.

'I'm in a rush,' I say to the sandwich woman.

She gives me a look that says I should have made my bloody mind up quicker then, but she says nothing and cracks on with assembling the portion-controlled amount of ham with a few slender slivers of tomato.

I grab the proffered sandwich bag gratefully, pay up and rush out of the door. At the end of the street, I see her turning the corner and sprint to catch up with her. She has such a commanding presence that she stands out in a crowd and it's easy to follow her down the narrow, cobbled lane. At the end she opens a door and goes into one of the shops. Keeping up my pursuit, I see she's gone into a ritzy-looking hairdressing salon.

I keep on walking and then lean against the wall just past the door and, still clutching my sandwich bag, catch my breath. Grief, I'm really not as fit as I think I am. TV detectives never get out of puff so quickly.

Once the blood has stopped pounding in my head, I risk a peep inside the salon. Inside looks even more chi-chi and probably has chi-chi prices to match. I have no idea what I'm doing, my body is on autopilot as I push open the door and walk in. A loud ding! announces my arrival. My love rival is sitting at one of the cutting stations chatting to an unspeakably trendy stylist. The stylist takes her to the back of the salon to get her hair washed. I wonder what she's having done, because, quite frankly, I've never seen anyone with more immaculate hair and I thought I was fussy about mine.

'Can I help you?' a tiny person all dressed in black asks me. 'Do you have an appointment?'

'No,' I say. 'Do you mind if I wait for my friend?'

She glances into the salon. 'Who's your friend?'

'She's over there,' I say. 'Getting her hair washed.'

'Oh, Neve!'

Neve.

'She's great, isn't she?' she breathes, admiration in her voice.

I know that certain people would agree with her. 'Yes.' I'm amazed that women like her too and it makes me think if I've ever heard anyone speak about me with admiration.

'Have you known her long?'

'Not really.'

'She'll be about half an hour,' the impressionable young girl says. 'Do you want to sit over there?' She points to a hard, black leather sofa.

'That's fine.'

'Tea? Coffee? Can I get you a magazine?'

'No. No. Nothing, thanks.'

'What's your name?'

'Lyssa.'

She swings away from me. 'I'll tell her you're here.'

'No,' I say. 'Don't do that. Don't disturb her. I'll just wait.'

'Okay.'

The stylist brings Neve back to the station and she sits down. She still looks impressive even with a towel wrapped round her head—cow. I watch her with slack-jawed intent. I can't get comfortable on this sofa. It's like sitting on a block of concrete and the back's too low, forcing me to sit upright as if I'm on a spike. So what do I do now? I know who she is. I know what she looks like. I know her name. I know that she has taken my boyfriend away from me.

The stylist has started cutting now. Tiny nibbles at Neve's perfect hair. She looks like a woman unconcerned by other people's troubles. And it seems to me the world would be a nicer place if we humans weren't so cruel or so indifferent to each other. The stylist is smiling at her as she chatters. I wonder what she's telling her? Is she confiding that her new boyfriend has just moved in? Is she revealing that he already had a girlfriend who is now desperately unhappy? Is she revelling in the fact that she has won him over someone else? Neve flicks her head about a lot when she talks, which must make the hairdresser feel like stabbing her with the scissors. Or perhaps it's just me who feels that way.

I can't stand this any longer, so I slide out of my seat, unseen, and go back out into the street. The air is cold after the hot fug, the lacquer and perm-lotion scent of the salon. And I feel dizzy with relief that I'm no longer in there.

Walking back along the street, towards Dunston & Bradley's office, I consider what my next move might be. I could wait for Jake, confront him now, but I just haven't got any strength left. I feel drained, exhausted and as if I've been punched in the gut. My rib cage feels nearly as bruised as my ego. The sandwich bag is damp under my grasp and my fingers are getting cramp from holding it too tightly. There's no way I'm ever going to be able to eat the contents.

I pass the sandwich bar and decide to go back inside. There's no queue now as the brief lunchtime frenzy is mercifully over.

'A cup of tea, please,' I say and wait patiently, gathering little bags of sugar and miniature cartons of full-fat milk and plastic stirrers to pass the time.

I pay and take the cup of tea outside. Across the street, the old dosser is curled up on the park bench. I imagine that I can smell him from here, but I think it's because all my senses are on red alert. The traffic is stopped at a crossing and I dash across the road.

As I approach the tramp, his eyes widen in what might be fear. He sits up abruptly.

'Here,' I say, as I give him the tea and the sandwich. 'I hope you like ham.'

And before I start to cry at the indignity of it all, I walk away.

Chapter Sixteen

Jake sat at his desk worrying about eggs. Boiled eggs, fried eggs, poached eggs, yodelling eggs with legs. All sorts of eggs. The egg campaign was not going well. The Egg Marketing Board had hated his last presentation, which he had to admit hadn't even turned *him* on and he'd been very half-hearted in his selling of it.

He was getting so desperate, he'd even approached Pip for some help this morning, which was strictly against his nature, but he felt he needed a new pair of eyes to give this the once-over and his friend could normally be relied upon to come up with the goods. Albeit sometimes rather wacky goods. Pip had been unusually terse and unhelpful and had given him the brush-off. It had left Jake feeling unsettled and he was sure Pip had been avoiding him for the rest of the day.

Neve came back into the office.

'Hey,' he said. 'The hair looks good.'

She gave him a twirl. 'Thanks.'

Lyssa always complained that he never noticed when she had her hair done and he wanted to do things differently this time. He had to admit though, they'd not got off to a great start. Neve had spent their first weekend with everyone other than him. In an unwelcome repeat of Saturday, most of Neve's Sunday had been taken up by training and seeing friends while he kicked around the apartment wondering what to do. He was trying very hard not to let his tension show.

Neve perched on his desk. 'I'm sorry we didn't have much time together this weekend,' she said, with what Jake felt was surprising insight. 'It won't be for long. My training will tail off once I've done the Everest trek and I'll make more effort to schedule you into my plans.'

Schedule him into her plans? *More effort* to schedule him into her plans? Something in the way Neve said that made his stomach turn jittery. Shouldn't she be trying to schedule everything else into *their* plans?

'I've been thinking.' Let's face it, he'd had plenty of time to do that in the last few days. Jake lowered his voice. 'Why don't I do this Everest thing with you?'

Neve threw back her head and laughed.

Jake couldn't help his frown. 'What?'

'You are joking?'

'I think it would be fun.'

'Fun?' Neve laughed some more—so much so that heads in the department were starting to crane. 'Have you ever climbed a mountain?'

'Not as such.' He'd taken a train up Snowdon on a family holiday in Wales as a kid. That must surely count for something. 'But I'm quite fit. You're not climbing Everest. You're only going to Base Camp. Isn't that at the bottom? How difficult can it be?'

'Why do you think I'm spending hours and hours in the gym?'

'Because you're a masochist who wants to look good in your mountain gear?' Jake gave her a lecherous look.

'You're being ridiculous,' Neve snapped. 'We're supposed to be keeping this a secret. Won't everyone guess if we start going away on trips together?'

'We'll be discreet,' he said. 'We have been up to now.'

'No,' Neve said. 'I won't have it.'

'What?'

'I won't have it. I won't have you muscling in on my plans. I always go with the same group. You'll change the dynamics.'

He had hoped she'd feel he'd change them for the better, but clearly it wasn't going to be so.

'Are you sure I'm not muscling in on your *life* too much?'

'Don't be ridiculous,' Neve said with a tut. 'I hate insecure men. Don't lay this one on me.'

'You do want me around?'

'Of course I do!' Neve's voice softened. 'Of course I do.'

Jake checked that no one was too close to overhear them. 'I spent the entire weekend farting round the flat, not knowing what to do with myself.'

'That's your problem, Jake. You walked out without any of your stuff.'

'I know,' he conceded defeat. He was never going to win an argument with Neve. Several creative meetings had already flagged that one up to him. 'I'm going to ring Lyssa and see if I can go round there tonight to collect some gear.'

'Good,' she said. 'I'll try to make you some room in the wardrobes.'

He bit back a sarcastic comment.

Neve leaned closer to him. 'Look, I'm not great at relationships,' she admitted. 'I've spent too much time on my own. Like Frank Sinatra, I need to do things my way.'

Jake smiled. 'I'm beginning to see that.'

'It'll be fine,' Neve said.

'Yeah.' Jake wanted to hold her and he wondered how long they would really be able to keep their relationship a secret from their work colleagues and, more importantly, from their bosses. 'Are you any good with eggs?'

'I might be.' Neve smiled.

'Give me a hand then,' Jake pleaded. 'I'm sinking here.'

Neve pulled up a chair. 'Sure.'

Pip walked past, head down, studying a clutch of papers.

'Hey, Pip,' Neve said. 'Want to come and look at this campaign with us?'

'Busy,' Pip said. 'Maybe later.' And he hastened his pace.

'What's eating him?' she asked.

'I don't know,' Jake pondered. 'I'd already asked him for help, but he turned me down.'

'So I'm second choice?' Neve didn't look too impressed. Now she knew how he felt.

'Perhaps he's jealous,' Jake said. 'Now that we're officially together.'

'Pip?' she said. 'No. Pip's cool.'

Was he? Jake thought. His eyes followed his friend out of the room and he wondered how close his jealousy theory was to the truth. It was an undeniable fact that something was definitely bugging Pip.

Chapter seventeen

I am calm. There is a big bubble of calm floating inside me. I'm so calm, I'm surprising myself. Jake phoned this afternoon, while I was at work, and asked if he could come round this evening. I'm trying to feel furious at him, but instead I just feel horribly, horribly disappointed and let down. Where I thought there'd be anger and pain, there's only deadness and a resigned acceptance and, maybe lurking in there, some sort of relief that this is not entirely my fault.

I've spent half an hour on the phone to Edie and it was she who helped to talk me into this collected state of suspended anxiety. This is not the usual order of things. My sister is normally completely hopeless in a crisis and I'm normally the one she runs to when anything needs sorting out, but, my goodness, has she come through for me this time.

I've poured myself a glass of white wine and am sipping it relatively contentedly—if I ignore the anxious niggle I've had in my stomach since Jake left—when there's a knock at the front door. I wipe my palms on my trousers and check my appearance in the mirror by the door, then I open it and let Jake in.

'Hi,' he said and he looks very sheepish. As well he might.

'You didn't need to knock,' I say. 'This is still your home.'

'It doesn't feel right.'

'None of it does.' I gesture at the bottle of wine. 'Do you want a drink?'

'No,' Jake says. 'I can't stay long.'

'I thought we were going to talk things through.'

'I've just come to collect some stuff, Lyssa, and then I'll be out of your hair.'

'I don't want you out of my hair. I want to sort out what we're doing and why we're doing it.'

Jake flops down in a chair like a sulky five-year-old and suddenly my calm aura departs and I get a surge of irritation so strong that I could slap him. And I can quite categorically state that I have never *ever* felt like slapping him before.

I go to pick up my wine, but my hand is shaking. 'How are you getting on at Pip's?'

'Fine,' he says. 'I'm sleeping on a futon in the spare room. I think "futon" is Japanese for small uncomfortable mat on the floor.' He tries a laugh, but it sounds very sickly.

'Oh, poor you.' I pout sympathetically.

'I'm managing,' he says stoically.

'Does Simon still live there?'

'Yes,' Jake says. 'He's cool about it.'

'So where's Pip's spare room? I thought it was a two-bedroom flat.'

'Er… It is. The futon's in the lounge.'

'So you're not sleeping in the spare room. You're sleeping in the lounge?'

Jake bristles. 'It's only temporary.'

My patience with this pretence is running out. 'Is there anything you want to tell me, Jake?'

The sulky five-year-old is suddenly awake. 'Look. I'd better be going.' He pushes himself up from the chair.

'I know, Jake,' I say, and I sound so reasonable that I can hardly believe it's me speaking. 'I know who she is. I know that you work with her. I know that you're not at Pip's. I know that you're not sleeping in his lounge on a futon or anywhere else for that matter.'

Jake sits down again. 'You're bluffing.'

I feel overwhelming sadness for the lies that have crept into our life. 'I think you're the one who's been bluffing, Jake.'

'I'll have that drink,' my lying ex-boyfriend says.

Getting up to pour the wine gives me something to do. Something that stops me from wringing Jake's neck. I hand him the glass and he swills down the wine. 'I love her,' he says.

'You must do, to walk away from everything we've worked for.'

'I couldn't stand it anymore,' Jake says. 'The whole baby thing. I'd just had enough.'

'Why didn't you say?'

'I did,' Jake insists. 'You never listened. You just kept banging on about my sluggish sperm.'

'It's important to me.'

'More so than I am,' Jake says quietly.

Some more of my calmness seeps away. 'I can't believe this. We've been going on for months having this torturous treatment and all the time you wanted to be with someone else—you *were* with someone else! And then you give me some line about wanting time away from me. Time away from me to be in someone else's knickers!'

Jake says nothing, but his face has gone grey.

'No wonder your sperm are sluggish,' I spit. 'They're probably guilt-ridden. Are they sluggish with her?'

'That was below the belt.' And then he realised what he'd said. 'I've had enough of this,' he announces and suddenly he looks sad and weary too. 'It's over between us.'

'I'd gathered that.'

'I did everything I could, Lyssa,' he continues defensively.

'I'd beg to differ.'

'It wasn't intentional,' Jake says. 'I didn't deliberately set out to have an affair. These things happen.'

'Do they?' I'm not so sure. 'Was she just walking past one day and suddenly you found yourself shagging her over the desk?'

The horrified look on Jake's face tells me that I'm not a million miles wide of the mark. Good grief.

'We just weren't on the same wavelength anymore,' Jake blusters on.

'And she is?'

'She's different,' he says. 'She's not like you. She wants what I want.'

And I hesitate to suggest that it might be a good kicking.

'She has interests outside the contents of Mothercare,' Jake says, twisting the knife. 'She's gritty. She's ballsy.'

'She looks like she could throw a javelin to Olympic standard.'

'You've seen her?'

'Of course I have,' I say. 'I've seen you together.'

'Then you'll know why I'm attracted to her.'

It's my turn to stay silent.

'Our lives had reduced down to nothing,' Jake says. 'You have lost your verve for life. All you think about is getting pregnant. Men don't care about having babies. We might pretend to. It might even amuse us for a while, but we don't really care. Not like women care.'

'Does she want children?'

Jake laughs. 'No. Neve wants to climb mountains and surf fifty-foot waves. She has very broad horizons.'

She has broad hips too, but I think it's best not to mention that at this juncture.

'She's going to Everest soon.' There's a tinge of pride in his voice. 'The woman has a lot of guts.'

I think it takes a lot of guts to let your boyfriend inject your arse with a cocktail of fertility hormones, but I don't mention that either.

'So, that's it,' I say. 'You didn't need time to think. It sounds as if you've thought a lot about it already.'

'I have,' Jake admits.

'I'll go to Edie's while you get your things together,' I say. 'I can't bear to watch you leave again.'

'I'm sorry about this, Lyssa. I did love you. If things had been different…'

'If I hadn't wanted a baby?'

'Maybe.'

'I think that's the saddest thing out of all this, Jake. I could forgive the lying and the cheating—probably. But it's the fact that we've spent so much time and energy and money pursuing a dream that I didn't know was mine alone. When were you going to tell me?'

'I tried,' he says. 'I did try. But you didn't want to listen.'

'I'll get my coat,' I say. 'I'll stay at Edie's for a couple of hours...that should give you enough time to move out permanently.'

I get up and walk to the cupboard under the stairs where we keep our coats and I pull out the warmest one I can lay hands on because I feel chilled down to the bone.

Jake is standing too. He looks smaller than I remember. He seems to have shrunk over the last few days. And I feel like I'm shrivelling inside where no one can see it.

'You haven't exactly been straight with me, either,' Jake says.

I blink back my tears.

'You can't lay all this at my feet, Lyssa,' he says and there's a catch in his voice. 'This inability to have children has all been blamed on me and my sluggish sperm, but that's not the whole story, is it?'

I feel as if the breath has been knocked out of me.

'All the time you've been telling me that there's nothing wrong with you, that everything's fine and in working order. But that's not quite true, is it?'

I am speechless with shock.

'I read the consultant's report, Lyssa. The one you hid from me. Everything's not fine at all. I've always felt that you blamed me, but you've not been straight. I think you owe me an explanation.'

'I don't think I owe you anything,' I say quietly and walk out of the door.

Chapter eighteen

Edie sent Lee to the off-licence for some wine the minute I arrived at their house, shaken and sobbing. We are showing our appreciation by drinking it very enthusiastically. Rather sensibly, Lee has now disappeared somewhere to do something with wallpaper. Two more glasses and we'll be shredding the entire male species. He has also been put in charge of the children so that we can commence the dissemination of my relationship in relative peace.

'Jake says I've lost my verve for life,' I tell my sister, sounding very much like someone who has indeed lost their verve for life.

'What does Jake know,' she says.

'Jake says she's a very *ballsy* woman.'

'You have had your own testicular moments.'

I curl further into myself on the sofa. 'She's going to climb Everest.'

'Well, I hope she gets eaten by a big, hairy-arsed bloody buggery Yeti.'

I wouldn't admit this out loud at a cocktail party—or to my sister—but I'm not entirely sure where Everest is. I know it's the biggest mountain in the world—I'm not that stupid. It is, isn't it? I'm sure it is. But I'd be hard pressed to put a pin in it on the map.

I do know that they have Yetis there though. I hope she gets eaten by one too. Slowly. A bit at a time. With her nice hairdo last.

'She's like Action Woman,' I moan. 'I bet she does bare-knuckle fighting and arm-wrestling in her spare time. She's got a much bigger bum than I have.'

'Well,' Edie says. 'Bottoms are the new boobs.'

'Oh really? And you know about these things?'

'Yes. My fourteen-year-old daughter tells me all I need to know about the world outside. I live my life vicariously through her.' Edie stares wistfully into the middle distance as she considers her lot. 'Any idea how long it's been going on?'

'I didn't ask for specifics, but for quite some time, I think. Certainly during our last two IVF attempts. That's when Jake started working late and going out for a drink with "colleagues" every Friday night.' His most overused phrase was 'I'll just have one and then I'll be straight home.' That 'one' seemed to last him about four hours. But then again, he never specified what that 'one' was. I'd assumed it was a bottle of overpriced beer. If I'd realised the 'one' was a furtive knee-trembler with his new girlfriend, then I wouldn't have watched the clock so anxiously waiting for his return.

'What a bastard,' Edie says. 'And to think I always liked Jake, despite what Mum thinks of him.'

'I quite liked him too,' I say with a heavy-hearted huff. 'I can't believe that when I was preciously hoarding up eggs like the Easter Bunny, he was out there splashing his sperm around willy-nilly.'

'No wonder his sperm-count was low if he was sharing them out between two women.'

My face crumples.

'Oh sorry.' Edie tops up my glass and puts her arm round me. 'Drink more,' she advises. 'It'll help you to forget.'

Drinking more usually helped Edie to get pregnant again, but she seems to have forgotten.

This is an awful situation and I can't tell Edie that it isn't entirely Jake's fault. Jake's not entirely wrong, somewhere in all this

I have to shoulder some of the blame too. I sink back into the cushions and close my eyes. I wish this sofa would eat me whole so that I would never have to deal with anything ever again. But as hard as I wish, the sofa just won't oblige.

I try to think back to guilt-free days. It's a long time ago. Since then, I've had to face this head-on. Every day. Some days it's so far in the background that it doesn't hurt at all. On other days it's right at the front of my brain, bashing against the inside of my skull like some demented cuckoo trying to head-butt its way out of a clock. I can't come clean. Not after all this time. Jake has poked a finger into my dark, dark secret. He has prised up the corner and now I feel I can never stick it back down again. Everyone has dark secrets. Show me someone who says they haven't got a skeleton or two in their cupboards and I'll show you a natural blond over the age of thirty.

Jake's right. I've been lying to him. But perhaps I've been lying to myself even more. At the beginning of our IVF marathon, I paid privately for an appointment with the consultant without telling Jake. The result was that he confirmed that I was damaged inside. I have scarred Fallopian tubes. Horribly scarred. And I know how they got like that. I didn't tell Jake. I didn't want Jake to know. I didn't want anyone to know. I still don't.

'Mum's worried about you,' Edie says.

I'm sure Mum *is* worried about me, but only up to a point. My mother worries about herself an awful lot more. She's always been more concerned about herself and her life than either me or Edie. When Edie was pregnant—for the first time—my mother took to her bed for days on end, wailing and moaning about what the neighbours would think and what terrible daughters we were. We were both teenagers—frightened teenagers. Edie because she was pregnant and had no idea what to do. Me because I could tell that it was falling to me to look after my sister, as I always had. When we've needed my mother, she's never been there. She has steel-grey hair and steel-grey eyes, but her nerves are made of a completely different substance. She has a voice that can reduce bank managers and checkout assistants to tears, but crumbles the minute there's a hint of a crisis in her own world. We can't depend on my mother, she depends on us.

I look at the toys scattered on Edie's lounge floor, the stack of children's videos by the telly and I wonder what my lounge would have looked like if I'd had a child. And the most terrible thing about all this is that I had my chance and I blew it. I blew it in the biggest way imaginable. No one knows this. Not Edie. Not my mother. Not Jake.

We'd all only just recovered from the shock of Edie's first pregnancy when she was at it again. She was eighteen and I was in my final year at university. My mother went ballistic, took to her bed with another attack of the vapours and insisted that this time Edie and Lee 'do the right thing' and get married. In the run-up to my finals, I came home, sorted my mother out, sorted Edie out, sorted the wedding out and when that was all over, went back to university and sorted myself out.

It was all too much. My mother would have had a nervous breakdown at the very least. In the midst of all the panic, tears and organising no one noticed that I was throwing up every morning. No one questioned why the very sight or smell of food sent me scuttling for the bathroom. All the attention was on Edie and her forthcoming event—it didn't occur to anyone that I might be having my own happy little incident.

I'd had a three-month affair with a well-to-do law student called Eamon. The earth hadn't exactly moved, but it did quiver for a little while and I wondered briefly if he might be The One. When I told him I was pregnant he disappeared on his Vespa scooter in a cloud of dust and I never saw him again. He was never in when I called at his digs and he never answered my letters. What he did do was push an envelope containing five hundred quid under my door one day when I was out, with a note saying his family would be scandalised. He told me to have an abortion. And I did. Without questioning whether it was really what *I* wanted. It seemed the most sensible thing to do at the time. I had always been the sensible one.

'More wine?' Edie asks.

I nod. To be blindingly drunk would be nice right now.

'What are you thinking about?'

'Oh, nothing much.' I smile at her to convince her I'm all right. Even now I can't bring myself to tell her the truth. This secret has to stay mine alone. Edie would be mortified and blame herself entirely and then she'd tell my mother who would probably have a heart attack—or feign one—and then she'd blame everyone else but herself. 'I'm just trying to get my head round a few things.'

The abortion was a disaster. The worst thing I have ever done in my entire life. It ripped out my heart as well as my baby. But I was twenty-two. I thought it would hurt too many people. I never considered the hurt it would cause me.

My child would have been twelve now—I don't even know if the baby was a boy or a girl. I thought I'd wait a few years, until I was more mature, before I set about replacing the void it created in my life. When you're young, you think that you have your fertility under control. You think that you'll have a great career, then find a nice man, settle down and when the time is right, start a family. But Mother Nature is spiteful and cruel. The great career leaves you so exhausted that you've no time to find a nice man. The nice man might never appear or he might turn out to be not-so-nice and run off with a work colleague at an inopportune moment. Or he might have been wearing his underpants too tight and have sluggish sperm. When you think the time is right Mother Nature has already been working on shrinking your ovaries and tinkering about with your hormones, so that becoming pregnant turns into a battle of science and technology over your own body.

The abortion left me with scarred Fallopian tubes—so the consultant said—but it left other parts of me scarred far worse than that. And my punishment now is that I can't have the one thing I want more than anything—that which I let go with so little thought.

Edie tops up her own glass. 'Crash over here tonight?'

'Yes.' My mother is right. Being alone isn't easy. I can't face going back to look at Jake's side of the wardrobe empty.

'You'll be okay,' Edie says softly.

'Yes.' I nod.

'You always are, Lyssa,' she continues, now sounding more than a little slurred. 'You're the strong one. The survivor.'

Nothing makes me want to lie down and weep more than someone calling me a survivor.

'You need to be kind to yourself for a while,' Edie suggests. 'At least tell me you're going to drop the baby thing for the time being.'

'I haven't got any choice, have I? One side of my nice, big double bed will be noticeably empty from now on.' I get a pang of loneliness and anger as I think of Jake out of my life and with someone else. Someone else with a bigger bottom and more arm muscles than me.

I remember Monica telling me that penguins only have sex once a year. It looks like I'm going to be joining them.

Chapter nineteen

I had to get up at the crack of dawn, go home, get changed and then drag myself into work. The longer I spend as a commuter, the harder it gets.

I'm sitting nursing my carton of Starbucks coffee, staring at my wonderful view and trying to work myself up to editing an article on the diary of a pregnant mother—'It's a Mum's Life!' Every title I write has an exclamation mark at the end of it. If I ever buck the trend and leave it off, Monica always puts one there anyway as if it's something I've forgotten and I'm not staging my own quiet rebellion.

Monica edges her way towards my desk. Her forehead is wrinkled in a very serious-looking frown. It's too late for me to pretend I'm working, so I take another sip of my coffee instead.

My friend and boss pulls up a chair and slides in next to me. This is also a bad sign as normally she shouts at me from the front of my desk or perches on it, depending whether she has good news or bad news to impart.

'How's it going?' Mon asks.

'Average,' I say. 'Pretty average.'

'Have you heard from Jake?'

'Yes.' I press my lips together tightly, which I've always found is a good way of suppressing those nasty emotions when they sneak up unbidden. 'He came and took all his stuff last night. He's now a permanent resident with Miss Iron Arse.'

'Bummer,' Monica says.

They're not blaming me quite so much for our relationship breakdown now that they know Jake has been duplicitous. I could milk this, if only I had the energy to.

My smile is tired. 'Things can only get better.'

Monica fidgets in her chair. 'That's what I want to talk to you about.' My friend looks as if she'd rather not be discussing whatever it is with me at all. 'I want you to see this as a positive step.'

Which means that I'm guaranteed not to.

'Go on,' I say with a certain amount of weary resignation in my tone.

'We've decided that it might be a good idea for you to move across to *My Divorce* for a while.'

'Who's *we*?'

'We think it would be a good idea for you to take a break from all this baby guff.'

'And immerse myself in divorce instead?' This actually makes me laugh out loud. I've often wondered if people go into shops and buy *My Divorce* brazenly. Or do they sneak it to the counter in the manner of people who normally buy things from the top shelf?

'We're thinking of you,' Monica says. She reaches out and squeezes my arm. 'You've had a rough time recently. A change of scenery might help.'

'I'm not giving up my great view.' I'd fight to the death to keep this desk.

'I meant metaphorical scenery.'

'So I can stay here?' Who will check how many times the river police and the half-empty tourist boats go past every day if I'm not here to do it?

'We can discuss that,' Monica assures me. Which means that some covetous bitch has her eye on my turf for sure.

'Is this a promotion?'

'Not exactly.'

'Does it involve more pay?'

'No.'

'I bet it involves more work.'

'*My Divorce* is a slightly busier magazine than ours.'

Mmm… So, I'm supposed to view this as a positive step. It's not a promotion. It involves no more pay. But it does involve more work. In other words it's a sideways move so that they don't have to look at my maudlin face and I may have to give up my great desk too.

'I don't want to do it,' I say.

'Well…' Monica is now very shifty. 'It's sort of been agreed.'

'By who?'

'Management.'

It's at times like these when I regret the weakening of the trade unions. None of us are members here, even though we all should be. If we were I'd march down to some bolshy shop steward bristling with indignation and get her to fight in my corner for me. Instead, I say, 'Okay.'

'I think you'll enjoy it.'

I think I won't. 'Why are you doing this to me?'

'We think it's for the best, Lyssa. You were getting a bit… desperate.'

'Desperate.' I didn't just wake up one morning and decide to be desperate. It's been creeping up on me for some time. With each passing year, I guess I realise that time is running out for me. And I know that you read all the time in the papers—and in *My Baby*—about post-menopausal women who are pregnant thanks to the miracle of technology. But is there any joy to be had in becoming one of the growing rash of 'grannymothers'? I'm not sure that I want to be pushing a pram around when I'm a white-haired coffin-dodger living off my pension. What if I get Alzheimer's? I might not even remember that I've got a baby!

'When is this wonderful, positive move going to happen?'

'Next week.'

If I wanted to change jobs, I'd apply to one of those glamorous magazines where you get Jimmy Choo shoes and SpaceNK cosmetics and Tiffany jewellery as freebies. What sort of freebies am I going to get on *My Divorce*?

I'm getting fed up of being dependent on everyone else's whims—Jake's, management's, Mother Nature's. I cast a wistful look out of the window. 'No one's getting my desk,' I say in as menacing a way as possible.

Chapter twenty

I have heard nothing from Jake all week. I've been rattling round the house on my own every night. And I'm considering erecting a barbed-wire fence around my desk. I did, however, make not one, but *two* momentous decisions on the train on the way home on Monday night. It is the result of the first one which finds me wearing a co-ordinated Lycra ensemble. A treadmill may not seem at first glance like a life-changing piece of equipment but it's a start.

I'm not happy. I have no boyfriend. No baby. And no job satisfaction. I thought all of these things would make me happy, but as some of them aren't immediately apparent on the horizon, I'm going to have to do something to make myself happy in other ways. Enter renewed gym membership and renewed determination to use it.

The sad thing about Jake is that I'd expected him to ring. I thought he might have given a little call just to check that I hadn't committed suicide because of him. Isn't it strange that one day you can walk away from someone who has been a large part of your life for a long time and not give them a second thought—not even to check whether they're dead? I have spent too much time nibbling my fingernails and wearing a track in the carpet waiting for him to ring.

That's why I'm at the gym. Which is nearly as momentous as the other decision I've reached. For the last two or possibly even three years, I've been paying nigh on a hundred quid a month to belong to this blasted place and I think it's fair to say that I haven't had my money's worth. But all this is to change. If Neve can look as if she can compete in three triathlons before breakfast then so can I. I'm going to get fit if it kills me. And it might well do. If not, I will be transformed into a lean, mean, athletic machine before my very eyes. I haven't been for so long that they've made me fill in one of their tiresome questionnaires all over again—the type that's designed especially to make you feel like Mrs Flabby Bottom. And I'm sure the staff have got younger and more beautiful. Still, everyone knows that mindless exercise is the best cure for depression. So, bring on the sunshine!

I'm also going to give up my quest to become an earth mother. I've had enough hints over the last week or so that it's time to let it rest. My boyfriend, my family, my friends and even the management at work are cheesed off with me, so it's abundantly clear that I need to address that too.

I am going to take a much more philosophical attitude to my predicament. If it is meant to happen it would happen. I'm not going to play God with syringes and temperature charts and injections. I must take note of the statistics. IVF does not work in a terrifying ninety-five per cent of cases and it is hideously, hideously expensive. Only a hundred years ago, scientists didn't even know how babies were conceived! Of course, they knew how the outside bit worked, but they hadn't a clue what really went on after that. And look what they get up to now. They take embryos in, out, fiddle them about without a second thought. Is that progress? It reminds me of the old joke—what's the difference between God and a doctor? God doesn't think He's a doctor. Ha, ha. Or maybe not so funny anymore. It all sounds terrifying to me and yet I'm letting these men—and invariably they are men—tweak with all my internal bits and bobs in order to produce a baby for me. The scientists can now create a baby from an embryo that's never been born itself and so we wander ever closer to Frankenstein territory. The ethical complications to all this tomfoolery are even starting to spook me.

Having a child is not the be-all and end-all to my existence. Not anymore. I'm not sure what is, but I'm about to embark on a voyage of discovery. I have to accept the fact that we all have demons and it's up to the individual whether you keep them in control or let them control you. Mine are going to go back in their box and the lid is going to be battened down firmly.

There are a lot of scary-looking women at this gym. Women who look like Neve. Women with rippling biceps. Determined women pumping their arms like pistons. Women who do not look overly concerned with their ageing ovaries. I wonder if they'll be like me in a few years' time, turned soft with advancing years and having to redefine their role in life when they find the one they most want is suddenly not available to them. Anyway, I'm not going to think about babies. I'm going to give this treadmill what for and develop thighs that can crush walnuts.

I take a deep breath and get on the treadmill, pressing the big, red button marked START. It's the sort of big red button that sets off bombs in James Bond movies. The treadmill starts to move and, rather tentatively, I start to march along with it. The treadmill picks up speed, slightly faster than I do. Am I really so out of condition? Ooo. Shit. I can't walk that fast!

This may not be a ground-breaking start to my new, improved life, but at least I'm doing something. I am going to do great things with the rest of my years on this planet. I haven't quite decided what yet. But something. Something that doesn't involve rocking chairs and knitting. Something out of the ordinary. This is my decision. I have no special skills. I've had no awe-inspiring experiences. My life, so far, has been singularly lacking in heady sensation. All that will change. I'm going to look at Jake's leaving as some sort of unexpected liberation from drudgery. Honestly, I am. I gasp some hot air into my labouring lungs. But for now, I'm going to concentrate on keeping up with this bloody machine.

★ ★ ★

Jake and Neve were pulling hard, side by side on rowing machines, and Jake realised that he'd have to make certain adjustments to his concept of togetherness. He'd learned already that he had absolutely no way of beating Neve, so the only way to ever get to spend any time with her was to join her. When he was with Lyssa, he'd always felt guilty about the amount of time he devoted to his chosen sports. Now the boot was on the other foot and Neve seemed to suffer no such pangs. She was utterly single-minded in her dedication to her goal and no one, least of all a sulky boyfriend, was about to get in her way.

Neve was panting rather attractively, perfectly placed sweat staining her grey designer sports vest. She was a stunning woman. And stunningly competitive too. Jake's arms were killing him and his chest was burning and tightening, but Neve was showing no signs of letting up. There was no way he could let a girl beat him. He gritted his teeth and kicked out.

'We need to finish off the egg campaign tomorrow,' he shouted over to her—more in an effort to distract her than out of a true desire to discuss work matters.

'I did it this afternoon.' Neve didn't even glance up.

'Oh,' Jake said. He'd seen her with her head down at her desk, but it hadn't crossed his mind to ask why. 'Okay. We'll look over it together in the morning and then pass it in to Alec for the once-over.'

Alec was the creative director. He was Pip's boss and generally known as a hard bastard. Alec was the only person who could intimidate Jake without really trying. Perhaps it was because he always made him feel as if he tried too hard to impress him.

'I saw him this afternoon,' Neve said casually.

Jake stopped rowing—partly because he was about to die, partly because he was in shock.

Neve stopped too. She grabbed a towel and ran it over her neck and face. Suddenly, she caught Jake's stunned gaze. 'What?'

'You didn't give him the presentation?'

'Yeah,' she said. 'Do you have a problem with that?'

Jake thought that he did. 'That was my campaign.'

'We were working on it together. I did some extra stuff this afternoon. You seemed to be busy. I didn't want to bother you.'

'We should have presented it together.' *I* should have presented it, he thought. It was *my* project. It made him feel like a kid getting jealous because someone else was playing with his ball. He bit back any other comments he might have wanted to make.

'No harm done,' Neve said. 'Alec liked it. He thought it was inspired.'

Jake brightened. 'Did he?' He wished he'd been there to hear Alec say that he'd thought it was inspired. Alec was generally sparing with praise.

'Yes,' she continued. 'He said he was impressed by our teamwork.'

'He did, did he?' Jake smirked to himself. Little did Alec know exactly how much teamwork they did together. Jake suspected one or both of them would be for the high jump if Alec ever caught wind of what.

'What else did he say?'

Neve shrugged. 'Not much.' She stretched her arms above her head. 'Are you finished?'

'Yeah,' Jake said. 'Shall we grab something to eat on the way home?' He was sure that there would be absolutely nothing of note in the fridge. He'd have to make a major sortie to the supermarket this weekend. They couldn't spend their entire lives existing on Blue Sapphire vodka and champagne.

'I've got a few errands to run,' Neve said casually. 'I'll catch up with you later.'

Jake glanced at the big stainless-steel clock on the wall of the gym. It was nearly nine o'clock. 'Now?'

Neve pouted her lips. 'Now.'

He knew better than to ask exactly what errands needed to be done at nine o'clock at night. 'I thought we could cuddle up on the sofa together.'

'Later,' she said rather dismissively.

Jake tried not to look hurt. Even though he'd been back to the house in St Albans and had relocated all his stuff to Neve's—and how painful that had been—he still didn't feel like a permanent fixture there. If he'd been a puppy, Neve would have been prosecuted by the RSPCA for neglect by now.

His girlfriend came over and kissed him slowly, nipping at the skin as their lips parted. It was still hard to think of her in those terms. Would Neve ever truly be 'his'? She smiled at him. 'I won't be long,' she said.

Before he could argue she walked away, trailing her towel behind her. Jake frowned. Takeaways for one were becoming less appealing all the time. Alec might not be impressed if he knew the amount of teamwork they were doing together, but from Jake's point of view, he wasn't sure that they were doing nearly enough.

Chapter twenty-one

Everest looks very high. Even the base camp appears to be a bit of a misnomer. It seems a hell of a way up to me. It also looks as if you need to have very bad taste in clothes to climb to it. In the photograph, they are all wearing serviceable red anoraks and cheery bobble hats. I might want to do something exciting with my life, something that will inspire future boyfriends—if there ever are any—to speak of me with pride. I glance at the expedition brochure again. Trepidation sets in. In a moment of sheer madness, I phoned up an adventure travel company on impulse and requested it. All I wanted to do was have a little look at where Neve was going. Really. Though I now feel it may have been an impulse too far. Do people actually do this sort of thing with their two weeks' holiday? What happened to the joy of frying yourself on a beach with nothing more taxing than a bit of chick lit to exercise your brain? Why does everyone now have the urge to fill their lives with the exotic, the challenging and the downright dangerous? And even more pertinent—why do *I* now have the urge to do it?

The answer is that I want to do something that's going to make people go 'wow!'. I want them to say, 'Hey—you know that Lyssa? You'll never guess what she did right after her boyfriend dumped her.' I want to do something jaw-droppingly awe-inspiring. I just don't want to do it while wearing an anorak. On the plus side there are a lot of men in the brochure and not many women. Probably because most women would have more sense—particularly dress sense. If a man has enough stamina to go on an expedition like this, it might well mean that he has very frisky sperm. And when it comes down to it, everyone has to take their bobble hats off in bed. Well, they would if they want to get in bed with me.

Things seem to have been moving apace. This is my last day on *My Baby*. Next Monday morning I will be an employee of *My Divorce* and the vexed subject of me moving away from my lovely desk has yet to rear its ugly head.

Monica and Charlotte are taking me to lunch to wish me luck and I think I'll need it a little bit more than they expect. At the other end of the office, I can see them gathering up their bits and pieces and heading towards me. I stuff the brochure with big, high mountains on the cover into my desk drawer and feign innocence as they approach me.

'Ready?' Monica says.

And I am.

We totter *en masse* along the Embankment, clutching each other's arms, heads down against the wind. The lilac-grey clouds look as if they're taking part in a Formula One race across the sky. I keep an eye on the brisk, gusting breeze as it tries to whip a cappuccino froth onto the Thames and then we duck into one of the side streets to our favourite little restaurant for moments of celebration. Every excuse and we're down here—birthdays, anniversaries, moving to unsuitable jobs, life-changing announcements. It's a Spanish restaurant with a deeply unoriginal name—Pueblo—and it serves great tapas and a wonderful creamy, fragrant soup made of garlic and bread. I've tried numerous times to make it at home, but it doesn't taste wonderful, it tastes remarkably like garlic and soggy bread. The restaurant only has half a dozen tables, so I've no idea how it manages to keep going in this part of London. We squeeze into our special place in the corner, just by the window. Whenever I think of leaving, it's the views out of windows that I'll miss the most. Does this mean I spend most of my time staring out of them watching as life passes me by? Monica goes into ultra-efficient mode and rattles off a list of tapas to tempt us, while I sit and look at the grey people, in grey coats, heads tucked down like tortoises as they plod along, shoulders hunched against the elements. People don't walk like this in hot countries, do they? They swing along, heads high, shoulders back, embracing the sun. They whiz around on inline skates and bikes and skateboards and generally look as if they're having a lot of fun. Today the wind feels strong enough to turn your eyeballs inside out.

Pedro, the lovely swarthy Spanish waiter who has a look of Antonio Banderas—particularly after a drink or two—brings us a bottle of wine, which means that no work will be done this afternoon. And do I care? I do not.

'Are you looking forward to next week?' Charlotte ventures.

'Yes.' I can quite categorically state that I am.

'I don't want you to leave *My Baby*,' Charlotte says as Monica plays mother with the wine bottle. 'But I think a change will do you good.'

'So do I.' I raise my glass and take a swig.

Pedro arrives balancing a tray full of tiny terracotta dishes that are giving off delicious wafts of heavenly smells. I do think for the first time since Jake left that my appetite has come back and a smile spreads across my face.

'What are you grinning at?' Monica says, diving into one of the dishes before poor Pedro can get it anywhere near the table.

I feel a tremble of excitement inside. It's years since I felt like this. Probably since Jake and I first started going out and we couldn't wait to race home from restaurants to touch each other naked. We had a lot of half-eaten meals in those days. And I feel sad that somewhere along the way we lost that, the sheer pleasure of each other. But not even those thoughts can dampen my spirits today.

'I think we should propose a toast,' Monica says.

'Hear, hear.' Charlotte lifts her glass in agreement.

I have another drink in preparation.

'To Lyssa,' Monica starts. 'The *Baby Blues* page will not be the same without you.'

'To Lyssa,' Charlotte picks up. 'A great friend. A great editor.'

'We're going to miss you,' Monica says.

I'm going to miss them too. This is a big move. For the first time I feel a flutter of apprehension. It will be the first time I've spoken my intentions out loud.

'To *My Divorce*,' Monica says, and throws back her wine.

'To *My Divorce*,' Charlotte echoes, and does likewise.

I have another drink just for the hell of it. I didn't go near a drop of alcohol all the time I was trying to get pregnant and I think I should, therefore, try to make up for lost time.

'You'll love it,' Monica effuses. 'They're a fab bunch. Not as fab as us, of course, but fab nevertheless.'

'And we can still have girly lunches together,' Charlotte assures me.

'They do, however, want you to move desks,' Monica says as if this revelation is going to be a surprise to me. I always knew it was on the cards. Too many people have their eye on my prime spot. I bet my mate Monica is up there at the top of the list. She hangs her head slightly. 'Are you worried about that?'

'No.' And I'm not. Really, I'm not.

She sags slightly with relief. 'I'm sooo pleased,' she says. 'I'd sort of had my sights trained on it, to be truthful.'

'I guessed as much.'

'You'll still love me when I'm gazing out of your great view?'

'Maybe.' I want her to know that I'm not a complete pushover.

'Well…' Monica rubs her hands together and casts a greedy eye over the tapas dishes. 'Shall we tuck in before this lot gets cold?'

They both spear a tasty morsel.

'This is nice, isn't it?' Charlotte mumbles.

I take another leisurely drink. 'I'm not going to work for *My Divorce*.'

Their food stops halfway to their mouths.

Monica doesn't look overly amused. 'What?'

Charlotte's chin has hit the floor.

'I'm not going to work for *My Divorce*.' You can read as many books as you like about empowerment, but there's nothing quite like doing something empowering to give you a buzz. My veins are positively fizzing. I think I could quite happily spend the afternoon just repeating that phrase. It feels like some sort of meditation mantra. I couldn't honestly see myself spending my days editing articles suggesting *'How To Make Your Divorce Party Swing'* or *'The Power of Pre-Nuptial Agreements'*. I don't think editing articles about the breakdown of relationships could hardly be considered 'moving forward' in my current situation.

'What do you mean?' Monica says, seeming to struggle with her powers of speech.

I'm quite enjoying this. I take a deep breath, because I want to appear absolutely confident when I say it. 'I'm leaving.'

Monica's chin joins Charlotte's on the carpet.

I sit back and smile, tasting my wine, which is fabulous and fruity and is certainly hitting the right spot.

'Leaving?' Monica stutters. 'You can't leave!'

'I think you'll find I can.'

'Where are you going?' my incredulous friend wants to know. 'Have you been having secret interviews and not telling us, you cow?'

'I bet you've got some glammy job lined up,' Charlotte says. 'And are going to make us green with envy. If you get free designer clothes, I'm going to beat you to death with this wine bottle.'

'I haven't got a new job,' I say. 'I'm just leaving.'

'To do what?' Monica is nearly shrieking. 'Are you going to look for another job?'

'I'm leaving today, Monica.'

'You can't!' She's apoplectic. I sometimes forget that occasionally she is more management than mate. 'You must be on three months' notice.'

'And what can they do, Mon? Stop my pay? Sue me?' I shrug as if I haven't a care in the world.

'Why?' she says. 'Why are you doing this?'

'I don't want to write about divorces. That would be too, too depressing.'

'What if I ask them to keep you on *My Baby*?'

'I don't want to write about babies either.'

'What!' This is from both of them.

'Everyone's right, I've been too focused on having a baby for too long. I've done nothing with my life but moon over the contents of Baby Gap. I'm going to do something positive, for myself. I'm going to have an adventure.'

'An adventure?'

'An adventure,' I echo. And I hope to goodness that's what it's going to be.

Chapter twenty-two

The doorbell rings and I plod down the stairs. When I open the door my sister is standing there. She breezes past me. 'Lee said you'd left a message saying you wanted to talk to me.' Edie throws her bag down on the sofa. 'I thought I'd break free from the sink and see if there was still a world outside my front door or whether it was all now a charred, black wasteland.' Edie stops in her tracks. 'Are you going out?'

'No.'

'Then why have you got a rucksack on your back?'

I'm also wearing shorts and a vest and sweating like a pig, but she hasn't noticed this.

'Why are you wearing shorts and a vest and sweating like a pig?'

I can't help but giggle. 'I'm training.'

'I am too,' she says. 'To be an alcoholic. Get some booze out, sis. Anything. I don't care what colour.'

'Aren't you going to ask me what I'm training for?'

Edie settles herself in the comfiest armchair. 'What are you training for?' she obliges.

I present myself in a theatrical manner. 'I'm off to Nepal!'

My sister looks unimpressed. 'Where's that?'

I try another tack. Strike another theatrical pose. 'I'm going trekking in the Himalayas!'

'They're hills, aren't they?'

'Got it in one!'

Edie shoots out of the armchair. 'Are you insane?'

'Possibly.' If she saw that I had six tins of Heinz Big Soup in my rucksack and had been marching up and down the stairs for the last hour trying to turn my thighs into steel bars, she'd definitely think I was. I have also been singing 'Eye of the Tiger' in the style of the *Rocky* films, to myself, out loud. Are these generally considered the actions of a rational woman?

'Where did this come from?'

'Everyone's been nagging me to get off the baby treadmill. Jake's naffed off because of it. I've no commitments. There's a bit of money left in the savings account that was going to be used for our next IVF attempt which I can now blow.'

My sister is looking wide-eyed and incredulous.

'What?' I say. 'Why not?'

'It's a bit sudden.'

'I thought you'd be pleased.' If everyone reacts like this, then my faith in myself is going to take a bit of a wobble.

'I am,' she says, sinking back into her chair. 'I think.' Edie puffs out a long breath, clearly trying to make some sense of this. She rakes the mop that she calls hair. 'The Himalayas…' she breathes. 'They're so…*hilly*.'

'Hills have a tendency to be,' I point out. 'I thought it would be a challenge.'

'Good grief,' she says, 'it will be. Are you sure you're fit enough for this?'

I slip off my rucksack. I have no intention of showing her my tins of soup. I have never carried a heavy weight on my back in my life, so I thought I'd better put a bit of practice in. 'That's why I'm getting myself into shape.'

'Wait, wait!' Edie says, a cloud crossing over her eyebrows. She fixes me with a censorious stare. 'This isn't because the Amazonian-type woman who's nicked your boyfriend is going there?' My sister's eyes bug out of her head. 'You've not booked on the same expedition? You're not going to *stalk* her up hills?'

'I'm not that mad,' I huff. Although I have wondered myself. I'd been poring over all the brochures I've acquired with the thought that anything she can do, I can do better. And then I realised I probably couldn't when it came to climbing mountains, but by then I was hooked on the idea of getting out of my box to do something different. I'm missing Jake so much that I can't just sit around here waiting for him to come back. I could, however, have opted for a few weeks in a five-star health spa in Thailand instead. But it's a bit late to be thinking like that now. I flop down in the chair next to Edie. 'Do you think I'd put myself through this extreme privation just to prove a point?'

'What extreme privation?'

'Well, I'm going to have to walk everywhere.'

Edie looks somewhat less than sympathetic. 'That's usual for a trek, I'd assume.'

'And I'll be living in a tent.'

'A tent? Now I do need a strong drink. You've never been in a tent in your entire life.'

'I have so!'

'Once, Lyssa,' my sister reminds me. 'One night. We bleated and badgered Mum until she let us borrow the next-door neighbours' tent to sleep in the garden—one measly night—and then not even the whole of it. We spent weeks persuading her, and you—*you*—chickened out at half past ten because you thought the bogeyman was going to come and get us.'

'I was twelve. You were eight. You kept telling me ghost stories until I was scared shitless. And now I'm older and wiser and know that the bogeyman doesn't exist.' The meanest men in the world you'll come across are generally the ones you live with.

'Where are you going to plug in your hairdryer?'

Ooo. Hadn't thought about that one. My sister gives me a knowing look. 'The Himalayas are no place for super-smooth straightening irons,' she says with menace.

Gulp.

'How many hours a day are you going to trek?'

Believe me, I went through the brochure until I found a trek that had the word EASY next to it in great big letters. But it still looks like an awful lot of walking compared to my usual twenty-minute stomp to the train station.

'Are you going to be sharing your tent with an utter wombat?'

'Hah!' I have sorted that out at least. 'I've booked a tent all to myself.'

'Luxury,' Edie says, failing to hide her sarcasm.

'And someone else puts it up for you.'

'I'm *so* tempted to join you,' she adds. 'Why didn't you make your point by sodding off to a five-star spa in Thailand?'

There's no way I'm going to admit that, rather belated, this is crossing my mind. 'I've done that stuff before,' I say bravely. 'There's no challenge in that.'

'I might have come with you then,' Edie offers. 'Two whole weeks without the kids.' Edie closes her eyes.

'I…'

'Don't speak,' she instructs. 'I just want to hold that thought for a few moments. Two weeks without kids…'

'Be pleased for me,' I beg.

She opens her eyes again and is still looking fazed by this.

'I'll get that wine.' I go through to the kitchen. My legs are killing me already and I've only been going up and down the stairs with my soup for one night. Edie follows me.

'I *am* pleased for you,' she says. 'Really, I am.'

'I need a break,' I explain. 'I just want to get away from all this. From Jake, from hormone injections, from fertility-enhancing nasal sprays, from my job. They wanted to move me sideways on to *My Divorce*.' I hope my desperate look encompasses all I feel about that. 'I'm utterly fed up.' I'm into my stride now. 'I wanted a complete change.'

'You'll certainly get that,' Edie concurs. She finds some glasses in the cupboard and plonks them in front of me. Her need for liquid refreshment seems to be reaching crisis point. 'When do you go?'

'Er…' I'd sort of hoped she wouldn't ask that. She gives me her most scary stare. The one she normally reserves for her children. I cave in and blurt out, 'Next week.'

'Blimey,' she says. 'That is quick. You'll never be fit enough. You're going to have to bribe one of those Sherpa chappies into carrying you.'

I have a feeling she may be right. About the first bit, if not the second.

'And the office were happy for you to take a holiday at such short notice?'

'Er…' I sort of hoped she wouldn't ask that either. 'I've resigned,' I admit. 'Today. And then I walked out.'

Edie is blinking lots, but not speaking at all.

I rush on. 'And then they rang me up when I got home and said I could have a sabbatical—fully paid—as it was obvious that I was under extreme stress. I think Monica told them I was planning to sue them for constructive dismissal or sex discrimination or something. I wasn't, but it means my job will be sitting waiting for me when I come back. On whichever magazine I choose.' Personally, I think that's a bit of a result.

'Is this really my perfect, sensible sister speaking?' My sibling is suitably gobsmacked. 'You quit your job to go and yomp up a hill or two?'

I shrug. 'Perhaps my perfect and sensible days are coming to an end.' And perhaps Jake will love me again if I'm an Action Woman who no longer has a toddler fixation.

My sister scratches her head. 'Exactly how long are you planning to go for?'

'A month,' I say. 'Just a month.'

'A month.' I'm sure I can see fear in Edie's face. 'In a tent? Bloody hell. Rather you than me.'

I slump against the counter. My knees are all wobbly-fied. My shoulders are aching a bit from my rucksack too. 'Do you really think I'm mad?'

'Quite,' my sister says. She comes and puts her arms around me. 'But I love you for it. And I love you for trying. I'm not sure that I'd have the guts to do it.'

'I'm not sure I have.'

'At least you're giving it a go,' my baby sister says. 'You'll be fine. Just don't talk to any strange yaks.'

We both laugh, but I know that my laughter sounds just that little bit nervous.

Edie waves her empty glass at me. 'We should open some champagne. Toast your new idiocy…sorry…independence.'

'We have got a bottle on ice.' Edie and I exchange a glance at the 'we'. It was the one I put in the fridge on the day that Jake walked out. Seems rather ironic really.

'Crack it open then,' she insists.

I do and as I pour the creamy bubbles into our glasses, I say, 'This is nice. It does feel like a celebration.'

'It feels to me like something that will piss a couple of people off no end,' Edie counters. 'I'm not sure who I'd be more worried about telling,' she says. 'Jake, or Mum.'

And suddenly that feels more disconcerting than conquering any Himalayan foothill.

Chapter twenty-three

A week is not, I've found, a very long time to prepare yourself for such a momentous trip. Go on a beach holiday and all you need are a few bikinis and a sarong—maybe a natty pair of flip-flops. Nipping off to Nepal is not in the same league. The Himalayas are not so accommodating when it comes to equipment requirements. I went out on Monday and threw myself on the mercy of a very lovely young man in the local Outdoor Shop. After several hours of trying on walking boots and down jackets and discussing the various merits of four-season sleeping bags, I came out of the shop several hundred pounds lighter and several bags heavier.

When I got home, I tried on all my new gear again in the privacy of my own lounge. It was truly alarming. I fear that I might look more like one of those anoraked, bobble-hatted types in the expedition brochure than I care to imagine. Plus I can hardly move, let alone march up a hill.

Still, I'm committed now—or should be—and I'm having a going-away party to mark the occasion. A select few. My sister, hubby Lee and their brood, doting mother who has not yet been told the purpose of the party, and Pip. That's it. That's my send-off party. I'm not sure why I invited Pip. Except that he's been nice to me and has even called a couple of times to see if I was okay—which is more than can be said about Jake, from whom I've heard bugger all.

Edie and her entourage have arrived already. My mother always likes to make a late entrance. My sister's kids have the entire contents of my new wardrobe spread out on the lounge floor and are taking it in turns to try it on. It's causing them great hilarity, which is not the response I'd hoped for. Liam is wearing my new wraparound, mountain-strength sunglasses. My nephew is stumbling round, groping the furniture—as well he might. Honestly, they're so dark I can hardly see out of them. I'm going to need the services of a guide dog if I'm not to walk straight off the edge of a mountain when I'm wearing them. Which would not be a good start to my trip. Something else for me to worry about! Lee, lost without any DIY to do, is taking a moment of respite to read the small ads in the local free newspaper.

'I tried to do Nepali-themed food,' I say to Edie, 'but Sainsbury's didn't oblige.'

'All they eat is yak,' she replies, Archie hanging from her hip. 'Yak meat, yak butter, yak milk, yak yoghurt. You'll come back looking like a yak.'

'How do you know this, font of all knowledge?'

'I saw it on the National Geographic channel.'

Pip arrives. I think he's very brave to have agreed to share the same air space with my family. *I'm* fairly reluctant to do it sometimes. He kisses me as he comes through the door and gives me a tentative squeeze. I take his motorbike helmet and the ton weight of his jacket. My inability to bear even moderately heavy loads is beginning to worry me.

'Oh, my word,' my friend says as he picks his way through the pile of equipment and children on the floor. 'This looks like serious stuff.'

'I know,' I say. 'I'm not sure what to do with half of it yet.'

'I'm not sure I would,' he admits.

As well as tons of equipment and clothing, I'm taking loads of books in case no one talks to me. Pip picks one up and examines it. 'Interesting reading matter,' he observes. 'Possibly not the best selection for someone who's going to spend a month in a tent.'

As well as the obligatory guidebook, I've chosen only paperbacks that feature murder, horror and serial killers.

'Ah yes,' I say, 'but there are no children, no angelic babies, no romantic heroes, no happy families—especially after the serial killer calls—and definitely no happy endings.'

Pip laughs. 'Then they're very appropriate.' He rubs his chin and ponders. 'Where exactly are you going to put them?'

'Goodness only knows.' I haven't worked that out yet. I'm hoping my rucksack performs miracles and holds all that is stuffed into it.

'Look,' I say, pulling my attention back to my guest. 'You can make a run for it now if you'd like before my relatives get their claws into you. It could be a wise move.'

'Nonsense,' Pip says. 'I wanted to be here to wish you *bon voyage*.'

'Come and meet my sister then,' I suggest as I'm not sure what else to do with him and Edie's eyes look as if they may be about to shoot out of her head. 'Edie meet Pip. Pip, Edie.'

'Pleased to meet you,' Pip says and looks as if he would shake hands with her, but her one hand is clutching a wine glass and the other a small child.

'You too,' Edie says. 'What do you make of this?'

She points Archie in the direction of my clothing mountain. Pip turns to check out the full-colour glory of my trekking gear again—as if he can't quite believe how terribly unstylish it is. Mind you, Pip's wearing a shirt that looks like the purple wrapper off the nut whirl in a tin of Quality Street. My mother will view this with the utmost suspicion. She does not normally mix with men in purple, metallic shirts.

Edie mouths to me, *'He's gorgeous!'* just as Pip turns back.

He has the grace to look embarrassed while my sister turns a deep shade of mortification and tries to melt into the walls. I feel myself flush too.

'Daisy!' Edie says. 'Stop trying to jam that boot on your head!'

She looks apologetically at us. 'Excuse me.' And dashes off to beat or berate her children.

'Sorry about that,' I offer. 'And she's the least embarrassing of all of them.'

'It's okay,' Pip laughs. 'It's an everyday occurrence, women falling at my feet.'

'Yeah, right!'

'She's lovely,' Pip comments, his eyes following my sister. 'Just like you.' Then he's distracted by the untidy heap of mountain-type clothing on the floor. 'Brave girl,' Pip says to me, deftly changing the subject. He flicks a thumb at the stacks of gear.

'Well, you encouraged me to do something with my life. So you're partly responsible.'

Pip lowers his voice. 'I suggested you take a lover, not jack in your job and clear off for the foreseeable future.'

'It feels like the right thing to be doing, Pip.' I have no other explanation.

'Then go for it,' he says and puts his arm round my shoulders. From the other side of the room, my sister winks at me. 'I, for one, admire you.'

'You might be the only one,' I say. But I like the thought of being admired. Isn't that what I wanted? 'Oh hell!' I'm certainly not going to be admired for my hostess skills. 'I haven't even offered you a drink.'

'Your mind is clearly on loftier pursuits.'

'Wine?'

'No,' Pip says. 'I'm on the bike. I'll have orange juice or something.'

'Come and see what I've got.' I go through to the kitchen to find something non-alcoholic for my abstemious guest. Pip follows.

As I pour him a glass of juice, he leans very aesthetically against my fridge. 'So. Now that we're alone. How are you?'

'Oh, fine.'

As I hand over his glass, he touches my fingers and forces me to meet his eyes. 'How are you *really*?'

'Er...really, I'm missing Jake so much it hurts, I'm utterly terrified about this trip. And I'm frightened that my sister may be right and I'll have to eat yak products for a month.'

'You'll be fine.' Pip smiles softly. 'It'll be character building.'

'That's what I'm most afraid of.' I fuss about getting some wine and putting away the juice, then when I can bear it no longer, I blurt out, 'How's love's young dream?'

'Jake?' Pip rubs his chin. 'Also finding out that not all's necessarily fair in love and war.'

'Oh?'

'I'm staying with my original assessment,' Pip says. 'If I were a betting man, I'd put a fiver on them splitting up before Christmas.'

It's near the end of November now. Which means that by the time I come back from my adventure, I'll only have to wait a short time before Jake comes scurrying back. My heart gives a little leap of joy.

But before we can discuss it further, my mother arrives and breezes into the kitchen. She eyes Pip with something that looks like contempt and to his credit he pretends not to notice. My mother tosses down her handbag and proceeds to peel off her gloves with what can only be described as purpose.

'Edie's just told me what all that clutter is.' Thanks, Edie. 'What on earth are you thinking of?'

'I thought it would be a change. Something to put on the CV. Something to tell the grandchildren.'

'You've got to have your own children before you can be a grandmother,' she notes and gives Pip another once-over to check whether he might be a suitable candidate.

'I thought you'd be pleased.' I thought no such thing.

'I would be, darling,' she says, hand on my arm. 'You know I support you in everything you do.' I bite back the comment, Since when? My mother suddenly looks a little faint. 'What's Mummy going to do without you, darling?' That's more like it.

'I'm sure you'll manage,' I say lightly. 'I'll be back before you know it.'

'I *do* hope so,' my martyred parent says mysteriously.

To distract herself from her plight, Cecilia trails an exploratory finger over my work surfaces, which are often found wanting in the cleanliness stakes. 'But aren't you doing it all with rather indecent haste?'

'Spontaneity,' I say. 'It's something that's been lacking in my life for too long. I thought this would take my mind off things.'

My mother looks doubtful. At that point, Daisy comes into the room. She's wearing my down jacket, which touches the floor, and has my bobble hat wedged over her eyes. 'I'm a Yeti, Grandma,' my niece says and growls ferociously to prove it.

'Yes,' she says. 'Aunty Lyssa will know all about those in a few weeks.'

From behind my mother's shoulder, Pip catches my eye. He gives me an approving look.

'I thought it would be fun,' I say rather lamely. I can only hope that I'm right.

Everyone else has gone, except my sister. She somehow persuaded her husband to take the children home without her—primarily on the pretence that she was going to stay here and help me clear up the mess. Her children have eaten me out of house and home, so clearing up mainly involves drinking the dregs of wine from the half a dozen bottles we managed to open.

I'm washing up some serving dishes that are too big to go into the dishwasher. Edie has her feet up on the kitchen table, glass of wine nestling on her chest.

'Thank goodness they're gone,' she sighs. 'I love my kids, but I wish that you could take the batteries out of them for a while. They wear me out.'

'You don't know how lucky you are,' I say.

'Don't start that again, Lyssa,' she warns. 'Anyway, you're one to call the kettle black. You seemed pretty lucky yourself a little while ago.'

I give her a puzzled look.

'Pip,' she says. 'I've heard you talk about him, but you didn't tell me he was so swoon-making.'

'He's all right,' I say.

'All right! Your red-blooded male alert mechanism clearly hasn't been reset yet.'

'You're a married woman who doesn't get out much. You're impressionable.'

'I'll say so.' She goes all dreamy. 'Do you think he's got the hots for you?'

'No. He's a mate,' I insist. Give my sister an inch and she'll take a mile—just like my mother.

'Maybe he could be more?' She gives me a suggestive leer.

'No,' I say. 'I asked him to sleep with me and he wasn't interested.'

'What?' Edie nearly spits out her wine.

'That's what we young, free and single women do these days,' I toss over my shoulder. I don't tell her that it was in jest.

'You're a dark horse,' Edie mutters. 'I'm not sure what's come over my big sister in the last week.'

'A mild rebellion born out of necessity,' I say wearily.

'I wouldn't say no to him,' my sister says into her glass.

'Well, he did say that he thought you were lovely.'

Edie sits up. 'Did he?'

I smile at her. 'I saw him give you the once-over across the crowded room.'

'Really?' Edie sips her wine thoughtfully. 'I thought I caught him looking at me a couple of times.'

'There you go.'

'Well, if you're not interested,' she says briskly, 'I suggest that you stand aside and make way for someone who is.'

'You're married and I'm not interested. But you're right. Pip's lovely. He's just not Jake.'

'I hope you're not going to sit round on your bum waiting for that scoundrel to come back.'

'I'm going to Nepal. I don't think that can be classed as sitting on my bum.' Actually, I'm beginning to worry that I'll not be doing enough of it.

I put down the tea towel and join my sister in polishing off the remaining wine. 'Pip thinks it won't last.'

'He may be right,' Edie agrees, 'but you can't put your life on hold for Jake indefinitely.' My sister gets a peculiar look in her eye. 'I hope you meet some big, hairy-arsed yak shepherd who'll shag you senseless.'

Knowing my luck, that's all I'll meet.

Chapter twenty-four

Jake was sitting staring vacantly at his computer screen when Pip sloped into the office.

'Hey!' Jake shouted over.

Pip stopped in his tracks and, after a noticeable hesitation, came towards him. Jake wondered briefly if his friend had been going straight to his desk instead of coming over to shoot the breeze as they normally did.

'Hi,' Pip said and sat on the corner of his desk.

'Good weekend?'

'Yeah,' Pip said. 'Not bad. You?'

Jake looked round. 'Not great.' Neve wasn't at her desk. They'd travelled in together, but she'd disappeared the minute they'd arrived and was still nowhere in sight.

'Home alone again?'

'Yes,' Jake said. He nibbled the end of his pen. 'Is it me, mate? Am I being too demanding?'

'Is that what she said?'

'Not in as many words,' Jake admitted, 'but I think that's what she's getting at.' Jake puffed out his cheeks. 'I hate women. They're just too...too...*different*.'

'They'd be worse if they were the same as us, mate.'

'Yeah.' But maybe that was half the problem. Neve was exactly like a bloke. Not in the looks department, obviously—but she behaved like a bloke. She wanted to spend her weekends at the gym and out with her mates. She had no idea about shopping—unless it was in designer boutiques—and he didn't think she'd ever been involved with the working end of a vacuum cleaner. There wasn't a single duster in the apartment. It wasn't that the place was a mess, far from it—but whoever cleaned it clearly had to bring all their own stuff with them. Women weren't supposed to be like this. Lyssa had never been like this. Lyssa had tackled all domestic duties with something approaching joy. He was sure she had.

Jake opened the brown paper bag that Pip had put on his desk and examined the contents. 'Mmm.' He helped himself to a chocolate croissant while Pip looked on with a pained expression.

'Still no food at Neve Towers?'

'Cupboards full of the stuff,' Jake said. He had actually eaten breakfast, but only because he'd spent a good part of his leisure time pushing a shopping trolley around the supermarket with all the other reluctantly domesticated mugs. Jake bit into the pastry. It was very tasty. 'I'm doing this for the benefit of your waistline.'

'You are charm itself,' Pip said. 'So what did you get up to?'

'Tagged along after Neve at the gym, which I'm not sure she was overly keen on,' he admitted. 'Not so easy to flirt with the hunky instructors if you've got the old man in tow.' Jake gave a philosophical shrug.

He'd had this vision of doing coupley things with Neve—romantic strolls in Hyde Park, cosy lunches in chi-chi bistros, snuggling up at night on the sofa. The sort of thing he'd done with Lyssa before 'baby' became the most frequently used word in her vocabulary.

Women generally wanted their man to be around, while Neve was obsessively independent. Most of the time he just felt as if he was in the way. If that was the case, he had no idea why she'd asked him to live with her at all. Or maybe it had been he who'd suggested it? To be fair, Neve hadn't mentioned any other long-term relationships to him—but then she hadn't mentioned much to him as they spent so little time together. Perhaps this was all too new to her.

'She went out with her mates on Saturday night while I watched *Saturday Football Special* with a bag of sour cream and onion Kettle chips and two cans of Miller Lite.'

'Mmm,' Pip said.

'Mmm, indeed,' Jake said. 'Still, I shouldn't complain.' Although he wasn't exactly sure why not. 'What did you get up to?'

Pip shifted on his desk. 'Not a lot.'

'It can't have been less than I did, mate,' Jake said with a sigh. Then he grinned. 'Or are you being evasive because there was a lovely lady involved?'

'Yes,' Pip said.

Jake sat up at his desk. 'Oh?'

His friend chewed at his lip thoughtfully and took his time before answering. 'I was at Lyssa's yesterday.'

Jake sat a bit more upright. '*My* Lyssa's?'

'Your *ex*-Lyssa's.'

Jake felt vaguely put out. 'What were you doing there?'

'If you'd thought to call her at all, you probably would have found out.'

'I've been busy,' Jake said and sounded too defensive even for his own ears.

Pip looked at him as if to say, 'You've just told me you did fuck-all this weekend.'

'I didn't want to upset her,' Jake corrected quickly. 'Was she okay?' He tried to look suitably penitent. 'I'd hate to think of her moping around because of me.'

'No,' Pip said. 'I can't say she was moping around.'

Jake forced a smile. 'You're not thinking of…'

Pip raised his eyebrows in question.

'You know…you're not thinking of…*you* and Lyssa?'

Pip pondered for a moment. 'Maybe,' he said. 'Why? Would it be a problem?'

'For me?' Jake said. 'Why would it be a problem for me?'

'Quite,' Pip pointed out. 'You've moved on to bigger and better and more athletic things, remember?'

'Yeah,' Jake said. 'Yeah, I guess I have.' But his stomach had started churning all the same and he was sure that it was simply because of all the fast food he'd consumed over the last few weeks.

'I might ask her if she fancies a date….' Pip stared levelly at him. 'When she comes back.'

'Comes back?' Jake asked. 'Comes back from where?'

'Nepal,' Pip said. 'The Himalayas, to be precise.'

Jake felt himself go pale. Very pale. 'What the hell's she going to the Himalayas for?' He could hardly speak.

'Why not?' Pip shrugged. 'Seems to be a popular thing to do.' And Jake couldn't help but hear the slight irony in his voice.

'Yes, but not for Lyssa! She's…she's…she's not the type!'

Pip seemed to be suppressing a smile. 'Perhaps she's thinking of becoming "that type".'

'She can't.' Jake could feel panic rising in him. 'She wears nail varnish. And make-up. Every day.'

Pip didn't look the slightest bit concerned. But then Pip wasn't her boyfriend. Yet. And come to think of it, neither was *he*, anymore. 'Who's she going with?'

'No one,' Pip supplied. 'She's going alone.'

Jake nearly gasped out loud. 'Do you think she's unhinged?'

Pip laughed. 'No.' His friend was suddenly serious. 'I think she's more together than I've ever seen her.'

Jake shook his head. 'I've got to talk to her. She can't do this.'

'I think you'll find she can,' Pip said. 'She's jacked in her job and she's off.'

Jake's heart had started to pound. He thought he might be having an anxiety attack. The only time he ever felt this bad was trying to keep up with Neve in the gym. 'Jacked in her job!' Jake put his head in his hands. 'She's completely lost it.'

'Why do you think it's great that Neve is doing the same sort of thing, but with Lyssa you view it as a catastrophe?'

'They are very different women,' Jake said. 'Lyssa won't be able to manage on her own. Neve doesn't need anyone.' The thought nipped painfully at his subconscious. He shot an accusing glance at Pip. 'I can't believe you didn't tell me sooner.'

'I didn't think you were that interested anymore.'

'She can't do this. She's very vulnerable. I need to talk her out of it. I'm going round there tonight.'

'Then you'll be too late.'

Jake heard himself squeak with terror. Where did that come from?

Pip glanced at his watch with rather less haste than Jake would have liked. 'She'll be on her way to the airport in the next couple of hours.'

Jake stood up. 'Then I'm going right now.'

It was Pip's turn to look surprised. 'What about the presentation to the Egg Marketing Board?'

Jake frowned. 'What about it?'

'The suits are due in soon.'

The frown deepened. 'Says who?'

'Says Neve.' Pip was frowning too. 'She's set it up with Alec. Didn't she tell you?'

'No,' Jake said, and he couldn't quite vocalise the emotions that this particular piece of knowledge stirred up inside. 'She didn't mention it.' Despite the fact they'd sat on the same Tube train all the way into work. What the hell was she playing at?

'I'm out of here,' Jake said.

'Ring her.'

'She won't talk to me,' Jake said. 'I know what she's like.' Or at least he thought he did.

'You'll miss the meeting,' Pip warned.

'I don't think I was invited anyway,' Jake said, shrugging on his coat. 'And do you know something, Pip? Suddenly that doesn't seem quite so important. I'm going to try and catch Lyssa. I want to stop her from making the biggest mistake of her life.'

And he wasn't altogether sure he hadn't just made an equally disastrous bloomer himself.

Chapter twenty-five

I open the door and Jake is standing there. He's out of puff and red-faced. His hair's a mess and he looks dreadful. There are dark circles round his eyes and they're probably as a result of having sex in every room of the house with the nubile Neve. He looks washed out and exhausted. And I want to feel pleased about this, but I can't.

'What do you want?'

Jake pushes into the lounge. 'Pip told me about your hare-brained plan,' he pants.

He stops abruptly as he sees my brand spanking new kit bag and my rucksack and my rather startlingly coloured anorak. 'Good Lord,' he breathes.

'I can't stand here chatting,' I say as pleasantly as I can manage. 'I'm off to the airport.'

'You can't go,' Jake says. There is real terror in his eyes.

'Why?' I say. 'And don't mention anything about yaks or Yetis. It's all been done.'

It seems strange to see him standing here again. I feel uncomfortable with him and not as if I've spent the last four years with him. It's as if that was my old life and this is the new, biologically improved me.

'Have you actually thought this through?'

'Of course I have.'

'What are you going to do when you get there?'

'Trek,' I say. 'It isn't as demanding a trip as *Neve's*.' I can't help sounding barbed. 'But it will suit me.'

'You wouldn't even go for a walk round the duck pond in Verulamium Park without an hour's protest.'

'My,' I say brightly, 'how things change!' I hope Jake doesn't spot my leery bobble hat.

'You're not one of life's active people.'

I make no comment, but set about doing busy things involving baggage tags and rucksacks.

'Where will you plug in your hairdryer?'

'Is that all anyone thinks about me?' I have to admit this is the one thing that is worrying me most. That and having to go to the toilet behind a bush. Lack of civilised sanitary facilities has always been one of my main reasons for eschewing the great outdoors.

Jake's shoulders sag and he slumps into the chair. 'Don't do this,' he says. 'Please don't do this.'

And for a moment, I nearly forget that I'm not supposed to love him anymore. I can't stand this space, this void, between us. I look at his face and it is creased with concern. And, bizarrely, I think it's concern for me. This is a man who up until the day he left lay with his arms around me while he slept—is that usually a sign of someone who has a mistress?

'I feel this is all my fault,' Jake says.

I feel it is all Jake's fault too. 'You washed your hands of me, Jake,' I say flatly. 'You left when I needed you most.'

Jake hangs his head.

'You needed a change and you went for it without another thought.' I was feeling really wobbly about this, but Jake's concerns are only serving to make me determined to be positive. 'It's time for me to do the same. A complete change.'

Jake sits and doesn't say anything. He looks into the middle distance and then turns and stares out of the window.

'I have stuff to do, Jake,' I say.

He sits forward in his seat and I think the circles round his eyes have darkened. 'Let me take you to the airport.'

'No. No way.' I shake my head. 'I wouldn't even let Edie or Mum come. I've had enough emotional goodbyes recently.'

Jake stands and heads for the door. And it's all I can do not to cry.

My heartbreakingly gorgeous ex-lover opens the door. 'Lyssa, if you could turn back the clock, would you?'

'To when?' I ask lightly. 'To last week? To pre-IVF days? To when you still loved me? To before I ever laid eyes on you?'

'I hope this works out for you,' Jake says sadly.

I can't speak. It's too risky.

'I still care for you,' he adds.

'Go.' 'Go' is the shortest complete sentence in the English language and it's also the saddest.

Jake goes.

I sigh heavily and press the tears back into my eyes. Picking up the last few bits and pieces, I stuff them into my rucksack, which is bulging alarmingly at the seams. It's no good, I can't take all this crap. I have never been one for packing light and it's still slightly worrying that I'm faced with carrying all this lot by myself. Despite the fact that I've abandoned my usual paraphernalia of folic acid supplements, hormone injections, sniffer drugs, pregnancy tests, I've still got far too much unnecessary kit. Apart from my trusty guidebook, the reading matter has gone—no joyous tales of serial killers to keep me amused in the dead of the night at three thousand metres—I'm just going to have to force myself to be sociable. Even with that lot out, I'm still going to have to leave something else behind. I pull out my hairdryer and put it in the middle of the floor in a reverential way. If I'm going to do without something, it might as well be something symbolic.

Chapter twenty-six

I'm thirty-four years old and although I've been on a plane kerzillions of times, I've never actually flown alone. How bizarre is that in this age of supposed emancipation? And it's quite an ordeal. Jake normally sorts out all the money and tickets and the passports and checks we have the right gate number. My duties were always restricted to plundering the tax-free shop for perfume and booze bargains. Such are my nerves that I develop a pathological fear of losing my boarding card, and until we take off and the pilot announces that we are definitely headed for Kathmandu, I'm convinced I've made a complete hash of it and am on the wrong plane and will end up in balmy Benidorm in my Arctic-strength anorak.

I spend the entire time during the flight, not watching *Scooby Doo* or any of the other movie selections, or catching up on my sleep or reading my *Lonely Planet* travel guide to see exactly what I'm letting myself in for, but trying to suss out who my fellow travellers might be. Everyone who has a pasty white face and a loud-coloured anorak is a suspect. Its only when we approach Kathmandu and the majestic sweep of the snow-tipped Himalayan foothills comes into view that my anxiety turns to excitement. There's something quite exhilarating in feeling the fear and doing it anyway. And in a blinding flash of bravado, I know I can do this. I can do this alone.

At Kathmandu airport I identify a shuffling bunch of Brits as my travelling companions. They look as ill at ease as I do and that helps me to relax too. I'm not alone in my apprehension. This motley crew are the people I'm going to spend the next month with and they don't look too scary after all. Not one of them looks hideously fit. Hurrah! Following some cursory nods and tentative 'hellos' and nitpicky complaints about airline food, we're shepherded through to the rickety domestic terminal and onto the tiniest aircraft I've ever seen by a smiling man who's no bigger than my nine-year-old nephew. The whole thing looks as if it might be held together by string. Cheap string. And probably not enough of it. All of our luggage is pushed inside the aircraft with us and we set off again, amid the rucksacks and kit bags, bouncing down the runway in the slipstream of a jet.

Half an hour later, we land again—this time in Pokhara airport, which looks rather like a home counties village hall. My legs are shaking as we get off the plane and I'm trying not to think that I've now been travelling for more hours than I have fingers to count them on and am on the point of hallucinating. This isn't helped by the fact that there's a huge cow asleep in the arrivals hall and we dodge round her as we lug our bags out to a colourful coach.

Our transport is painted bright blue and pink and its chrome is so highly polished that you can see your face in it. Mine doesn't look particularly inspiring. As a swarm of smiling Nepali men take our bags from us and load them onto the roof, I can see that less attention has been lavished on its braking system. Two blocks of wood wedged under the wheels are all that stop us from rolling down the nearest hill and into oblivion. It's not a comforting thought that we're soon to be winding our way round mountain roads in this.

Machhapuchhre—the snow-capped, razor-edged 'Fishtail' peak—stands at the head of Phewa Tal Lake and pierces the cloudless blue sky whilst towering majestically over the small touristy town. This is my first glimpse of the Himalayas from the ground and I feel as if I've finally arrived. I do, however, hope that we're not going to attempt to walk up anything even remotely that high.

'Hey.' A vision of manly loveliness approaches us proffering a friendly wave. And I know that I have tipped over the edge and am now in full hallucination mode. Perhaps the cow was, after all, a figment of my imagination too. This certainly isn't the raddled, old yak shepherd of Edie's dreams. 'I'm Dean,' he says to us all with a broad smile and some kind of hybrid American accent. 'I'm going to be your guide for the trip.'

One of my main worries about this adventure was whether I'd like my fellow travellers—I hadn't bargained on liking one a bit too much. I thought our guide would be some gnarled, ancient man of the mountains—a brother to the yak shepherd. It hadn't crossed my mind that he might be a babe.

Dean is working his way round the group, checking off names, shaking hands. He comes to me.

'Lyssa Allen,' I supply. My lips are very dry. I always get completely dehydrated on planes. That's the only reason. Believe me.

His smile widens. Oh, my good grief. In a land where, so far, everyone seems to have been relatively toothless, it's a particularly nice smile. 'Hi. Great to meet you.'

He takes my hand and gives it a welcoming squeeze. His fingers are rough and calloused and I wonder if maybe he works in the fields or something when he's not guiding unfit bands of Brits. His hair is black and unruly and looks as if it's been chewed by a wild bear or styled by a blind barber. He has soft brown eyes the colour of freshly dug earth and when he's not smiling—which seems as if it's a fairly rare occurrence—pale, delicate lines radiate from the corners of his eyes where the sun has failed to kiss. He has an enviably healthy tan, which probably makes him look slightly craggy and maybe older than his years. There's no evidence of psychedelic trekker-type clothing. Dean is wearing combat trousers, a black tee-shirt, black boots and an army dog tag. He looks very cute. I'm sure I recognise him from a trendy aftershave advert. But it doesn't appear as if his look has been put together as an image statement—he gives the impression he's just flung on the clothes nearest to hand from his bedroom floor. I try to stop staring at him.

'First time you've done anything like this?' he says.

'Does it show?'

Dean shrugs. 'You look a little nervous.'

I hug my arms round myself. 'I am.'

'There's no need to be,' Dean assures me. 'I'll look after you every step of the way.' I could put it down to my new anorak, but suddenly I feel very warm. 'You'll be fine.' He ticks me off his list and cranks up that smile again. 'We'll have a lot of fun.'

Will we? Oh my good grief!

Chapter twenty-seven

'Are you going to sulk all night?' Neve asked.

'Quite probably,' Jake said and restructured his sulking posture. Neve was sitting on a chair, while he was taking up as much of the sofa as he could manage.

'We've been over this a dozen times today.' She was getting more tetchy by the minute and Jake didn't think she had any right to. Her voice sounded hollow and hard-edged as it bounced off the walls in the cavernous main room of the apartment. It was like living in the reception area of an architect's office. He hadn't realised how much affinity he had for carpet until he didn't have it anymore. 'I thought you'd lost interest in the egg project.'

Neve snapped off the television with the remote control.

'And I thought we were working on it together,' Jake said. 'So we were both labouring under a misapprehension.'

Neve said nothing.

'You didn't even tell me about the meeting you'd fixed up with Alec. How do you think that makes me feel?'

'I was going to tell you….' Even Neve didn't seem to think she sounded convincing.

'When exactly?'

'When I came over to your desk and Pip told me that you'd just gone chasing off after Lyssa.'

'So minutes before it was due to start? Why didn't you tell me days before or the night before or when we were on the Tube together all the way into work?'

'It slipped my mind.'

'No, Neve,' Jake said. 'Nothing that important slips your mind.' If one of the guys had done this to him, Jake would have decked him first and asked questions later.

'Why didn't you tell me you were rushing off to hold your ex-girlfriend's hand?'

'The first I knew about that was from Pip too. She's off on some madcap trek in the Himalayas.' He cast an accusing glance in her direction. 'She clearly hasn't thought it through properly.'

'Good for her,' Neve stated. 'You said she never did anything interesting. Perhaps she'll love it. She's her own person now.' Neve shot an equally accusing glance back at him.

'I was trying to stop her from making a big mistake,' Jake pointed out. 'I was trying to help her. Not stitch her up.'

'Is that what you think I was doing to you?'

'Is there any other explanation?'

Neve flicked her hair back and glared at the wall. He'd come back from seeing Lyssa, depressed and feeling displaced, only to find the egg meeting was over. The egg presentation—the presentation he'd worked for months to prepare—had been nicely hijacked by the love of his life. He'd sat and stewed all afternoon, tasting bile and wondering quite where he'd gone wrong in life.

'I shouldn't discuss this with you,' Neve said.

'It's my bloody project!'

'This is confidential,' she continued, ignoring his protest. 'Alec is concerned about you.'

Jake pushed himself up on his elbow. 'About me?'

Neve lowered her eyes. 'He doesn't think you've been giving work one hundred per cent commitment.'

'I've had a lot on my mind,' Jake said. 'As well you know.'

'I think he's caught wind about us too,' she admitted. 'There's been some gossip in the office. I think some of the guys know.'

Jake sagged back. This was dreadful news. Alec had never liked him and always seemed to be looking for some reason to hang him out to dry. An affair with Neve could be just the ammunition he was looking for. Then again, in a rather perverse way Jake was glad that the guys in the office knew he was shacked up with Neve. Despite her sleight of hand in whipping one of his projects out from under his nose, she was one hot chick. There would be some very green faces at Dunston & Bradley when this became common knowledge.

'I did this because I didn't want you to make any stupid mistakes in front of him,' Neve said. She sounded earnest enough. 'The last presentation was a stinker, Jake. And you know it.'

Neve was right. He was lucky that Alec hadn't taken the project off him there and then. He was going to have to get back on track at the office, otherwise they would be making him hit the road. All day long his mind had been drifting to Lyssa and wondering what she was doing now. She should be there by now, ready to start her new adventure—without him. He only hoped that she'd be okay.

Neve stood up, stretching her long legs. There had been no mention of going to the gym tonight. 'I'll make us some cappuccino,' she said. Jake couldn't get up any enthusiasm. 'Or shall we have some champagne?'

'Neither for me,' he said.

Neve slid onto his lap and twined her fingers through his hair. She kissed along the edge of his jaw, her hot breath teasing up towards his ear. 'What about an early night?'

He didn't want cappuccino. He didn't want champagne. He didn't want to make love. He didn't want to be sitting on a sofa that was exquisitely designed but as comfortable as a concrete slab. And he didn't want Neve thinking that she could get round him so easily when he was still harbouring the sneaking suspicion that she had well and truly stitched him up like a kipper.

Sensing his lack of response, Neve eased away from him and

went into the kitchen. He looked round the apartment. It was fabulous to look at, but it had no heart. Only a few weeks ago he had thought all this was exactly what he wanted. Now he wasn't so sure at all. But if he didn't want all this, exactly what *did* he want?

Chapter twenty-eight

A dozen or more of the Nepali porters get on top of the bus along with the luggage and a basket of struggling chickens and three pumpkins while the rest of us squash inside. Someone pulls the blocks of wood out from under the wheels and we're off again.

I find a seat near the back and jam myself in—Nepali legs are clearly a lot shorter than European ones. Our bumpy journey jogs along dusty dirt roads that cry for the want of Tarmac. We're accompanied by the strains of a counterfeit George Michael cassette played at the wrong speed and the inside of the bus is madly decorated like a council house at Christmas. Tassels and streamers of every different shade of lurid swing wildly along with the motion of the bus and our porters clap along to George who hiccups as we hit every hump, bump and pothole in the road. I'm too stunned to speak. I cling on to my rucksack for protection and, in the stifling temperature, cook quietly in my own juices without the benefit of air-conditioning.

We squeeze our way through the suburbs of Pokhara, winding at wild speeds through the roads crammed with ragged people bartering for their daily food outside equally ragged shops. It's seriously bad karma to hit one of the sacred cows wandering down the centre of the streets, but no one seems to have told our driver this and I'm sure he avoids them and the crowds of people by sheer good luck rather than good management.

Soon we leave behind the sound of honking car horns and climb further as the dirt track gets narrower and the shops and cheek-by-jowl, breeze-block houses give way to open fields and mudbrick, one-roomed homes clustered into tiny villages. We lurch to a standstill at the outer reaches of one of the villages just as I'm reaching the limit of my travelling ability, moments before the onset of nausea.

Dean stands up. 'This is it, folks!' He claps his hands. 'The start of our trek. All you need is your rucksack. The porters will take the rest of your luggage and meet us at tonight's camp.'

Ooo. This is indeed *it*.

I feel there should be a fanfare of trumpets or a drumroll or something significant to mark this moment—but there isn't, so I shoehorn myself out of my seat and we dutifully file off the bus and then hang around like lemmings. Some look like distinctly more enthusiastic lemmings than others. Most of the group are older than me, which is sort of comforting. I hope if I look completely pathetic then they might take pity on me and not march off too quickly. I hate old people who are fitness freaks—it sort of goes against the grain of things, doesn't it? Everyone else seems to be in pairs—not couples necessarily, but at least linked to another human being, and that makes me feel sad. The porters have formed a chain and are man-handling our bags from the roof of the bus. A group of children from the village run out of the fields and stand and eye us shyly.

'*Namaste,*' Dean says, and clasps his hands as if in prayer.

'*Namaste,*' the children chorus.

'This is the only word you need to know,' Dean tells us. 'Literally, it means I respect the God in you—but is used for anything from good morning to I hope a donkey pees on your grandmother.'

'*Namaste.*' I risk my first word in Nepali and all the children shriek in delight, clutching each other in their hilarity. Clearly my Nepali accent needs work.

We fuss about with our rucksacks and trekking poles. I've never used a trekking pole before—it's not essential equipment in London—but the man in the Outdoor Shop told me that I must have one. So have one I did. My credit card and I had both lost the will to argue by that point. I'm not sure what I'm going to use it for yet, but maybe it will come in handy for fighting off frisky yaks.

'This is Sanjeev Sherpa,' Dean shouts. 'Our Sirdar, or captain, for the trek. He'll be leading the walk today. We'll have a gentle start.' I'm sure he looks specifically at me. 'A couple of hours to lunch and then another three hours this afternoon.' When I went to school, that was around five hours' walking—which doesn't sound all that gentle to me. I don't know if Dean sees my look of terror, but he quickly adds, 'And it's mainly flat.' How much is 'mainly?' I'd like to know.

'Okay,' he says. 'Wagons ho!' Seems as if I'm about to find out. The porters are loaded up. Without exception, they're tiny, wiry guys wearing flip-flops and a variety of tee-shirts advertising alcoholic drinks from around the globe—Budweiser, Castlemaine XXXX, Stella Artois and Boddingtons. As well as the luggage, they're carrying all our tents, food and cooking equipment including the kitchen sink and a large, metal stove that looks as if it has already seen a bit of action. Most of them have huge wicker baskets slung across their backs, the weight taken on bands around their heads. They're singing, joking and laughing and I'm not sure why, given the enormous loads they're lifting. I'm struggling with the weight of my rucksack and realise that I should have trained with considerably more than six tins of soup in it.

Sanjeev Sherpa leads the way and, like nervous sheep, we follow. I fall into line and the village children drop in behind me, giggling madly. There's not one of them has a clean face and they are clearly strangers to a hairbrush as they all sport a tangle of black, bird's-nest hair, but each one of them has a beautiful beaming smile and the biggest, happiest eyes I've ever seen. A tiny little girl slips a sticky hand into mine and we head off out of the village.

'What is your name?' she asks in impeccable English.

'Lyssa. And yours?'

'Sajani,' she says and tugs me forward. 'I am six.'

'I am thirty-four.'

Sajani giggles. 'You are very old.'

Some days I would agree with her.

In the fields the women are working, cutting the pale, golden corn with knives. They stop and wave at us, laughing and shouting '*Namaste*!' as we trail past. We walk along the edge of the cultivated terraces, balancing on narrow ridges just wide enough for one person. The sun is high and strong, the sky is clear and cloudless, the air unimaginably pure. Overhead, the black silhouettes of eagles and buzzards circle lazily in the sunshine. And I'm not sure whether I should view the presence of wheeling buzzards as a comment on my trekking ability. The Seti Khola River flows by twenty feet below us at the bottom of the terrace. The river isn't solid, flat and grey like the Thames, it's a ribbon of pale blue water, the shifting, sparkling colour of opals. Its rushing sound is the only discernible noise. The sun beats down on my neck, warming my bones, and I sigh and wipe my handkerchief across my forehead. The land here is more beautiful than I ever could have imagined. It may have a very unfit audience, but that doesn't mean I'm not appreciative.

Dean is walking behind me and as he gets nearer I hear him whistling softly under his breath. I turn and grin at him. He winks at me. 'That's better,' he says. 'It's the first time I've seen you smile. I hope there's going to be more where that came from.'

'I think so,' I answer and a weight lifts from my heart. My little friend skips along beside me, her tiny hand so trusting in mine as she leads me along and I suddenly realise that my nerves have melted clean away. My step is confident and free. Dean grins back at me. I haven't felt this light or carefree in a very long time. There's a serious danger that I might actually be enjoying myself.

Dean reaches down to Sajani and swings her onto his strong shoulders, both of them chattering away in Nepalese.

'What is she saying?' I ask when I hear Dean laugh.

'Sajani thinks you are a very beautiful woman,' he answers. Then he catches my eye. 'And I told her that I agree.'

I'm so shocked that I nearly fall off the path and into the paddy field. Dean and Sajani giggle again as he grabs me and holds me steady.

'Hey,' Dean says, 'I'd better keep my compliments to myself if that's the effect they have. We don't want any accidents on your first day. Otherwise, I might have to swing you up onto my shoulders too.'

'I'm fine,' I say, straightening my baseball cap with a nervous cough. 'Absolutely fine. Just fine.'

I wonder what my sister would think if she could see me now.

Chapter twenty-nine

'Have we arranged to meet here so that you can tell me why you've got a pouty lip?' Pip crossed his legs and sipped at his Peroni beer.

Jake gazed out of the window of the Pig in Muck pub, out over a road gridlocked by taxis in every shade of the rainbow except the traditional black. This was a trendy place where advertising and media types mingled with City boys in the meagre fifteen minutes that generally counted as a lunch-break. It could take all of that time to get served in here. Today they had been lucky. Two beers and two rather limp sausage sandwiches were providing adequate sustenance. Jake chewed on his before he said thoughtfully: 'My heart is a burdened thing.'

'Oh dear,' Pip said. 'This doesn't sound good.'

Jake turned from the window, returning his wistful stare to his friend instead. 'You know that Neve nicked the egg project from under my nose.'

'I did know that, I'm afraid,' Pip told him.

Jake sighed heavily.

'I'd be very careful there,' his friend warned. 'She's stolen your heart and now she seems to be working the same magic on your client portfolio.'

'You don't trust her, do you?'

'Not as far as I could throw her,' Pip said. 'It was a very nifty piece of work, if you don't mind me saying.'

'I do mind,' Jake said. 'That's the problem. Does everyone else know?'

Pip leaned back and folded his arms. 'Depends who you mean by everyone else.'

'Most of the office.'

'*All* of the office,' Pip confirmed.

'Damn.' Jake puffed out a disgruntled breath. 'They must think I'm an idiot.'

'Put it down to jealousy. I think most of them would be delirious to get near enough to Neve to have her nick their projects.'

'I've got nothing much on the cards,' Jake moaned. 'Do you think Alec is passing me by?'

'You need to talk to Alec about this, Jake.'

Jake straightened up. 'That means you know more than you're telling me.'

'I know that this relationship isn't doing you any obvious favours.'

'What am I going to do?' Jake shook his head as if that would help clear the fug that had somehow settled in his brain in recent weeks.

'I am the last person to ask for advice about women.'

'You're older and wiser than I am,' Jake pointed out. 'Well, older.'

'I think wiser is more pertinent,' Pip said. 'I'm not the one shagging his workmate.'

'It seemed like a really good idea at the time.'

'Most of the biggest cock-ups in the world usually do.' Pip tasted his beer again. 'No pun intended, mate.'

Jake hung his head.

Pip, sensing his despair, took sympathy on him and changed tack. 'Did you manage to catch up with Lyssa before she left?'

'Yes,' Jake said. 'She looked so…so happy.'

'That's good.'

And it was good. Wasn't it? It was just that it was also a little bit unexpected. He was the one who was supposed to have upset the apple-cart. He was the one who had moved on. And yet here he was wallowing around in the smelly mud of emotions while Lyssa seemed to have got her act together pretty damn quickly. A bit too quickly, if you asked him. Wasn't a relationship split supposed to be devastating? Shouldn't there be a period of mourning or something to mark its passing? Should your ex-girlfriend really be jumping on the next available plane to start some sort of half-arsed adventure when she'd never been remotely moved to do that sort of thing before? Lyssa seemed to have got over him so *quickly*. And that was something he hadn't really bargained for at all.

Chapter thirty

You can't believe how relieved I am when I see a little line of blue tents appear on the horizon. I think that must say something about my state of mind as I would not normally be looking forward to spending the night in a tent, I'm pretty sure of that. How my expectations have changed. Am I the same woman who went to pot because she'd no electricity for two days!

Our snugly proportioned accommodation for the night—and for the next four weeks—has been pitched by the banks of the river. From this distance they look like colourful butterflies settled in a meadow. As we approach, trudging down the hill, knees complaining, I can see the porters scuttling about, a hive of activity. There's a welcoming fire going and steam rising from a battalion of big metal pans. My stomach groans in anticipation.

Dean catches up with me again. 'We'll be there soon,' he says. 'Feeling okay?'

I nod. Apart from being pink-faced and having a pleasant overexertion throb in all body parts, I'm fine.

'You've done really well.'

I think that's a bit of an optimistic assessment—my own view would be that I've survived my first day. My little friend Sajani left us at the outskirts of her village, but another gaggle of smiling children await our arrival at the camp. They're armed with a washing-up bowl full of cold water from the river in which chilled bottles of Coca-Cola float and, even more incongruously, San Miguel beer brewed in Nepal rather than Benidorm. They surround us like a swarm of friendly bees in moments and when Sanjeev Sherpa tells us that they've walked five miles from the nearest village to bring us these welcome refreshments, only the hardest of hearts could resist parting with a few pence for a bottle of Coke. Even though it's two years past its sell-by date and the caps are rusted shut.

I buy a Coke for Dean too and pass it to him. We both sit on a welcoming boulder and he takes the tops off, wiping away the slightly rusty ring of dust from the surface on his tee-shirt before we gulp them gratefully. 'Most of the villages don't have clean drinking water,' he says sadly, wiping his mouth with the back of his hand. 'Though you're never far away from a multinational soft drink.' He studies the label on his bottle as if mystified by the ways of the world.

I lean back, enjoying the weakening, last rays of sun on my face. 'Have you been here long?'

Dean stares out across the Seti Khola—where blue-throated bee-eaters and white-capped river chats scoot across the surface in the gathering twilight. 'Ten years,' he says, looking fairly amazed about that too. 'I came out here after college as a volunteer on a conservation project and never went back.'

He looks at me for a reaction.

'Very noble.'

'The folks back home seem to view it as very insane.'

'Where's home?'

'Good question,' he says with a faint laugh. 'California originally. Now I think it's probably here.'

'You don't sound very Californian.'

'Everyone says I have a weird accent.' He laughs again and I don't correct him. He does have a weird accent—slightly mangled American. 'I speak mainly Nepali these days. Most of my English conversation is with British and Aussie tourists in the trekking season.'

I think the cold cola on my throat is loosening my tongue and making me talkative. 'Do you ever miss America?'

Dean shakes his head. 'The thought of going back to the cut and thrust of "civilization" scares me to death. We have no stress here—other than the stress of keeping fed and warm. The simplicity of life is very seductive.' We watch the sun sinking behind the peak of Machhapuchhre, casting a golden glow over the wispy clouds flirting with the mountain. 'I get up with the sun, work in the fields, help prepare the evening meal, meet with the village elders, sing some traditional songs, dance a little, drink a bit more and go to bed with the sun.' He shrugs, slightly embarrassed, as if there's no more to add. I can quite safely say that I've never seen anyone with such relaxed shoulders. Or such broad ones, come to think of it. 'A nine-to-five number at Citibank holds little appeal now.'

Dusk is gathering over our campsite. The children stop their game of football played with a tightly wound ball of long grass—no skateboards here, no snazzy aluminium micro-scooters, no Beyblades, no PlayStations, just a grass football. As the light fades, they collect their washing-up bowl and wave us a cheery goodbye as they head off into the gloom with not even a torch to light their way. And it strikes me that it may be a hard life, but at least they have the freedom to roam about unaccompanied when everyone at home is terrified of letting their kids out of their sight these days. Strangers round here are seen as a welcome novelty by the children rather than a threat.

The Sherpas are moving round the tents, singing songs. Dean smiles at me. He points his empty Coke bottle at what appears to be my tent. 'Your en suite bathroom has arrived,' he says. Sanjeev Sherpa places a metal pan of steaming hot water on the ground outside and beckons me. My bag is waiting too. 'You'd better go before it gets cold.'

I ease myself from the boulder. Every joint I have has stiffened up and I think the pan of water would only be any good if it was two feet deep and six feet long and I could lie in it for an hour with some muscle-soothing bubble bath and a glass of fine white wine. 'Ooo,' I say as my knees object to standing up again.

Dean smiles. 'You'll be fine,' he says. 'Really you will.'

I wonder if he can tell I've come here with a heavy heart. I start to hobble away, trying to look as if I'm not ninety-two years old. Dean takes my rucksack from me with a grin. 'You'll loosen up.'

I'm not sure if he's talking about my body or me in general. We fall in step next to each other—okay, he slows down to my pace—and we walk across to the tents. 'I tock the liberty of having Sanjeev pitch my tent next to yours,' Dean says. He suddenly comes over all shy. 'I want to look after you.'

I sigh heavily with something that I think is relief and say, 'Thanks.' What I should add is that it sounds like a rather nice prospect.

Chapter thirty-one

Edie chewed her lip as she looked at the clock. 'I wonder if Lyssa's all right.'

Lee dragged his attention away from his Southern-style curly chips and the elderly episode of *Star Trek—The Next Generation* that was on television. 'She'll be fine. Your sister's a very capable woman.'

'She's not thinking straight at the moment,' Edie countered. 'I'm worried for her. I wish I could ring her.'

'It'll do her good to get away.'

A selection of their children lay in a line on the floor also watching the antics of Jean-Luc Picard and his intergalactic shenanigans. Kelly was upstairs, the beat of her Robbie Williams CD loud enough to vibrate the ceiling light. Lee was eating his reheated dinner from a tray balanced precariously on his lap. Archie was wedged between them, sucking the nose off one of Daisy's cast-off Beanie Babies. Edie always thought that they should try to eat together more often as a family, but idealism and realism never quite seemed to collide in this house and Lee was so often late home from work that the children would end up biting the legs off the furniture if they had to wait for him. Lee did something in computers. Edie was never quite sure what. She was only glad that it paid well as they managed to get through money like water with this lot who did insist on growing at alarming rates. Edie was positive that she and Lyssa had never grown at such a reckless speed—but that may have been due to the fact that most of their diet had been formed by a rather eclectic and limited selection of dishes churned out, more often than not, by her rather intense older sister. Toast had featured heavily on the menu for several years. Her heart did a worried little palpitation as she thought of Lyssa thousands of miles from home, all alone. Despite the fact that all her children were computer wizards—with the notable exception of Archie, who no doubt would join them in due course—she'd never found the time to master even the basics of email. Perhaps she'd blackmail one of the kids into sending a message for her, just to make sure Lyssa was managing okay. Though quite what she'd do if her sister wasn't managing, heaven only knows—worry a bit more, she supposed.

'Lee…'

'Mmm…'

'Do you wish we'd never had…*these*?'

Her husband looked at her, chip half-chewed.

'You know…if we hadn't had children and we'd done something more with our lives.'

'I heard that, Mummy,' Daisy said.

'Be quiet and watch the television. I'm talking to Daddy.'

'What more do you want to do?'

Edie teased out a strand of her hair and nibbled it. 'I don't know.'

Daddy seemed rather perplexed. 'It's a bit late to be thinking like that now.'

'I know,' Edie admitted. 'I was just doing a bit of "what if".'

'I don't think about it,' Lee said.

'I don't really,' Edie agreed. She spent most of her time thinking what to feed them all for dinner that night. 'It's just with Lyssa going off. It started me wondering. Do you wish we'd travelled before we settled down?'

'Not really,' Lee said. 'I like Devon.'

Which was just as well because they went there every year for their annual two-week holiday.

'I like Devon too.' It was always being voted Britain's favourite county in one poll or another, so there was something reassuringly affirming in that. 'But it's not Nepal, is it? Or Cancún? Or Peru?'

'You don't need any jabs to go to Devon.'

'No.' And she couldn't see the kids getting overexcited about travelling for hours on a cramped plane to see the mind-boggling treasures of the Incas She thought their minds might be considerably less than boggled. All they needed to keep them happy was sand, a bucket and spade, a few hours without rain and a constant supply of junk food. But did that keep her happy?

'What do you think we'll do when the kids leave home?'

'Hang out the flags, throw a big party and celebrate our good fortune.'

'I heard that, Daddy,' Daisy said without looking round.

Edie tried to stop Archie from wriggling. 'Do you think we'll still go to Devon then?'

Lee put down his knife and fork. 'Is this leading up to something?'

'No,' Edie said. 'Not really.'

They watched Jean-Luc Picard shoot some more aliens in the name of peace.

'We never talk anymore,' Edie said.

'We're talking now.'

'I mean *really* talk.'

'Good grief,' Lee said. 'I wish Captain Picard would get on with it. I've got to go out to the shed soon and put a top coat of varnish on those shelves.'

'Is this what our life is reduced to?' Edie said. 'Bloody *Star Trek* and varnishing shelves?'

'Yes,' Lee said, kissing her on the nose. 'Dinner was fab. Thanks.' He stood up and left the room.

'Bollocks,' Edie muttered as he went.

'I heard that, Mummy,' Daisy said.

Chapter thirty-two

I roll out my sleeping bag and lie down on its soft contours in my tent, staring at a tiny spider that's already taken up residence in the point of the roof. And I guess there's a more technical term than 'point'. Inside, there's just about room for me, my stuff, my very smelly hiking boots and my trusty trekking pole. My home back in England could never be described as palatial in proportion, but this is taking downsizing to extremes. Quite how I would have accommodated a tent mate, I'm not sure. It would have been very cosy. It's very cosy with just me in it.

With a bit of huffing, puffing and expert manoeuvring I've managed to have a decent wash from my bowl of pleasantly hot water. The air brushes over my naked skin, chilling the droplets of water clinging to it. Outside, the temperature is plummeting quickly with the sinking of the sun. The lurid anorak is going to come in very useful. The light is fading fast too. And I miss Jake. He used to like to dry my back for me, lying next to me on the bed, caressing me gently with a towel, kissing the places he'd dried—did he do this all the time he was with Neve? I shake away the thought and give myself a good therapeutic and very unromantic scrubbing with my specially designed trekking towel, which is about six inches square but will soak up an entire bucket of water if required—something like that. The luxury of a change of clothes is something I'm denied, so I pull on my dusty trousers once again just as someone bangs a spoon against a pan to signal that dinner is served.

Two kerosene lamps burn in the bright green tent that doubles as our dining room and night-time accommodation for our happy band of porters and kitchen crew. Most of the party are already assembled and tucking into plates of popcorn, which seems an incongruous thing out here in the middle of nowhere—my only other experience of popcorn is in the massive multiplex cinemas at home, but it appears that it's a local delicacy around here. The sky is blacker than I've ever seen, daubed with milky bands of stars. I now know why the Green Party complains about Britain being saturated by light pollution. However, I'm very glad that the young man at the Outdoor Shop equipped me with a hands-free torch that straps to my head; otherwise, I wouldn't be able to see beyond the end of my nose—and as I have quite a small nose, that isn't very far at all. I might look like a miner, but at least I won't fall in a hole. This man has thought of my every need—some I didn't know I'd have; I think I'm going to ask him to marry me the minute I get home. Assuming, of course, that I make it home alive after the next four weeks and they're not just shipping bits of me back in a box.

I follow the unsteady beam of my torch and take up my place on a little camp stool at the table set for the twelve of us. Two of the porters sit near the tent and one beats gently on a drum while the other sings a traditional song. The wood of the campfire hisses and spits showers of bright orange embers into the night like fireworks.

Dean appears out of the darkness and comes to join us. Is it my imagination or does he make a beeline for the seat next to me? We're all still self-conscious and not bonded into the little group I'm sure we'll become over the next few weeks.

Our cook is Mr Bom and he is the most immaculately turned-out man I've ever seen—particularly given the fact that he's had to walk all the way here like the rest of us. Mr Bom is the epitome of spruce. He's wearing what my mother would describe as smart slacks, a checked shirt and a tie that would do a civil servant proud. He has shiny hair and a shiny face and it's split into a wide grin as he brings us one of the huge pumpkins filled with home-made soup and sets it down with a flourish. The aroma is heavenly and I realise how hungry I am. That's mountain air for you.

The Sherpas graciously serve us our soup while we go about the stilted business of introducing ourselves to our fellow travellers. They're not all pairs as I previously assumed. There are only two brave couples and six of us pesky single-types. On closer inspection, a few of the unmarrieds look as if they have always been single and are destined to remain forever single. I wonder does this type of holiday—if you can call it that—attract the romantically disaffected? First up is David Smythe who's fiftyish at a guess. He takes great pleasure in announcing that he works in a growth industry—as a divorce lawyer. Much hilarity all round—I guess we're all being polite at this stage in the proceedings. I wonder idly does he have copies of *My Divorce* scattered about his waiting room. He's a long streak of nothing beneath a smattering of grey hair and is wearing fairly well-scuffed trekking gear. But, despite his down-at-heel Berghaus boots, he probably owns a Surrey mansion. Sharing a tent with Dave—lucky bloke—is Jim Darker. He looks like a master criminal with a shaven head, earring and bulging biceps but is, in fact, an undercover police officer for the National Crime Squad. I wouldn't want to meet him in a dark alley if I were a criminal, but I bet he's got a great line in seedy anecdotes.

I'm having terrible trouble concentrating on all this—not because it isn't interesting, but it's just that I can feel Dean's thigh pressed up against mine. I have to put this in context—this is not a very big tent and there are a lot of us squashed in it. I don't think this is a deliberate ploy on his part. His thighs, however, are very hot. He's laughing a lot and every time he does his stool jiggles and as a result his leg rubs against mine. It's very distracting.

Two other guys are sharing a tent. One is a train driver from Essex called Graham. He says he never normally tells people he's a train driver, because anyone who has ever commuted pounces on him and blames him for all of their horrible experiences at the hands of Railtrack. He says it's worse than being a GP. Which is a shame because the guy he's sharing with *is* a GP—a very handy profession in my view. His name is Ian and he's smiling and affable. We immediately complain to him about our blisters, bunions and insect bites. He says that is why he normally tells everyone he is a train driver. Ian is good-natured, eats all his dinner and is the type of man I'd like for my doctor. I can tell just by looking at him that he'd be much more understanding of my child-free predicament than my current miserable bastard who has three kids all of whom he seems to hate with a passion.

The only other single woman is Saffron. I probably need to go no further. She is more than likely the sort of woman I'm going to end up being. Saffron is strident, childless and very slightly mad. She's already told us that she's holding a full complement of homeopathic substances—but is she holding a full complement of brain cells? I'm not entirely sure. She's come to dinner wearing a jewel-coloured floaty kaftan that looks slightly incongruous in the mountains. Saffron works as a relationship counsellor and I'm going to avoid getting into conversation with her like the plague. I'm fully expecting her to be vegetarian. I thought I had run away from everything, but I may have just had a vision of my future if I don't change my ways. She is my Bob Marley's ghost—or do I mean Jacob Marley? I'm glad that Saffron too has opted for a solo tent experience, otherwise I'd be sharing with her and I think there's a lesson to be learned there.

Of the two couples, Tony and Tania are the most nauseating—but it is a close-run thing. They must be the wrong side of forty, but act like teenagers and are so deliriously in love it is very sick-making—it makes me wonder whether anyone ever looked at Jake and me and thought that. Tony is an eye surgeon and wears bottle-bottom glasses. Tania is a chocolate taster for a Knightsbridge department store whose name is familiar to all Americans. How jammy a job is that? Despite her profession, she has a figure like a bird—and I'm talking tiny little sparrow here, not hulking great vulture. They finish each other's sentences and he eats all her vegetables, while she eats all his fattening stuff. The woman is quite obviously some sort of metabolic freak. They hold hands all the time and giggle at each other as if sharing private jokes. I'm feeling very excluded here, but of course, they're completely oblivious. I'm glad my tent isn't pitched next to theirs because they're probably going to be at it all night.

I suppose on all of these group-type expeditions there are going to be people you are never going to want to see again in your entire life. And Felicity and Felix are such people. They live in Hampstead—celeb central. Felicity is a voice coach and over-pronounces everything and talks as if she's addressing the back of the stalls. She insists that she's had all the top stars—metaphorically speaking—although she can't name any of them because of client confidentiality. Oh, that old chestnut. She does however mention the 'Welsh Beauty' and the 'Dimpled Hollywood Legend' more times than I'd consider discreet. She looks theatrical and I can just see her and Saffron sharing homeopathic elixirs. Neither of them is as young as they think they are. Felicity's husband, Felix, is a conceptual artist and I feel very threatened by him because I don't understand conceptual art at all. I'm one of these Barbarians who thinks it's a load of old nonsense, but can't argue enough to defend my stance, which even I will admit is largely based on ignorance. I thought that awful multi-coloured ceiling panel affair which won the Turner Prize a few years ago looked like something out of a 1960s working-men's club—but I fully understand that I am deemed to be missing the point. They both look too *avant garde* to have been bothered with that fuddy-duddy institution of marriage or to trouble themselves with a holiday in a tent. Strange. And when the Sherpas clear away the delicious soup and replace it with a spicy, pungent chicken dish, a speciality of Nepal, Saffron tucks in with gusto—which just goes to show that you can never judge a book by its cover.

So—all of life is here. That leaves poor old me, Lyssa Allen—

unlucky in work, unlucky in love. Depressed, heart-broken single and child-free zone. Although I'm alone, in another way I'm feeling strangely comforted to be travelling with this mish-mash of humanity.

We finish the chicken—all of it. The plates are so clean that they probably won't need to wash them and then Mr Bom brings us a metal dish of tinned fruit salad—the one with the livid red cocktail cherries in it that everyone's grandmother used to serve. And we all tuck in because it tastes so much better here with the Himalayas in the background and because some poor sod has carried it on his back all the way here.

The Sherpas finish us off completely with steaming mugs of Nepalese black tea which tastes wonderful—smoky and refreshing. Now that we're all too fat to move, we waddle outside to sit by the campfire so that the porters can move into the dining tent and bed down for the night.

Tony and Tania head straight back to their tent because they clearly can't wait to get down to it, but the rest of us assemble round the fire, leaning into the warmth. There are some mats on the ground to shield us from the chill and I'm gratified to see that my lovely guide takes his place by my side again. I'm not deluding myself, but it could be the fact that I'm single, relatively young and not completely barking that he's finding being joined at the hip to me quite attractive. And I'm certainly not complaining.

The foothills nestling round us form a magnificent backdrop to the camp; the night is cold and inordinately still. A couple of the porters join us and quietly continue to sing traditional songs, blending one into the other with only a modicum of 'what shall we sing next' discussion. It's sad, isn't it, that we Brits don't have much in the way of tradition left? Unless, of course, you count Morris dancers, and the less I say about grown men jumping around with bells on their legs and hitting each other with fake pigs' bladders the better. Most of us would be hard-pushed to know the words to the National Anthem. And it's not exactly a rousing tune at the best of times, is it? I blame it on the advent of television that none of us sit round the piano singing 'Roll Out the Barrel' anymore. And the poorer we are for it.

As well as no running water, these villages have no electricity and consequently no television, no phones, no internet. I haven't heard a single mobile phone ring since I got here. It feels like a kind of sensory deprivation and it certainly takes a bit of getting used to. There's no traffic either—because there are no roads. The only noise is the sound of the river, the occasional dog barking in one of the villages and the murmur of my companions. I have no idea who Ulrika Jonsson is sleeping with, I don't know if Madonna has bought another house and I'm surprised how easy it's been to wean myself off my weekly dose of *24.* Jack Bauer will save the world—it's a forgone conclusion. Are they really going to kill off Keifer Sutherland when he looks so fab when he's angst-ridden and knee-deep in terrorists? I don't think so.

I also have no idea what Jake is doing, and that's what feels most peculiar. Whatever he's doing though, I'm sure he's having a high old time without me.

Chapter thirty-three

Jake put his head round the door of Alec's office. 'You wanted to see me?'

Alec was looking out of his corner-office window at his fabulous view across London. He turned and bared his teeth at Jake, which in other circumstances might have been considered a smile. 'Jake,' he said in a welcoming tone. 'Come in. Sit down.'

Jake sat down. Alec returned to his desk, lowered himself into his executive leather swivel chair and spread his hands wide. 'How are things going?' There was a slight wink in Alec's eye that Jake assumed meant he was feeling chummy. Alec was at his most terrifying when he was being chummy.

Jake nodded emphatically. 'Fine.'

Alec nodded in unison with him.

'Fine,' Jake repeated.

Alec made a steeple of his hands and rubbed them together. 'Except a little bird tells me that it's not, is it?'

Jake wondered which little bird that might be. 'I've been having some personal problems,' he admitted reluctantly. 'But they're sorted. I'm getting them sorted.'

'It's affecting your work, Jake,' Alec said, his worried frown underlining the seriousness of his words. 'I'm concerned.'

You're all heart, Jake felt like saying, but kept quiet. 'This egg project has been a nightmare,' he agreed. 'I just could not find it in my heart to make eggs sexy.' Honesty, he'd discovered a little too late, might be as good a policy as any. 'They just didn't get my blood stirring.'

Alec looked at him levelly. 'They stirred some people's blood.'

Neve again. 'I asked Neve to help me out. A fresh pair of eyes. She ran with it,' Jake said. 'I was happy for her to do it.' Not strictly true, but he didn't want Alec to know his domestic situation. If he hadn't been sleeping with Neve, he probably would have branded her a manipulative bitch.

'She rescued the situation, Jake,' Alec pointed out. 'She got you out of the shit.'

Not quite, it seemed.

'I need another project,' Jake said. 'Something sexy. Something savvy. I've got ideas for the new Blow aftershave. I know we got the contract.' It was a big one and everyone in the office would be chasing it.

Alec pursed his lips and nodded slowly.

Jake sat forward on his seat. Positive body language. 'I want to get back into the fray.'

Alec nodded some more. 'That project has already been assigned.'

Jake felt it like a body slam. This was news. 'Assigned? When? To whom?' And then suddenly he didn't need to ask. 'Neve.'

'Yes,' his boss said. 'Neve.'

Jake sat and stewed while all the time trying to keep his face neutral.

'She's good,' Alec said. 'Very good. We need more people like her. People who aren't afraid to go after what they want.'

He gave Jake a mysterious look. Jake tried a smile in return.

Alec stood up and wandered back to his window. 'You need to think about your situation here, Jake,' he said, back towards him. 'Dunston & Bradley only want players on its team.'

Jake was a player. He'd always been a player. He was one of the most ambitious people in the office—bar Alec. And, of course, Neve. His plan had been to hold on to his boss's coat-tails and go with him for the ride. He'd wanted to make himself invaluable to Alec and couldn't believe how this had all gone so wrong.

'Think about what you really want, Jake,' Alec advised.

As if he hadn't been doing that every day and every night.

'Maybe you've lost your edge,' his boss continued. 'Maybe you need some time out.'

This did not have a good feeling about it. He was being asked to jump before he was pushed. Alec wanted him out. And it sounded as if he wanted him out sooner rather than later.

Jake stood up. He suddenly felt dizzy and his vision was doing that in and out thing that normally only occurs after several pints of brewed hops. Pip would know what to do. He needed to talk to Pip. They couldn't just get rid of him like that. Could they? He'd done nothing wrong. Everyone liked him here. He was a popular member of the team. No one would stab him in the back. As he reached Alec's door, his blood chilled slightly. There was only one thorn in his side at Dunston & Bradley, and that was the woman who, up until this moment, he thought he loved.

Chapter thirty-four

The others are deep in conversation, but it's passing me by. Dean rolls over and lies on his stomach facing me, toasting his toes by the fire. 'It's a good place to run away to.'

'So transparent, hey?'

He leans on his elbow and studies my face in the firelight. 'I recognise the pain from past experience.'

'Ah.'

Dean pulls a bottle of San Miguel from the depths of his down jacket. He wiggles his eyebrows in a devilish fashion.

'The alcohol route to curing pain?'

'It never works,' he says with a shake of his dark, messy hair. 'I just think you've earned a small treat today. You haven't come here to beat yourself up.'

I wonder what I have really come for. Dean rummages in his jacket again and from his Swiss Army knife extracts a bottle opener. I always wondered what people used these for, but now I know. It's really a Swiss Army cocktail set. He flips the lid from the bottle, tips the remnants of our black tea from the metal mugs and refills them with frothing beer. We clank them together and raise our mugs.

Dean takes a draught. 'Want to talk about it?'

'There's not much to say.'

My new-found friend takes my hands and examines my fingers. 'No ring,' he concludes. 'Divorced?'

'No.' I shake my head. 'Never married.'

'Kids?'

I shake my head again, as my power of speech seems to have disappeared.

'That's something to be thankful for then,' Dean says.

'Yes.' I can't even consider complex explanations at this stage, and think that if Jake and I had managed against all odds to produce a child then something good might have come out of it. Of course, I voice none of this.

'So what happened?' Dean may have a convoluted accent, but he still has his American directness.

'We wanted different things from life.' I avoid his eyes. 'Jake found them with someone else.'

'Jake?'

I nod. 'Boyfriend of four years. Blond bombshell–dropper and all-round bad egg.'

'He'll live to regret it,' Dean tells me sagely. 'Betty Jane Brightman did.'

I giggle. 'Who the hell's Betty Jane Brightman?'

Dean smiles. 'She was my sweetheart right through college. We were at UCLA together.' That's about the only American university I've heard of—that and Princeton and of course Harvard. 'She was majoring in media and film. I was studying social anthropology.'

We both laugh.

'Yeah,' he continues. 'Maybe I should have spotted the differences then.' His eyes glitter in the flickering flames. 'I'm the only guy from California I know who never wanted anything to do with the film industry.'

'So Betty Jane's married to a movie star?'

'No, she dumped me for my best friend, who's now a Realtor.' Dean shrugs as if to say it takes all sorts. 'I was offered a chance to come out here with the volunteer programme and jumped at it. I had no commitments, there was no need to even think twice. My first year was spent compiling research of the different kinds of herbs that the villagers use for medicine. I fell in love with the place.'

I wonder who else he fell in love with.

'I bumped into Betty Jane once on a visit home. She said she wished she'd never let me go. She said my former buddy had got fat and lazy. All he ever wanted to talk about was selling beach-front homes.' He draws on his beer again. 'She said we could have been married with two kids and living in the Valley. Woo!' Dean laughs. 'I think she did me the best favour of my life.'

He looks up at the stars in open admiration. I smile at him. His nose is pudgy, and if he were still living in California I bet he'd have had it changed by now. 'So you see, every cloud does have a silver lining.'

'Don't you miss your folks?'

Dean shakes his head. 'We're not that close. It's one of the things I regret. Now that I'm out here, I realise how important a sense of community is. There's no feeling like that in L.A. Your neighbours are more likely to shoot you than help you out.' He glances over at me and gives me a broad grin. 'Or maybe that's just where I come from.'

Sanjeev Sherpa comes over and gives Dean another bottle of beer. He places his hand on his shoulder. 'Brother,' is all that he says. Dean goes through the ritual of opening it and pouring it into our cups again. My eyes are getting rolly from the warmth of the fire and cumulative effects of the fresh air and bottled beverages.

'I had a pretty idyllic childhood,' he continues as he hands me my mug. 'The sun and surf make up for a lot of other shortfalls. I wanted for nothing—except parents who could get their act together. My folks were childhood sweethearts, but they split when I was still young. They like each other better now and they've both remarried—several times. Neither of them has been out here. I just don't think they'd get it. My father always asks me what I drive. When I say "no car, no roads," he thinks I'm kidding him.'

'Is there a Betty Jane replacement out here?' I guess I should find out before I find myself lusting after another hopeless case. And I do think I might be suffering from a mild onset of lust.

'No.' He looks fairly adamant. 'All the local women have arranged marriages from about the age of ten to the boy next door. I don't get a look in. Most of them would run a mile from getting mixed up with a crazy American. In a lot of ways I'm still an outsider. I guess I always will be.'

'So what do you do for fun?' I think that sounds a bit more provocative than I intend it to.

'I live just outside Pokhara, and every now and then I stay in town for a few days. Let off a little steam. There's a steady flow of trekkers to keep me amused.'

I look away from him.

'I didn't mean it to sound like that,' he says. 'Here, you offer commitment, you don't fool around. I have the occasional date, not much more.'

I'm not sure that I believe him. I bet he has a stream of carefree, sun-bleached, buxom Aussie trekkers beating a path to his door. 'Don't you miss all that?'

'Not really. Sometimes I get lonely. I think I've become more spiritual since I've been here,' he says. 'Does that sound too wacko?'

I shake my head.

'The people here are so beautiful and humble, it forces you to reassess your behaviour too. The only gods I worshipped before were movie stars. These people live by old laws. I'm more gentle now and, I hope, more caring.'

I relax. I've never had a conversation like this with Jake. Or at least not for a long time. I don't know what drives him anymore. Is it greed, ambition, desire? Whatever it is, I'm sure his actions aren't primarily motivated by compassion and spirituality. I feel I know more about what makes Dean tick in a few short hours than I did in four years with the man I was planning to settle down and have children with. It's a scary thought. I guess you can spend a lot of time avoiding conversation when there's so much more to fill your lives with—books, newspapers, cinema, TV, theatre, dinners with friends, shopping. It's amazing how the old arts come back when there's really nothing else to do.

'I've talked too much.' Dean sounds sorry.

'No,' I say. 'Not at all.' I turn to face him. 'I was just thinking how nice it is. How long since I've talked like this. I'm out of practice.'

A breeze blows up and I shiver.

'It's getting late,' Dean says. 'We have a long day tomorrow.'

When I look up, the others have already gone to their tents. I can see their head torches moving around under the canvas and the murmur of low voices, the rasping of zips. The porters are settled down for the night, all huddled together for warmth in the dining tent.

Dean helps me up. There is a pleasant tiredness seeping through all my bones. 'Mmm,' I say in agreement. 'It's late.'

My guide helps me back to my tent. He leaves me at my door—or flap to be more accurate—and gives my hand a squeeze.

'Goodnight,' he says. 'I'll be right next door if you need me.'

I'm not sure if that thought makes me feel better or not. He disappears and ducks into his tent. I follow suit, crouching down in the cramped space. Sitting on my sleeping bag, I start to get undressed. I'm not sure how many clothes I'm happy removing whilst sleeping in a field, so I've brought some cosy, fleecy pyjamas with Tiggers all over them—not a great look for a thirty-four-year-old possibly, but comfort takes precedence over all other considerations these days. I can't believe how many trappings of my former life I've been persuaded to leave behind—I've no make-up on, so there's no lengthy process involving make-up removal, I've only got bottled water with me, so teeth brushing even with the best intentions is a bit cursory. I've got no epilator, no Perfect Pout, no hair gel, no straightening products, no anti-wrinkle cream. My ablutions severely curtailed, I'm in my sleeping bag and tucked up within seconds.

I can hear Dean moving around in his tent, humming gently to himself. This is very disconcerting, but I can hear him peeling off his clothes. At this moment, I think being blessed with a vivid imagination is actually a bit of a curse. The sound of his trouser zipper makes me gulp, then I hear the sound of his sleeping-bag zipper, followed by much wriggling as he snuggles inside. He clicks his torch off and I'm lying perfectly still, frozen. I can hear my own breathing and I can hear Dean's too.

His voice comes through the darkness. 'Night, Lyssa,' he whispers.

'Night,' I answer. Dean fidgets until he gets himself comfortable. I'm not comfortable at all. I feel all bandaged up in my narrow mummy bag. It's ages since I've worn pyjamas and they're all wrapped round my legs like tourniquets. Gradually, the sounds of movement in the camp die down and the spots of torch light disappear.

And as I go to turn off my own head torch, my eye catches sight of my watch and I see, with something approaching shock, that it's not yet eight o'clock. I can't think of the last time I was in bed before *EastEnders*.

Chapter thirty-five

'You're not sulking again, are you?' Neve said.

Jake wasn't sulking. Not as such. It was just that he didn't know exactly what he wanted to say to Neve. He hadn't managed to see Pip, who was out on a client visit all afternoon and, even though Jake had texted him, his friend hadn't replied.

It was late and Neve had persuaded him to stop at a restaurant on the way home to grab some dinner. The fridge was suffering another food crisis, as he hadn't managed to get to the supermarket this week and Neve, as usual, hadn't given it another thought. He might not be showing the results of it, in Alec's eyes, but he'd certainly been putting the hours in. Jake regarded his surroundings. The place was minimalist to the nth degree. The walls were decorated with tiny, white ceramic tiles and white paintings. All the fittings were stainless steel and frosted glass and the waitresses wore white. They were sitting rigid and upright on steel chairs. It felt like having dinner in a morgue. There was some sort of bland jazz oozing from the sound system and Jake couldn't believe that they'd often slipped away to eat together in here in the first throes of their love. What on earth had possessed them to view it as the right place for a romantic assignation? He felt like he needed another sweater on.

The atmosphere between them was decidedly cool too. They'd been eating in silence like an old married couple who'd run out of things to say to each other.

Neve picked at her pasta. 'I'm not trying to stitch you up,' she said again. 'No matter what you might want to believe.'

He couldn't think of any other way to explain it.

'I'm trying to shield you from Alec,' she carried on. 'You're not flavour of the month at the moment.'

Anywhere, it would seem.

'Let's face it,' Neve said. Her countenance had set like stone. 'You've not exactly been pulling your weight at the office. In a lean company like Dunston & Bradley, it's going to be noticed.'

Why, when he was wanting her to offer him words of comfort, was she insisting on cudgelling him with every sentence? 'There were reasons for that,' he said calmly.

'And now Lyssa's gone,' Neve pointed out, 'you're not under pressure from her anymore to play happy families. We can get on with our lives.'

'Our' seemed a bit of an optimistic term. Nothing could swerve Neve from her chosen path. Jake sighed inwardly. He had ordered some sort of fancy bollocks—spinach and pork and tomatoes arranged as a stack. It was tiny and fiddly and he'd never had less appetite. Every mouthful felt as if it was choking him.

He never felt connected to Neve. She always seemed to be at arm's length, just out of his grip. When they were snatching a few illicit hours together, he'd put it down to that. Now that, in theory, they were able to spend all of their time together, they didn't seem to be getting any closer—quite the contrary. He still couldn't find any words he wanted to say to her.

Neve heaved a theatrical sigh of relief that made several diners at adjacent tables turn and look at them. They probably thought they were a couple on the verge of relationship meltdown, splitting up. Perhaps they were.

'Look,' Neve said, 'I'm going away for a few days.' She put her fork down. 'Business,' she added when there was no response from him. 'Milan.'

'Is it to do with the Blow account?' he said, not trying to disguise the sarcasm in his voice.

'Yes,' Neve huffed. 'I *was* going to tell you.'

Jake just wondered when.

Chapter thirty-six

At exactly 6.00 a.m. and before it's light, Sanjeev Sherpa pops his head through my tent flap. 'Hot tea.' His smiling face is a welcome sight. And he puts my tin mug of tea on the ground, along with a bowl of hot water. 'Breakfast in fifteen minutes, sister,' he says, and disappears to repeat the process in the next tent.

'Thanks, Sanjeev,' comes out rather belatedly and accompanied by a yawn.

Pushing myself out of my sleeping bag, I try to rearrange my Harpo Marx–mad hair. I hardly slept a wink last night. My sleeping bag felt like a suffocating cocoon, my body was too hot and my head was too cold. I had a ridge in my sleeping bag exactly where my shoulders wanted to be. There was a chorus of snores coming from all of the other tents, like some kind of novelty orchestra act. I was, however, pleased to note that there were no antisocial sounds coming from my immediate neighbour's tent. I pull the tea and the bowl of water towards me, switching onto autopilot as I go through the washing motions.

It was dark last night. So dark that it kept me awake—if that makes sense. There was no light pollution from nearby street lights—nothing. Just a sliver of moon and rash of stars. Every time

I tried to slide into dreamland, I stuttered and stumbled and jerked myself awake. Someone once told me that when you have that feeling it's your heart stopping momentarily and that your body causes the jerk to restart it—that's never helped me to relax. Quite frankly, that's far too much information. And although I was lying on the floor I held on to my sleeping bag to try to stop me falling. But it was no good—I tripped as I tried to reach Jake heading for the door, I staggered from the kerbside as I followed an elusive Neve, I slipped on the steps as I climbed the foothills of the Himalayas and Dean reached out to catch me. I just kept falling, falling, falling until finally sleep found me. I think that was about half an hour ago. I did, however, manage to survive the night without having to struggle through the darkness to pee in a hole in the ground that passes as a loo and I'd class that as a result.

Breakfast is set out on a trestle table with the mountains to one side and the river to the other. I think it's quite possible that during the night I have died and gone to heaven. Dawn is breaking and everything is pink and rosy. In this light, the snow on the mountains makes them look as if they're tipped by strawberry ice cream.

Dean is already seated. His hair is damp and curling round his face. He's clearly more adept with his bowl of water than I am. And, call me shallow, I am missing my hairdryer. Marginally more than Jake at the moment.

'Hey,' Dean says and pats the camp stool next to him. He is too chipper by half. 'Sleep well?'

'Wonderfully.'

He gives me a wry smile. 'I heard you tossing and turning.'

It feels sort of protective that he was listening out for me in the night. 'I'm not used to sleeping alone,' I say and then add hastily, 'or in a tent. This is the first time I've camped.' There's no way I'm going to recount the one failed backyard expedition I had with my spiteful sister. At the thought of Edie, I get a pang for home. I wonder if my mother is surviving without me or whether she and her younger daughter have slaughtered each other yet.

'It gets easier,' Dean assures me before I can conjure up the image of a bloodbath in my mum's lounge. 'After a few days you'll get into the flow and wonder why you ever lived in a house.'

Before I can dispute that, Sanjeev arrives with a tray of hot, creamy rice pudding, studded with coconut and nuts and raisins. The rest of the group straggle out to join us and it's clear that the first night in a tent hasn't been particularly restful for the others either. I devour the rice pudding—and to think I used to fight eating this at school. I had hoped that I was going to return from this holiday as slender as a reed with supermodel-thin thighs. At this rate I'm going to be as fat as a house and struggling to fit in my one-man tent by the end of the first week. I console myself with the fact that my appetite will find its level after a few days and I won't be so desperate to consume everything put in front of me. It's a long time since I've been so enthusiastic about food. When we've finished the rice pudding, pancakes and scrambled eggs magically appear. My appetite goes into overdrive. Some hope!

The porters are already breaking camp and making up the day's loads. The bags are packed, the tents are being folded. The breakfast pans have been washed and stowed in wicker baskets ready for transportation to the next open-air kitchen. I would love it if some of these people came home with me and got me ready for work every morning. My legs are aching, but pleasantly so. The sun is up, peeping over the hills and chasing the cold away. We finish our breakfasts as the first string of porters skitter away, taking the footpath at a full run. Just watching them makes me feel exhausted—not to mention deeply inadequate.

At a more leisurely pace, we don our rucksacks and I don't know what I've got in here—I know it's not the kitchen sink because I've seen someone else carrying that. I'm becoming acutely aware that everyone is wearing utility clothing in shades of khaki and beige—except me. Despite the best efforts of the man at the Outdoor Shop, I shunned the utility, zip-off trousers in mud shades and put together my very own mountain ensemble. Which means that I'm wearing Miu Miu embroidered combat pants, a

Kookai tee-shirt and a pink baseball cap with a diamante star on the front.

Dean grins at me. 'Are you going for the award for the most glamorous trekker?'

'It wasn't my intention.' In fact, I'd rather look like a fit bit who could run up hills and eat Yetis for breakfast. Striking a blow for fashion maybe wasn't the best idea I've ever had.

'You'd win,' my guide says. He winks at me. 'Hands down.'

I think it's a compliment.

Still glancing over his shoulder at me, Dean herds us together and then Sanjeev takes up the lead as we set off just before the little hand reaches seven. I'm surprised that I can make my eyelids open, let alone force my reluctant legs to walk.

We make our way out of the village, swinging over the frothing river on an extraordinarily rickety, rope suspension bridge with several essential planks missing. Once that has been safely, if somewhat nervously, navigated, we then head up a steep slope through paddy fields where already the smartly dressed women in richly embroidered saris and Nike trainers are working, harvesting the rice. Children with faces the colour of creamy caffé latte are running up and down the path shouting *'Namaste!'* as they pass, carrying baskets laden with firewood, ears of corn and complaining chickens squawking loudly. A little boy in a Dick Tracy tee-shirt and Snoopy shorts stops and smiles shyly as he hands me a marigold flower, before running away chuckling madly. These kids could melt the most frosty of hearts and mine is already dissolving like an ice cream in the full blast of a fan-heater. My sister's kids are noisy, robust, loud and, to a man, constantly demanding. These children are open, innocent, gently insistent. They don't wear Nikes. They don't wear shoes at all. Nor do they have the latest labels, just a ragtag of clothing that looks like the leftovers in an Oxfam shop. They follow us laughing through the villages, running in the dusty lanes, not frightened to hold the hands of pale-faced strangers; they give us marigolds, pretty quartz stones and golden smiles from filthy faces.

Our route takes in lush paths overhung with the welcome shade of oak trees, ramshackle villages where everyone rushes out to wave at us. The stone steps are made for tiny Nepalese feet not European clodhoppers and test the thighs and calves to the limit. Never again will I fear a StairMaster. Farmers work the fields, using ancient methods to thresh the cereal, driving a team of oxen over the yellow stalks to separate the precious seeds. Outside the houses groups of women thresh the millet using the power of their feet while they chat and giggle to each other.

I can feel my stress peeling away with every turn in the path we take. The sun is fully up and the temperature is soaring, but the warm rays feel wonderful on my back. I've spent so much of my life rushing from one place to the next, winding myself up to a pitch over nothing, that I've rarely stopped just to watch the world go by. This is the perfect panacea to Western living and I can see why Dean has chosen not to go back to the rat race. One thing for sure is that no matter how hard you try, the rats will always win. It feels as if I'm in a Disney version of life—overblown colours, cute faces, everyone laughing and smiling, immaculately drawn backdrops. When did London become so monochrome? The red buses are the only things I can think of that add colour to the landscape.

We stop to catch our breath and take on some welcome water. The snow-capped peaks of Annapurna South, Lamjung and Machhapuchhre keep the keen photographers in the group entertained. Sanjeev comes round and hands out hot, fragrant cloves to chew on. They're strong, spicy and an acquired taste.

'You don't look so sad today, sister,' he says and I guess he's right. How can I be sad with scenery like this? It's a million miles away from *My Baby* and *My Divorce* and my real life. The air is so clear and invigorating it feels as if it's got an extra oxygen molecule and any thought of aching legs is soon dispelled. Mainly because my mind is focused on my lungs, which are threatening to explode.

Dean drops his rucksack next to me. He's been chatting with some of the others in the group this morning, but I wanted to keep my own counsel and just take in the sights. I'm huffing and puffing so much that I'm not sure I've got enough breath left for talking either.

'It's beautiful here, isn't it?' he says.

'Marvellous.' I could lie down here and quite gladly never move again. Dean is framed by the mountains, there's a healthy flush to his cheeks and his eyes sparkle in the perfect light. 'Wait,' I say. 'Don't move a muscle.' Ferreting round in my rucksack, I dig out my camera and take a snap of Dean looking suitably gorgeous. This will make my sister weep with envy. 'I'll email you a copy.'

'Let me take one of you,' he says and while I strike a pose, he snaps away. 'Mail me that too,' he says and we both blush a bit.

And just when it might be getting cosy between us, the sight of a camera means we're immediately surrounded by village children who are keen to have their photo taken and practise their English. It's so nice that they have no fear of outsiders here and their open trust is bewitching. They chatter away as I take their photos and then they all stand obediently in line while they view themselves on the screen of my digital camera. One young girl with a dirty face, no shoes and a Marks & Spencer glittery party dress tugs at my heartstrings. I smooth her hair and she covers her mouth, giggling at her image on the screen, and I wonder if these pangs of longing will ever go away.

Chapter thirty-seven

The office was quiet, almost peaceful, before the usual hubbub started. Jake leaned back in his chair and stared at the air-conditioning vents in the ceiling. Still he couldn't make the scrambled bits of his brain come back together and form a cohesive shape.

The swing door crashed open and Pip, cradling his motorbike helmet and a battered briefcase, came in.

'Couldn't sleep?' Pip wandered over and perched on Jake's desk. He peeled off his leather jacket to reveal a shirt blooming with floribunda roses. It was an assault on Jake's already delicate senses.

'No,' Jake admitted miserably. 'Neve got up at some ungodly hour to go to Milan. I thought it might give me an opportunity to get back in Alec's good books if he saw me here at the crack of dawn.'

Pip said nothing.

'Did you know she'd been put on the Blow account?'

Pip nodded. A few more of the conscientious staff drifted in via the coffee machine.

'Thanks for telling me.'

'I thought it was better if it came from Neve,' Pip said.

'Well, I'm not sure she was in a tearing hurry to tell me either.'

'No one wants to be the harbinger of doom, mate,' his friend said. 'She knew you wouldn't be happy. *I* knew you wouldn't be happy.'

In a bizarre way—after moaning that she was never at home—Jake had been glad to have the house to himself. He needed to clear his head and do some serious thinking about where his future lay. The opinion was starting in his fuddled cranium that great sex did not necessarily make for a fulfilling relationship. Jake cursed himself. Maybe it was a bit late in the day to be discovering cornflakes-box philosophy. Besides, his problems weren't just confined to his personal life—from the look of things his professional prospects weren't shaping up too great at the moment either. Jake checked there was no one in earshot—you could never be too careful in this place these days. 'I think Alec is trying to get rid of me,' he confided.

Pip rubbed his chin shiftily.

'Oh bollocks, man!' Jake thumped his desk with his fist. Heads turned. He lowered his voice. 'You knew that too.'

'There are always rumours,' his friend said.

'And what else do the water-cooler gang say?'

'It's never pretty, is it,' Pip reasoned. 'You shouldn't take any notice of office gossip.'

'I haven't heard *any* of it!' Jake admitted. Which was alarming because he'd always thought he had his finger on the pulse. It could only be because all of the office gossip was about *him*. 'What shall I do, mate?' He lowered his voice further. 'I feel like I'm drowning. I need help.'

Pip sighed. 'I'm a friend, aren't I?'

'Yes,' Jake said. 'The only one in this bloody place.'

'Then remember this is coming from a friend.'

Jake felt himself go cold even though the air-conditioning wasn't blasting out like normal.

'You've dug yourself a very big hole by getting involved with Neve,' Pip said flatly.

This wasn't what he wanted to hear, despite the fact that he was rapidly coming to the same conclusion. 'How do I start to get out of it?'

'It's going to take one hell of a big shovel.'

'Do you think Alec knows about me and Neve?'

Pip chose his words carefully. 'I think it's a forgone conclusion.'

'Damn! I think I need to go in to see him,' Jake said. 'Get things straight.' He had to confront this head on. If he just let bad feelings fester between him and Alec, things would only get worse. This was a nightmare and he hadn't realised how much of a support Lyssa had been when it came to the tricky politics of business. She always listened to him, offered sensible advice and generally propped him up when he needed it. His stomach twisted slightly at the thought of her. It hadn't all been about babies and sperm samples.

'What are you planning to say to Alec?' Pip spoke into his thoughts.

'I don't know,' Jake sighed. 'But I'm going to strike while the iron's hot. I'll do it today.'

'Not possible,' Pip said, shaking his head.

'Why?' Jake asked. 'Do you know something else that I don't?'

'Probably, mate.' Pip chewed at his lip. He gave his friend a sympathetic glance. 'Alec is in Milan too.'

Chapter thirty-eight

I have survived another day. And that feels like no mean achievement. We've trekked for about seven hours and I'm pretty sure that's farther than I've ever walked in my entire life. The path took us through oak and rhododendron forests and I've vowed that one day I'll come back in the spring when the primulas and orchids are in full bloom. I spend the afternoon walking with Dave the divorce lawyer and Jim the undercover cop—I've discovered they have disastrous love lives too and that makes me feel a lot better. I couldn't face Tony and Tania, as they are too loved up and I thought it might take the shine off my good mood. Saffron has hooked up with Felix and Felicity and they've been putting the world to right since they discovered they are all posh socialists. Ian and Graham have been surprisingly macho and are striding ahead with Sanjeev Sherpa and Dean while another Sherpa guide, Tek, is left to round up the stragglers. I think there must have been a mirage of cold beer urging them on. A hot bath and a quick rubdown with some Deep Heat would work for me.

Tonight's camp is in an open meadow within striking distance of the village of Sikklis and dominated by a fantastic view of the peak of Machhapuchhre. The thought of being in a tent again holds less dread—particularly as I've noticed I'm parked next to Dean once more.

I've gratefully dumped all my gear, thus rendering my humble abode an instant bombsite, and am airing my hot, throbbing feet while I sit and drink my smoky, black tea. My major preoccupation is wondering which bits of me I can get into my bowl of water and in what order. I want to wash my hair but there's no way I'd do it after my feet have been anywhere near it. Is this really the same woman who is used to a shower every morning and a bubble bath every night? Dean saunters up to me.

'You look like you're contemplating the cares of the world,' he says as he sits down.

'No.' I give him a wry smile. 'I'm contemplating much loftier issues.'

He waits for me to continue.

'I don't know whether to wash my feet or my hair. Or quite how I'm going to manage it.'

'Ah,' he says. 'Typical townie. I can help you there.' He wanders off and comes back moments later with his bowl of water, as yet untouched. 'I'll wash your hair for you.'

'Oh.' Ooo!

'Normal protocol goes a little by the wayside on this type of trip,' he advises me. 'Take off your shirt.'

Gulp. I take off my shirt, leaving on my sleeveless tee-shirt underneath. In the villages it's polite for women to cover their legs and arms, but in the camp, where standards are more relaxed, it's possible to have knees and elbows on show. The breeze feels good on my skin. We're higher here—the air is thinner and much colder. I hand Dean my eco-friendly, bio-degradable shampoo, which doesn't smell nearly as nice as my usual rose-petal aromatherapy stuff at ten quid a bottle. Kneeling down, I bend over the bowl. Dean pours water over my hair, followed by shampoo and then slowly starts to massage my scalp with fingers that are clearly designed for the job.

'Does that feel good?'

'Mmm.' I try to sound appreciative, but not as if I'm really getting off on this—which, of course, I am! I have a horrible feeling that somewhere along the line in the last four years, Jake and I simply ceased to touch each other. Was that all to do with the mechanical process of trying for a baby, or had we stopped touching before that? Jake has never shampooed my hair and has never shown the slightest inclination to do so. Is that unusual? I think we missed out. At this moment, shampooing has taken on a very sensual turn. Didn't Robert Redford wash Meryl Streep's hair in *Out of Africa*?—if he didn't, I'm sure he should have done.

'Enough?' Dean asks.

It seems improper to suggest that he might like to continue for another hour or two. I wonder if I could persuade him to massage my feet. 'Yes, fine. Thanks.'

He rinses my hair and hands me a towel. I feel slightly dizzy. It may be the altitude or it may be that I've been bending over, but I'm not so sure.

Dean smiles. 'I'll see you at dinner.'

I look out over the camp, trying not to watch him as he returns to his own tent. At the end of the row, I see Saffron struggling to wash her hair. I might go over and offer to help her—and call me a selfish old cow, but I'm quite glad that Dean didn't.

Chapter thirty-nine

Edie opened the door and looked surprised to see Jake standing there.

'You are *such* a muppet!' she said to him with an exasperated puff.

'Nice to see you too, Edie.' He dug his hands deeper into his pockets and let his lip droop lower. 'Can I come in?'

'Only if you want fish fingers and baked beans. I'm about to dish up.'

'My favourite,' Jake said and followed her inside.

Edie walked away from the door, dragging Archie behind her who was screaming blue murder and was attached to her leg like a snot-nosed limpet. 'He's been like this all day,' she shouted over her shoulder. 'I've given up trying to dislodge him.'

The rest of Edie's numerous children were sitting at the kitchen table shouting at each other and hitting each other with spoons. The grill pan with a mountain of fish fingers piled on it waited patiently.

'Keeping Captain Birdseye in business?' Jake said as he shrugged out of his coat.

'Yeah. That man's going to enjoy a prosperous retirement thanks to this lot.' Edie dragged the screaming Archie across the floor to the cooker. 'Sit down,' Edie instructed Jake as if she were speaking to another one of the children. Jake did as he was told. 'Say hello to Uncle Jake.'

'Hello to Uncle Jake,' everyone said, including him.

Daisy sidled round to Jake's side of the table. 'When I grow up I'm going to be one of Girlth Aloud.' She cast a hateful glance at her harried parent whilst performing a dance routine. 'And then I'll be able to eat all the ithe cream I want.'

'Splendid idea,' Jake said. 'Except that your management team will want you to stay ridiculously thin if you're a pop idol and *they* won't let you eat ice cream either.'

Daisy frowned.

'See?' Edie said. 'It's not just Mummy who's a pain in the bottom. Uncle Jake is too.' She jiggled the fish fingers under the grill.

Kelly stamped in. 'I hate this house,' she shouted. As an afterthought she noticed Jake's presence. 'Oh hi, Uncle Jake.' She kissed him on the cheek. 'I hate everyone here.'

Jake gave her a squeeze. 'How's the world's most beautiful teenager?'

Kelly blushed. She was wearing an unfeasibly short skirt and had unfeasibly long legs and it was frightening to think that only recently she'd been a gawky, coy eleven-year-old schoolgirl with plaits and without breasts. When had she gone from being a child to a hormonal woman? And it scared him to death to think that one day he could have a daughter who looked and behaved exactly like this.

'Take me home to live with you,' she said to Jake.

'You get arrested for that sort of thing these days,' he said.

Kelly scowled her most fearsome scowl. 'I'm not allowed to do anything.'

'You're not allowed to stay out until two in the morning.'

'Katy Marchmont is.'

Edie put her fingers in her ears and started to sing in the style of Julie Andrews. *'You are fifteen, going on thirty-five. I—I am si-ick of you…!'*

'Losers.' Kelly stamped out again. Daisy slid onto Jake's knee.

'And to think Lyssa wants all this,' Edie said. 'How could you not find that irresistible?'

'Your kids would be enough to put anyone off,' Jake said. 'Except you two.'

Edie banged out some plates and whizzed the fish fingers onto them, followed by a splot of baked beans. Her culinary skills seemed to lack a certain finesse. Yet for all the hustle and bustle and boisterousness, he was surprised to admit it was a far sight better being here among the cut and thrust of real life than in Neve's icy, clinical box. Edie plonked a bowl of jacket potatoes in the middle of the table and dished out the plates. 'Has everyone washed their hands?'

Everyone nodded.

'Liars,' Edie said. 'For what we are about to receive, et cetera....'

Feeding commenced.

Jake waited for the crush to die down and then helped himself to a jacket potato. He felt himself sinking and, for some ridiculous reason, close to tears. Perhaps it was the fact that Edie had welcomed him back into the fold in her own inimitable way when she could easily have left him standing out in the cold. And he hadn't realised how much that meant to him. They might not be blood-related or linked by way of the formality of marriage, but he thought of Edie as his sister-in-law by default and her kids were the closest he was going to get to nephews and nieces. Certainly with the way things lay at the moment, anyway. 'Thanks for this, Edie.'

He loved family life. He loved the thought of having his own family life. It was just the practicalities and the reality of it all that took the shine off it a bit.

'Have you heard anything from Lyssa?' Jake asked as nonchalantly as he could manage.

'Of course I haven't,' Edie said. 'She's not likely to be sending postcards from halfway up the Himalayas or wherever she is.'

'No,' Jake agreed.

'I blame this on you,' Edie said. 'This is all because of that action-packed *Neve*.' She mouthed the word.

'Ith Neve your new girlfriend?' Daisy said, mouth full of fish finger.

Edie gave him a now-see-what-you've-done look.

'Er…'

Daisy pouted. 'Don't you love Aunty Lytha anymore?'

'Yes,' Jake said sincerely. 'Yes, I do.'

Edie's eyebrows shot up at that. 'Look, you lot. You can have some ice cream later.' Moans all round. 'Go and do something. Preferably something useful. And preferably something that involves feeding one of the dozen neglected pets that inhabit this place.'

Reluctantly the kids climbed down from the table and scattered about the house. When they'd gone, Edie regarded him coolly.

'Don't look at me like that.'

'I have six children, this look is automatic.'

Jake pushed his plate away from him.

'I gather that all is not love's young dream.'

'No,' he admitted. 'I'm very confused.'

'You're a bloke. What do you expect?'

'I feel as if I've made a real mess of things.' He glanced up at Edie and grinned. 'I know. I'm a bloke. What do I expect?'

Lyssa's sister sighed. 'I'm not sure I'm the right person to come to looking for sympathy.'

'I need to contact her,' Jake said. 'I want to know what she's thinking.'

'If I were her, I'd be thinking you're a wanker.'

'I've tried her mobile,' he said. 'It's not working.'

'She's not in bloody Kensington High Street, Jake. She's up a mountain somewhere. She's gone without her hairdryer. Don't you realise how serious this is?'

'What can I do?'

'Get your act together. She's going to be gone for a while yet. When she comes back, you need to have decided exactly what it is you do want.'

'She will come back, won't she?'

'Can you see Lyssa staying anywhere that's out of reach of Starbucks coffee for too long?'

'No,' Jake said. 'But then I never imagined in my wildest dreams that she'd do this anyway.'

'Me neither,' Edie said. 'My sister isn't one for surprises. That's normally my forte.' She cast a glance at Archie as if to confirm it. 'Sort it out, Jake. Sort it out before she comes back.'

'I will,' Jake said. 'I promise you.' One way or the other.

'I can't begin to see why, but the poor deluded woman still loves you.'

Jake felt a lump catch in his throat and it was nothing to do with the indigestibility of Edie's cooking.

'I'd better be going,' he said. Though he wasn't sure he wanted to. It wouldn't have taken too much persuasion for him to settle down here for the night, but Edie wasn't offering. 'I've got stuff to do.'

'Me too. Clothes to iron. Children to torture.'

He stood up. 'Can I ask you one thing, Edie?'

'Yes,' she said. 'As long as it doesn't involve borrowing money.'

'Do you ever regret having kids?'

They both looked down at Archie, who was licking the kitchen floor. 'Every day,' she said. 'But I still wouldn't be without them.'

Was that the answer he wanted to hear? Probably not. He wanted to hear how much children enriched your life and that you never hankered after the days when you were young, free and single and had money to blow on skiing holidays. Why did kids have to be such a big compromise in one's life?

'Now can I ask *you* something?'

'Yes. As long as you don't grill me like those fish fingers.'

'No, no,' Edie said. 'Nothing like that. I just wondered...' She coughed slightly. 'How's Pip?'

'Pip?'

'I met him at Lyssa's *bon voyage* party.'

'Oh.' That hurt more than he liked to admit to. Lyssa had thrown a *bon voyage* party and hadn't invited him—surely she should have, if only for old time's sake.

'There were just a few of us there,' Edie said, reading his mind. 'Mainly family.'

'And Pip.'

'Yeah. And Pip. Is he okay?'

Jake shrugged. 'He's fine.'

'Oh. Good,' she said, tucking her hair behind her ear. 'Good. Give him my regards.'

'Yeah,' Jake said. 'Will do.'

Edie followed him to the door, a now placid and probably bug-ridden Archie trailing in her wake. They faced each other uncomfortably.

'Thanks for everything. And for the fish fingers. They were great.'

'Charmer,' Edie said as she wrapped her arms round him.

Jake hugged her tightly. How could he have screwed this up so badly?

'We love you. You're family. Come round anytime. You know you're always welcome. Except if you hurt my big sister again,' she warned. 'Then I'll kill you.'

Chapter Forty

Last night's meal was obviously a fluke. Today—as I'd been warned by my mother, my sister and all of my office colleagues—the dish of the day is dried yak. And I have to say, contrary to popular rumour, it isn't half bad. Saffron, who I'm still convinced is a closet vegetarian, is certainly tucking in again. The yak casserole is accompanied by noodles, plates of green beans and copious amounts of rakshi, the local distilled rice wine. It all makes for a heady mix. Maybe it's the mountain air or maybe it's because it's exactly like rocket fuel, but the rakshi is going straight to my head. The other thing is, because of all the IVF stuff, I've been on a strict diet of abstinence for longer than I care to remember—no alcohol, no blue cheese, no raw eggs, no tuna fish. Now this is no longer an issue, bring it all on! I say. Particularly the alcohol.

After dinner we take our fold-up stools out into the night air and I think it's telling that the group already leave a space for Dean beside me. Some of the local villagers have come to join us for the evening, walking a mere two miles to entertain us, and bringing with them traditional drums and penny whistles. The Sherpas bring the kerosene lamps out of the dining tent and gather round, laughing boisterously in a way that shows they too have been enjoying the raw warmth of the rakshi. Some of the younger men start to lead a dance in the middle of the group as the villagers sing and clap. They twirl madly, twisting their bodies, spinning and spinning. The few women porters on the trek huddle at the back, eyeing them shyly. The huge sweep of the Milky Way provides the disco lights above us, sparkling brightly from horizon to horizon.

'Come and dance,' Dean says.

'No. No, I can't.' Typical British reticence kicks in. 'I don't know what to do.'

'How hard does it look?' he coaxes. 'Everyone's had too much to drink to take any notice.' He pulls me to my feet. 'Nepali people love to dance.'

Already, Saffron is strutting her funky stuff. She's clearly been to one of those New Age 'circle dancing' courses and is gyrating like a thing possessed. Dave is her reluctant partner; he's dancing with all the flair and rhythm of the average British male. I let Dean lead me to the centre of the dancing—safe in the middle, away from mocking observers that might just be waiting to pour scorn on my skills. Like who? Reluctantly, I try a few tentative twirls.

'A natural,' he says, laughing.

Oh, sod it! What have I got to lose? Felix and Felicity are already up and she's prancing around like Kate Bush on a bad day. He's doing Mick Jagger circa 1967. I'm sure if my dad were still around, even he'd be able to dance better than that. I try to join the fray. Try as I might, twirling does not come easy. My whole body is rigid with tension. When did that happen? I seem to have become so out of touch with myself. Dean whirls around me and I surrender myself to the elements and to my partner.

The music flows from one song to another seamlessly and we spin until I'm even dizzier than I was before. 'I have to sit down!'

'Okay,' Dean says. 'You've proved you can do it.'

And I *can* do it. Me—whose idea of a good night out is dinner in a sophisticated little restaurant or maybe a few glasses of Chardonnay in a prissy wine bar. I've never twirled around in a starlit field before, swigging beer and local gut-rot from a tin mug.

The girls take up the song and sing a couple of choruses, followed by the young men who chant in response.

I lean over to Dean. 'What are they singing?'

'This is a courtship song,' he explains, looking slightly sheepish. 'One of the girls is looking for a husband. It's very cheeky.' He gives an embarrassed shrug. 'The women say what they want, and the men answer. Tonight, one of them is likely to find himself with a wife.'

'Beats dancing round your handbag at the disco.'

'It's probably just a variation of it,' Dean rationalises. 'Single women wear those colourful, striped aprons at the back to show that they're still available. It's unusual to have women porters,' he says. 'It isn't considered a fitting job for an unattached female. This would be frowned upon in their villages. These girls are really striking a blow for feminism.'

'Good for them.'

There's much shrieking and giggling. A bowl of what looks like rice pudding is being handed round. Some of the boys are trying to smear it on the girls' foreheads. There's a lot of wrestling going on. Sanjeev and Dean guffaw as they watch.

'That's tika,' Dean tells me. 'It's a mixture of rice, yak yoghurt and honey.'

The bowl is handed to Dean. Sanjeev looks on wide-eyed.

'And it has a significance, right?'

Dean nods.

'I offer this to you if I like you.' His eyes meet mine. 'If I *like* you a lot.' He traces his thumb through the white, pungent mixture and holds it up to me. 'If you accept it,' he adds, 'it means that you return the affection. That you…*like*…me a lot too.'

I lower my head towards him and Dean smears the tika between my eyebrows.

'That smells truly awful,' I say.

Dean smiles softly. 'No one ever said that love would smell of roses.'

No, they certainly didn't. I feel rather self-conscious now that I'm wearing rice pudding on my head.

'I want to kiss you,' Dean whispers.

I'm not objecting.

'Public displays of affection are frowned upon.' He gives a nervous half-laugh. 'We'll have to wait.'

He takes my hand and leads me in a dance again. I'm sincerely hoping not for too long.

Chapter Forty-One

Jake returned to Neve's flat alone. He'd stopped and had a few beers in one of the busy, impersonal bars down the road rather than face his own company, but now it was nearly midnight and time to go to bed. His footsteps echoed throughout the place, bouncing off the walls and the wooden floor. He threw his coat over the sofa, opened the fridge and grabbed another can of beer. This place could definitely do with a few kids running round, a stereo playing, some background noise. You could set up a brilliant toy railway track up here. Good heavens, what was he saying? Wasn't this the very thing that had filled him with so much dread?

There was no message on the answerphone from Neve—hardly surprising since he'd been in a stinking mood when she'd left this morning. He should call her. Try to build some bridges. Even if their relationship wasn't quite turning out to be the bed of roses he'd envisaged, they'd still have to work together whatever happened. And he owed it to everyone to at least give this a chance. Lyssa wouldn't be home for a few more weeks yet; he had plenty of time to work out where he really wanted to be.

Jake rummaged in his briefcase. He'd managed to inveigle the name and telephone number of the hotel in Milan out of Alec's assistant—Neve, probably in a fit of pique, hadn't bothered to leave it for him. He checked his watch. Would it be too late to phone her now? Jake had no idea of her schedule in Milan—if she'd got any early-morning power breakfasts, he was clearly the last person she'd planned to tell about it. He picked up the phone. This was no good—he had to be in a more conciliatory mood if he was going to ring her at all. Long-distance fighting was never a good idea. Jake took a couple of deep breaths to calm himself. Followed by a couple of deep draughts of beer. He punched in the number of the hotel and asked for Neve Chandler's room.

The phone in the room was answered after a couple of rings. 'Hello.' It was a man's voice.

'Oh,' Jake said. 'Is Neve Chandler there?'

'Er...' the man said. 'Who's calling?'

'What?' Jake scratched his head. It wasn't a great telephone line. Sometimes you can dial halfway round the world and talk to someone as clearly as if they were in the next room. This wasn't one of those times. This was a crackly, static-filled, Italian-type line. Nevertheless, it was a very familiar man's voice, Jake was sure. Almost sure. 'Who's that?' he asked.

'Sorry,' the man said hastily, 'you've got the wrong room.'

Before Jake could think of anything else to say, the line went dead.

He was stunned. That was definitely Alec. It was Alec in Neve's room. It was gone midnight in the UK—what time did that make it in Italy? Even later, Jake thought blackly. And Alec was in Neve's room. What should he do? Should he ring back? What if Neve answered this time? What would he want to say to her? Would he want to say anything at all with the possibility of Alec lurking in the background? Then again, what if the hotel operator *had* put him through to the wrong room?

Jake put the phone back on its cradle. This was terrible. Was Neve being unfaithful to him? And with Alec of all people! Didn't she realise what a compromising position that would put them all in? Jake laughed to himself. Talk about chickens coming home to roost. If Neve was giving him the runaround with another man, then this truly were his just deserts. This was exactly what he'd been doing to Lyssa—all the time she thought they were trying to start a family together. Did the fact that she was completely unaware of it make it any better? Jake felt shame colour his face. How could he have been such a bastard? There were a million different ways to rationalise it and none of them stood up to close scrutiny. He sat in Neve's flat while she was in another country and quite possibly getting it on with another man. He felt sick and as if he might be about to throw up all his Miller Lite. Infidelity didn't feel quite so great now that the Jimmy Choo was on the other foot.

Chapter Forty-two

So I'm lying in my tent and wondering 'now what?' It's probably a terrible insult to the Nepali culture, but I had to wipe the tika off, I'm afraid. It smelled disgusting and felt even worse and I hope this isn't a bad omen. As primitive mating rituals go, I don't think daubing the object of your desire in whiffy rice pudding is one that should be encouraged.

The party disbanded as rain started to fall. Since then it's got steadily heavier. First it was a gentle patter against the canvas and now it's pounding away. Even the obligatory howling dog seems to have gone inside for shelter. I can't even hear the snorers' rhapsody above the din. This is supposed to be the dry time of year, so I can't imagine what it must be like here in the monsoon season when the rain is torrential. The noise means that I can't hear anything from Dean's tent either. I'm lying here outwardly calm, but inwardly a mass of twanging elastic bands. I know that I'm waiting for something to happen and I know what I'd like it to be, but I'm just not sure. I'm not sure of anything, anymore.

There's a rustling at the canvas flap that I've laughingly come to regard as my front door. And this time, I've no fear that it's the bogeyman or serial killer.

'Lyssa,' he whispers my name.

'Yes.'

The tent zipper opens and Dean pops his head inside. Even in the darkness, I can see that his hair is wet and there's rain dripping down his nose and onto my sleeping bag. 'I came to see if you were okay.'

'Fine,' I say huskily.

Dean squeezes into my tent and suddenly there's not much room in here at all. I want to reach out and touch his damp curls.

'I thought you might be worried by the rain.'

'No.' I'm British—since when has rain ever bothered us? Now my late-night guest doesn't look sure what to do.

'Well,' I say. 'A little.'

If he's been lying there imagining me laid out seductively in a spaghetti-strap negligée then he must be cruelly disappointed. I'm in my fleecy Tigger jim-jams with my sleeping bag pulled up to my neck. Though I have, thankfully, taken off my socks.

'I think everyone else is asleep.' Dean's eyes are glittering darkly like the stars. He clears his throat. 'Could you do with some company?'

I hear myself gulp. 'Yes.'

And then we're on each other. Our lips hot and searching, frantic. I pull at his wet tee-shirt, ripping it as I do. He zips open my sleeping bag, jamming it halfway down.

'Goddammit!'

As I struggle out, he's tugging at my pyjamas. I start to giggle.

'Ssh. Ssh.' Our thrashing about might be disguised by the pounding rain, but not if we're making enough noise to wake the dead. 'This is crazy,' Dean mutters thickly.

'I know.' I'm wriggling out of my pyjama bottoms and trying to tug Dean's belt off at the same time. Crashing to the ground, we scatter my tin mug, my washing bowl and my trekking pole. We seem to have grown more elbows than the standard quota. Dean kicks off his boots and we wrestle with his jeans, stifling our laughter. We probably sound like a couple of drunks and maybe we are. If someone was watching this from the outside it would probably look like fifty ferrets having a fist fight. He pulls off my pyjama top and holds me close, suddenly serious.

'I don't do this as a rule,' he pants, breathless. 'I haven't got any… I haven't come prepared.'

I put my finger to his lips. 'It doesn't matter,' I say. 'I can't…I can't get pregnant. I can't have children.' Good grief, this is the first time I've said that out loud—and certainly in these circumstances. And I can't believe that it doesn't feel too bad. In fact, for the first time I feel positively grateful!

'What about other risks?'

I don't care. I just want wild abandoned sex that doesn't involve charts and temperatures and injections. I want unsafe sex with a hunky stranger. I want sex that has no purpose but fun, fun, fun. I want to get hot and sweaty. I want to scratch and bite and fight and when we've done that I want to be soft and gentle and sexy and when we've done that I want to do it all over again! 'Well, you could stay outside the sleeping bag and I could stay inside… but it would be a lot less fun.'

We fall on each other, giggling again.

Dean smooths back my mad hair. 'Are you sure you want to do this?'

'Absolutely.'

We struggle and wriggle some more until we're both naked and then the kissing begins in earnest. Dean has a fabulous body, strong and lean. The rain beats harder and harder on the canvas, Dean's hands are all over me, caressing, exploring, and I let myself drown in the sensations. I am no longer a desperate, unhappy, unpregnant person—I am reckless, shagging Mountain Woman!

Chapter Forty-three

I wish I could say that I had a massive hangover or some regrets. But I have neither. This morning the rain has gone, the birds are tweeting and I'm having breakfast outdoors in the foothills of the Himalayas. I have that warm feeling in my tummy that comes from really good porridge and great sex. Life really does not get any better.

I'm very happy there was a torrential downpour that lasted until dawn. Believe me, Dean and I took full advantage of it. I think it's fair to say that the rakshi successfully removed the majority of my inhibitions. Then we fell asleep in each other's arms and he crawled quietly away with more kissing just before Sanjeev—bless him—brought my early-morning tea. Every fibre of my body is zinging and I guess we both might have a few bruises, but it was a lot of fun. And somehow this feels like more than irresponsible, illicit sex—I can't readily put it into words, but it feels like some sort of release, too. I can see now that I've been utterly focussed on one thing to the exclusion of all else and had forgotten the sheer joy that moist, writhing bodies can generate just for the sake of it.

Not that my ex-boyfriend featured much in last night's fray, but this morning I understand why Jake was totally pissed off with me. And I feel bad that it's taken another man to show me that. But, hey, not that bad! Something has sparked in my heart that has been missing for far too long. And I feel that I'm hiding this badly. If I need to hide it at all. I'm wandering round the camp gaily singing to myself. I had a pee in a smelly, eco-friendly loo (hole in the ground) just now along with the resident mice and I didn't care a jot. Funny, that.

Everyone else is on their second bowl of porridge when Dean emerges from his tent. He looks like a creature from the deep and as if he's had no sleep at all. But as he approaches, I can see that there's a contented smirk on his face.

Jim does a wolf whistle as he comes closer. 'Did the rain keep you two awake?'

Ah. Perhaps the rain wasn't as loud as we thought. Or perhaps we were louder than *we* thought. Both Dean and I flush to our hair roots. So at least one person was witness to our nocturnal activities. He's not an undercover cop for nothing. Then everyone at the table giggles and bursts into a spontaneous round of applause.

'It's the mountain air, dear,' Saffron says and pats my arm.

I think it was more to do with our guide being a particularly gorgeous specimen of humanity—but I say nothing to incriminate myself.

'I fancied a bit too,' she adds with a wistful look in her eye. 'It's all that physical exertion. It gets the hormones twitching.'

Saffron moves up and lets Dean sit next to me.

'Hi,' he says sheepishly.

This is torture in the full glare of the rest of the group. 'Hi.'

He slides his hand under the table and squeezes my leg. And that's nearly enough to start me off again. I've never jumped into bed—or sleeping bag if we're going to be technically accurate—with a stranger before and I'm not sure how to behave. I've been in a committed relationship for too long and, therefore, I haven't a clue about modern sexual etiquette. If I were younger, perhaps I would. If I were younger, perhaps I wouldn't care!

'Are you as tired as you look?' I murmur as close to Dean as possible without attracting attention.

'No,' he says. 'I feel great.' My new lover gives me a shy smile. 'Thanks.'

'You're welcome.'

'No regrets?'

'None whatsoever.'

'I guess we weren't as sneaky as we thought.'

'No.' And the thought flashes through my mind that I should have taken some lessons from Jake, who seems to be the king of being sneaky.

Dean reaches out and takes my hand under the table. 'Our paths might cross for a very short time, Lyssa,' he says quietly. 'I think we should make the most of every day.'

I meet Dean's eyes and hold them with a steady gaze. 'And every night.'

He laughs and presses my hand in his. 'That goes without saying.'

Chapter Forty-Four

Archie was asleep. At long last. Daisy was at her friend's house and the others were still at school. Peace reigned. For another half hour at least. Edie sipped her cup of coffee and gazed at the mound of cheap mince that would soon, with the aid of a few bottles of ready-made sauce, be transformed into the Firth family's all-time favourite Italian extravaganza, lasagne. She would be assured of clean plates tonight.

Edie checked her watch. If she was going to carry out her harebrained plan and do this, she'd need to do it now. It was rare that she had half an hour alone and if she was going to seize the opportunity, she didn't have a moment to waste. The coffee was making her buzzy—a heady mixture of excitement and agitation.

She chewed at her lip for a few indecisive seconds before crossing the kitchen to pick up the phone. She pulled the crumpled piece of paper out of her jeans pocket and smoothed it down on the work surface. And with a deep breath, she dialled the number.

'Hi,' she said when the call was answered. Her breathing was slightly uneven. 'Can I speak to Pip Henshall, please?'

This was a mad, bad thing, she thought as she waited for the receptionist to put her through to Pip's office.

'Pip Henshall speaking.'

At the sound of his voice, Edie felt her courage creep away and hide under the kitchen table. 'Hi,' she said nervously. 'It's Edie. Lyssa's sister.'

'Oh hi,' Pip said, sounding suitably surprised. As well he might, Edie thought. 'Good to hear from you.'

'I'm sorry to bother you at work.' She forced herself on.

'No. Not at all. It's fine.' Pip assured her. 'Have you heard anything from Lyssa?'

He sounded very anxious to know. 'No,' Edie said. 'No, I haven't.'

'I hope she's having a great time.'

'Me too.' The conversation halted.

'So,' Pip asked, 'what can I do for you?'

'Well...I was wondering whether you might like to meet up for lunch sometime,' she babbled. 'Sometime soon. Maybe. If you're not too busy.'

'Lunch?'

'I'm worried about Jake,' she said hurriedly. 'Jake and Lyssa. I thought...well...I thought...being his friend and all that...'

'You want to talk about Jake and Lyssa?'

'Well...yes.'

'Oh,' Pip said. 'Oh. Okay. When do you want to meet up?'

So, it was as easy as that. 'Soon,' Edie said. 'Let's do it soon. I thought I could come into the City.'

She heard the flicking of pages, which she presumed was Pip checking his diary. 'Work's manic,' he said. 'Lunch never involves much more than a quick sandwich on the run. Why don't we meet up tomorrow?'

'Tomorrow? Saturday?'

'I've plenty of time then,' Pip said. 'I thought that would be better for you with the kids.'

'Oh yes, right. The kids.'

'I can jump on the bike and come up to you,' he offered. 'It'll give me an excuse to go for a ride.'

She should be pleased about this. She knew she should. But Edie had envisaged a quiet little lunch far away from her own stamping ground—maybe followed by a blissfully unhindered afternoon of shopping all to herself. 'I'd rather come to you,' she said weakly.

'I wouldn't dream of it,' Pip insisted. 'Do you know a good place?'

'Yes.' Good grief, when was the last time she'd been out for a bijou little lunch? The only time they ever went out to eat these days was with the kids and that was usually to Pizza Hut or Burger King.

Edie trawled her brain and netted the first name that came to mind. It was a pseudo-French place just off the main high street that was always getting decent reviews in the local paper. *'Ménage à Trois.'* She almost choked on the words as she said them. Good grief, was there any significance in this? What had her horoscope said this morning? There were a dozen other restaurants in the centre of town that were equally respected. Why had she chosen the only one with a loaded name? Was this a fateful portent that she should take notice of? She repeated it, hoping that it was indeed a good place, and she swallowed hard as she heard Pip scribble the name down.

'Sounds fun.'

'Yes.' Edie chuckled nervously. Was he flirting with her?

'And rather suitable, don't you think?' Pip said with a laugh.

Yes, Edie thought, but not for the same reasons you're assuming.

'I'll see you there at one o'clock.'

'One o'clock's fine,' she said, hoping that it would be.

'Great,' Pip said. 'Until tomorrow.'

'Yes.' Edie hung up. At that exact moment Archie screamed his discontent at being awake and lacking entertainment for five minutes. Back to earth. Back to reality. Edie sighed as she went upstairs to get her son, the conversation with Pip replaying in her head. Until tomorrow.

Chapter Forty-Five

Felix and Felicity talk a lot about Tibet. I think they've possibly come to the wrong country and, instead of visiting Nepal, should have gone to Tibet instead. They once met the Dalai Lama and it seems to have had a profound effect on them—and, subsequently, their spending habits. Every time a Tibetan trader comes into one of the camps or villages, they are pounced on by Felix and Felicity, who commiserate in broken voices about the atrocities committed in their homeland and, to prove that they're earnest, they buy lots of tacky jewellery. We were allowed ten kilos of baggage and I should think they've already bought the equivalent of that in beads, bangles and trinkets. The sum and total of my knowledge of Tibet is from watching *Seven Years in Tibet* at the local cinema and I only went to see that because Brad Pitt was in it. And I would agree with anyone who cared to voice the opinion that my knowledge of world crises is somewhat shallow. But this is what travel does for you—in the words of all travel brochures, whether it be Cornwall or Kathmandu, travel does indeed expand your horizons. The only thing that travel has normally expanded for me is my waistline. I've decided that if you can trot the globe without en suite facilities that's when you can start to feel more worthy.

And this has been an eye-opener for me. Not least because I've discovered that I can manage perfectly well without a hairdryer or Touche Eclat concealer. I'm enjoying rubbing shoulders with nature. I've rediscovered my joy at the night sky, even though I can't work out where the major constellations are because they're all in different places over here. You simply can't do this at home because of all the light pollution from the street lamps.

Why is it that we assume our way of life is better? Does it really make us superior beings because we have Sky Digital, gas-guzzling motor cars, power showers and Prozac? The villages might not have electricity, but is it better to spend the evenings singing traditional songs and chatting to the village elders or sitting comatose on a comfy sofa watching *Pop Idol*, oblivious to the lost art of conversation?

There's no divorce, no old people's homes, no psychiatrists, no Weight Watchers' clubs and I'm not sure that the Nepali people are the poorer for it. The other thing I've found that I can manage without is Jake. Whether that's down to the fact that I've found an even more wonderful—albeit temporary—replacement in Dean, I've yet to decide.

My new lover and I walk together today, but we can't hold hands or cuddle—even though it's patently obvious to all but the seriously uninterested that we'd like to—because, culturally, it isn't the done thing. He slows his step so that I can keep up with him and we keep our arms as close together as we can manage without touching, which I have to say is rather romantic.

'What are the things you miss most about the States?'

Dean shrugs. 'Not much. When I'm at home in the village I eat dhal bhaat for breakfast every day—a kind of lentil porridge. It's taken me a long time to learn to love it.' He smiles wryly. 'Sometimes I crave bacon, but it's forbidden. Also, there's no dentist for miles—I haven't seen one in ten years. As an American, I can't quite get used to that. All that money my parents spent on an orthodontist when I was a kid has gone to waste.' His lips spread in a smile, showing off a perfect set of teeth. 'I also miss central heating in the winter. You don't realise how cosy life is in California until you leave it. Wall-to-wall sunshine and air-conditioning. My house is as draughty as hell and it can get real cold up here. The only air-conditioning comes from the foot-wide gap between the top of my walls and the roof.' He gives me a coy look from beneath his eyelashes. 'Now I'm a whining Yank.'

'Not really,' I say. 'It must be a very different culture. I'm just finding it hard to picture you in a house!' Though I have a very interesting vision of him in a tent.

Dean laughs. 'I can be quite domesticated sometimes,' he insists. 'The conservation project I'm working on provides a tiny place for me at a minimal rent because I don't get a salary.'

'No salary?' I can't keep the horrified look off my face.

'Rockefeller I ain't,' he teases.

I have to overcome my British aversion to talking about money. 'What do you live on?'

'I do some teaching, a little bit of guiding in the season.' He nods at the party ahead of us as if to prove it. 'I take some photographs and try to sell them to *Lonely Planet*. A bit of this. Even less of that.'

'Wow.'

'I can be fairly sure that women aren't after me for my money,' he says. 'Look where I do my day job, though.' Dean gestures at the mountains that surround us. 'It makes it a lot easier to give up the material things in life.'

I can imagine it. But would I be brave enough to try it? How many of us would? I'm feeling particularly virtuous that I'm coping without hair-styling products for a few weeks. What does that say about me?

'Once you're off the treadmill, it's not that hard to adjust,' he assured me. 'It's other people viewing from the outside who find it harder to accept.'

I can imagine that too.

We've walked for miles again. My knees aren't quite sure what's hit them. Sanjeev led us on a steep descent from the camp through chestnut forests, which was really tough going as the sun was hot and high and the forests steamed from last night's rain, pushing the humidity up to punishing levels. The group has fallen into a comfortable pace that suits us all. We tramp across a dozen or more rickety suspension bridges swinging high above the raging waters of the Sardi Khola and I take each one with a more confident air, even though we're dodging herds of goats and old women carrying baskets stacked high with maize like mobile haystacks—and none of them has any intention of stopping for anyone. I feel I have a touch of the Indiana Jones about me.

We follow the course of the river through ever-changing scenery. The journey here is flatter, cutting across terraced paddy fields and past the natural hives of wild bees the size of satellite dishes that cling to the side of rock overhangs, rippling with activity.

'We've got a rest day tomorrow,' Dean informs me. 'We can slip off alone and go to my village for a while.'

I can think of nothing better than the prospect of slipping off alone. 'I'd like that.'

'Me too,' he says.

There's an awful lot of longing in my lover's dark eyes and I feel a rush of desire. My libido has come back with a vengeance and I hadn't realised that it had been missing. Jake and I might have had a regular and active sex life—but it was hardly frenzied or fun. And this might sound blunt, but basically I can't wait to get at it. At last, I've found an infinitely better therapy than shoe shopping!

'I have a treat in store for us tonight too,' he whispers conspiratorially. And now I really can't wait.

Chapter Forty-six

We camp by the river again and I sit on a rock by the rushing waters, jotting in my diary. I want to remember every moment of this trip and, so far, it's been beyond my expectations. And far from feeling any animosity towards Jake and Neve, there's something inside of me that wants to thank them for creating the circumstances that led to me coming here. I can hardly believe I'm saying that myself. I hope that things are working out for them and that Jake is happy. But not too happy, of course.

There's a kingfisher on a branch a few feet from me, its feathers beautifully iridescent even in the fading light, and white-capped river chats and blue-throated bee-eaters swoop low over the water looking for the insects to provide their evening meal. I can smell our cooking in the dozen industrial-sized pans that Mr Bom has on the go and I realise that we have a very easy life.

I hear a noise behind me and look up and smile. You can never stay alone for long in Nepal. Behind every bush there's a small child waiting to say hello. This time, there are three little girls standing in a line behind me.

I clasp my hands and bow. '*Namaste.*'

'*Namaste.*' They giggle together.

I turn over the page of my diary. 'What are your names?'

They reel off a list of incomprehensible names.

I offer the book. 'Come and write them down for me.' They show off their excellent grasp of English and best hand-writing skills, all the time inching closer to me on my rock, until all four of us are sitting together watching the sun sink.

'Looks like you have a little fan club.' Dean comes up and joins us. The girls get even more giggly and then with much waving drift off back to their village. 'You're good with kids.'

'Well…'

'Do you regret not being able to have any of your own?'

I nod. 'It's a sore point.'

'Sorry.'

'I'm coming to terms with it.' I gaze out over the river. 'This is helping a lot.'

Dean looks at me and sighs. 'I want to be alone with you.'

I lean against him and his lips brush my hair.

'Do you think the others mind that I'm neglecting them?'

'They seem perfectly capable of looking after themselves,' I say. We glance back at the camp and there's much washing of socks and tee-shirts in progress. 'And I think Sanjeev is making up for any of your shortcomings.' I grin at him.

'I haven't felt like this in a long while,' he says and I'm not sure that he sounds too happy about it.

'Let's enjoy the time we have.'

His fingers reach up and toy with my hair. 'I need another shampoo,' I say.

'Oh, I can do much, much better than that,' Dean says with a wink.

I could get seriously addicted to this rakshi if it didn't taste quite so much like neat petrol. Tonight's entertainment, after the obligatory traditional Nepali songs and dancing, is being provided by a bunch of strait-laced Brits whose tongues have been artificially loosened due to excessive consumption of the local hooch. Saffron started off the proceedings while we were still relatively sober with a rendition of two folk songs that were probably sung by Lindisfarne or some other long-haired bunch in the 1970s. Her voice was all wobbly and she did actually put her finger in her ear in the ilk of all good folk singers, which was quite scary. She ate the mutton curry tonight as if it was going out of fashion, but I'm still not convinced that it isn't a front. She's far too 'Greenpeace' to be a real carnivore.

Dave and Jim sing the theme tune from *Auf Wiedersehen Pet* in mock-Geordie accents and the poor porters look more bemused at our cabaret by the minute. I feel none of this is suitable recompense for their heart-warming songs of love, beauty and sacrifice handed down through generations—and I suspect they feel the same. The time for my party trick is fast approaching. Dean pulls my hand.

'I can't do this,' I protest. 'Really, I can't.'

He shows no mercy. 'Go, girl!'

The last time I sang in public, I was at St Stephen's School and I was in the second-year choir—quite some time ago by anyone's calculation. I've always avoided karaoke like the plague, deeming it totally uncool and generally demeaning to all concerned. In my adult years I've always been more of an appreciative-audience type rather than an active participant. Now I'm going to attempt to sing without the help of background music or even a song sheet. There are very few tunes that I could even contemplate, given the circumstances.

I stand in the circle, petrified—you could hear a pin drop, I'll swear it. At least I've had a huge amount to drink and in a few weeks' time I'll never have to face any of these people ever again. Everyone is looking very expectant. I clear my throat.

I have chosen the anthem of all recently dumped women as my vocal début. The grandmother of all 'get lost' songs. I launch forth into 'I Will Survive', thanking Gloria Gaynor for her services to karaoke and heartbroken girlies everywhere. I do it rather enthusiastically, calling on my vast experience of therapeutic nights at some disco or another, bolstering myself or one of my dear friends after yet another failed relationship. I can't believe it was a man who wrote this song.

Rather supportively, the group start to clap along with me. I don't care now; the full anaesthetic powers of the rakshi have kicked in and I grab a hapless trekking pole lying nearby and use it as my microphone substitute, Freddie Mercury–style. Even the porters sit up straight. Saffron sings along—bless her, I love her cotton socks. A couple of the porters start to giggle. Dean joins in and starts twirling in Nepali fashion and I croon louder and louder. A few of the crew join him and then everyone is on their feet, whooping and hollering and hoping that 'I will survive' long enough for my big finale. Which, buoyed by my success, I do as if it's my last-night concert of a world rock tour.

When I've finished, we all collapse on the ground laughing and cheering. I think the porters can't take any more as they quickly grab their instruments and launch into a rousing Nepalese lament before we subject them to any more 1970s disco hits or any other music that will make their trousers turn immediately into flares. We join them to twirl and twirl some more until the stars are going round and round of their own accord.

Dean holds my hands. 'You are one hell of a woman.'

I'm a bit unsteady on my pins. 'Ah well,' I say, trying to be modest. 'I'll survive.'

'Of that I have absolutely no doubt.' He checks that the group are happy entertaining themselves. 'Come with me,' he says, and he leads me away from the camp and into the rich, enveloping darkness.

We wander away from the safety of the line of little blue tents—which is no mean feat in the pitch black—leaving the sounds of singing and laughter drifting on the air behind us as we follow the banks of the river until we are completely alone.

'Over here,' Dean says and helps me to scramble over the pebbly, water-smoothed rocks that form the shore. We cross the river, jumping from boulder to boulder. This is more activity than I've ever done in my life and I'm thankful that my eyes have adjusted to the darkness. I'm not frightened at all as Dean's strong hands guide me and hold me steady. When we reach the other side, we wend our way into a secluded inlet whose entrance is guarded by huge, monolithic boulders. We edge in, the sides of the cliff closing in on either side of us. Ferns and dripping greenery all but cover us with a natural canopy high over our heads. The air is still and warm, heavy with the pungent scent of fresh foliage.

'This is my secret place,' he says. 'I'm the only person who knows of its existence.'

'Really?'

'Well…' I can see his cheeky smile even in the dark. 'Me and several dozen Nepali villagers.'

I smile back. Dean wraps his arms round me. 'I've wanted to do this all day,' he murmurs in my ear.

I feel myself sigh and relax. 'Me too.'

Our lips meet and we kiss hungrily.

'Take off your clothes,' Dean instructs. Perhaps he sees my eyebrows shoot up in surprise, because he laughs out loud. 'Trust me. You'll be safe here. No one comes here at night.' He laughs again. 'Except me.'

I feel a thrill of anticipation. 'Okay.' My fingers fumble as I start to open my shirt.

'Here,' Dean says. 'Let me help you.'

I surrender as he peels off my clothes, covering me with kisses as he does so. He throws off his own clothes until we're both naked and then he beckons me to follow him and we weave through some more rocks until we reach a small clearing that contains a clear pool of water. Steam is rising from the surface.

'Good grief, this is fabulous.'

'I thought you'd like it.'

'I love it!'

Dean takes my hand and leads me into the water. My muscles are crying out for this. 'Oh, it's so warm.'

My lover joins me. 'It's a natural hot spring.'

'It's bliss.'

'The villagers use it during the day, but now we have the place to ourselves.'

We float together and Dean takes me in his arms.

I kiss him, tasting the water on his lips. 'Thank you for bringing me here.'

He kisses me again, long and hard, then smooths my damp hair from my forehead. 'It's supposed to have magical restorative properties.'

I lay my body along the length of his. 'Mmm. Do you know,' I say with a smile, 'I'm sure I can feel something happening already.'

Chapter Forty-seven

Neve had returned from Milan. And to say that there was an atmosphere between them was somewhat understating the fact. If it got any chillier between them, Jake was going to have to turn the central heating up to full blast. 'Atmospheres' seemed to be their speciality. He'd had days to think about what to say to her and still the words hadn't managed to form coherent, meaningful sentences in his brain.

Neve had breezed in, all smiles, around ten o'clock, and when he hadn't responded to her, she'd gone into a huff. His girlfriend had given him a perfunctory kiss on the lips and now was in the bedroom unpacking her case. He had an irrational urge to barge in there and go through the laundry basket to check her underwear for signs of illicit unions with Alec. Was this what she'd driven him to?

Jake was pretending to watch television when Neve came back into the room. She opened the fridge, rummaging around for food. He'd deliberately not gone shopping just to spite her, and that was never a good sign in a relationship, was it? Lyssa had always maintained that for a relationship to work you had to be more concerned about the other person's happiness than your own. He could see the wisdom in her words now. And how little notice he'd taken of them.

As a conciliatory move, Jake clicked off the television and walked over to the sleek marble slab that formed the kitchen counter. He perched on a bar stool and watched Neve as she prepared a rather wilted-looking salad for herself with some dried-up remnants of blue cheese. She was studiously ignoring him.

'So,' he said. 'How was Milan?'

Neve stopped trying to find some lettuce leaves that hadn't gone brown at the edges and looked at him. 'Fine,' she said. 'Milan was fine.'

'They liked your work on the Blow account?'

'Yes,' Neve replied tightly. 'They were very impressed with my work.'

Jake felt his guts twist. 'And Alec? Was he impressed with your work?'

Neve hesitated momentarily.

'Why didn't you tell me Alec was going with you?'

'Because I knew you'd react in exactly this way.'

'Didn't you think I'd put two and two together when I found out he wasn't in the office?'

Neve's mouth set in a sulky pout.

'Was he in your room when I called?'

Another hesitation. 'Yes.'

'And what was he doing there?'

Neve pulled open the fridge again and took out a half-empty bottle of white wine. She waved it at Jake to offer him some. He shook his head, even though the lure of strong drink was tempting.

'You haven't answered my question.'

Neve slugged back her wine. 'That's none of your business, Jake.'

'Oh, I think it is,' he said. 'What was it, a late-night meeting? Was he going through your briefs for you?'

'You can stop that right now,' Neve warned. 'You have no right to interrogate me.'

'I'm not interrogating you,' Jake said, trying to sound as reasonable as possible. Which was difficult because he didn't feel like being reasonable at all. 'I simply want to know if you're sleeping with someone else.'

'That's got nothing to do with you.'

'Neve,' Jake pointed out, 'you have just been away with another man for several days. I think I have a right to know.'

Neve's head snapped up. 'I didn't think this was an exclusive relationship.'

'And I didn't think you were shagging the boss.'

'Well, now you know,' she said softly.

Jake struggled to find his breath. 'How long has it been going on?'

'Does it matter, Jake?' Neve wanted to know. 'Does it really matter?'

It did matter, but he couldn't articulate why. Had Neve been seeing Alec all the time he'd been deceiving Lyssa? The thought made him feel sick to his stomach. He had very strong suspicions that she had. How could she have done this to him? Had he really been such a complete idiot?

When he didn't speak, Neve said, 'Yes, it's been going on for some time. I like him, Jake. Alec is a lot of fun.'

'Not to mention the quick route to promotion.'

'I think that's unnecessary,' Neve said darkly. 'I'm earning everything I have by my own merit.'

'But you'll never be able to prove that, will you?' Jake said. 'Everyone will think you've got the Blow account because you were sleeping with the boss.'

Neve said nothing, but he could see her chest heaving with indignation. At this moment she looked truly pathetic to him. And it was highly likely that he could be viewed in the same way.

'Is there anything else you want to tell me?' he said.

Neve folded her arms. 'Yes.' She took another swig of her wine and Jake noticed that her hand was shaking. 'As a matter of fact, there is,' she said. 'I'm pregnant.'

Jake felt all the blood drain from his face. He stood up, unsteady on his feet. 'Whose baby is it?'

He couldn't believe that they were having this conversation. Part of him felt as if he'd stepped out of reality. He went to the other side of the counter to look at Neve.

'I don't know,' she admitted. 'That's why I'm getting rid of it.'

'That's very kind of you to tell me.'

'I didn't want you to hear it from anyone else.' She'd missed the irony in his voice.

Her stomach was washboard flat, as always. No hint of burgeoning pregnancy. She caught him looking at her. 'I'm not very far gone,' she said crisply.

'Have you told Alec?'

'Yes, and he agrees with me. He's not ready to be a father.'

'His wife and kids must be pleased.'

Now it was Neve's turn to look rattled. 'I'd be a hopeless mother,' she said. 'I don't suppose you want it either.'

Did he want a baby with Neve? This is what he and Lyssa had been totally focused on for the last year or more, and now, out of the blue, the chance of fatherhood had literally fallen into his lap. Why couldn't it have happened so easily for him and Lyssa? Maybe they wouldn't be in this stupid situation now. What if it was his child? What if his sperm weren't sluggish after all? What if they were all strong, athletic swimmers? Jeez, what a conundrum. 'That "it" is a person,' he pointed out. 'A life.'

'It's a clump of cells, Jake. Get real.' Neve's face was set hard. 'Ten minutes and it'll be gone.' She made a disgusting sucky, vacuuming noise.

'You'll regret it,' Jake said softly. 'Think about it very carefully or you'll regret it for the rest of your life.'

'I don't think so,' Neve said. 'I can always get one out of a test tube if I want one.'

'It doesn't always work like that,' Jake said sadly. If anyone knew that, he did. Life was so unfair. Lyssa's struggle to become a mother. Neve casting it off as if it were an irritating insect. Something to be brushed off the skin. He felt stupid admitting it, even to himself, but he'd never realised how important this was. 'There's nothing I can say to change your mind?'

'What can you say? That you want me to have a baby—which may or may not be yours—marry me and live happily ever after?' Neve threw back her head and laughed at the very thought of it.

'I'm young, single, loaded and loving it. I've got bags of time before I get tied down with babies. What I need now is freedom.'

'I gave up everything that was dear to me to be here with you.'

'I don't think so. You were desperate for me, Jake. I hardly had to encourage you.'

'I left Lyssa for you.' Right when she needed me most.

'And it was very sweet of you....'

'Sweet?' His façade of being reasonable suddenly split open. Jake was apoplectic with rage. 'Sweet! I've ruined her life for you.'

Neve snorted. 'I think that's being a bit dramatic.'

'Do you?' He could feel anger boiling inside him. His fists were clenching against his will. 'Well, I think *this* is being a bit dramatic.'

Systematically, one by one, he pulled open each cupboard door and swept all of Neve's trendy, white crockery from the shelves and let it smash to smithereens on the wooden floor. The bits he missed, he picked out individually and hurled across the room to smash against the wall. There was a noise like someone howling like a wolf and Jake thought that it might well have been him.

Neve had curled into herself, sheltering from the shards of plates and cups and hideously expensive bowls against the fridge. When he'd finished, Jake stood, breathing heavily.

His girlfriend uncurled herself. When she spoke, her voice was heavy with sarcasm. 'Feeling better now?'

Jake's breath was refusing to return to normal. His lungs were painful and pounding against the inside of his chest. Blood was flooding his brain and he was absolutely sure there was a red mist in front of his eyes. He could barely make himself speak. 'Yes.'

'Fine,' Neve said. 'Now fuck off.'

Chapter Forty-eight

I lie on my back on the sleeping bag, adjusting Dean's arm so that he holds me closer. He makes a snuffly protest in his sleep. I kiss his nose and watch his chest rise and fall with his steady, even breath. I have a horrible feeling that I'm falling in love with this man. It feels too soon and too silly, but there's only so much I can blame on the mind-expanding powers of rakshi and soothing thermal baths. A few short weeks ago I thought I could never love anyone as much as I loved Jake and was destined to spend the rest of my life in a limbo-land somewhere between Jake and happiness. I can't believe how much things have changed. I look at Dean and trace my fingers over his skin and smile as I make him snuffle again.

We stayed in the pool until we were all relaxed and wrinkly and loved up and then came back to my tent and made love all night—well, most of it. I wasn't counting, but I was pretty impressed. And Dean might insist he's out of practice, but I'd say it was like riding a bike—it all seems to be coming back to him rather rapidly. Not that I'm complaining. Far from it.

It's still dark, but outside the tent I can hear the sounds of the breakfast being prepared, the faint clattering of pans, the chatter of the kitchen boys. The porters are rising from their sleep too, as always laughing and joking. Dean snuggles down next to me. He needs to be going, as Sanjeev will be here with my tea any minute.

On cue Sanjeev pokes his head into the tent. If he's taken aback at the sight of my company, he doesn't show it. Dean's eyes flicker open.

'Come, come, sister, brother,' he urges. 'The sun is soon up and I think it will be very beautiful.'

'We're with you,' Dean mutters and drags himself up. He rubs his cheek sleepily against mine and he's all rough and stubbly and I think I might love him more for it. 'Wanna see the sunrise?'

'I'd love to.'

'I was worried you might say that.' He kisses me and then pulls his combat pants towards him. We wriggle into our clothes and crawl out of the tent. The rest of the group are waking and mobilising too, judging by the rustling sounds emanating from beneath the line of blue canvas.

'You go up to the ridge alone,' Sanjeev says with a knowing smile. 'I'll take the rest of the group farther along the valley. Quick. You haven't got much time.'

Dean and I head for the ridge and, with me puffing like some knackered old steam engine, we scramble steadily to the top of a knife-like ridge that splits two valleys. I'm all in favour of pre-breakfast climbing being banned until we reach the top, when the view literally takes my breath away. The sky is banded with red and blue streaks and the sun is just peeping over the horizon, tinting the snow on the Annapurnas the colour of lemon cake frosting. Thick white mist swirls in the valley like big downy, puffball clouds. Eagles wheel above them and there's not a sound, save an intermittent burst of birdsong. It's so fabulous that I could cry.

Dean puts his arms round me. 'Worth the climb, hey?'

'Yes,' I sniff emotionally. 'Well worth it.'

He finds us a suitably comfy rock to sit on and we cuddle together, fending off the cold nip in the air. The sun eases itself higher, slowly, slowly, and the mountains are banded with confetti-pink flashes like a slideshow. There's a crack of sound like a gunshot.

'Avalanche,' Dean says and points to Lamjung where a slab of snow the size of a football pitch loosens itself and slides majestically down the mountain, flowing like water and puffing billows of snowflakes in the air. The golden rays of the sun fan out to highlight peaks and crevasses.

'I never want to go home,' I breathe.

'Lyssa—' Dean takes my face in his hands and looks at me squarely '—I never want you to either.'

Chapter Forty-nine

'Oh my word.' Lee looked up and nearly dropped his hammer.

'What?' Edie said, feeling herself flush as she came down the stairs. She felt as if she was making a grand entrance in the *Ziegfeld Follies*.

Archie was busy thrashing hell out of his xylophone and didn't miss a beat with his little plastic hammer. Lyssa had bought the brightly coloured instrument for him on his last birthday. Only someone without children would think of buying such a nerve-shreddingly noisy toy. Its tinny sound echoed round Edie's brain and bounced off the fillings in her teeth.

Lee finished bashing the nail into the wall before he turned again. 'Where did you say you were going?'

'To lunch,' Edie said. 'I'm going out to lunch.'

'With your mother?'

'Don't you listen to anything, Lee?'

'No,' Lee said. 'Tell me again. And speak to me like I'm a five year old. You know that gets me going.'

Edie tutted her annoyance. 'I'm having lunch with Jake's friend.'

'Paul?'

'Pip. He wanted to talk about Jake and Lyssa. See if I can help with the situation.'

'I thought they'd split up and that Jake was shacked up with some other bird?'

'That's a very succinct assessment,' she said, bristling.

'Sounds pretty irreconcilable.'

'But it may not be a completely lost cause. Pip thought we should at least try.' Edie hoped she wasn't blushing too much.

'Lyssa will be home before too long,' Lee said. 'Can't she sort it out herself when she gets back?'

'It may be too late then,' Edie said in what she hoped was a cryptic manner. 'I could hardly say no.'

'Well, he won't know what's hit him,' Lee observed. 'You look like you're auditioning for a part in *Saturday Night Fever*.'

'Thanks.' Edie had thought her outfit was really trendy when she'd bought it. Now as she looked at the short, geometric-print dress in the harsh light of day, she wasn't altogether sure. It would probably look a lot better on Kelly or anyone under twenty-five.

'What are those two white things hanging out of the end of it?'

'My legs,' Edie supplied.

'Good grief,' Lee said. 'Really? When did I last see those?'

'When did you last ask nicely?' his wife retorted.

'I think you look pretty, Mummy,' Daisy offered as she chased her rabbit, Justin—after Justin Timberlake—down the hall.

'Thank you,' Edie said. 'That doesn't mean Justin can stay in the house. Take him out to the garden.'

Daisy picked up the rabbit and stomped out.

'Do you think you could take Archie to your mother's on the way?'

'No,' Edie said. 'You'll have to look after him.'

'Oh, Edie, I've got loads to do. I can't sit and watch Archie all the time.'

'You promised,' Edie reminded him. 'Anyway, how often do I leave you with the kids? Get Kelly to watch him.'

Her daughter shot down the stairs. 'Not me,' she said. 'I'm out of here.' And before Edie could protest, the front door slammed in her wake.

'Where's she going?' Edie demanded.

'You don't think she told me, do you?' Lee said. 'But judging by the amount of make-up she was wearing, it will probably involve making some poor, unsuspecting youth feel inadequate.'

'What are the others up to?'

'No good of some description,' Lee said with a smile. 'When I last saw Anna, she was trying to tattoo her tummy with a marker pen. Liam and Mark are in the garden pretending to play football while trampling what few surviving green things we have left.'

Archie filled the gap with several off-key, staccato bursts. 'Archie, stop that,' she snapped.

Archie promptly burst into tears.

For some stupid reason, Edie felt tears springing to her eyes too. 'We really have lost our grip on this lot.'

Lee put his hammer down and lifted up their screaming son, who promptly stopped.

'Did we ever have one?' Lee said, and then, when he saw her lip wobble, added more kindly, 'I don't know what you worry about. They're fine. They're never going to win any awards for exemplary behaviour or bedroom-tidying skills, but they're good kids.'

He came over to her and put his arms round her waist, squashing Archie between them. 'You look lovely,' he said. 'Have you done something to your hair too?'

Edie prised herself away from his arms. Lee handed over Archie, and Edie slung him in his customary place on her hip. 'I thought I'd better make an effort,' she said. She was also wearing make-up for the first time since dinosaurs roamed the earth. Needless to say, she'd had to nick it all from Kelly's stash.

'I just hope he's taking you somewhere posh,' her husband said.

Edie fussed getting her coat and handbag together. 'I'm not sure.' *Ménage à Trois!* She couldn't even bring herself to think it, let alone say it.

'You ought to try that French place.' Her husband smiled innocently. 'Otherwise you'll turn a few heads in Burger King.'

'I'll try not to be too long,' Edie said.

'Take your time,' Lee said. 'You never go out. You should do it more often. Enjoy yourself.'

'It'll probably be really dull,' Edie said.

'Hey,' Lee said tenderly. 'Don't rush back for us. We can manage.'

'Thanks,' Edie said, not knowing whether that made her feel better or worse. She kissed her husband on the cheek.

Lee chucked their son under his chin. 'You know that I love you, don't you?' he said.

Edie studied her handbag. 'Yes.'

'I'd do anything for you and the kids.'

'I know.'

'And you feel the same?'

Edie hung her head. 'Of course.'

'Be an angel, then,' Lee said. 'Take Archie to your mother's.'

Chapter Fifty

So that we didn't suffer too much, Sanjeev climbed the ridge too, bringing us a kettle of hot black tea, rolled pancakes with local honey and two boiled eggs each. And I have to say, this is the most memorable picnic I've ever had. We sit still for ages, enjoying our food and the solitude. The light changes second by second until the full glory of the Himalayas is revealed.

Dean leans his head against mine. 'Happy?'

I can't think of a time in recent years when I was more happy. 'Very.'

'Me too,' he says and I melt a little bit more.

The next few days are officially rest days—although I'm not sure that getting up at 5.30 a.m. constitutes a rest in anyone's book. Sanjeev is leading the other members of the group on an optional walk. Being enthusiastic souls, they are all going along. Dean and I have opted to stay back in the camp—ostensibly to do some chores but, of course, we're planning to do our own explorations. Some of them involving the surrounding countryside. Some of them involving a bit of loitering within the tent. Tee-hee!

When the sun is fully up and the warmth is coming back to the air and our bones, we take a long, slow walk back to the camp hand in hand. The place is a hive of activity. Some of the porters are entertaining themselves by playing cards—indulging the Nepali habit of gambling away most of their meagre pay, Dean tells me. The others have strung up a washing line and are busy rinsing out their clothes in the metal washing pans. As there are no designer cut-price shopping malls or multiplex cinemas within striking distance to occupy us, I can feel a frenzied bout of laundry coming on myself.

So as part of our first romantic day alone-ish together, we get down to the dirty business of washing our socks and pants. And I guess it couldn't be classed as a particularly lovey-dovey way to spend our time, but my perceptions of a lot of things have changed since I arrived here—romance being one of them.

I sort out my tent, air my boots and repack my rucksack for the thousandth time and anyone watching this process would think that I was an old hand at this camping lark, I'm sure they would. Chores finished, we share lunch with the porters before setting off on a trail towards the village of Sikklis.

The track is a narrow stone path that winds up from the camp and within minutes I'm puffing away and thanking the God of Trekking Poles for finding me the man in the Outdoor Shop. We stand aside in an open, thatched hut to watch as a shepherd drives a reluctant herd of goats to lower pastures. The inside of the hut is covered in blood red, Maoist anti-government slogans, reminding me that not everyone here is happy with their lot. One man's paradise is so often another man's hell.

After another steep climb, we reach a small plateau and the full vista of the Himalayas is laid out before us. A steady stream of spindrift blows from the top of Annapurna II and I can feel the chill of the snow from the very top of the mountains stinging my cheeks. The foothills feel so close that I'm sure if I stretched far enough I could touch them. We find a grassy bank and lie down with our backs against a warm, smooth rock. Dean takes my hand and we close our eyes, basking in the sunshine.

After a while Dean kisses my cheek. 'Penny for them?'

'I was thinking about my family,' I say.

'You're missing home?'

'No,' I say. 'Not at all.' And in one way that's quite a surprise. I've hardly given the folks back home a second thought. 'I was just wondering what they'd think of all this.' I snuggle into Dean. 'They thought I was mad to come out here. I'm the sensible one. The coper. Ms Reliable. I'm not given to flights of fancy.'

'Maybe that's because you've never had the chance.'

That's exactly the reason. But then how many of us can afford to take time off the treadmill of modern life to think about what we really want to do? Most people are just too busy trying to get through the days to consider whether sitting in an office somewhere shuffling paper to pay off their mega-mortgage is how they truly want to spend their days. It's taken one hell of a jolt for me to do it.

'You're very lucky,' I say. 'I have no idea what I want to do with my life.'

'Luck has nothing to do with it,' Dean says. 'It's about seizing opportunities until you find something that excites you.'

I don't know what excites me anymore. The only thing I wanted more than anything I can't have. That leaves me feeling sort of adrift. 'I do a very dull job.'

'Chuck it and do something else,' Dean suggests with the ease of someone who has no fear of doing that.

'Some people are adventurous and some people go on holiday to the same hotel in the same place every year,' I say. 'I think it's indicative that Jake and I went to the same resort in Thailand for four years on the trot.' I think it's even more indicative that it was *my* choice.

'People are comfortable with familiarity,' Dean says. 'There's nothing wrong with that unless you start to find it stifles you. Are you close to your family?'

'Mmm. I have a mad mother, one younger sister, Edie, and a gaggle of small relatives.'

'And they rely on you?'

'Totally.'

'They could probably manage without you if they had to. People do.'

'I'm not so sure.' Would Edie be able to manage if she didn't have me to call on every day for something? What about my mother? Edie would never be able to deal with Mum on her own. 'My sister's got six kids. They take a lot of managing.'

'Six?'

'The miracle of contraception has somehow managed to pass her by.'

'Is that hard to cope with?' Dean asks.

'Not really.' I risk a smile. 'Although it does seem a little unfair sometimes. I'm sure that Edie's husband only has to leave his underpants near their bed and she gets pregnant. She must have inherited all the procreation genes in our family.' I pluck absently at the grass. 'It does mean, however, that my nieces and nephews are more than happy to act as surrogate children. Particularly if it involves bribery with expensive gifts.'

'Kids here are still a vital part of the community,' Dean says. 'They work the fields with their parents. They provide for them when they get older. On the rare occasions I go back to California, I sometimes think that children are seen as an unnecessary luxury these days. They certainly don't seem to provide the joy for their parents that these little ones do here. I guess everything these days is a juggling act between career and family life. More often than not, career wins.'

'That's so sad.' But horribly true. 'Do you want to settle down?'

Dean laughs. 'Sure.' He toys with my fingers, avoiding my eyes. 'But I'm hardly classic eligible-bachelor material. I have no career prospects. No investment portfolio. I make twenty-eight dollars a month.' He meets my gaze. 'I have nothing to offer.'

'I don't agree.' Our lips meet and they're warm from the sunshine. 'You have your heart.' I trace my fingers over his chest. 'No woman could ask for more than that.'

Chapter Fifty-One

Jake did as he was told and fucked off. Early in the morning. Before Neve was awake.

He'd spent the night on the hard, unyielding sofa, sleepless with rage and shivering for the lack of a blanket. As the first hint of the cold, white dawn sneaked its way through the slatted wooden blinds, he'd forced his rigid body up and had crept round, stuffing what gear he could lay his hands on into his holdall, desperately hoping that he wouldn't wake Neve and then he'd have to face her all over again. The last thing he wanted to see was her hard, smirking face. She lay immobile in the bed. Jake wasn't sure whether she was actually asleep or just—like everything else, it seemed—faking it. But he didn't care. There was nothing more he wanted to say to her. He watched her from the doorway, curled up in the duvet, not a crease of worry on her smooth face. There was no doubt that she was a beautiful woman, but there had never been more truth in the saying that beauty is only skin deep. It was impossible to love someone whose heart was as soft and caring as a concrete block. But then could it have been love he'd felt for her when she had managed to decimate it so successfully in one sentence? There is indeed a very fine line between love and hate and Jake knew that he'd crossed it.

He knew that he was going to have to face her at work, but he had two whole days to think how he was going to handle that one. And Pip would help. Pip would know what to do. He'd give his friend a call as soon as he got back to the house in St Albans and dished the grisly dirt on his predicament. He should have listened to Pip months ago. His friend had warned him that Neve was bad news. Oh, how right he'd been—and then some! Okay, so he was going to have to put up with a lot of 'I-told-you-so' looks, but to become an object of ridicule among his friends was the least he deserved.

As he reached the front door, he looked at the immaculate interior of the apartment with its designer this and one-off thats. His emotions were so depleted that he didn't even feel like smashing any of it anymore. All he wondered was how he could ever have envisaged making this sterile box his home. Jake felt his door keys, cold in his hand, and left them on the table.

The street was deserted—no sign of shattered lives lurking behind the Georgian frontages—and he clomped to the car and threw his holdall in the boot. He rested his head on the steering wheel before pulling himself together and easing the car out into the road. He just wanted to be out of here—back at home. And, if he could manufacture some sort of miracle—back with Lyssa.

Chapter Fifty-two

Edie noticed Pip's eyes widen with alarm as she approached. He stood up to greet her, clutching at the white-starched napkin on his lap.

'Hi,' she said, trying to overcome her shyness with a stab of bravado.

'Hi,' Pip said, still looking stunned.

'This is nice.' Her eyes took in the room. The trendy décor, the trendy food, the trendy people and the lack of accompanying not very trendy babies.

Pip scratched his chin. 'And who's this little fellow?' A shadow crossed his eyes. 'It is a fellow?'

No one had ever mistaken Archie with his fat, ruddy cheeks and his shock of blond hair for a girl before. Clearly Pip wasn't experienced in the realms of childcare.

'This is Archie,' Edie said, praying that her son might have a sudden change of personality and behave for once.

'Truck!' Archie said and threw his big red one on the floor to emphasise the fact.

'Yes,' Pip said, bending to pick it up. 'I couldn't have put it better myself.'

Edie struggled to pull out her chair and Pip rushed to her side. 'Where are you going to put it…him?'

'I don't know,' Edie said, searching the room. 'Do they have any baby chairs?'

'Baby chairs…' Pip looked as if this was an alien concept to him. 'I thought this was your local haunt?'

'No,' Edie said. 'I've never been here before in my life.' She didn't like to tell him that anywhere she went these days had to have chicken nuggets on the menu.

The café *Ménage à Trois*, on the other hand, was a chic hommage to all things stereotypically French. Like Edie would know. The only French things she ever came in close contact with were mega-size bags of frozen French fries when they were on special offer in Iceland. But that's what it said in the local rag, so who was she to argue. There were arty black-and-white photographs of onion-sellers in berets atop their *bicyclettes* adorning the walls, so that was French enough for her. Her one and only time away from British soil had been on a day trip on the ferry to Calais for some cheap Christmas shopping with Lyssa. She was so excited to get away for the day that she'd been sick even before she left home. A force-nine gale in the English Channel had encouraged her further and she'd spent her entire inaugural visit to a foreign land throwing up in a grotty loo in a soulless hypermarket while Lyssa bought French bread and Camembert and other stuff that she could just have easily got from Sainbury's. Since then, Edie had never quite got to grips with the fact that she was supposed to be a European and, therefore, should have a better appreciation of her continental brothers. Soft, heavily accented music oozed from the speakers and, as Edith Piaf and Vanessa Paradis were the only two French female singers she'd ever heard of, Edie assumed it must be one of them. Trying to stop terror from paralysing her, she focussed again on her new friend. 'I understand it's very good though.'

Pip called a waitress over. She was tall, skinny and dressed from head to toe in black Lycra with the addition of a crisp white apron, laced a dozen times round her impossibly thin waist. That was not the waist of a woman who had borne six children, Edie noted. Pip pointed at Archie as if he couldn't quite fathom what he was. 'Do you have any chairs suitable for…?'

The girl's eyes widened. 'I don't know,' she admitted. 'We don't normally get many… I'll find out….' And she disappeared hastily.

'Truck!' Archie shouted at the couple on the next table. They recoiled in horror and then glared at Edie as if she were the worst kind of mother for letting her child speak out loud in public. The waitress returned with a high chair that looked as if it had never been used and reluctantly set about manhandling it into place. When she'd finished her performance, Edie stuck Archie in the top of it. He promptly screamed loudly, so she snatched him out, sat down and stuck him on her lap. Pip looked dazed.

'He'll be all right in a minute,' Edie promised, jiggling Archie up and down on her knee, hard enough to make him sick.

Pip sat down and gulped at his drink.

'I was supposed to leave him with my mother,' Edie explained, still jiggling 'But she'd gone out.' She felt like killing—first her mother for being unavailable when she needed her and then Lee. Why couldn't her husband have just looked after their son for a couple of hours so she could have some freedom? Was it too much to ask? She looked at Pip guiltily. Freedom to do what exactly?

'It's fine,' Pip said, sounding as if it wasn't fine at all. If he'd been harbouring any thoughts of a cosy lunch between the two of them—like she had—they must have flown straight out of the window the minute he saw Archie wrapped round her. 'I haven't had a lot to do with children.' He looked as if it wasn't a regret.

He extended a tentative finger towards her son, but then withdrew it quickly when Archie looked as if he might be inclined to bite it. 'Lyssa said you have loads of kids.'

'Six,' Edie said, suddenly appreciating that out in the normal world it was 'loads'.

'Wow.' She was sure she saw Pip's eyeballs rotate. 'Six.' It was breathed more in horror than admiration. 'So all those kids at the party were yours?'

'Every last one of them.'

'Wow,' Pip breathed again.

Edie felt tears prick at her eyes. This wasn't how it was supposed to be. This wasn't how it was supposed to be at all.

She tried Archie in the high chair again and, more by good luck than good management, this time he acquiesced. Edie gave a nervous laugh.

'Drink,' Pip said. 'Can I get you a drink?'

'White wine, please,' Edie said. A bottle or two wouldn't go amiss.

The waitress approached them again cautiously, giving Archie a wide berth, and took their order.

'Can you bring some ice cream, please?' Edie said, without adding 'fast'. It was a tried and tested way of pacifying Archie.

Pip was looking gorgeous. He was wearing black velvet trousers and a black-and-white shirt that looked like the pattern of interference on a television screen. Everyone here was unspeakably well dressed, most clad in black, themed to complement their surroundings and none of them wearing loud, geometric-print dresses. Edie felt like a country hick up from the sticks. She wondered if she'd ever been trendy. Or had being pregnant with alarming regularity since she was a teenager somehow blighted her 'trendy' sensors? Now she never had the money or the cause to be the height of fashion. She left that to her fourteen-year-old daughter and that was a truly terrifying thought.

Groups of giggly women—who could still get away with the title of 'girls'—were out 'doing lunch' at tables all around them. They were roughly the same age as Edie and yet they looked as if they hadn't a care in the world. Not one of them looked as if they might be blessed with copious offspring. Not one of them looked as if they had the wherewithal to cram a screaming toddler into a Pampers nappy. Without exception, they were immaculately groomed and wildly glamorous. One or two of them cast overt admiring glances at Pip—who, thankfully, seemed oblivious to their attentions.

The waitress returned with their drinks and Archie's ice cream, which she handed to him at arm's length and then scuttled away with their food order.

They both watched as Archie manhandled his spoon and set about the messy business of making ice cream meet with mouth.

'How old are your kids?'

Edie held up a hand. 'I'd rather forget all about my brood today.' There was no way she was going to admit that she was the mother of a rapidly aging teenwoman monster. To fill the silence, Archie decided it was a great idea to bang his big, red truck on the wooden top of the high chair and sing 'Baa-baa, Black Sheep' at the top of his voice, completely drowning out the mellow efforts of whichever *chanteuse* it was, whilst waving a sticky-icky spoon around. Edie ignored him. Pip seemed to find it harder to do so. 'I don't get much free time without them.' One hanger-on didn't really count, did it?

'No,' Pip said. 'It must be impossible.'

'Well.' Edie tried for coy. She mustn't appear completely unavailable. 'Not entirely impossible.'

'So,' he said after a few moments of being pinned to his seat by the incessant noise of Archie's imaginative percussion. 'You wanted to talk about Lyssa and Jake?'

'Oh yes,' Edie said. 'Jake and Lyssa.'

They looked at each other. Pip rather expectantly, she thought. He was very handsome when he was frowning.

'Have you heard anything from Lyssa yet?'

'No.' He'd asked her that yesterday.

'Aren't you getting a bit worried by now?'

'No,' Edie insisted. 'I'm sure Lyssa's fine.' And then she remembered why she was supposed to be there. 'Of course, I'm a bit concerned. She was in a terrible state when she left. I hope she's done nothing foolish.'

'Lyssa doesn't strike me as the foolish type.'

'No,' Edie agreed. 'She's not.' She lowered her eyelashes. 'But love can do very strange things to a woman.'

Archie started to lick his truck.

Pip was mesmerised. 'So I've heard.'

Careless of his spoon, Archie flicked a lump of ice cream from the tip of it, which sailed in slow motion through the air towards Pip.

Edie gasped. The ice-cream landed with a wet plop on Pip's trousers. Her lunch date jumped up and dabbed at them with his napkin.

'Oh grief,' Edie cried. 'I'm sorry. I'm sorry.'

'It doesn't matter.' Pip, realising he was attracting attention, sat back down.

'They're velvet, aren't they?'

'Yes,' Pip said.

'Real velvet.'

'Yes,' he repeated. 'Look, it doesn't matter. They'll dry clean, I expect. It was my fault for wearing them.'

A silence hung between them, only perforated by Archie's singing. Several diners had started tut-tutting. Her son, of course, was completely unperturbed by the fuss he was causing.

'So,' Edie finally said. 'How's Jake?'

'Still acting like a twat.' Pip looked shocked at his choice of words. 'Sorry,' he apologised to Archie. 'Sorry.'

'Twat,' Archie said, seizing with both hands any sign of a forbidden word. 'Twat, twat, twat.' He turned to the couple on the next table, grinning his toothy grin. 'TWAT!'

They both paled.

'Archie, be quiet,' Edie urged. She tried to renew his interest in the big red truck. 'Be a good boy.'

'Sorry,' Pip offered.

'He's normally very good,' Edie said. 'I think he's over-excited.' Like me.

Their food arrived. Heartbreakingly small portions, delicately arranged on pure white porcelain. She hadn't seen food like this in years. Her menus revolved round industrial-sized portions for monster children's appetites. Chips and spaghetti Bolognese featured too large in her life. Her heart sank to her uncomfortable platform shoes. What on earth was she doing here? Who was she trying to fool? Pip and she would never have the slightest thing in common. He was probably *au fait* with all things French. He looked like the type who was comfortable on all five continents. She pushed at an oh-so-tiny asparagus tip with her fork. 'Do you see me as a woman, Pip?'

Her companion's fork stopped halfway to his mouth. 'Er…'

'It isn't a trick question.'

He let his fork fall.

'Do you see me as a woman?'

His Adam's apple bobbed nervously at this sudden turn in the conversation. 'Yes.'

'An attractive woman?'

Pip shot a surreptitious glance at Archie. 'Yes.'

'Yes, if it wasn't for the fact that I'm saddled with six children?'

'It probably comes into the equation,' Pip hedged.

She flopped back in her seat.

'Edie,' Pip ventured. 'Is there a point to this?'

'Yes,' she admitted, steeling herself. 'I thought you might be interested in…seeing…me.'

'Seeing you?'

She shrugged. 'Sometimes. Every now and again.'

Pip's jaw had dropped open.

Edie lowered her voice. 'I thought there was a spark between us,' she said. 'At Lyssa's farewell party. I thought there was a spark of attraction.'

Pip's jaw didn't move.

Edie's slender grip on her confidence slipped away from her. 'I've read this wrong, haven't I?'

'Er…' Pip said. 'Yes. You have, rather.'

'Oh.' Edie fiddled with her napkin. 'I've never done seducing before,' she admitted. 'I've been rather too busy. I haven't had any practice. I don't know what to say.'

'I don't think you should say anything.'

'Oh.' Edie sagged. 'So you wouldn't consider it?'

Pip seemed to recover some of his equilibrium. 'Edie, you are a very attractive woman. Very attractive. There's no doubt about that. But you're married. Married with several children.'

'I can get away,' she said. They both looked at Archie. 'Sometimes.'

'Look.' Pip shook his head. 'I'm sorry if you thought I'd led you on. But I'm not that kind of guy. I'm hopeless at commitment, but I do sort of like monogamy. You and your sister are both very beautiful….'

My sister. Lyssa. Edie could hear her brain going whirr-whirr-thunk. It *was* Lyssa all those sideways longing looks were aimed at. She should have stuck by her original assessment. It was only Lyssa insisting that they were just friends which had convinced her otherwise. 'Oh my word,' she said. 'It's Lyssa. She's the one you've fallen for.'

Pip flushed.

'Oh, my word. Oh, my word. How can I have been so stupid? Of course it's Lyssa! Why wouldn't it be?'

Pip looked sheepish. 'I have to admit I don't really have a vested interest in seeing Lyssa and Jake get back together.'

Edie could have wept. 'Now I feel very foolish.'

'Don't,' Pip said. 'Don't. It's an easy mistake.'

'Ah, you get women every day asking if you want to have an affair with them?'

'Not every day,' Pip said with a smile. They both laughed. 'And I am flattered but…'

Archie piped up again. 'Twat!'

'This is my life,' Edie said with a weary sigh. 'Old before my time with half a dozen kids in tow. I can't blame you for not wanting to get involved.'

Pip reached out and took her hand. 'Do you know what I'd do if I were you?'

Edie shook her head.

'Go home, organise a babysitter and take your husband out on the town tonight. Tell him how much you love him and then both get blindly drunk and dance until dawn.'

'That's your recipe for getting some excitement back into my sad little life?'

'If you want to be seen as a woman again, it's better that it's through your husband's eyes. That way is a lot less painful in the long run.'

'But a lot less fun.'

'I'd put it to the test first,' Pip advised.

Edie puffed expansively. 'I guess you're right.'

'I am,' Pip said. He took her hand and kissed it tenderly. 'But that doesn't mean that I'm not very flattered.'

Edie blushed. 'I can't believe I've been so stupid.'

'Grandma!' Archie shouted.

Edie wheeled round. Her eyes widened in horror. Pressing her face against the full-length window of the restaurant was indeed the last person she'd expected to see. Her mother. She dropped Pip's hand like a hot brick. Even more surprising, lurking behind her frowning parent was a rather dashing man in smart slacks.

Chapter Fifty-three

Dean and I are taking a hike to his village—a mere two hours away—where he's going to show me his home and introduce me to some of his friends. I feel quite nervous about it, as if I'm going to meet his parents—except his parents, of course, are safely out of the way in the US of A. And I think it indicates an inherent switch in my perspective that it's not the four-hour round trip by foot that I'm finding daunting.

'Are you ready to make tracks?' Dean says.

'Yes.' The thought of a day alone together is utter bliss.

We trek gently downhill, away from the camp, and on the stretches where we are completely alone, hold hands as we walk. Monkeys swing through the trees above us, chattering as they go. The scenery is softening as we walk, along with my muscles. My tension feels like an onion skin—each day I manage to shed another layer and I didn't realise quite how many layers there were. My tension is one bloody big onion! It's not an iddly-piddly spring onion, it's a great hulking Spanish dobber.

We squeeze against the side of the narrow trail as a mule train of a dozen pack animals passes by, the bells of their colourful, plumed headdresses jingling and their hooves clip-clopping on the stones as they take essential supplies to the highland areas by the only route that's available in the Annapurna region. How the lucky 10 per cent of the world's population who own cars take them for granted!

The last part of the walk is down a wide meadow and we pick our way down slippery stone steps enjoying the open vista above Bengas Tal Lake. Tiny houses cling to the side of the hills like colourful Lego bricks.

As we approach the village, the children run down from the fields shouting, *'Gora! Gora!'* Foreigner! Foreigner!

'These are some of the kids that I teach,' Dean says as they hit us at full tilt and wrap themselves round his legs.

So, clearly, the chant is for my benefit. They swarm round me, noisier than the wild bees, all smiles and shouting.

Two sticky hands curl round mine and I'm led into the main street—the only street. There's no road at all here, not even a dusty track, just a sweeping curve of grass opening out to a field that falls away over the side of the mountain. The houses are smarter than the ones in the other villages we've passed through, the mud-brick outsides painted in vibrant shades of blue and orange topped with tidy, thatched roofs. The gardens are well tended and filled with large ripe produce—cabbage, sweet potatoes, peppers, aubergines, chillis and the more exotic and unexpected, bananas, squash, lemons and tangerines. Out on the porches the women are sprucing up their homes, swishing away the dust with brooms made of twigs while others sit in groups singing and kneading dough to make chapattis.

'They'll have been cooking for days,' Dean tells me. 'Everyone is getting ready to celebrate Tihar—the Festival of the Brothers—this afternoon. Nepal has a hundred and ten festivals and holidays every year—all a great excuse to eat too much and drink too much and take time off work.'

'A bit like Christmas then.'

'A lot like Christmas, but a hundred and nine times more often.'

'That doesn't bear thinking about.' Once a year is far too often for me. I'm sure I'd love Christmas if it only came round every five years.

'It's great. Everyone gets very overexcited.' Dean flashes me a reassuring look. 'It'll be a lot of fun. You'll love it.'

The women giggle bashfully and wish us *'namaste'* as we pass.

We wander farther down the street until we reach a tiny thatched house. It looks as if there's one room downstairs and one upstairs. It's well tended and there's a blackened, brick-built range on the front porch. Next to the house stands a tall wooden rack containing ears of corn drying in the sunshine. There's a black baby goat curled up asleep and half a dozen plump chickens strut and peck around it.

'Well,' Dean says with a smile. 'This is it. Welcome to my life.'

I suppose if I'm absolutely honest, Dean's house is a bit of a shock. It's as far away from my twee little home in St Albans as I can possibly imagine. Although it's small, the rooms are neat and tidy, but 'basic' is the word that most readily springs to mind. The floors are bare stone and the walls bare brick. A garish Bruce Springsteen poster supplies the only relief, shouting out the legend *Born in the USA*, and I gather that's Dean's touch. There's one living room that has two roughly carved wooden armchairs and a small Buddhist shrine in the corner. The bathroom contains a squat loo and a metal basin and I gather that water has to be brought from the communal well, as there's a bucket with a rope attached to it in evidence but no taps. Open wooden stairs lead to the only bedroom, which contains a double platform for a bed covered by worn but clean sheets and a mosquito net. There's a wonky cupboard, a raffia mat on the floor, a kerosene lamp and a stack of well-thumbed English-language paperbacks by the bed.

'It's nice,' I say, and it makes me realise how spoiled I am. Electricity at the flick of a switch. Turn a tap and out comes water.

Dean blushes. 'My other house is a forty-acre estate in the country.'

'It's great, really.' I give him a hug.

'It serves me well,' he says. 'Except in the winter when it's the coldest place on earth.'

'I'll be able to picture you here when I go home'

He places a finger to my lips. 'No talk of that now,' he insists. 'We've got a party to go to.'

When we emerge from the house into the bright sunshine once more, the women are in the process of draping strings of marigold flowers from house to house—a sort of natural bunting. Giggling children place garlands of marigolds round our necks as we make our way to the centre of the village. A makeshift trestle table pulled from the only café is being loaded with food and drink—dishes of dhal bhaat, platters of boiled rice studded with morsels of chicken and yak beef, momos, little parcels of pasta filled with meat and vegetables, spicy snacks of jelebis and laddus. Jugs of the robust distilled beer, chhang, and the local hooch, rakshi, are being passed round and someone hands Dean and me two metal cups half-filled with the brew. I can feel a hangover coming on just smelling it. Last time I got drunk on this it got me into a lot of trouble! For which I'm now very grateful. I look across at Dean and grin happily.

A group of men have gathered under the now vacant thatched roof of the café with their musical instruments and have started up a vibrant, lilting tune. The villagers, all decked out in their Sunday best, gather round, clapping and singing along. To my embarrassment Dean pulls me into the centre of the circle and starts twirling me round, causing great hilarity all round.

'Strut that funky stuff, girl!' he orders as he spins me.

After watching for a while for their amusement, the villagers join in twisting and spinning, taking the celebration and whipping it up another gear.

As darkness falls, the music continues and we've eaten and drunk our fill and have danced until we dropped. The stars come out, sprinkling the blackness of the sky with diamond pinpricks, and I realise that at this moment I wouldn't want to be anywhere else.

Chapter Fifty-Four

Lee was pulling at the neck of his shirt. 'What exactly is the purpose of this?'

'Nothing,' Edie said, adjusting her hair. 'We're going out—alone—to have a good time.'

'But we never do that,' Lee said, checking that there was nothing untoward in his teeth in the dressing table mirror. He suddenly looked up. 'Have I forgotten our anniversary?'

'No.'

Her husband breathed a sigh of relief. 'Thank goodness.' A look of panic sprang up in his eyes. 'It's not your birthday?'

'No,' Eddie said. She went and wrapped her arms round him. 'I just thought it was time we went out together, forgot about the kids, kicked up our heels.'

Lee looked uncertain.

'Kelly will be fine. She's been bribed with pizza and hard cash. And threatened with a slow and painful death if she misbehaves. We'll have the mobile with us if there are any problems.'

'And where are we going?'

'We're going out for dinner and then on to a nightclub.'

'A nightclub.' Lee shuddered. 'Does that mean I'll be required to dance?'

'Until your feet drop off.'

'My feet might have forgotten what to do.'

'We've got all night for them to remember.'

'That's what I was afraid of,' her husband said. 'I might have to get horribly drunk.'

'I'm relying on it.' Edie nuzzled into his neck.

'You're not going to take advantage of me while I'm under the influence of alcohol?'

'I think it's essential.'

Lee smiled at her. 'Why don't we do this going-out thing more often?'

'Because we can never get rid of the children and we're broke.'

'I knew there was a reason.'

Edie picked up her handbag. She'd recovered from feeling foolish about approaching Pip. Goodness only knows what had come over her, she was far too young to be blaming it on her hormones. Thankfully, he'd taken it in good form and had given her some sound advice into the bargain. Now all she had to do was find out how much her mother had seen. Contrary to expectations, when Edie had seen her she'd grabbed the hand of her anonymous male companion and had scuttled off in the opposite direction. No doubt she'd have something to say on the subject—her mother always did. She gave an inward sigh and wished it was time for Lyssa to come home.

'Are you ready then?'

'As I'll ever be,' Lee said, straightening his jacket.

As Edie headed towards the door, Lee grabbed her arm. He pulled her towards him and kissed her full on the lips. 'This is a great idea,' he said.

She didn't mention that he had another man to thank for her renewed enthusiasm in their relationship.

'Have I told you lately that you're a very beautiful woman, Mrs Firth?' her husband said.

'No,' Edie sighed. 'No, you haven't.'

'Then I must remedy that immediately,' he said. 'You are a very beautiful woman and I love you very much.' He kissed her tenderly.

'I love you too,' Edie said.

'You're just saying that because I'm the father of your incredibly beautiful and intelligent children.'

Edie buried her head in his neck. 'And what better reason is there than that?'

Chapter Fifty-Five

I can't feel my hangover until I start to lift my head from the pillow and then there are psychedelic colours inside my brain. I wonder if the whole village is similarly indisposed or is it just soft Westerners who can't handle their booze. Beside me Dean groans to show that he's awake. I let my head sink slowly down again and enjoy the relief that closing my eyes brings.

'Did we have a good time?' Dean asks. He's flat on his back, staring glassy-eyed at the inside of the thatched roof.

'We had a great time.'

'Thought so.' Dean sounds very fragile. 'That's why I can't remember it.'

'I think chhang is very evil stuff.'

'I agree,' Dean says. 'But these guys sure know how to throw a party.'

The wooden shutters are closed, so we haven't yet had to experience the full horror of direct sunlight. Outside, the sound of men working drifts across the fields—the bizarre haw-haw-haw call as they drive the buffalo to thresh the millet, followed by the echoing thwack of a stick on the beasts' rumps. Hangover or not, they're out there providing for their families. I guess the cycle of nature doesn't wait around for a clear head. There's the chatter of children's voices in the street.

Dean peers at his watch. 'School starts at ten o'clock,' he says. 'It gives the kids time to work in the fields with their parents. Most of them will have been out there since before dawn.'

I can just imagine Edie's brood dragging themselves out of their pits at dawn to do a few hours' hard graft before going to the local comprehensive—I don't think Kelly, like most teenagers, ever surfaces before noon. And it makes me think how easy our kids have it.

'Can we visit the school?'

'Sure, if you'd like to,' Dean says.

'I would.' I want to know everything I can about these lovely, hospitable, gentle people. 'We should think about getting up.'

'I guess we should.' Dean throws his arm across me, pinning me to the bed and covering my lips with insistent kisses. 'But not just yet.'

Chapter Fifty-six

Edie couldn't move. None of the normal reflexes she used for creating movement were working. Oh my word. Somewhere, somehow, between leaving the nightclub and waking up, she'd become paralysed. Everywhere. There was no feeling in her arms and legs, although there seemed to be far too much in her brain.

She turned her head. Her husband was lying next to her in the bed, prone and unmoving. He was still wearing his shirt and a faintly dazed expression. His eyes were open, but she wasn't sure if he was awake.

'I'm paralysed,' she muttered through lips that had also become thickened and numb.

'Paralytic more like,' Lee mumbled.

Edie groaned. She would kill Pip. When he had told her to go out and get drunk, he'd forgotten to tell her how bad hangovers felt the next day.

'My feet hurt,' her husband complained. They had danced, if not quite until dawn, then certainly until about three o'clock.

'My everything hurts,' Edie complained back.

Lee stuck his feet out of the bed. He was still wearing his shoes.

There was a gentle knock on the door, followed by it cannoning open and crashing against the wardrobe. Archie toddled in, chewing on his dummy and naked except for an artistic smear of Marmite. Daisy followed, gingerly, carrying a tray as if it were a case of dynamite. She took step after careful step until she reached the bed.

Edie struggled upright, and Lee, wearing his shirt and shoes, did the same.

'I brought you breakfatht in bed,' Daisy said, the words failing to break her utter concentration.

Edie formed her lips into speech shapes. 'Thank you, darling.'

Daisy placed the tray on the bed in front of them as if she were dismantling an unexploded bomb. Edie's red eyes took in the breakfast set before them. Lee, scratching his head, stopped in mid-itch. Edie tried to pin a smile on her face.

'Now eat it all up,' Daisy said brightly, using a phrase that Edie had heard far too often before. 'I made it all mythelf.' She smiled proudly. 'Exthept Archie helped a little bit.'

Archie rubbed his Marmite streak into his hair. Edie dreaded to think what her son's contribution might have been.

'Yum,' Lee said.

Breakfast consisted of two bowls of Smarties ice cream—and the rainbow-hued sweets looked particularly fluorescent this morning—which were accompanied by a plate of rather well-grilled fish fingers submerged beneath a slick of tomato ketchup, what was left of two burned squares of bread that may or may not have been fit for human consumption hiding beneath an inch of Marmite. More than likely her son's contribution. To finish off there were two glasses of Ribena Toothkind and a chunky Kit Kat each.

'Toast,' Lee declared, examining the offerings. 'How clever of you to get it so black.'

Daisy beamed.

'And so much Marmite.' Her husband beamed gratefully.

'I'm not that hungry…' Edie tried. 'Mummy's feeling a bit poorly.'

'Thith will make you feel better,' her daughter assured her.

'Eat it,' Lee muttered under his breath. 'She's gone to a lot of trouble. Eat it.'

'I'll die.'

Lee didn't move his teeth, which were set in a smile. 'It'll be in a good cause.'

Edie was horrified to think that her own culinary efforts might have inspired this, but she feared they might well have. Dutiful parents, they both grinned and picked up their spoons.

'Mmm, ice cream,' Edie said as the cold shock jarred all her teeth. Just the thing for a hangover. She hoped her daughter would grow up to have a drink problem and then she could get her own back on her manyfold.

Daisy stood over and watched as they struggled down every last morsel. Whoever said parenting was easy? When they'd finally finished and Daisy had deigned to take their tray away and had been persuaded to make them a cup of tea—following explicit instructions—Lee and Edie collapsed back onto their pillows, giggling. Lee pulled her into his arms.

'You're not going to be sick, are you?'

'I can't guarantee it.' She pushed the thought of the brightly coloured Smarties ice cream to the back of her mind.

'It was a good night, wasn't it?' Lee grinned at her.

'Yes,' she sighed happily. 'It was a great night.'

'We should do it more often.'

'Do you really think so?' Edie said. 'I'm not sure that I can stand the pace anymore.'

Lee wiggled his feet. 'I'm still not sure how I managed to get my trousers off without removing my shoes though.'

Edie looked up, smiling contentedly. Then suddenly her smile died. The ceiling fan above them whirred lazily, creating a welcome draught of refreshing air. It had been one of Lee's many DIY bargains from B&Q—an essential for those three giddy days of summer when it was too hot to sleep. Her husband followed her gaze and as his fuddled brain registered what was mesmerising her, they stared at each other with an expression of horror.

'Oh no,' Lee said. 'Oh no.'

'Oh yes,' Edie said. 'Oh yes.'

Hanging on the fan, swishing the air delicately, were her black lacy knickers and, in a blinding flash of clarity, they both remembered exactly how they got there.

Chapter Fifty-seven

Jake and Pip were queuing up in Bite Me! It was the lunchtime rush and packed as always. The secretaries and the suits shuffled forward to order their salad sandwiches.

'You've looked miserable all morning,' Pip observed, leaning against the wall.

'With good reason, mate,' Jake said. 'Bloody good reason.'

'Want to talk about it?'

'Yeah,' Jake said. 'But not in the office.' What he didn't want to admit was that he felt like crying. He hadn't cried since he was six and his mum had put Pindy-Pandy bear in the washing machine and both of its arms had dropped off. And, clearly, this was a rather more serious situation.

'Let's go to the bench across the road,' Pip suggested.

Having ordered and collected their sandwiches, they did just that. The wind whipped down the road, plummeting the temperature with a substantial chill factor. Pip pulled up the collar of his jacket and looked as if he hoped this wouldn't take long.

'I take it this is about Neve?'

'Yep.'

Pip dipped into his brown paper bag of sandwiches and examined the contents before biting into one. 'So, how did it go when she got home?'

Jake rubbed his chin. 'I thought it went well. In the circumstances.'

Pip continued munching.

'I smashed all her Jasper Conran crockery and she told me to fuck off out of her life.'

'There must have been quite interesting "circumstances".'

'Yes,' Jake said. 'She *is* sleeping with Alec—' he glanced at his shivering friend '—but then you already knew that.'

Pip said nothing.

'I don't suppose you knew she was pregnant?'

After a sharp intake of breath, Pip said, 'No, I wasn't aware of that.'

'Neither was I until last night.'

'Bummer,' Pip said.

'Double bummer,' Jake agreed.

His mate looked at him sympathetically. 'I can hardly bring myself to ask the next question.'

'Whose baby is it?' Jake shook his head. 'That's the question I'd like answered too.'

Pip raised his eyebrows. 'She doesn't know?'

'Speaks volumes, doesn't it?' Jake said sadly.

'Shit, mate,' Pip said. 'What are you going to do?'

'I've no idea.' The bit where his brain used to be had been replaced by a big, numb lump. 'She's having an abortion.'

Pip looked dumbstruck. 'That's heavy, mate.'

'Tell me about it.'

His friend abandoned his half-eaten sandwich. 'It might be for the best.'

'Do you think so?' Jake wasn't so sure. He wasn't so sure at all. 'What if the child is mine?'

'You could insist on DNA testing,' Pip suggested. 'At least then you'd know.'

'What difference would that make?' Jake said. 'She still wouldn't want the baby. I can think of some suitable names for Neve, and

"Earth Mother" isn't one of them. You can't bring a kid into the world like that.'

Jake felt himself sinking into depression. When did we start playing God with creation? Snuffing out babies without a second thought. Treating human life as a commodity. The act of creation as simple as merging the contents of two Petri dishes.

'I guess it's over between you?'

'It pretty much looks like it.'

'It wasn't shaping up too well when she nicked the Egg Marketing Board account from under your nose.'

'True,' said Jake. It seemed like small fry now in comparison to this latest betrayal. 'She said she was shielding me from Alec. I just didn't realise she was doing it by selflessly throwing her body in between us.'

Pip started to laugh wearily and he clapped Jake on the back. 'You've got to laugh, mate.'

'Have I?'

'You'll see the funny side of it,' Pip said, but he sounded forced. 'In years to come.'

Jake's laughing mechanism seemed to have been switched off. Perhaps he could have agreed more readily if he hadn't got Lyssa caught up in the whole sordid mess and lost her in the process. He'd spent a terrible weekend back at their house on his own, just wondering what to do to make it all right again.

'Come on,' Pip said. 'Let's go back inside. I'm freezing my knackers off here.'

Jake wished his knackers had frozen off years ago, then perhaps he wouldn't be trapped in the middle of this waking nightmare.

Still, as always, Pip was right. December wasn't the traditional time for sitting outdoors with sandwiches. It was strange, but Jake didn't feel cold. He didn't feel anything. Anything at all.

Chapter Fifty-eight

The school is set on a hill above the village. It's a small, one-storey building and there's a group of children playing in the potholed concrete square of the playground.

The children here are scrubbed and polished, wearing immaculate, if slightly worn, navy blue uniforms as they chase each other round and round. Some are clearly drowning in hand-me-downs. All the girls have their hair tied up in red ribbons and they look so adorable and so keen—again, something that doesn't instantly spring to mind when thinking of pupils at home.

They come and hang on Dean's arms and follow us inside.

The schoolhouse is as neat as a pin inside, but oh so basic. It's made up of half a dozen rooms and the walls are bare, the paint is faded and cracked, the rows of desks rudimentary. The classes are mixed, but the girls sit on one side and the boys sit on the other. They're also mixed in age—anything from seven year olds to the three shy women sitting at the back who are probably in their early thirties.

Their young Nepali teacher, Manuka, gladly gives up teaching her lesson to welcome Dean and me. He's clearly very popular here and I feel a surge of affection for him. Dean introduces me first in Nepalese and then in English. 'This is Lyssa and she's come to visit us all the way from England.'

The children find this hilarious and abandon their desks to crowd round me. One little, doe-eyed boy coyly hands me a crumpled book.

'Do you want to read for them?' Dean suggests.

'I'd love to.' And as soon as I've said it, I give the book the once-over and I have to say it's pretty dire. It's one of their English set texts and the book doesn't do justice to the children's grasp of language. Nevertheless, before I've even uttered a word, I'm surrounded by a rapt audience of smiling faces and I think if all pupils were as attentive then teaching wouldn't be a bad job. I do appreciate that some of their attention is due to my novelty value.

One of the smallest girls has wriggled her way onto my knee, threading her arms round my neck, as I read aloud the fairly rubbishy story about a frog looking for somewhere to live—but no one seems to care about the content. Even the older women have joined us cross-legged on the floor. Dean is sitting over in the corner, also surrounded by fans, and as I catch his eye I can see him grinning proudly.

There's a simplicity in his life that I'm starting to envy. And I'm also full of admiration at how he's been able to adapt to it. Coming from California, it must have been a bit of a culture shock to say the least. As much as it seems appealing, I'm not sure that I could give everything up for this. I think I'm just too grounded in consumerism to change my ways now, yet Dean seems to be the least materialistic person I've ever met. Take his house. There's absolutely nothing wrong with it. It's perfectly adequate. It has four solid walls, a roof, a fire and a bed. A nice verandah that doubles as a kitchen. But that's all it has. There's no gas cooker, no fridge, no electricity, no bath, no wall-to-wall laminate flooring, no CD player, no modern conveniences at all. No convenience! Unless you count the hole in the ground outside, of course. How many people used to a house stuffed full of Western comforts could cope with that on a permanent basis?

I finish my story and, led by my biggest fan, the children applaud—even the teenagers. How enchanting they are compared to our dull-eyed, bored kids. They cluster round me to show me their exercise books and, from what I've seen of my nieces' and nephews' homework, their curriculum looks like a scaled-down version of ours, which on their meagre resources is pretty impressive. When we finally manage to prise ourselves away, we leave behind a group of grinning faces, waving madly, and we wander out through the playground, shooing a few chickens out of our way until we're back on the street again.

'They're great kids,' Dean says. 'They have so little, but they want to learn so much.'

'They're adorable.'

'I teach them English,' he says shyly. 'And math. And probably bad habits.'

'They obviously love you.'

He squeezes my hand briefly and rather furtively. 'I'm easy to love.'

'I can vouch for that,' I say with a smile.

We carry on down the street, past houses where the women sit outside on straw mats in chattering groups, tiny babies cuddled on their laps while they sift through the harvested rice, carefully picking out each precious grain by hand. None of them look as worse for wear as we do. They giggle and shout greetings as we go by.

'We'll be the talk of the village,' Dean advises me. I expect he is anyway.

At the end of the street, standing rather grandly, there's one posh building in the village that turns out to belong to the conservation project that Dean works for. It's painted white and has a roof tiled with wood shingles. The building is surrounded by small plots of cultivated land.

A tiny man in a traditional woven topi hat comes out to greet us. After a *'namaste'* or two, he shakes Dean warmly by the hand. 'This is my boss, Mr Thakari,' Dean says.

The man, who is half Dean's size, laughs roundly at the idea. 'We are happy to have Mr Macaulay here,' he tells me. 'But he needs to be married with a wife and children of his own.' He gives me the once-over. 'It is not good for a man to be alone. I tell him this many times.'

This man and my mother would get on like a house on fire.

'You must come here, sister, to our village,' he continues, 'and make him a happy man. Can you not see how sad he is without a woman?' Mr Thakari breaks into uproarious laughter again. 'I will take you to the astrologer. Come, come. He will tell if it is auspicious for you to have a union.'

Dean flushes. 'I think it's time I showed you around,' he says. 'We're going to see the kitchen garden, Mr Thakari.'

'Namaste!'

Dean hurries me to the back of the conservation building. 'Sorry about that,' he says.

'It's okay. I get the same thing from my mother all the time.' I'm so looking forward to her trying to pair me off with all her bridge partners' loser sons when I get home.

'As a Westerner, you never quite stop being an oddity here,' Dean adds. 'Especially an unmarried Westerner.'

We walk into a neatly tended field filled with a variety of crops. 'We're experimenting with different types of fruit and vegetables to encourage the villagers to grow a wider range of produce,' Dean tells me with an enthusiasm born of keen commitment. 'And we're also establishing projects to bring clean water supplies to the area.'

It serves to make my work on *My Baby* look very sickly indeed. Does anyone really care how a minor celebrity felt during her birth experience? The awful thing is that at one time, not too many weeks ago, I would have said they did.

I've begun to realise that our way of life has a certain unreal quality to it—if you choose, you can sit on the sofa with a nice cup of tea and a few choccy biscuits watching a war, a famine, catastrophic floods and earthquakes, devastation on an amazing scale, unfold live on the BBC. All these images are brought to us in the comfort of our own homes. How weird is that?

Let's face it, we never even have to get our hands dirty with preparing our own food. It all comes sterile, flavour-free in acres of needless packaging for our convenience. Isn't the most bizarre statement on any food—'Grown for Taste'? Why else would you grow food? Vine-ripened tomatoes—'Grown for Taste'—what *is* that about? Anyone who wants to work the soil and turns over their suburban garden to an organic vegetable plot is considered slightly barking and as if they're stuck in the 1970s along with *The Good Life*. If Jake and I had decided to grow our own produce, half a dozen carrots would have filled up our measly plot. When you're shoving your shopping trolley round Sainsbury's you don't really stop to think about these things—how far we've been removed from the nasty business of real life. I'm normally in a rush to get home and watch *Trading Spaces*—which, and this is a terrifying admission, is the only time I stop and think that maybe there's a better way of doing things.

While my head tries to wrangle with the problems of the world, we wander round admiring the work and Dean offers words of advice and encouragement to the women, sharing a joke or two. I feel so proud of him that he can care so much to do this. I love him for his energy and his selflessness. I want to give him a big hug, but know I'll have to wait until later. Later, when we're alone and private in my love-shack tent. As if he can tell what I'm thinking, Dean turns and smiles at me. He indicates with a nod of his head that we should be going. So we do our round of '*namastes*', before we wave goodbye and move on.

'It must be nice to make a difference,' I say.

'A small difference,' Dean says modestly. 'But, yes, it's nice.'

'They obviously think a lot of you.'

'I guess they do,' he admits. 'And even though I'll always be a foreigner, I have a great sense of belonging here. You can't get much better than that.'

Do I have a great sense of belonging back home in St Albans? I don't know. I've never even met half of my neighbours. I'm on nodding terms with the people next door, but they're not the sort you could turn to in an emergency. They, as we like to say, keep themselves to themselves. Isn't it strange that we view this as a quality in those with whom we live in close proximity to? We know what each other does for work and that's about as far as it goes.

You could put it down to the fact that most of us in the street are commuters and we never catch a glimpse of each other from one year's end to the next. But is it more to do with an inherent lack of interest in the welfare of others these days? I bet none of them have even noticed that Jake and I have split up. Would they care anyway?

Dean breaks into my musings: 'We need to set off back, so that we'll make it before dark,' he says. 'Have you seen enough?'

And I have. I've seen enough to know that I'm falling in love. In love with this wonderful place. And with Dean.

Chapter Fifty-nine

Jake was in Alec's office. The silence could only be described as tense.

His boss had put the barrier of his desk between them both. Jake sat on a hard chair, keeping his hands under his thighs in case they were tempted, of their own volition, to punch the smarmy bastard's lights out. Alec, on the other hand, was standing up, pacing the carpet, clicking his pen on and off nervously.

'The thing is,' Alec continued, 'I'm not sure you're still in the loop, Jake.'

'Loop?'

Alec cleared his throat. 'I think it's fair to warn you that you may...*may*...be involved in some sort of departmental restructuring in the near future. I...*the board*...can't rule it out.'

'You mean I'm going to be fired.'

Alec chewed at his lip. 'I can see where you're coming from,' he said. 'But you have to appreciate, Jake, that this isn't personal.'

'It isn't personal?'

'Of course not.'

Jake crossed his arms and tried to keep his face impassive. 'So it's nothing to do with the fact we're both shagging Neve?'

Alec blanched. 'We're simply undertaking a cost-saving initiative.'

'In other words, start scouring the job ads, Jake.'

His boss failed to meet his eyes. 'It may be the wise thing to do.'

'Then I'd like a glowing reference,' Jake said.

'I'm not sure…'

'I'd like a glowing reference *now*,' Jake repeated calmly.

'I…'

'If I get one, I'll leave straight away without a fuss. I won't drag your name through the dirt. I won't tell everyone what a bastard you are and I won't go to *the board* with lurid tales of your misconduct.'

His adversary smiled tightly. 'I won't be blackmailed, Jake.'

'Oh, and I won't tell your wife either.' Jake returned his smile.

'I'll get Annabelle to forward one to you.'

'I don't want Annabelle to do it. I want you to do it,' Jake said. 'And I want you to do it *now*.'

Alec reluctantly sat at his desk. 'This is out of order.'

'I think you should know all about that.'

Alec's fingers were poised over his keyboard.

'I'll tell you what to write.'

'Now wait just a minute…'

'To whom it may concern,' Jake dictated.

Pursing his lips unhappily, Alec typed.

Jake stood up and paced the floor, US lawyer-style, 'Mr Jake Swift has been a valued and talented member of our team for many years….'

Alec glanced up at him. Snorted and then typed again.

Jake continued, 'His vision and originality are unsurpassed in the world of advertising.'

His boss could hardly bring himself to do it. Jake felt his lips twitch as he watched Alec's fingers clenched tightly over the keys. Serves the bastard right.

'His conduct and demeanour have always been exemplary.' Jake winked at him. 'More than we can say for some members of staff, hey?'

Alec fumed silently.

'We are desperately sorry to lose him. Desperate is d-e-s-p…'

'I can spell "desperate",' Alec said tersely and bashed away.

'Mr Swift would make a fine addition to any team.'

Alec snarled. He finished typing, hit the print button and, with a few clunks and a whirr, a copy came out of the printer in the corner of the office. Alec strode over to the printer and snatched the copy out.

'Sign it,' Jake said.

Alec's hand shook with rage as he did so. He handed the reference over to Jake.

'Thanks.' Jake gave it the once-over, folded the paper carefully and slipped it inside his jacket pocket.

'Is that all?' Alec snapped.

'No,' Jake said. 'There's just one last thing.'

He cannoned his fist into Alec's chin with as much force as he could manage. His boss reeled in shock before his knees buckled and he slithered peacefully to his shag pile carpet. Jake rubbed his knuckles. That was unbelievably painful, but it felt very, very good. He smiled to himself.

'Thanks, Alec,' he said as he stepped over his inert form and walked towards the door. 'Thanks for everything.'

Chapter sixty

Kathmandu is a hell-hole. But as hell-holes go, it's fascinating. Smelly, dirty, crowded, noisy, polluted and utterly fascinating. After the perfect peace and quiet of the foothills, the city batters my senses from all sides. Goodness only knows how I'm going to cope back in London—except that London doesn't have scabby cows wandering down the middle of Oxford Street or mad, one-legged men in orange robes chasing unsuspecting tourists with the hope of a few spare coins. Some things are similar to London—there is gridlocked traffic, but it's a mixture of ancient cars, creaking buses, tut-tut taxis, rickshaws, bikes, wandering animals and multi-hued backpackers. This might be a gentle introduction to life back in the big city smoke—from paradise to purgatory—but I'm still not exactly looking forward to my imminent return to civilisation.

I can't believe how quickly my time in Nepal has passed and now it's almost time to leave and I can hardly bear to think about it. Under Dean's expert tutelage the group had some rest and recuperation in Pokhara, then we spent two days white-water rafting on the boiling waters of the Trisuli River before flying to Jomsom and trekking some more in the Kingdom of Mustang in the Inner Himalaya. I feel as if I've really gone native in my time away. My body is toned and tanned—but only the bits you're allowed to expose. I've got freckles on my nose in lieu of make-up and hands the colour of mahogany. My hair is bleached by the sun instead of chemical highlights and I can't remember when I last plucked my eyebrows, even though I did bring my tweezers. Edie would be proud of me! My sandals have long lost their pristine look and are as dusty and battered as the rest of me. I've got hard skin on my feet for the first time in years. I'm also wearing a floaty, kaftan-type dress, the sort that I ridiculed Saffron for and the sort that I wouldn't be seen dead in at home. The sort that went out of style in the late 1960s. It's big and billowy and covers me from my head to my feet. It has all the sartorial elegance of a Boy Scout's marquee. And guess what? I don't give a stuff and I feel great.

We waved a tearful goodbye to our trekking crew, which gave me an unpleasant taste of things to come. As they departed, still smiling broadly, to their home villages, it was horrible to think that I might never see them again, but I really don't want to dwell on that. Our last few days have been spent in Kathmandu soaking up the history and culture of the place. There's so much more that I want to see. I've only scratched the surface of this wonderful country and it's leaving me with an itchy restlessness to return. And what can I say about Dean and me? Our relationship has grown closer all the time. I feel as if I've been with him forever and that Jake is a very distant and bad memory. I'm also trying hard to ignore the fact that our time together is rapidly running out.

I dodge a dozen rickshaw drivers with death wishes and weave between the sparring tut-tuts, clutching the dirt-cheap, jewel-coloured pashminas I've haggled over fiercely for Edie and my mother. Last-minute purchases, hurriedly bought as time now seems to have taken against me and is speeding up alarmingly as my call to go home comes ever nearer. I can feel the tendrils of my previous life reaching out to pull me back in—I've even started thinking of headlines for *My Baby* in my sleep, for heaven's sake! If I were a braver person, I might not go back. It would be simple—one email would do it. I could just extend my stay and back pack around Nepal for another month with my own personal guide. But the lure of commitments is tediously strong and Dean has his own life to continue back in his vibrant village. I can tell he wants to be back among the people there and not a bunch of holidaying Brits. We haven't discussed what he feels about my impending departure, but there's been a melancholy air in his demeanour for the past few days. Still, life goes on. There's work in the fields for him to do and his pupils are pining for him—I expect I'll be joining them soon. Besides, it would throw my family into complete consternation if I didn't bowl up home again and I get a pang of familial duty for Edie and, I never thought I'd hear myself say this, but I'm missing Mum terribly too.

I thread my way through the multitude of bodies crowding into the Durbar Square—an area of fifty or more temples dating back to the twelfth century where the exotic snarling heads of a plethora of golden deities glare down at the reverently superstitious populace. I glance at my watch. The air is hot and heavy with the scent of spices. Even though the sky is darkening into night, the streets are getting suffocatingly warm. A trickle of sweat runs down my back. Back in the land of electric light, coloured bulbs are illuminating the tacky souvenir shops as I hit the edge of the tourist area of Thamel. I'm meeting Dean and the group for dinner in a traditional Nepali restaurant and I can't believe that we're spending our last night in the company of the people we've so badly neglected over the last few weeks. And all credit to them for tolerating our excesses—secretly, I think they've rather enjoyed watching our romance play out before them. The lovely Sanjeev has done more than his fair share to keep them happy and I'll always be grateful to him for that. But I want Dean all to myself for one last time. I feel tears prick my eyes and vow not to think about it now.

I pass an ornately carved building that looks like a significant holy temple, until I see the incongruous Happy Meetings Internet Café sign nailed to the front of it. The temptation is too strong. I've resisted emailing home all of the time I've been here, even though there have been a couple of opportunities. Edie is probably out of her mind with worry by now and I'm sure it won't hurt to send her a message to say that I'm safe and well and coming home. I duck into the cool, dark interior and hand over my few rupees. I'm shown into the tiny computer room and sit at one of the three empty terminals available. I tap in my email address and wait while the steam-driven computers chug, chug, chug across cyberspace to find my Hotmail account. Eventually, with much waiting and twiddling of thumbs, it pops open in front of my eyes. As usual there's ten tons of junk mail telling me how to reduce my debts and where to get my Viagra and my breasts enlarged, but one message catches my eye and takes my breath away. My heart has started up a slow, steady thud inside my rib cage and it's nothing to do with the buildup of heat in the cybercafé. A message from Jake is blinking at me on the aged, fuzzy screen.

My hand trembles as I flick the mouse over the message and open it. All it says is:

Lyssa—things have changed. I don't know where to start. Contact me as soon as you can. Love, Jake.

I stare at the screen. What the hell's that supposed to mean? Things have changed? Jake has always been a good one for cryptic messages. My heart picks up a beat. Was Pip right all along? Has Jake's relationship with Neve come to a sticky end? I click the message closed as I really have no idea how to reply to it. Is this what I wanted to hear all along? I'm not sure how I should be reacting. My heart is still pounding and my stomach is sick and hollow. But my brain is refusing to provide any form of sensible analysis. How do I feel about Jake now? My palms are clammy with anxiety and my emotions are thrown into utter turmoil as I wonder what will be waiting for me when I return.

With unsteady fingers, I bash out a rather non-committal message to Edie with much blah, blah, blah in it. I grab my parcels and head out of the cybercafé. I'll have to rush now because I'm going to be late meeting Dean. *Dean*—I sigh inwardly. My heart knows how to react to this quandary. It still does a backflip every time I think of him.

Perhaps more than Jake is aware—things have definitely changed.

Chapter sixty-one

Jake didn't want to be doing this, but Pip had insisted. Gallery launches weren't really his type of thing—not that he'd been to one, but he was pretty sure that there were a whole lot of other things that were more his cup of tea. His spirits sagged some more as he saw the queue of people trying to push their way into the tiny backstreet shop.

Pip slapped him soundly on the back as they fell out of the taxi in Charlotte Street. 'You can't stay at home moping.'

'I can,' Jake said. 'If I'd done more staying at home and moping, perhaps I wouldn't be in this bloody stupid situation now.'

It was a freezing-cold night and, rubbing his hands together for some meagre warmth, Jake flicked up his collar against the icy air. He wondered whether it was warm in Nepal. He wondered where Lyssa was now. What would she be wearing? What would she be doing? Who would she be doing it with? Pip paid the taxi driver and they joined the throng of people on the pavement in the vain hope of getting a glass of flat champagne and a few limp canapés.

'It'll turn out okay,' Pip said jovially. 'You wait and see if it doesn't.'

'Do you really think Lyssa will take me back?'

'Well…'

'Would you, if I'd been such a prat?'

'I hate to disappoint you, Jakey mate, but you're not my type.' Pip indulged himself in some more jocular slapping. His friend was in a spectacularly good mood. Jake wished he could say the same of himself. He wasn't normally a heavy drinking man, but he'd been drowning his sorrows in cans of Miller Lite all day. He'd also been sitting at home looking at pictures of him and Lyssa on their last holiday in Thailand, but he wasn't about to admit that to anyone. She'd looked gorgeous and smiley and tanned in each photo and it had only served to make him feel much, much worse. It was as if he was seeing Lyssa with fresh eyes. What was that saying about scales falling off? Whoever had said it bloody well knew what they were talking about. He'd even felt moved to put a picture of Lyssa in his wallet and wear it next to his heart. With a bit of persuasion, he'd always considered himself reasonably romantic, but it had always been an effort, always forced. Now it felt real, sincere. Had it needed all this chaos to make him appreciate what he'd once taken for granted? Does the complacency of long-term familiarity mean that you become immune to the obvious charms of your lover? He was a bloke—how could he answer that? He just knew it would have been a lot more sensible if he'd stayed off the beer today and had got off his arse and phoned round some agencies to find himself a new job.

They finally reached the door of the gallery and, with Pip flashing his invitation, they were allowed through into an even bigger crowd. Pip knew everyone who was anyone and they all seemed to be here tonight. All pressed up against each other, air kissing and yah-yah-yah-ing. Jake was sweltering inside his suit and he could feel unpleasantly damp, warm sweat trickling down his back. This was torture. He wanted to lie down and cry or drink himself into oblivion. He didn't want to socialise—if that's what you could call squashing up against hundreds of nameless strangers.

Pip had become parted from him already and was chatting animatedly to some leggy blond who looked as if her daddy would be Well To Do. A waiter squeezed his way past and Jake whipped off a glass of champagne as he did so. As expected, rather than dancing on the tongue, it was as warm and palatable as his sweat and horribly flat. Jake let the crowd push him farther into the gallery. The exhibition on display—if that was the correct art world terminology—was a series of black-and-white photographs by someone he'd never heard of but who Pip assured him was 'the next big thing'. Pip always knew about 'the next big thing' whereas Jake never knew what 'the next big thing' was until everyone else did and then it wasn't a 'big thing' anymore.

Jake shuffled himself towards the wall, grabbing at a congealed miniature pizza as it sailed past on a silver tray. Not that he was any judge, but the photographs didn't look half bad to him. The price tags, which seemed to start at around £3,000, were less impressive. Perhaps he should polish up his old Canon. While he had nothing else to do, Jake studied the images—sharp collections of faces in close-up, mainly minor celebrities' eyelashes. That sort of stuff. They would have looked absolutely at home in Neve's apartment.

The crowd parted briefly and there she was, standing in front of him—like an apparition, as if conjured up by his thoughts. Jake spluttered out his champagne. Possibly not the impression he'd hoped to convey. Neve was standing there with a classically handsome man, a city-type in brown brogues whom he could imagine driving a Porsche. He did a quick scan. No Alec in sight.

'Well…' Jake said.

'Hi.' Neve smiled tightly.

'Boyfriend at home with his wife?'

Her companion's face darkened. 'Is this a friend of yours?'

Jake extended his hand. 'I'm the father of her unborn child,' he said politely. 'Possibly. Or possibly not. There are, apparently, a number of candidates. Are you one of them?'

Jake gave a forced laugh. His hand remained unshook, so he let it drop to his side.

'Have you any idea what he's talking about?' the man said.

'Yes, she does,' Jake informed him.

'If you really want to know…' Neve said, tension etched on her face. 'It was yours. I had its DNA checked before they flushed it.'

Jake felt the ground go soft beneath his feet.

Neve's eyes hardened. 'And it was a girl.' She sipped at her champagne. 'Happy now?'

'You bitch,' Jake managed to say even though his breath felt ragged.

'You're obviously more of a man than you thought,' she said.

'Darling,' the suit said. 'Is he bothering you?'

'Not anymore,' Neve said coolly and turned her back on him.

Jake didn't know what to do. He wanted to hit something, very hard. He wanted to say something—something that would make Neve realise what a terrible, terrible thing it was she had done. Instead, he felt himself stagger away. Fury and nausea were rising inside him in equal measures. He couldn't keep hold of his glass and he felt it slip through his fingers and crash to the floor. Several people turned to stare at him and then moved away from him, allowing him to stumble towards the door. Pictures and faces loomed towards him, all fuzzy and fractured. So this was what fainting felt like? He didn't think he'd ever done it before.

'Jake!' He heard Pip's concerned voice somewhere in the periphery, but continued to lurch for the entrance. He needed air. Lots of it. And then a gun. A gun would be good. He wanted to shoot that bitch for killing his child. He wanted to murder her as she'd murdered. An eye for an eye. A tooth for a tooth. A life for a life.

As he reached for the door, he could feel the tears start to come and he was gagging—his throat closing, choking. The mini pizza had been a bad, bad idea. Like so much else in his life recently. He crashed out through the crowds waiting to take his place for a chance of cheap champagne and launched himself at the gutter where somebody, it may have been him, was heartily sick. The street lights in Charlotte Street swam by him, blackness was coming and it was going to be lovely. It was going to blank out his brain so that he wouldn't have to think of dead babies. His dead baby. He let the air rush up and meet him.

Far, far away Pip's voice saying, 'Don't worry, I've got you, mate,' was the last thing he heard.

Chapter sixty-two

I take off my shoes and sit cross-legged on the floor beside Dean in the dark, low-beamed restaurant and I'm still feeling shaky. All the group are waiting for me and I force a smile as I glance round their beaming faces. They all look a lot more relaxed than when we started out and I wonder what they can read in my face.

I do have some guilty feelings about all my trekking companions whom I've so easily neglected. But after a month of travelling together they've all bonded to form their own little cliques now—which I'm standing slightly outside of because of the amount of bonding I've been doing with Dean. And I feel sad that I've not taken the time to explore the souls of these individuals, but then my own soul was in such a state when I arrived, I'm not sure that I'd have been capable. But they've been a lot of fun and they've given Dean and me plenty of space to find each other.

Dave the solicitor and Jim the criminal-looking policeman have become firm but unlikely friends. Believe me, being in close proximity in a tiny tent for a month can be a strange experience. Graham the train driver and lovely, cuddly doctor Ian have rubbed along quite well too. And, thank goodness, none of us have required Ian's professional services en route. Other than the odd blister, we are all relatively unscathed. Saffron has bonded with Felix and Felicity mainly due to their mutual dependency on homeopathic remedies, a penchant for chanting at inopportune moments and speaking in loud voices to Tibetan traders. They all feel that they've become more in touch with their spiritual side, which is nice. Saffron hasn't yet come out as a lesbian; in fact, I think she's rather disappointed that none of the single guys have made a play for her. But time is running out for her now—as it is for me. Tony and Tania are still as madly in love with each other to the exclusion of all else and I still feel very envious of their total absorption—particularly now that I've had a fleeting taste of it. How cruel is it that I've found someone so wonderful who lives a different life on the other side of the world?

I'm panting a bit as I ease my knees under the low table. 'Sorry I'm late,' I say.

My beautiful lover looks at me with concern. 'Are you okay?'

I nod. 'Fine.'

'You're shivering.'

'It's a little cold outside now.'

Dean doesn't look convinced. He lowers his voice. 'I've been worried about you.'

'I popped into an internet café to send an email to Edie. It took longer than I thought.'

'You haven't had bad news?'

Smiling waiters in colourful, traditional costumes swarm round us delivering metal dishes brimming with spicy mutton, slices of wild boar, steaming rice and tiny terracotta cups of rakshi. The others chatter on without us.

'No,' I say. 'It's just… I'm just…' My shoulders sag. 'I don't want to go home.' I lean against him. 'It's getting nearer and nearer and I can't stop it.'

'You'll be fine,' he whispers. 'You'll get home and forget all about me.'

'You're absolutely right,' I say flippantly. 'By tomorrow it will be Dean *who*?'

He gives me a rueful smile.

I wonder will that be the same for him. Will he forget me so easily? When he's back in his normal life in the village, will he still think of me? Will there be another, more attractive trekker running away from her life next time round to take my place in his bed? Will he whirl and twirl her until she forgets which way up she's supposed to be? Will he wash her hair and bathe her and love her all night? I sigh out loud.

'A penny for them,' Dean says.

'They're worth a whole lot more than that.' I force a smile. 'I don't want to be miserable and maudlin on our last night together.' I cast my eyes over the food. 'This looks wonderful,' I say.

Dean looks deep into my eyes then looks away, busying himself by dishing out some of the wonderfully aromatic meat. As he spoons it onto my plate, I realise that a knot of tension has grabbed my stomach and is gripping it like two tight fists. How I wish I had a crystal ball to see into the future.

'Thanks,' I say to Dean. Everyone else is tucking into their food with relish. 'I'm starving.' But, in truth, I have absolutely no appetite whatsoever.

'Me too,' Dean says.

And we both aimlessly push our food around with our forks.

Chapter sixty-three

'Hot, sweet tea,' Pip said as he handed over the cup.

'Just what the doctor ordered.' Jake tried to push himself upwards, but the soft contours of Pip's sofa were just too comforting.

'Feeling better?' Pip sat on the chair opposite and swigged from a bottle of beer.

'Quantify better.' His friend had managed to catch him as he fainted, but he'd still got a bruise on his head from somewhere, although his bruised feelings were infinitely worse. He didn't remember much about it, but apparently Pip had bundled him into a taxi and brought him straight back to his place.

'Simon's away in New York,' Pip said. 'I've purloined his bed for you. I'll put some clean sheets on. You can stay here overnight, or for as long as you like.'

'How ironic that I'm staying here now, when not too long ago I was saying that I was staying here when I wasn't. Am I making any sense?'

'If you are, it will be a first,' Pip said. 'How hard was that bang on your head?'

Jake laughed and it made all of him ache. 'I feel like a prat.'

'I'm sorry, mate,' Pip said. 'I'd no idea the lovely Neve would be there.'

'We might have guessed,' Jake said. 'She'd turn up at the opening of an envelope. Anything trendy, happening and free.'

'Yeah,' his friend agreed. 'It's a shame she doesn't apply the same criteria to her men. You'd never have stood a chance.'

'It was such a shock. I just hadn't envisaged seeing her so soon.' Jake forced himself up and found his cup of tea. He distracted himself by stirring it unnecessarily with his spoon. 'She said the baby was mine.' He avoided looking at his friend. 'But it's gone.' Jake could feel hot tears behind his eyes. 'Gone. She was a little girl.'

'Oh man,' Pip said. 'I'm sorry.'

'Me too.'

'I don't know what to say.'

'Something like if you play with fire, you should expect to get every shred of your skin flayed off in the flames.'

'You had no idea that it would turn out like this.'

He wondered if he had would he still have stomped in blindly with his size tens just for the thrill of an illicit affair. The awful thing was that at the time he hadn't even stopped to consider the repercussions.

'If it's any consolation, Neve's history at Dunston & Bradley,' Pip offered. 'The client hated her presentation on the Blow account. Alec is tiring of her demands already. I think he's worried that he'll get caught in the backlash.'

'Good old Alec. Still looking after number one.'

'Whatever way,' Pip said, 'my bet is that she'll be out of there by Friday.'

'It couldn't happen to a nicer woman.' Some women deserved to be mothers while some other women deserved all they had coming to them. And he had hoped that one day Neve would get hers. But even the knowledge of his ex-lover's demise at work couldn't fill the hollow that had sucked out the centre of him. There was only one thing that would make him feel whole again.

'I want Lyssa back,' Jake said. He wanted her back so that they could return to normal, stop living life upside down with her in another part of the world. He wanted to try for a baby again. And that would mean that he'd have to share the knowledge that he could become a father and that now it was something he wanted more than anything. More than anything except Lyssa. 'I want Lyssa back and I don't know what to do.'

'You'll think of something, mate,' Pip said. But Jake wasn't sure that he would.

Chapter sixty-four

'So this is it?' My rucksack is all ready and packed. It's sitting neatly by the foot of the bed and even that looks bloody miserable.

'Don't be so sad,' Dean says. 'Think of the fun we've had.'

'I am,' I say. 'I don't want it to stop.' I'm not ready for it to stop.

For the last few days we've been staying in a four-star hotel in Kathmandu, full-flavoured days of the Raj stuff, with uniformed doormen, Musak in the lifts and a real, live, flushing loo in the bathroom. Dean looks horribly out of place. He doesn't suit being in a wallpapered room, in a bed whose duvet matches the curtains. It's just not right—he's far too rugged. He looks much better in the mountains. It's some ungodly hour in the morning and already he's clean-shaven and his hair is freshly washed and he smells of vanilla bubble bath, rather than tents and sleeping bags and cheesy boots and sex. I can feel him slipping away from me already.

He puts his arms round me. 'I'm not coming to the airport,' he says.

I hear myself cry out.

'I can't,' he insists. 'I hate airports. It would be too awful. Too… too goddamn awful.'

'Anywhere's going to be awful. I want to stay with you to the very last minute.'

'There'll be people around…the rest of the group. It's better this way.'

I don't think any way is better. It all bloody hurts. There are so many things that I want to say and I don't know how to start. We've been lovers for a month now and yet we still haven't said we love each other. I can feel the words stretching between us like a spider's web, fine and fragile. And this is probably the wrong time to say it, so we let it hang there, suspended and unspoken.

I don't know if I can bear to be without him, watching him stomp up hills, pitch tents, light campfires and white-water raft. Goddammit, he's the nearest I'm ever going to get to a real-life Indiana Jones!

'It's time to go,' Dean tells me and we hold each other for one last time.

I cry pathetically. 'Thanks for everything.' What a stupid thing to say. It feels as if I'm talking to a stranger, not someone who's shared my sleeping bag every night.

'Keep in touch,' Dean says.

'Yes.' I sniff back my tears.

'I'll email you when I can.'

'Me too.' I'm aware that instead of schlepping into the spare bedroom at home as I would, this will involve Dean in a four-hour round trip to the nearest internet café in Pokhara. How soon will he grow tired of doing that?

My lover kisses my hair and then relaxes his hold on me. I want him to say something meaningful before the moment is gone. I want some wonderful, poetic sentence to remember him by.

'The coach will be waiting,' Dean says. He hoists my rucksack onto his back. 'Let's go.'

'Right.' I busy myself doing nothing, checking pockets for no reason, pulling up my socks, tightening my belt a notch.

Dean heads towards the door and I follow him, shoulders dropped, chin almost trailing the floor. Suddenly, he shrugs off my bag and I'm in his arms again, crying, crying, crying. We're clutching at each other, clutching at time, clutching at straws. I can quite honestly say that this feels a hundred times worse than Jake walking away.

Chapter sixty-five

Airline travel is disorientating. The flight from Kathmandu to Heathrow is nine hours in total. Nine long hours if you view it in terms of sitting in an unfeasibly cramped, economy seat with nothing but a tray of plastic food for solace. Nine very short hours in terms of catapulting me from my escapist, fantasy romance back into the grim reality that is my life. At least I got around to reading my trusty guidebook, which I haven't glanced at since I flew out. I pored over the most boring bits—the geological formation of the Himalayas, the chequered political history and the rules of the road in Nepal, which were covered in one paragraph. And it very, very nearly helped to take my mind off Dean and the miles that were opening up between us.

I didn't tell anyone when I was actually arriving as I thought I'd prefer to make my own way home. Now that I'm faced with slogging for the best part of two hours on the St Pancras to Bedford railway line—affectionately known as the Bedpan—to jolly old St Albans, I wish I'd phoned Edie and persuaded her to come and collect me.

My trusty and now rather battered backpack comes bumping round on the baggage carousel, looking as if the baggage handlers have had a boisterous game of football with it, and I hoist it onto my shoulders in what has become a familiar movement. And, weighty as it is, it's still nowhere near as heavy as my heart. I make my way out of the Arrivals Hall, through the green 'Nothing to Declare' channel even though I want to declare that I'm very unhappy to anyone who will listen.

I push out of the swing doors and into the main concourse, looking for the signs to the Heathrow Express to whisk me into London. There's a huge crowd of people all jostling for position as they wait expectantly, if not patiently, for loved ones, relatives or business colleagues. And there, jostling along with the best of them, holding a piece of crisp, white card with LYSSA ALLEN written on it in thick black marker pen, is Jake. He's standing behind the chrome barrier looking nervous. My heart has no idea what to do now—whether it should sink or beat faster, so it does a mixture of both, leaving me feeling dizzy and nauseous. His face brightens when he sees me. I'm not sure what my face is registering—beyond initial shock.

'Hi. Hi,' he says, pushing his way through the crowds to the side of the barrier where he stands in front of me.

'Hi.'

'Well. Well,' he says. 'You look...' He gives me the once-over, searching for the right words. Fucking miserable, I'd conclude. 'You look great.'

'Thanks.'

'I've come to take you home,' Jake says, sounding very earnest.

'Why?'

'Why?' He doesn't look as if he'd been expecting me to question his motives. Jake glances nervously at the crowd of people surrounding us.

'Yes. Why?'

'I've missed you,' he says plainly. Then he lowers his voice and checks no one else is listening. 'I realise I've messed up and I want to make it right. I sent you an email.'

'I saw it,' I tell him. 'It didn't say very much.'

He looks hurt. 'A lot has happened,' he informs me. I could well say the same thing. 'I checked with the airline when your plane was arriving,' he continues, pleased with his ingenuity. 'I wanted to surprise you.'

'You have.' I'll give him that much.

'Let me take your rucksack,' he offers.

'It's heavy.'

'I can manage.' I swing my rucksack from my back and hand it over. Jake staggers slightly under its weight.

'I warned you.' He shrugs my bag onto his shoulders and tries to look as if it weighs no more than a feather.

'The car's in the Short Stay multi-storey across the road,' he says. It seems as if Jake is about to reach for my hand, but I block the movement with my body and then fall into step beside him, a suitable distance apart. He looks disappointed. I don't know if he expected me to fall into his arms and be grateful, but I can't. I can't even manufacture it.

My ex-boyfriend tries a smile. He looks exhausted and there are fine, dry lines on his face and his eyes are shot through with red flecks that speak of sleeplessness.

'Did you take a day off work to do this?'

Jake chews his lip. 'In a manner of speaking.'

We exit the main doors and step out into the harsh grey light and the biting wind. The ferocity of it takes me aback and I wished I'd pulled my warm fleece out of my rucksack. I try not to shiver in case Jake feels moved to put his arm round me. The freezing air sucks all my breath away. I'd forgotten what a cold place Britain can be. The buildings are all black and white, hard-edged and intimidating, the taxis blasting backwards and forwards, impatient and aggressive. There's no warm, soft wind laden with exotic scents, no colourful statues of deities and no Dean. Jake heads off across the Zebra crossing to the car park and I trail behind him.

His car is sitting waiting and he throws my bag into the back. I haven't been in a car in weeks. We squash in next to each other. Everything feels alien and wrong. How long is it going to take me to get back into my life? He crunches the car into gear and we pull out of the car park.

Jake smiles at me in what he clearly thinks is a reassuring manner. 'Won't be long before you're home.'

And if that's meant to comfort me, it doesn't. Not one bit.

Chapter sixty-six

'We're here,' Jake says, just as I open my eyes.

Our journey home has been tense and tortured. There was a massive traffic jam on the M25—as always—and Jake's attempts to keep up a steady stream of conversation while saying nothing at all of any importance fell on deaf ears. I wanted to ask him what had happened between him and Neve, but simply couldn't bring myself to summon the necessary emotional energy. Instead, I decided to blank everything by closing my eyes and going to sleep. It seems that I did it rather successfully as we've now pulled up outside our neat little house in our neat little street.

Jake looks at me tenderly and I do wish he wouldn't as I'm really not sure what to make of it. 'Welcome home,' he says.

Home. I lever my stiff, travel-weary body out of the car, while Jake fusses with my bag and opens the front door for me. He's treating me as if I'm pregnant and a shaft of rich pain hits me.

The house seems so strange. Do I really live here? The place I call home seems so unfamiliar to me. I've expended so much time and energy over the last few years creating it and cajoling it into being a home, yet now I can't relate to it at all. It's fussy and smells of the artificial scent of pine glades from the air-freshening machine plugged into the wall. Why did I want my house to smell of pine glades?

There's an alarming pile of junk mail on top of the cupboard, all addressed to me and all entirely irrelevant to my life—apart from a few outstanding bills, I could have a dozen different credit cards, more loans than I could ever use, several-million-pound lottery wins that I, 'Lyssa Allen, have been chosen to receive!' and enough pizza delivery leaflets to wallpaper the lounge. Most of it can go directly into the bin.

Jake dumps my bag in the lounge. 'I'll put the kettle on.'

'I'll do it,' I say. 'I can manage.' I try to look at him kindly. 'Do you want a cup of tea before you go?'

A blank expression fixes on his face. 'Go?' he says. 'Go where?'

'Home.'

Jake looks round him slightly perplexed. 'This is my home.'

Now I'm the perplexed one. 'You left.'

He looks stung. 'And now I'm back.'

I let out a surprised and faintly bitter laugh. 'Just like that.'

'Neve and I...' He tails off and glances around him searching for inspiration. 'We...we split up.'

'I'm sorry to hear that,' I say.

'Are you?' Jake's knees sort of collapse and he sits heavily on the sofa. 'I thought you'd be pleased.'

'Did you?'

He looks vaguely stricken. 'I thought you'd want me to come back.'

Funny. So did I. Perhaps unwisely I choose not to reply.

'I've moved my stuff into the spare room,' Jake says. 'I didn't want to presume...'

'Presume?'

'I know it's going to take time,' he assures me. 'You'll have to learn to trust me again.'

I'm not sure if I've got that long. We stare at each other in silence.

'Say something,' Jake pleads.

I sit on the chair farthest away from him. It's soft and squishy and, like the horrible pine-scented room perfume, I can't believe I ever chose it. My mind is transported back to Dean's house with its stark room and hard, rough-carved wooden furniture, the aroma of earth and spices and sexy, man smells. Slowly, I blink the image away. 'This is all very sudden,' is all I can manage. 'I've only recently got used to the fact that you were gone.'

Jake looks crestfallen and I can't find it in me to comfort him. I don't know that I want him here. Maybe I need time on my own to think about exactly what I do want.

'What can I do?' I'm horrified to see that Jake's eyes are filling with tears. 'What can I do to make it right?'

My heart softens. 'I think you'd better put that kettle on after all.'

Chapter sixty-seven

I've had a long, hot soak in the bath and I'm feeling infinitely better. Better, if you don't count the fact that I'd rather be in Nepal than St Albans and that I'd rather it was Dean standing in front of me sporting an apron and a very silly grin instead of Jake.

My ex-boyfriend brandishes a wooden spoon at me. 'I've made us shepherd's pie.'

I wonder why. Never in my life have I expressed a particular partiality towards shepherd's pie. As far as I know, Jake has never before felt moved to cook it. But then there are a lot of things that I didn't know about Jake that I do now.

'Are you hungry?'

I wasn't, but I have to say that Jake's attempt at cooking smells rather wonderful and my appetite is coaxed into life. And I have to admit that it will be nice to eat meat that isn't yak. 'Yes,' I say, and in my comfiest, tattiest tracksuit and bare feet, pad after him into the kitchen.

He makes a great flourish of pulling out my chair and shuffling me into the table as I sit down. 'Wine?'

I nod and he pours out a glass of the finest ruby red claret, letting it glug enthusiastically from the bottle. It seems ages ago since

I took it in my mind to flood this place and, apart from a few unsightly bubbles on the ceiling, you'd hardly know that it happened. I sip the wine and it does taste good. Jake has used our 'best' glasses—the ones we get out on high-days and holidays. And I can't help but wonder why we have so many things. Have the years we've been together simply been spent accumulating material possessions? We have six different sets of wineglasses, for heaven's sake! Why do we need them? It means that every time we use them, I have to go through the rigmarole of washing and polishing them because they're invariably covered in dust—it's been so long since we last gave them an airing. I watch Jake as he flits animatedly round the kitchen, fishing out plates that he's even remembered to warm and fussing with dishes that I presume are for vegetables. 'Dinner won't be long,' he says with a twitch of his eye that could be a wink.

I have no idea who this chipper person is. But he's making me nervous. 'Fine.'

I cast a glance around the rest of the kitchen—anything rather than watch Jake metamorphose into Nigella Lawson. We've got more pans, plates and dishes than you can shake a stick at. How many can you use at once? Although I have to qualify that, as I note that Jake seems to have attempted to use all of them in the course of creating shepherd's pie. I feel I want to put all of my life in bin bags and just throw it on the local council dump. Or, even better, give it to someone who needs it more. I feel out of place here, out of time—like one of those time travellers who get the co-ordinates mixed up on their time machines and end up in the wrong location or the wrong century. Maybe world travel is too easy now and we don't give due reverence to being whisked out of our culture and plopped, unsuspecting of the impact it might have on our lives, into another one. I think British Airways have a lot to answer for. I can feel the wine making my eyelids heavy and perhaps it's just the dreaded jet lag that's making me feel so weird and displaced.

Jake pops the oven gloves on and whips open the oven door. 'Ta-da,' he says, as with a flourish he produces his creation. He oohs and aahs as he carries it to the table, the hot dish burning his fingers despite the protection of his asbestos gauntlets. He's being excessively chirpy and I wish I could rise to meet his enthusiasm.

My ex-boyfriend grins at me, expectant of praise.

'It looks lovely,' I oblige. And it does. The potato topping is golden and crisp, the scent of herby lamb mouth-watering.

'I'm going to learn to cook more things,' Jake promises as he dashes back for the dishes of vegetables. 'This is just a start I'm going to change.' He looks at me, worry etched into his forehead. 'I *have* changed.'

I don't know what to say.

'I want to do more for you,' he says. 'More for us.'

'Mmm.' I focus my attention on the food. He's being so considerate that I want to cry, but I can't break down because then he'll want to put his arms round me and I really, really couldn't cope with that. Why couldn't he have been like this months ago? Months ago when all I wanted was his baby and all he wanted was another woman. There's a huge void between us—a void that's been filled by other places and other people. Could we ever really get back to where we were before? And if we could, would I want to? I don't know if I sigh out loud, but Jake straightens slightly.

'I'll stop rabbiting,' my ex-boyfriend says. 'Otherwise it'll go cold.' Jake attacks the curls of potato with a spoon. 'I thought some good, old-fashioned British stodge would make you feel glad to be back.'

I smile gratefully, even though I think it's going to take an awful lot more than that.

Chapter sixty-eight

'Bloody hell,' Edie says as she opens the door. 'Look what the cat dragged in!'

We fall into each other's arms and I try to hug the life out of my sister.

'You smell like a yak,' my sibling continues.

'I do not,' I insist. 'I don't look like one either, so don't think of going there.'

'You look fabulous,' she says grudgingly, holding me away from her and running a critical eye over me. 'Tanned and fit. And *almost* relaxed.' Edie pulls me towards the kitchen. 'I've been on pins. Why didn't you let me know what time your flight landed, and I would have come to collect you.'

'Someone did collect me.'

Edie's eyebrows rise. 'Pip?'

'Pip?' I shake my head. 'No. Jake.'

'Ooo.'

'Ooo, indeed,' I agree. 'He's split up with action woman and has moved back into the house.'

'Fantastic!'

I'm taken aback. 'Is it?'

Edie frowns at me. 'I thought that's what you wanted?'

'So did I,' I say. 'A lot has happened in the last month.'

'And I want to hear all about it,' Edie tells me.

But then a shout goes up from behind me, 'Aunty Lyssa!' and I become a human totem pole as the majority of my nieces and nephews grab me by the legs and try to clamber up me.

'Leave the poor woman alone,' Edie instructs as they all ignore her.

'We've mithed you,' Daisy says, showering me with spittle now that her lisp is even more exaggerated due to the absence of two front teeth. She grins wider. 'I fell off Liam's skateboard,' she says by way of explanation.

'Tell her she can't go on it again, Mum,' my nephew pleads.

'You can't go on it again, Daisy,' my sister obliges.

'Aaww!' Daisy acts as if this is the biggest tragedy of her life so far—as well it may be. There'll come a time when she looks back on her past and wishes that she had nothing worse to worry about than restricted skateboard usage.

'Go on, scoot,' Edie says. 'Aunty Lyssa and I have lots to talk about and it's girly gossip, so we can't do it with you lot in the way.'

One by one they peel themselves away from me and then *en masse* crash upstairs like stampeding elephants. The silence they leave in their wake is deafening, only broken by Edie clinking china together as she goes about her tea-making duties. I look round the kitchen. My sister has loads of gadgets too—microwave, dishwasher, food processor, juicer, cappuccino maker, bread maker. I wonder how many of them she actually uses. I've never seen much evidence from the bread maker—no feather-light croissants or home-baked sun-dried, rustic tomato bread. Shop-bought, thick, white sliced is the variety that most frequently graces Edie's kitchen.

The room is lime green, because primary colours stimulate children—so she says—and I'm not sure how much more stimulation Edie's children need. They already seem to be ten points past hyperactive.

We are clearly in for a session as my sister raids her children's stash of biscuits and puts out a plate of chocolate digestives to accompany our pot of tea—reminding me that some British institutions are still utterly wonderful.

'So,' she says, biting into one. 'How was it?'

'Wonderful.' I select a digestive and start to lick the chocolate off it. 'All of it.'

'But you're glad to be back.'

'No.' I rub a hand over my forehead. 'Honestly, Edie,' I say, 'I'm sure I've got more problems now than I did before I went.' In fact, I know I have. 'Jake just seems to think that we can pick up where we left off....'

'And you can't?'

I focus my attention on my biscuit. 'There are complications.'

'Oh?' My sister is all ears. 'What's he called?'

Trust my darling Edie to cut to the chase. We both laugh. 'Dean,' I say. 'He's called Dean.'

'And the problem is?'

'He's dirt poor, he can't offer commitment and he lives in Nepal.'

'This is not sounding good,' Edie says. 'He'd better be hung like a donkey.'

'He is.'

'Fair play.' With a reluctant nod, my sister chooses and demolishes another biccy.

'We had a fabulous, fabulous fling,' I continue, trying to ignore the rather X-rated flashbacks that are popping up at this inopportune moment. 'But now that I'm back, I don't know if that's all that it was. A fling.'

'You haven't heard from him?'

'He hasn't got a phone,' I point out. 'He hasn't got electricity.'

'But he has other charms.'

'Lots of them.'

'Keep reminding me of this,' Edie says.

'He's wonderful,' I insist. 'Truly wonderful. You'd love him. He's all I've ever wanted in a man.'

'But with money, a penchant for commitment and not living on another continent.'

'Nothing's insurmountable.'

'Oh really?' Edie says cryptically. Her smile dies. 'I'd say some things are.'

I put my tea down. 'I take it we're no longer talking about my predicament.'

'No,' Edie says. 'I have a "predicament" of my own.'

I can feel my jaw drop. 'Oh no,' I say. 'Not *another* one!'

'Another one,' my sister confirms. 'I know you'll find this hard to believe. I'm pregnant again.'

'Are you sure?'

'Of course I am.'

'Have you done a pregnancy test?'

'No, I haven't,' she puffs. 'I've had six bloody kids, Lyssa. I don't need some ten-quid kit to tell me I'm knocked up again.'

I lower my voice. 'What are you going to do?'

'Do?' Edie says. 'I'm going to do what I always do, say goodbye to my ankles and balloon like a heifer for the next nine months until it drops.'

'But do you want it? Do you really want another child?'

'Children are the one thing I'm not short of,' Edie says, 'now you come to mention it.'

'You could always...' I draw a quick line across my throat, unable to speak the word.

'Don't be ridiculous,' she tuts. 'I couldn't do that. How could anyone?'

I lower my eyes.

'How could I do...*that*...when I know how desperately you want a baby?'

And the strange thing is until Edie brought it up, I hadn't even considered this as another example of how her gain reflected my loss. Would I have reacted differently a month ago?

My sister puts her hand on my arm. 'You're okay about it, aren't you?' she says.

'Yes, I'm fine.' Other than marvelling at my sister's propensity for accidental procreation, my emotions are all firmly intact. 'I'd be even more delirious for you if I thought it was what you wanted.'

My sister hangs her head. '*I'd* be delirious if I thought it was what I wanted.'

'How on earth did it happen?'

She looks at me askance. 'The usual way.'

'I thought you'd have given it up by now.'

'Actually,' she says, 'this is all your friend Pip's fault.'

'Pip?'

She hesitates slightly and I can see her flush. 'I had lunch with him while you were away….'

I give her a long, sideways glance. 'Oh yes?'

She looks at the table. 'We talked about you and Jake.'

'I thought my ears were burning out in Nepal.'

'He told me that Lee and I should go out for a wild night on the town and get roaring drunk.' Edie looks rather sheepish. 'We took him at his word. You know what I'm like when I've been at the vodka. We got a bit carried away.'

'Oh, Rabbit!' I say, reverting to her old nickname.

'Don't you "Oh, Rabbit" me,' she says. 'It's that randy old brother-in-law of yours. He took advantage of me. My knickers were on the ceiling fan before I knew what was happening.'

'Someone mention me?' Lee pops his head round the kitchen door. I rarely see my brother-in-law's full body as he's always rushing somewhere to knock a nail in or saw something in two. He sees me and comes over to give me a hug. 'Welcome home, darling.'

'I'm just telling Lyssa the happy news that we're 'with child' again.'

'Yeah,' Lee says. 'Lucky old us.'

'See?' Edie says. 'He's delighted. The proud father.'

'I'm moving into the shed,' Lee says affably.

Even with him in the shed and Edie in the bedroom, they'd still manage to get her up the duff somehow.

'Catch you later, sis.' And he's gone. That's about the deepest discussion you'll get with Lee on the pros and cons of multiple parenthood.

'If there's anything I can do to help...' I offer.

'Get back together with Jake,' she whines, 'then you can have this one.'

'Gee, thanks.'

'Really, I mean it. I'll do all the huffing and puffing and I'll just hand it over. I've no idea where we're going to put it. You'll get all the benefits and none of the stretch marks. It'll be the answer to both of our prayers.'

I think my sister is only half-joking. 'I'm not sure that it's so important to me anymore,' I admit.

'My word!' Edie says. 'I never thought I'd hear that from your lips. Are you sure you're all right? You haven't left anything else other than your heart in Nepal?'

'I don't know,' I say. But Edie's right. Somewhere in the mountains I've lost my heart and my obsession. I've just let them both go, floating off into the clouds. And whilst I'm missing one, the other I can definitely live without. Then a horrible thought occurs to me. Edie notices the fear in my eyes.

'I know what you're going to say...'

'Did you?' I ask. 'Did you tell Mum yet?'

'What?' Edie cries. 'Do you think I'm mad?'

'As it happens I do.'

'I'm trying to avoid it,' my sister admits. 'But then it's not been too difficult as our mother...our *wanton* mother...is rather preoccupied at the moment.'

'Our wanton mother?'

Edie leans forward conspiratorially. 'I saw her with a *man*,' she whispers gleefully. 'With a man in a blazer and slacks.' Edie nods as if that is condemning evidence enough.

'Mum? You must be hallucinating.'

'No. Straight up. I saw them in the town centre. It was Mum with a dishy fella hanging on her arm. Dishy, if you're of an age where you think Regis Philbin's a looker.'

This can't be right. My mother the man-hater? With a

bloke? The *only* man my mother would possibly consider giving houseroom to is Regis Philbin. 'Did she see you? What did she say?'

'Yes and nothing,' Edie says. 'I think we were avoiding each other until you came home.'

'Oh, thanks a bunch.' I sit back on my chair, stunned. This is even more shocking news than Edie being pregnant again. 'You know, you really ought to call her and tell her that she's going to be a grandmother. *Again.*'

'You can have too much of a good thing,' Edie says. 'Besides, I was waiting until I was out of the danger period.'

'What, three months?'

'No, out of danger from her shouting at me for being careless again.'

We both collapse into a heap of giggles.

'This *is* good news, Edie,' I say, holding my sister's hand.

'It is,' she says. 'Once the initial shock has worn off, I might agree with you. But I promise that I'll get my tubes tied after this one.'

'Maybe Lee should get his done as well.'

'That man is too fertile for his own good,' Edie pronounces. 'I think out-and-out castration is what's needed in his case.'

'I heard that,' Lee shouts from somewhere.

'One slip with that saw,' I warn, 'and he could do it himself.'

'I heard that too,' Lee calls.

'As we're on the subject of coming clean,' Edie notes, 'I take it you've 'fessed up about this fling with Nepal's most eligible bachelor?'

'I'm not sure that it's any of Jake's business.'

'For goodness' sake,' Edie says. 'He's been pining away without you. Have you noticed how much weight he's lost?'

I had, actually.

'You should at least let him know where he stands.'

I sag. 'I know.' Which is all very well, but I'm not exactly sure where *I* stand yet.

'He came round here for dinner while you were away. If you can call fish fingers and beans "dinner",' she adds. 'He was desperate without you. I know that he's come to his senses. Despite all that's happened, deep down he's always really loved you, Lyssa.'

'He's hidden it very well on occasions.'

'I know,' she says. 'But be realistic. Jake and you had a lot going for you as a couple before all this…nonsense…blew up.'

Is having an affair with another woman 'nonsense'? It seems like pretty painful nonsense to me. And it's all very well for my sister to pontificate, but her husband has never been anything other than utterly adoring and devoted. Could I just turn a blind eye to Jake's deceit and carry on as if nothing ever happened?

'How are you going to continue an affair with this bloke when he's halfway round the planet. Without a phone and without electricity.' My sister snaps the last biscuit in half and gives one of the pieces to me. 'Look, Lyssa.' She takes my hand. 'Jake realises he's made a terrible mistake.'

'He has,' I say. 'The trouble is, I don't want to make one too.'

Chapter sixty-nine

'I don't want to play poker, mate,' Jake said.

'Don't be ridiculous.' Pip chewed on his cigar as he pulled a plastic garden chair into his dealer's position. They always made Pip the dealer, as he was usually the only one who stayed sober long enough to remember what was going on. Pip pulled on his dark green, Perspex visor and steel, elasticated gaiters to keep his shirtsleeves back. These authentic 'props' had been bought on a gambling trip to Las Vegas especially for these occasions. You could never say that Pip did anything by halves. 'You always want to play poker,' his friend insisted. 'Your well-being depends on regular poker games.'

They played cards together once a month, always poker, taking it in turns to convert one room of their houses into a toxic wasteland, as it was compulsory to pass the evening smoking the biggest, fuck-offiest cigars they could find. The competition for the size of cigar was almost as hotly contested as the card game itself. Pip had won this time and was smoking something that looked as if it had been formed round a drainpipe and smelled as if it had lived in one.

'What *is* that thing?' Jake asked.

'This, my friend, was hand-rolled on the thigh of a dusky maiden,' Pip puffed expansively.

'It would have taken the thigh of a cellulitic elephant to roll that.'

'I hear someone very jealous speaking,' Pip said, cutting the cards with something approaching skill.

Pip exhaled deeply. Jake tried not to inhale. The aroma smelled faintly of elephant dung too and the fog of cigar smoke was already making him feel nauseous. These were always long and very drunken sessions, weaving on to the wee small hours and already, not past nine o'clock, Jake was ready to go home.

Jake and Pip were in Aidan's garage in a salubrious suburb of North London. They were banned from the inside of Aidan's house by Aidan's wife, who hated the smell of cigar smoke. At the moment he could sympathise with her. Aidan's dining-room table had been moved into the garage and covered, rather appropriately, with green baize and they'd all helped Aidan to move the lawnmower, the kids' bikes, the assorted garden implements and half-used pots of paint out of the way to make room for their card school. Aidan had also invited Dan and Max from Dunston & Bradley, who were also regular players. They'd obviously heard by now of his own untimely demise and of Neve's rumoured departure, but they still greeted and treated him like a mate, a chum, a pal, rather than a has-been, a washout and a loser—which was closer to how he felt. But somehow he felt out of the circle now—a little, lonely spur jutting off to one side.

The truth was there wasn't a lot he was interested in at the moment. He couldn't stop thinking about Lyssa for long enough. They were pussyfooting around each other as if they were embarrassed strangers and he had no idea how to break the impasse they seemed to have reached. Every time he tried to talk to Lyssa, she bolted out of the room, or if he cornered her for long enough to splutter out a sentence, it came out so, so wrong that he wished he hadn't bothered.

'Gentlemen,' Pip said, clenching his teeth round his cigar. 'Time to lose all of your money.'

Jake, Aidan, Max and Dan shuffled their garden chairs until they were cosily ensconced round the table.

Pip rubbed his hands together and then flexed his fingers, cracking each of them in turn. 'Time to show your cash,' Pip said.

Each man pulled out a bulging bag of pennies and put it on the table. Once upon a time they used to play for big money, serious money. When they were all young, free and single they'd think nothing of blowing five hundred quid or a grand in a night, more sometimes—if they were particularly drunk. But now, apart from Jake and Pip, all the guys were sprogged up and paying out for heavy, heavy mortgages, so the stakes had become suitably more modest. It was hardly *Lock, Stock and Two Smoking Barrels* territory, Jake thought. If only he'd been as cautious in gambling with other areas of his life.

Aidan's thirteen-year-old son, Ethan, acted as barman for the night—until it was his bedtime. Ethan was already wise enough to charge them each ten pence every time he was called from the kitchen to bring them another cold beer. Sometimes Jake's £1.20 bar bill he'd racked up wasn't even covered by his winnings. But it wasn't about winning, it was about taking part. He normally loved the camaraderie, the tantrums, sometimes the tears, the threat of a beered-up brawl. Tonight he didn't want camaraderie. He didn't want to be in Aidan's garage. Jake wanted to be at home in his own garage with his own wife who hated cigar smoke and his own thirteen-year-old son whom he could press into eager slavery. He wanted more than anything else—even winning the cigar competition—to be middle-class, married and a man with a future.

'Five pences in the pot, gentlemen,' Pip said. The others all shuffled forward keenly and they tossed their money into the middle of the table. 'House rules—aces high, two low pairs beat a high pair, minimum stake ten pence, ten pence to change your cards, no fisticuffs, no IOUs, no offering to throw in your wives or girlfriends in lieu of your debts, the dealer's decision is final!'

Jake was never sure whether they played by what you could call 'classic' poker rules. He always had the feeling that Pip made it up as he went along and that, mostly, it was to his own advantage.

'Jake,' Pip butted into his reverie. 'Put your poker face on, mate.

If you just sit there and look like a miserable bastard all night, that's not fair. We'll have no chance.'

Jake used to think he had a great poker face—lying to everyone, bluffing his way through life. Somehow the art of organised deception held little thrall for him now. Pip flicked out the cards. Jake, not surprisingly, had been dealt a very shitty hand. Not even a single pair or a decent high card.

They all fanned out their hands, studying them intently. Jake forced himself to look at the cards again. Pip stared at Dan. 'Change?'

Dan threw in his ten pence. 'Hit me with two.'

Pip obliged and doled out two fresh cards.

'Aidan?'

'I'll take three,' he said, also parting with his cash.

'Any for you, Max?'

Max looked smug. 'I'll stick.'

There was a sharp intake of breath. Max also hadn't mastered the art of a poker face and it was transparent to everyone when he was holding great cards.

'Jakey-boy?'

Jake threw down all five of his cards. 'Give me a new set.'

They all looked at him in disgust.

'What?' he said. 'It was a crap hand. There's nothing in the rules that says I can't change them all.'

Pip chewed anxiously on his cigar and fixed Jake with a stare. 'And there's nothing to say this won't be crap either,' he advised. 'You've got to work with what you've got. Don't throw your hand in so easily.' Jake knew that his friend wasn't talking about the card game. Nevertheless, he silently dished out five new cards.

As Pip had predicted, they were no better. In fact they were infinitely worse. Didn't that have a ring to it? Jack in the old one, get a new one that's ten times more stinky.

'Dan-Dan?'

'I'm in.' Dan put another ten pence on the table.

'I'll see your ten and raise you ten,' Aidan said. There were approving noises all round.

Max looked even more smug. 'I'll see your twenty and raise you twenty.'

Everyone sucked in their breath. Fighting talk.

'Jake?'

'I'm folding.' Jake threw down his hand.

'You can't fold,' Pip said.

'I can,' Jake said. 'I have.'

'That's pathetic,' his friend shouted. 'You're not even trying.' Their eyes met in a mutual glare. 'If you're not going to play properly, we might as well go and get Aidan's kids' pack of Happy Families or play Snap.'

'I am playing properly,' Jake protested.

'Bollocks,' Pip snorted.

Jake sat back and folded his arms. 'I'm just lulling you into a false sense of security.' But he knew in his heart that he wasn't playing properly—that he hadn't been playing properly for a very long time.

By the time they stopped for another beer and pee break, Jake was £3.20 down and feeling very morose. He had been dealt crap cards and had folded in every single hand they'd played. It was fair to say he was not on a winning streak. He felt it was a due reflection of his life. Pip pulled him to one side. 'You've got to snap out of this, mate,' his friend said quietly. 'It's doing no one any good.'

'I can't help it,' Jake whispered. 'I can't do this anymore. I can't concentrate on anything.'

Pip leaned against the lawnmower. 'Things aren't getting any better at home?'

'Worse, if anything.' Jake admitted. He grabbed his friend by the arm. 'Talk to her, Pip.'

'No, no, no.'

'Yes, yes, yes.' Jake felt himself brighten. 'She'll listen to you. She respects you. She *adores* you.'

'I don't think so.'

'She *does*.'

'Don't ask me to do this, my friend,' Pip begged. 'I am not the right man. Not by a long chalk.'

'You are. You'll know what to say, Pip,' Jake said. 'You always do.'

'There's something I should tell you….'

'What?'

'I…'

'What?' Jake was shocked. What else could there be? 'If I can't win Lyssa back, I haven't a clue what I'll do. You have to help me. I don't know if I can cope with anything else, Pip.'

'It's nothing.' Pip shook his head. 'Forget I said anything.'

His friend buried his face in his big cigar, concentrating intensely. Jake didn't know what to say—and that clearly made two of them. And he was relying on his friend to talk Lyssa round.

The other guys were shuffling in their garden chairs, fidgeting impatiently. 'We'd better get back to the table,' Pip offered.

Jake trailed after his friend. For a man who always said the right thing, inspiring words seemed to be eluding him.

Chapter seventy

Going back to work is a huge shock. No one brought me black tea in bed this morning to gently cajole me into life. I had to make my own breakfast—which consisted of two measly Weetabix rather than the sumptuous spread of pancakes, porridge and creamy rice pudding that I and my growling stomach have grown accustomed to.

I've forgotten all of the small routines that I used to perform completely automatically. I even had to stop and think about how I went about buying a train ticket. Needless to say, my early-morning commuter train is packed to the rafters, and it was infinitely better to be getting up at the crack of dawn to go and view mountain vistas and glorious sunrises in the Himalayas than it is to be squashed against someone's sweaty armpit all the way into the city of London. I've never seen a sunrise in St Albans despite living there for most of my life. It makes me wonder why.

I thought my memories of Nepal would start to grow dim, that a faint veil would come down over them or the fluttery curtain of day-to-day living would flick back and forth, obscuring them from view. But, if anything, they've grown brighter and sharper in contrast to my own life. And I'm holding on to them like treasured childhood possessions that I really can't bear to let go. And the brightest of all my memories is Dean.

I'm squeezed out of Embankment Underground station like toothpaste out of a tube, and cross the Hungerford Bridge to the offices of *My Baby* and *My Divorce*. It's a freezing-cold day, but not freezing with the tang of snow-capped peaks, just bone-jarringly freezing with an icy wind that's creeping inside the vulnerable openings of my coat, the neck, the ends of the sleeves—it's teasing inside the hem above my boots to numb my knees. I wish it were my brain that would go numb instead. And I wish these were flat, clonky walking boots instead of three-inch tottering things. I'm determined to abandon all hint of the sensible, maternity-type clothing I was so diligently collecting, so my pre-pregnancy flattie boots are shoved in the back of my wardrobe and all my impractical heels have now been hastily reorganised to centre stage on the Allen shoe-rack in order to enhance my attempt to glam up again. Another thing I'd forgotten in my brief absence from real life was how hard and how uncomfortable stilettos are. At this moment I'm regretting my rashness. I should have eased myself gently back into ridiculous fashion toe-crushers. The balls of my feet are burning and my calves feel as if they're about to cramp. No wonder they're called killer heels.

The sky is dappled grey and white with black splotches like a piebald horse, and every single person, without exception, is huddled into a big, black overcoat. The rhythmical, plodding footsteps clonk on the steel bridge like the march of some mindless automaton. The whole landscape looks like a photographic negative and I can't help feeling that I'm trapped in the wrong life.

I get to the office and, such is the harshness of the weather, even the hardened smokers have abandoned their post and I don't see Monica and Charlotte until I stomp, steaming, into the stuffy, overheated offices. They both shriek when they see me and rush over from their desks.

'Ohmigod! Ohmigod!' Charlotte trills. 'You're back!'

I'd emailed them to warn them of my imminent return to incarceration in the world of minor-magazine publishing, but given their reaction, I don't think they really expected me to turn up. They jump around me, clapping happily, and welcoming me as if I'm the prodigal son returning to the fold.

Charlotte starts to unwind my scarf, while Monica takes my coat, fussing round me. My boss ushers me to my seat. Like Jake, she's treating me as if I'm pregnant—and the thought doesn't even give me a moment's anxiety.

'We saved your desk for you.' Monica checks it for dust.

I look at my clean and tidy desk with my fabulous view and fail to feel any spark of excitement.

'Although I did keep it warm while you were away,' she admits. 'It's a great desk.'

I look out over the pewter ribbon of the river and at the clock on the art deco Ministry of Defence building across the water. It's not yet nine o'clock. I think I can see that clock far too clearly. I sit down at my clutter-free workspace and smooth my hands over its alien surface.

'Charlotte,' Monica says. 'Go and get Lyssa some coffee.'

Charlotte scoots away. I wonder how long this treatment will last. I'll give it until lunchtime.

Monica perches on the edge of my desk. 'Have you made a decision yet?'

'About what?' Jake? Dean? My life? Monica knows so little of these things, but again she probably will by lunchtime. I didn't give the girls a second thought while I was away, but now that I'm here, I realise that I have, in a strange way, missed them. I feel myself slipping under the waves of my previous existence.

'About what?' She laughs. 'Silly!'

I look at her blankly.

'It's big-decision time,' she says. 'Ta-da! *My Baby* or *My Divorce*?' She holds the choice up to me as if it's a prize in a game show.

'Oh,' I say. 'That.'

She looks at me as if I'm mad, and I can see the thought go through her mind that I may not have got my act together anymore than when I left. 'How was Nepal?' she asks tentatively.

I get a flashback of lush fields, rice terraces, towering peaks and dark brown eyes. 'Fabulous.'

'And it helped?'

If she means did running away from my problems solve them, then no, it didn't help, not at all. I've realised now that you can't run away from problems; you simply swap one set of difficult circumstances for another. 'Yes,' I say. 'It helped.'

'Good.' She looks immensely relieved.

Charlotte returns with my coffee, which I sip gratefully enjoying the fact that the scalding liquid at least makes me experience some sort of sensation.

'Did you decide?' Charlotte asks eagerly. 'Which mag are you going to plump for?'

'I don't mind,' I say. 'I'll fit in with whatever works best for the company.'

They exchange a worried glance.

'No, really,' I say. 'I don't mind. I'll slot back in here or I'll move my arse over there.' I point to a desk in the *My Divorce* section of the office and shrug.

Monica frowns. 'Are you sure you don't mind?'

'No.' I try a smile. 'I'm just happy to be back.' What I really mean is that I don't give a toss about either and I know that I need to get out of here as soon as humanly possible.

They both come behind me and give a group hug. 'It's fantastic to see you back,' they say in unison.

I only wish that I could say the same thing.

Chapter seventy-one

'Come to do Jake's dirty work?' I say to Pip as he meets me just outside the door to my office block at lunchtime.

'Yes,' Pip says and gives me a sheepish glance.

'Thought so.'

Pip is leaning on a low brick wall by the steps to the building. He's wearing an exquisitely tailored, black, mob boss overcoat and a charcoal-grey suit with a frilled, pink shirt that makes him look like a macho, thug fop. And, despite his individualistic dress sense, I realise that I've missed Pip rather more than I'd like to admit to. It was great to get his phone call this morning on my first day back—and not simply because it broke up the endless stretch of boredom that loomed before lunch and meant I could escape for some brief respite.

He comes and puts his arms round me, giving me a brotherly squeeze. 'You look absolutely fantastic.'

'Thanks.' I feel myself blush slightly under his scrutiny. I link my arm in his, and we start to make our way back over the foot-bridge to the Embankment.

'Shall we eat?'

'No,' I say. 'Unless you're hungry?'

'Not particularly,' Pip says.

'Let's just walk then.' I glance towards him. 'I take it there are "things" you want to say to me.'

'More than you can imagine,' Pip admits with an uneasy laugh.

The sun has made a rare appearance, poking its head through the blanket of cloud, and it's brought the joggers out. Middle-aged, grey men with knobbly knees skirt round us, panting unpleasantly under their towelling Mark Knopfler headbands while sprightly young girls with impossibly tight tracksuits and Sony Discmans clamped to their sides follow in pursuit. Slivers of gilt glimmer on the domes of the tall buildings, lighting up the city with rare golden streaks.

'Was Nepal all you hoped for?' Pip says.

'More than.'

'I missed you,' he says, looking out over the Thames. 'I thought about you a lot while you were away.'

'That's nice.' It feels good to be outside, even though it's so cold I can see my breath puffing out in front of me. I need a head-clearing walk. And it's strange that a few weeks ago my body ached from unaccustomed physical exertion and now it is stiffening up for the lack of it.

I don't know how I struggled through the morning, but struggle I did. Manfully. The whole time I felt so restless it was making my skin itch, as if I had ants crawling over me. It was decreed that I should move on to *My Divorce*, but to ease my transition, I've been allowed to keep my desk for the first month. I think everyone was scared that if I continued on *My Baby* and got back into the swing of potty-training problems, my obsession with small, pudgy babies would return with a vengeance. But I don't think it will. I can't explain what's changed inside me, but I no longer want a child at any cost. If I try to rationalise it to myself, I could say that it was seeing the happy, smiling faces of the children in Nepal—the children who have so little and give so much. It's a harsh comparison with the kids here, who have so much and constantly want so much more. Do I really want to bring a child into this life? Do I want to expend all my best efforts into parenting only to have them crushed by a child who thinks I'm failing if it doesn't have the latest designer trainers? If I want something cute and cuddly to love, would I be better off with a guinea pig or a Jack Russell?

Edie's impending and, as always, unexpected pregnancy has made me think again about my rocky relationship with Jake. My sister has one hundred per cent support from her husband, Lee—why should I be content to settle for anything less? I can admit to myself now that Jake was never as keen on trying for a family as I was, and that's no basis on which to start out. On the other hand, I was heartily sick of having my bum constantly injected with hormones and I now realise that it's within my own control to stop it all.

I suppose I felt such a desperate rush to procreate because I never wanted to end up as one of those forty-year-old career women who in a late flurry, have a baby just before the hormones give up and then alienate everyone around them by acting as if they are the only person ever to have given birth. And I'm now the first to admit it was becoming a close-run thing. We have a very slender window of fertility between teen-mum and pensioner-parent. I'm thirty-four and not getting any younger. Plus, I wanted to stay at home and look after my children. I had no intention of turning into one of these harried-looking mothers who are trying to juggle a demanding career and equally demanding children and making a mess of both. I've no idea how Jake would have felt about that—but I could have a better stab at a guess now. Do men really want a little wife and mother at home these days? I don't quite know what we've done to ourselves as a society, but all our roles seem topsy-turvy. Women may think they've achieved equality, but all it seems to mean is that we can swear, drink until we fall over, have sex indiscriminately, work all the hours God sends for less pay and have babies with anyone's sperm we choose. And for what? What exactly have we achieved by this defeminisation of ourselves? Most men's idea of a perfect woman these days seems to be a bloke with breasts. It is so much more simple when one of you has to go out and work in the fields and the other stays at home making chapattis, feeding the kids and the animals and doing the washing in the local stream. Each role is equally valid and vital to the good of the community and there're no blurred lines of demarcation. Things have become a lot more complicated since we lost all that.

I'm also beginning to question whether, just because I can't produce children naturally, I really have the right to 'create' one? What did infertile couples used to do before all this jiggery-pokery was invented? Did they lie down and die, bemoaning the infringement of their human rights, or did they just get on with life and contribute to society in other useful ways? How many Guide leaders are childless? I wonder. Someone must have statistics somewhere. I've no longer got the drive to struggle on with absurdly high expectations, paying out thousands to fertility clinics, which, all studies seem to show, have relatively low success rates. Plus, I've been very good at avoiding the complex moral issues that donor sperm might involve, so I'm not going to start now. Except to say that it's all very well handing over a few anonymous tadpoles when you're short of a few bob at university, but do you really want that same tadpole knocking at your front door when it's grown up into a strapping eighteen-year-old with, 'Who's the Daddy?' tattooed on his arm? See? Who am I trying to kid? One morning back at *My Baby* and I'm forced to confront these issues all over again. My head is already spinning round of its own volition rather like Linda Blair's in *The Exorcist*.

Pip is unaware of my inner turmoil as we make our way down towards the footpath by the river, mingling with the City-types as they eat their snatched lunchtime sandwiches on the move. We pass the smart, red-brick building of the City of London School and hear the high-pitched trill of boys' singing drifting from the open windows, along with the noise of a violin being tortured by inexpert hands. There's a semicircle of wooden benches set among a small, walled garden of dark green shrubs that are thriving healthily even in the polluted environment of London—and I guess some things will flourish wherever they are. Me? I'm not so sure now. Pip steers me towards the benches and we sit down, still arm in arm.

'Jake's floundering without you,' Pip says plainly.

'Good.'

'You don't mean that.'

I soften. 'No,' I say, 'you're right. I don't.'

'He wants you back, Lyssa,' his friend entreats. 'But he has no idea how to go about it.'

'Then perhaps he shouldn't have given me up quite so easily,' I point out.

'I'm sure with hindsight that he's well aware of it.'

I turn to Pip. 'And what about me?' I watch the grey gulls wheel soundlessly over the white-tipped water. 'What if I've realised—with hindsight—that Jake was a pretty crappy boyfriend?'

'Is that what you really think?'

A couple, quite clearly in love come giggling along the path and sit down on the bench next to us, cuddling up close. Pigeons settle and peck around their feet, searching for leftover crumbs. Usually, I love this part of London, down by the river, away from the crowds. I never tire of the ever-changing shape of the skyline and the unsteady blade of the new Millennium Bridge that, after its rather shaky start, cuts cleanly across the river carrying tourists to the uncompromising block of the Tate Modern. It's my standard lunchtime escape in summer when the deadlines and headlines of *My Baby* all get too much. Today the view washes over me and fails to add any levity to my heavy spirit.

'Jake doesn't know the whole story,' I say with a sigh that's taken by the wind.

Pip moves his head closer to me and stares into my eyes with a look of concern.

'I met someone else in Nepal,' I continue flatly.

Jake's friend says nothing.

'I thought that I could never love anyone as much as Jake,' I confess, pulling my collar up against the winter chill. 'But I was wrong.' I let my mind wander, thinking about Dean. 'It's very easy when you meet someone wonderful.'

'I know,' Pip says.

'Oh yes?' I grin at him. 'Something *you'd* like to tell *me*?'

'Not particularly.' Pip unlinks his arm from mine and lays it casually across the back of the bench. For a moment, it looks as if he might stroke my hair and then his hand stills.

'Come on!' I nudge him in the ribs. 'Have you met someone too?'

'Yes.' He sighs heavily.

'And is she wonderful?'

'Oh yes,' Pip says. 'I think so.'

'How long have you been seeing her?'

'I'm not exactly seeing her,' Pip admits. He shifts uncomfortably on the bench. I smile to myself. Men are so pathetic when it comes to discussing their own emotions. Although I have to say, Pip is better than most. It's quite funny seeing him squirm. 'We're just friends.'

'But you'd like it to go further?'

'I'd love it to.' Pip scratches at his stubble. 'But I think it's unlikely.'

'She must be mad!'

'Oh, she probably is,' Pip agrees. 'She also happens to be in love with someone else.'

'That's always tricky.'

'Yeah,' Pip continues, 'but I've only just found that out. I was labouring under the illusion that there might be room in her life for me one day.'

'Bummer!'

'And if that isn't enough,' Pip says, 'my best mate is head over heels for her too.'

'Lucky lady,' I say. 'She must be very special.'

'She is.'

'But where does that leave you?'

'I have absolutely no idea, Lyssa.'

I give him a kiss on the cheek. 'You'll work something out,' I say. 'You're utterly gorgeous. How could she resist you?'

'I'm at a loss to know,' he says with an over-bright laugh. 'Still, you don't want to hear about my futile yearnings. Tell me all about this new man.'

And I do—spilling the beans on Dean is something that doesn't require much encouragement. I almost feel moved to pull out a photo of Dean, but then realise that although Charlotte and Monica might well coo over him, Pip is highly unlikely to. Instead, I wisely rely purely on my powers of description to bring my lover to life. Pip digests all my love-lorn ramblings without comment.

'So what are you going to do?' he asks when I finally stop babbling.

The only bit I've left out is the fact that Dean hasn't replied to any of my emails since I've been back. Something that I'm finding increasingly worrying. Perhaps out of sight is indeed out of mind.

'I don't know.' The distance between us seems insurmountable. 'We'll find a way,' I say more bravely than I feel. 'If we both feel the same, we'll find a way.' And, if I had it, I'd pay a million pounds to know what was going through Dean's head right now.

'You ought to tell Jake about this guy,' Pip advises. We blokes like to know exactly how hopeless our situation is.'

'I don't know….'

'At least he'd realise what he was up against then.'

'We're not exactly communicating very well,' I tell him.

'I know,' Pip says. 'There are things he needs to talk to you about too.'

'Like what?' I pull my coat around me. Suddenly I'm feeling very cold. 'I thought you were his appointed spokesperson.'

'Not for this,' Pip says. 'This is too important. You need to speak to Jake.'

And that's something that I'm trying steadfastly to avoid.

Chapter seventy-two

'I don't want to come out.' I'm tidying my desk and getting ready to face the long trek home again. 'Really, I don't.'

'You do,' Monica insists. 'Even if it's just for a short while.'

'We've got to celebrate your first day back at work,' Charlotte chips in.

I'm not sure that 'celebrate' is the word I would have chosen. Or 'work', if it comes to that matter. Ignoring the mounting pile of copy and letters accumulating on my desk, I spent most of my afternoon compiling an email to Dean. One, like Goldilocks's porridge, that was not too hot and not too cold. One that smacked of shared intimacy but wasn't too desperate and gushing. It's bloody difficult, I tell you.

'Just one quick drink,' Monica cajoles. 'Maybe two.'

'You've told us nothing about your trip yet,' Charlotte says. 'We were thwarted in our lunchtime gossiping session. We saw you going off over the river wrapped round Pip.'

I can feel that I'm losing this battle.

'If you go straight home, you'll only have to look at Jake's miserable face,' my friend informs me with a wag of her finger. And, I have to say, she has a valid point. My conversation with Pip has left me feeling disturbed, and I don't really want to go out to a party to avoid contact with Jake.

'Just one drink then,' I say.

'Hurray!' they both shout.

And I know in my bones that it means I'm going to crawl home pissed and maudlin just before midnight.

All the bars in the City are crammed. Despite the fact that it's December, there are people spilling out onto the pavement, clutching bottles of designer beer and champagne. This does not bode well. I wonder why none of them are in a rush to go home, even on a freezing-cold night like this. Perhaps too many have their equivalent of 'Jake' waiting at home. Or perhaps they have no one at all.

Monica decides on a suitable watering hole for us down one of the narrow back lanes—Wine and Whatnot—and, elbows out, we jostle and barge our way into the smoke-filled bar. I'm too old to be doing this. A quiet drink in a country pub is more my style these days. I'm seriously thinking about buying a Labrador to take for rambling walks, that's how bad it is.

The bar is one of those long, thin London places with no room to move but with its walls decked out with dozens of massive mirrors in the hope of conning you into believing that there is room to move. There's no music blaring out; the background soft jazz is all but drowned out by the clamour of conversations. There are blue leather sofas and blue halogen lights—subdued to coal-mine proportions—and a granite, drink-soaked floor. There's as much modern art on the walls as there are stains on the tiles. Established in 1870, a plaque on the wall states—ruined in the 1990s, I'd like to add. The after-work crowd are out in force. Co-ordinated clothing is definitely optional for the men—pinstripe suits and pink-checked Thomas Pink shirts teamed with spotted red ties seem to be *de rigueur.* Where did all the Old School go with their charcoal chalk-stripe suits, bowler hats and rolled umbrellas? The women wear a uniform of tight, black Armani with overly short skirts. They all have bleached blond hair and talk in ear-splitting, yah-yah voices. We struggle through a sea of laptops and black leather briefcases abandoned on the floor. Monica and Charlotte form a front-line push to the bar, while I huddle pathetically behind them. I'm not sure I need a drink this much. I look at my watch—six o'clock. What time is it in Nepal? Nearly midnight. Dean will have been in bed for hours. I wish I were with him—and not for the more obvious reasons. I wonder if he's alone.

Monica and Charlotte finally manage to get served and Monica splashes out on a bottle of champagne, ostensibly as a welcome-back present, but I'd like to bet a pound that it appears on next month's *My Baby*'s expenses sheet. One of the few perks of being a boss, I guess. Too late to bag a sofa, we fight our way over to one of those tiny tables that you have to stand up at, and Charlotte plonks down the glasses. Monica pops the cork and they both cheer. I have to admit to a little cheer myself.

We've barely taken a sip when three smoothy City blokes in sharp suits and mismatched ties move in on us.

'Celebrating, ladies?' the smoothiest of all says.

'Our friend Lyssa has just returned from the wilderness,' Monica announces. 'We're welcoming her back.'

They raise their glasses in a toast to me. 'Welcome back, Lyssa.'

Monica and Charlotte echo it. 'Welcome back!'

'Cheers.' I raise my glass in return. Monica and Charlotte are already girly and giggly, despite the fact they haven't even had time to do much more than inhale the vapours of the champagne yet. It seems that now they are considerably less interested in my escapades in Nepal than in what these three young studs might have to offer.

This is clearly the end of our girly bonding, as the studs, in return, seem to have set their sights on us. The three smoothies sidle round us to start their campaign of divide and conquer.

'Hi,' one of the guys shouts at me over the din. 'So where have you been?'

'Nepal,' I oblige, shouting back.

'Oh,' he yells. 'Interesting.' He looks not the slightest bit interested. 'I thought you might have been on *I'm a Celebrity, Get Me Out of Here*!'

'No,' I yell back. 'Unfortunately not.'

'Oh.'

My feet hurt too much for me to be bothered to be polite. This is desperately hard work. And I feel that I'm far too old for this chatting-up business. Is this what I have to look forward to in life after Jake? Will I go back to being a desperate single trying to pull dubious men in dubious bars? In order to commiserate with myself, I throw back some more champagne.

Monica and Charlotte are flirting wildly with their hunks, all thought of me, their needy friend whom they persuaded here against her will, conveniently forgotten. The man who has attached himself to me leans forward and speaks quietly. 'Shall we get out of here?' he says. He flicks his eyes over me so that I can be in no doubt of the message he means to convey. He's clearly not into prolonged foreplay.

'No, thanks.'

He sneers just enough to really piss me off. 'You're not shy, are you?'

'No,' I say. 'I'm fussy.'

His sneer dies and he pushes away from me, muttering something that's probably very uncomplimentary to his mates as he passes. He turns back and gives me an unpleasant snarl and the finger.

Oh, what a shame! I can't help but smile. It looks as if I'm not going to get lucky tonight after all.

Chapter seventy-three

We polish off three bottles of champagne. Monica will never get all of those through on expenses and I must remember to stump up for one in the morning.

I'm not in a great mood. I've been hanging around on the fringes of my friends' conversations, but it was obvious that they weren't planning to give up available men that easily. I amused myself by plodding my way through rather too many glasses of fizz to numb my pain, before excusing myself and heading home alone.

I totter down the darkened, narrow streets. The City is dead at this time of night, when all the party animals are ensconced in bars and everyone else with any sense is already at home. All the shops are closed and shuttered—Xpress Copies, Londonsandwich.com, Wily Wine Merchants. There are never any people around—or taxis. I head off to somewhere more populated, regretting that I have a long, late train journey home too. When I'm old and grey and hobbling round in comfy slippers, I will be able to pinpoint this as the very night my bunions started. I am just *so* going to have to sort out my life.

A taxi whizzes past, ignoring my frantic attempts to hail it. And I plod along some more. I'm not far from St Paul's Cathedral and the Underground station but I hate taking the Tube at night because I'm always getting groped by drunken men in pinstripe suits and would rather go straight to the mainline station, but needs must.

Passing a group of children—well, teenagers—I wonder what they're doing out, hanging round the streets on a freezing winter's night. I bet their parents have no idea where they are or what they're up to. Gone are the days when children stayed at home in the evening entertaining themselves with colouring books and board games. There are four of them, and two of them have on only hooded sweatshirts, and I marvel at the ability of kids not to feel the cold. Perhaps they hope their baseball caps will keep them warm. They're leaning up against the wall near inside the entrance to a dark, narrow alley way, oozing attitude, and it looks to me as if they're scratching graffiti onto the brickwork, but I can't be sure.

'Hello, darling,' one of them shouts as I walk past. 'Want a good time?'

They all laugh, silly boys' giggles.

It brings a smile to my face too. My second offer tonight. Lucky me. I laugh, too—at the sheer nerve of them! I don't think any one of them is old enough to shave yet. What are kids these days coming to? But before I have a chance to formulate a suitably cheeky riposte, they're on me. One of them kicks me in the back and I fall to the pavement. Someone is yanking on my hair and my handbag. Out of instinct rather than a desire to protect my bag, I pull it towards me and earn myself a blow from a well-aimed foot to my stomach. They have their hoods up on their sweatshirts but I can still see the anger in their bitter, young faces.

'Come on! Come on! Get it!' one of them shouts, panic in his not-yet-broken voice.

I want to scream, but I can't as I'm winded and I think it's shock that's preventing any sound from forming. These are children! I can't believe what they're doing to me. My hand is stomped on by a designer trainer and, as a reflex, I let go of my bag and am relieved to hear them running away down the street.

I try to get up but I can't move. My back and my stomach throb with exquisite pain. There's sticky blood on my face, but I don't know how it got there. Maybe I hit my head on the pavement when I fell. Forcing myself to my hands and knees, I crawl along on all fours. I start to cry and I don't want to. I don't want these horrible, vicious little boys to have made me cry. And, for all that, they've got a few measly quid and an out-of-date mobile phone.

A taxi pulls up next to me at the side of the road, and the chugging noise of its diesel engine might as well be the sound of the cavalry arriving. Now my weeping changes from fear to relief.

Next to me, a pair of big boots appears. 'All right, love?'

I nod, unable to speak.

'There, there. Up you get.' Two bulky arms reach out for me, but seem unsure which bit they should get hold of. I reach out my now swollen hand and take his arm. He gently hoists me up. 'I saw the little buggers run off,' the taxi driver says. He helps me to pull down my coat and gently brushes away some dirt. 'Get in the cab, love.'

'I haven't got any money.' My voice is gruff and squeaky and not quite joined up.

'Don't worry yourself about that.' The outside of the cab is painted with a leopard skin design, advertising something but I don't know what. All I can see are the words *It's a jungle out there*! How true is that? How horribly, depressingly, awfully, bloody true is that? He opens the door for me. 'We need to get you looked at. You've got a nasty graze on your head.'

'They kicked me,' I say.

'Evil little bastards,' my saviour comments as he loads me gingerly into the back seat.

'Thank you,' I mumble through my tears. 'Thank you so much.'

'Just try to rest for a minute,' he says. 'We'll get you to the hospital as soon as we can.'

He hands me his phone. 'Have you got someone you can call to come and get you?'

I nod and it makes my head hurt. The taxi driver jumps into

the cab and pulls away. I can feel myself wince as we hit the potholes in the road. I take the phone and punch in the only number that my frozen brain can think of.

Chapter seventy-four

Jake makes a dramatic entrance through the door of the Accident & Emergency Department and everyone turns to look at him. My ex-boyfriend must have driven here at warp speed, because it's not much more than an hour since I phoned him. He scans the waiting room and his face turns white when he sees me sitting amid several other bleeding people. He strides over to me, his face a mass of anxiety.

'What did they do to you?' he says.

'They mugged me,' I reply quietly, sipping my third cup of putrid machine tea since arriving at the Royal London Hospital. My shock, anger and fear have been replaced with a horrible sickness and disappointment in my fellow human beings. I can't remember when I've ever felt so low in my entire life. Putting my tea down, I stand up. 'Thanks for coming.'

Jake looks stricken. He goes to hug me, but I put my hand up to stop him. I'm not sure that I can cope with physical contact—I might just break down again. His hands, as well as mine, are shaking.

'I got kicked in the stomach,' I say. 'Don't touch me.'

I was 'lucky'. It's a quiet night in A&E and I've already seen the doctor, albeit a junior one, who didn't look much older than my muggers. Nothing is broken, apparently, but a lot of me is bruised. The taxi driver who came to my rescue was so kind that it made me cry even more and he very nearly managed to restore my shattered faith in humanity.

'Are you okay to leave now?' Jake says.

'Yes.' All I want is to get home and slip into a nice, hot bath.

'The car's outside.' Jake carefully takes my arm and, like the walking wounded, I limp gratefully after him.

We drive home in silence with me drifting in and out of sleep and it reminds me of our journey back from the airport, except I have a more valid reason now. My hand is vibrating with pain, but the tablets I've been given are taking the edge off everything else. I hug my arms around my body in the passenger seat, tenderly massaging my shoulders, and curse myself for my misfortune, wondering what I could have done to prevent this sorry incident.

Jake pulls up outside the house and then leads me inside. 'I'll make some tea,' he says.

I've had enough tea to float a ship. 'Thanks.'

'Have you eaten?'

I shake my head. 'I'm not hungry.' My stomach still feels tender and nauseous, but I think it's just shock rather than any permanent damage. 'I'm going to get straight into the bath.'

'Good idea,' Jake says.

I head up the stairs, each step a gargantuan effort. The light in the bathroom seems too bright and makes my pupils contract. It's not a pretty sight that greets me in the mirror. There's someone looking vaguely vampiric staring back at me. I've got the bloom of a big, blue bruise on my cheek and a piece of gauze taped to my forehead covering a gritty graze. There's blood in my hair and no colour in my cheeks. I turn on the bath taps, desperate for the soothing relief of hot water. Everything aches as I ease off my clothes. I'm going to burn them, burn them all. I'm going to take them into the garden and put them on a bonfire. This is awful, I feel violated and I have to keep reminding myself to keep this all in proportion. I've been mugged by some scabby teenagers out to make a few bob—this sort of thing happens every day to all kinds of people. It's not the end of the world. But it feels pretty close to it at the moment.

I lower myself into the bath and let the water work its healing powers on my injuries. And as I lie back and the water flows over my shoulders, there's a timid knock at the door and Jake pops his head round. It seems strange for a man who was my lover, my friend, for so many years, to be so formal with me now. 'I've brought your tea.'

'Thanks.' He puts the cup on the side of the bath and then hovers.

'You look pretty rough,' he says.

'I'll be all right after a good night's sleep.'

'You should tell the police.' He sits down on the loo seat next to me.

'Why?' I cross my hands over my chest and I see Jake avert his eyes. 'And add my name to the growing statistics? They won't do anything about it,' I say with a touch of resignation in my voice. 'They were kids. Young kids. Thirteen or fourteen at the most. The sort of boys Kelly goes out with.' The sort of kids we once hoped to have, I want to say. 'Even if the police managed to catch them, they'd get away with nothing more than a slap on the wrist. You know what it's like. What would be the point?'

'I wish I could get my hands on them,' Jake says.

I sigh. 'I wish *I* could.' I wish I could have done something at the time. I wish I hadn't been so bloody helpless.

'I don't know what this country's coming to,' Jake says miserably.

'Me neither.' I want to be back in the fields and foothills with nothing more to worry about than whether I'd managed to catch a good snap of a flitting kingfisher on my camera.

There's very little petty crime in Nepal. Buddhists, quite sensibly in my opinion, believe in karma—what you give out, you'll get back in spades. I wish it were the same here, where criminals appear to get away with whatever they like—usually backed by some loony judge who's never heard of mobile phones. Wouldn't it be wonderful if the young thugs here believed that their punishment would fit their crime? Then they'd be worried about some old granny turning up and spraying graffiti on their front door or running a key down the side of their precious car. That would be justice in my mind.

'I know this isn't a good time,' Jake continues, 'but we need to sit down together and talk. There are things I need to say.'

I rest my head back on the rolled edge of the bath, which digs into the tense muscles of my neck. 'Pip's already told me.'

Jake straightens. 'About the baby?'

I twist round to look at him, sitting up out of the water. 'What baby?'

His colour drains to match my own. He doesn't speak for a very long time. 'Neve was pregnant.'

I feel as if I've been punched in the stomach all over again. Kicked while I'm down. Fresh, hot tears spring to my eyes. '*Was* pregnant?'

'She had an abortion.' Jake hangs his head. 'But it was mine, Lyssa. I was the father.'

'You're right,' I say, closing my eyes in the hope that everything will go away. 'This isn't a good time.'

Chapter seventy-five

It's three o'clock in the morning and I've had two bouts of restless sleep and two nightmares. I'm awake and sweating ice-cold droplets all over the pillow. My first nightmare involved a dozen hulking, great, blank-faced thugs circling me and taking it in turns to hit me, but they were all wearing baby bonnets and were hitting me with Pooh Bear rattles. In my second nightmare, I was at an antenatal class where I was the only woman who wasn't pregnant and no one liked to tell me. They were all fat and waddling, like Edie is just before she drops, and wearing tent-like maternity clothes. I was wearing tight-fitting Lycra and high heels and trying to join in a conversation about piles and swollen ankles when it was obvious to everyone else that I had no idea what I was talking about, so they decided to mug me too. How sad can you get?

I lie shivering beneath my duvet. How can I turn my brain off? I need more painkilling drugs—or maybe I need less.

There's no point lying here tossing and turning, so I pull on my dressing-gown and pad downstairs. I couldn't talk to Jake after his bombshell. All I could do was crawl into bed and hope for a swift and pleasant death. There was no way I could make sense of it all after what had just happened.

In the kitchen, I root about in the back of the cupboard. Somewhere we've got the remnants of a tub of Horlicks, which I bought when Jake was going through a hard time at work and couldn't sleep. Having found it, I check it's still in date—I wouldn't like to have survived my earlier suicidal thoughts only to poison myself with out-of-date Horlicks. That would be too cruel a fate. I then pour some milk into a pan and bring it to the boil. I'm not sure that I even like Horlicks, but I plan to drink it anyway. I have no idea what else to do.

In the darkness, I go through to the lounge and look out of the window and am surprised that even at this time in the morning there are lights on in other houses down the street and I wonder if it's other people struggling with their lives, pacing the floor with nothing but milky drinks for solace. Research shows that we're all suspicious of the people we live in close proximity to these days, mainly because we're such a transient population, split from our family core by the practicalities of employment and economics. And it strikes me again that I really haven't a clue who my neighbours are—there's a retired doctor a few doors down and the obligatory gay couple—but that's as far as it goes. I have no idea what their names are. If we ever get a letter misdelivered, we never know where its true intended home is, so just send it back 'not known at this address'. Doesn't that tell you something? The concept of community has somehow lost its way round here. We don't have barbecues together, we don't pop into each other's houses borrowing cups of sugar, we don't string our homes with marigolds during festivals. It seems we very rarely have anything to celebrate. The closest I've seen to a wild display of liberation and happiness round here is next door's dog when he sticks his head out of the window of their car as they drive away down the street. Virtually the only time we catch more than a fleeting glimpse of each other is when there's a sudden rush of spring weather and we all dash out on a Sunday morning to wash our cars and deadhead the winter flowers. It's not much in the way of bonding. I wonder, would they bother to stop and help someone being mugged?

I can't face turning on the light, so I sit in the dark and try not to think. After a few minutes, I hear footsteps on the stairs and turn to find Jake standing there. 'I couldn't sleep either,' he says.

'I can make you some Horlicks.'

Jake nods and we head into the kitchen. I go through the routine of making his drink, while he sits at the table and watches me without speaking. When the milk has boiled, I hand over his cup and sit down opposite him.

'That was a bit of a conversation stopper,' I manage eventually.

'I know,' he says, stirring his milk. 'I didn't mean to blurt it out. It was stupid of me.'

'It sounds as if Neve has been more stupid.'

'We've both behaved very badly,' he admits. 'And I've been sacked. Well, I resigned, but it was only a matter of time.' He gives me a sheepish glance. 'She was sleeping with my boss too.'

'Busy girl.'

'That's all over now. And she's got the bullet as well.'

This is giving me a headache. 'What a very tawdry tale.'

'I know. How did we ever make such a mess of things?' I would, if I had any fight left in me, dispute the word 'we'. But I guess he may have a point. Jake drags his fingers through his hair. 'I didn't mean for any of it to turn out like this.'

'No,' I agree. 'I don't suppose you did.'

'But in a strange way,' he continues, 'it's been good for us.'

I'm not going to ask Jake to qualify the word 'good' either.

'It's made me realise how much I want to be with you.' Jake reaches out for my hand—the one that doesn't look as if it's been whacked by a mallet. He toys with my fingertips and I haven't the strength to move them. 'And then tonight—' Jake's voice cracks. 'I couldn't bear it if anything happened to you.' He rubs his hands over his eyes and I can see that they're red-rimmed. 'I want us to get married. Right away. We've messed around for too long. I can get a new job. A better job. I've had a couple of interviews and they were very keen. I got a great reference—'

I look up at him in surprise.

'I forced Alec to type it before I hit him.'

I smile, though I don't think it reaches my lips. That's fairly typical of Jake.

'The thing with Neve,' he says haltingly, 'it confirms that I can become a dad.' It obviously pains him to speak of it. He fights to hold on to his control before he continues. 'I want children. I know that now. I want loads of them. And we can do it.' He sounds very impassioned. 'Together, we can do it.'

This would be a good time for me to confess everything to Jake. Tell him about my abortion and why I cared so desperately about becoming a mother. I should tell him. Wipe the slate clean between us. Stand us back on equal ground. But I can't. I can't be that intimate with him anymore. And that was a very different me from the one who's facing him now.

We sit and look at each other, one of us with a very expectant look on his face. My fingers curl round my cup, searching for some warmth. The throbbing pulse in my hand is echoed in my head.

'Say something,' he urges.

The words take an age to push through my hurt. 'I don't know that I want it anymore.'

Jake looks stunned.

'I met someone else.' Someone wonderful. 'In Nepal.'

'I don't care,' Jake says. 'I don't care what you've done. Even if you slept with him—'

Jake's naiveté stuns me. I think of Dean and me, laughing in my sleeping bag, making love in the hot spring, sleeping in his makeshift bed. Why does Jake think that time has stood still for me?

'I'm the one who's here and he's…where?'

A long way away from me. And the distance between us seems to be growing with each passing day.

'We'll have a fresh start.' Jake presses on regardless.

How can I begin an explanation that encompasses all the changes that have taken place inside of me when I'm not absolutely certain of what they are myself? 'It isn't that easy.'

'It is,' he insists. 'Lyssa, I want you to marry me. I want you to be my wife. And I won't stop asking until you say yes.'

'I've changed, Jake.'

'You've only been gone a month,' he says. 'You can't have.'

But he's wrong, I have.

Chapter seventy-six

What am I going to do? It's a question that's weighing heavily on my mind.

At five o'clock this morning, still lying awake, I was almost convinced that Jake was right and that I could forget about Neve and Dean and everything else and we could go back to how we used to be. I could submerge myself in the familiar—the tried, if not necessarily the trusted. However, in the cold light of day, I know that, no matter how persuasive Jake might be, he could also be seriously misguided.

He brought me breakfast in bed in an effort to endear himself further—a soft-boiled egg and toast soldiers—comfort food for the delicate and ailing. And I'm certainly both of those. I can't help but remember that he was boiling eggs on the wretched morning when all this started and he walked away from me. How long ago does that seem? Jake's memory isn't, it appears, as razor-sharp as mine, as he clearly hasn't formed any emotional attachment to this particular food. My ex-boyfriend plumped my pillows and smoothed my duvet. He put my magazines, the telephone and the television remote control where I could reach them so that I wouldn't have to stretch too far. I nearly cried at his tenderness—which certainly isn't too little, but it may be too late.

Then Jake, virtually as pale as I am, reluctantly left for an important interview he'd already arranged and I wished him well, because I really do. After eating my egg, I had to phone in to work to tell Monica my tale of woe and explain that I wouldn't be gracing the offices of *My Baby* today or for the next few days. Of course, she was horrified by what had happened to me, but I suspect she was even more horrified that their impromptu 'dates' had glugged as much of their champagne as they could sink and then had cleared off into the night without so much as a thank you. A much more sophisticated form of mugging in my opinion.

I'm too shaky inside to do very much today, although my physical wounds are faring much better. I've got a bruise on my cheek that's the colour of a squashed canary and a red-speckled graze on my head. My hand has returned to somewhere approaching normal size, and although it's an attractive shade of mauve, there seems to be no permanent damage done. I guess the same can't be said for my personal life. I snuggle down into the duvet and flick on the television. It's a long time since I've had the luxury of watching daytime television, but having channel-hopped through the entire range of programming and finding nothing remotely interesting to hold my attention, I flick it off again and try some of the magazines instead.

I'm halfway through *House Beautiful* and learning how to use pastels to transform my home when the phone rings. I roll over, trying not to crush my hand in the process, and reach out for it. 'Hello.'

'Hi.' The line is crackly, but the American voice at the end of it is unmistakable.

'Dean?' I sit up in bed and try to straighten my hair and my pyjamas.

'Is this a good time?' he says. 'I thought I might catch you before you left for work.'

'I'm not going into the office today.'

'Oh. That's good, isn't it?'

'It's wonderful.'

'What's it like being home again?'

'Dreadful.'

I can hear his distant laugh and it turns my insides out. 'Is it okay to talk?' he asks.

'It's fine,' I reply, a tear escaping from beneath my eyelashes. 'I'd nearly given up on you.'

'We've had a tough time here,' he says with an expressive noise. 'There was some unseasonal rain last week that caused one hell of a mudslide and blocked the mountain path. I've spent the past five days with the villagers digging us out. This is the first time since you left that I've been able to walk down to Pokhara.'

I forget that Dean has more elemental problems to contend with.

'I thought you might have been worried,' Dean says.

I hold the phone closer to me, trying to squeeze nearer to him, even if it's just by a few millimetres. 'I was very worried.'

'I read all your emails,' he says. 'You sound very bright and breezy.'

Pressing my lips together, I answer, 'Maybe you shouldn't believe everything you read.'

I can feel his concern coming down the line. 'Have you been okay?'

'Great,' I say without conviction. 'And you?'

There's a long pause and I think the phone might have gone dead.

'No,' he says with a lengthy sigh. 'I guess I'm not great.' There's another long, staticky gap, which my heart fills by beating loudly. 'I'm missing you.'

I can't stop the tears from falling. 'I miss you too.'

'Oh, Lyssa,' he breathes. And I know there are a thousand things we need to say and can't. 'Any chance that you're going to come back and visit me?'

'I'd love to.'

Dean's voice softens. 'Make it real soon,' my gorgeous lover says.

And I know in an instant exactly where my heart lies.

Chapter seventy-seven

'I can't stay,' I say to Monica. She's pulled up her chair so that it's right next to my desk.

'I think we'd gathered that already,' she replies.

I couldn't face going back into the office for a whole week after I'd been mugged, and when I did I was scared of the crowds pushing and shoving around me, scared of anyone who so much as bumped into me. It seemed as if my scars marked me out as someone who could no longer look after herself, and I don't want to spend my life swamped by hostile strangers and delinquent children who care nothing about me. I've never felt frightened in London before, but I do now and I don't want to be here any longer. I want to belong somewhere—somewhere quiet, surrounded by friends, where my life will have a purpose. And I know with every ounce of my being that I'm no longer capable of being a city girl—four cruel teenage boys have beaten the last vestiges of it out of me.

I feel terrible about deceiving Jake, as he's clucked around me like a mother hen, trying to prove that he's wonderful husband material. And the fact that he thinks he can change my mind by sheer will and a few well-cooked meals has almost broken my heart. But, the fact of the matter is, as soon as he was out of the house, I've been on the internet planning and plotting my escape behind his back. I'm not proud of it, but I know that it's what I have to do. I turn my attention back to Monica.

'I'm doing it for charity,' I offer meekly.

'Oh yeah?' My friend looks singularly unimpressed. 'Couldn't you just stick a few quid in a collecting box like everyone else does?'

On the internet, I've found a voluntary organisation, Teacher Placements in Nepal, that will—unsurprisingly, given their name—arrange a teaching post for me in Nepal. They'll provide me with accommodation and all the training I need to get started. All I have to do is raise an awful lot of money as soon as I possibly can.

'I need two thousand pounds, Mon.'

'And that guarantees your placement?'

'Yes.' I cringe slightly. 'And I'm looking to you lot to provide it.'

'Ooo,' my boss says. 'Then we'd better set up some kind of sponsored drinking session pretty quickly. That'll be the fastest way to raise money round here.'

'You're a very understanding boss,' I say, giving her a hug and a kiss on the cheek.

'And I'm a very concerned friend,' she says, puffing out a sigh. 'Are you sure you're doing this for the right reasons?'

'I don't know.' I can feel excitement and terror in equal measures bubbling up inside of me. I haven't told anyone else about this yet—including Dean—and it feels so strange to hear it coming out of my own mouth. 'But I've seen a different way of living and I have to try it.'

'Well,' Monica says, 'you can't say fairer than that.'

'Plus, you get my view on a permanent basis.' We both look out of the window and across the grey expanse of the Thames.

'Cool.' Monica cheers up considerably. She rubs her hands together. 'I suppose one of us ought to do some work today.'

'Thanks, Mon.'

'By the way,' she says as she stands up, 'where do you want to have your leaving do?'

And I have to say that I think that's the least of my worries.

Chapter seventy-eight

'How did your first day back go?' Jake says brightly. He has on his frilly apron again and a lasagne in his hands, which he slides with a practised flourish into the gaping oven.

I strip off my coat and throw down my bag, massaging my temples as I do so. 'Jake, sit down,' I say. 'We need to talk.' I hate saying that, it makes me sound like some bit-part actress in a soap opera, but try as I might I couldn't think of another way to broach this.

'Do you want a glass of wine?' He waves a glass at me. 'I opened a nice bottle of red to let it breathe.' He shows me the bottle and sniffs appreciatively at it. 'Mmm. Wonderful.'

'No,' I say. 'No wine. Thanks.'

'Do you want me to grate some parmesan for the lasagne? I nipped up to the high street this afternoon, into that new Italian deli, and bought some really nice cheeses.'

'Jake.' How do I stop him chattering? 'Just sit down. Please. This is important.'

He comes and sits down at the table. 'Dinner won't be long.'

'I won't be long either,' I promise.

Jake looks at me expectantly. There's a new lightness to his spirit and I can hardly bring myself to crush it, but I guess there's no easy way to do this. Whenever a relationship breaks down, one person is always going to be more hurt than the other. Last time it was me. This time it's Jake's turn. I wonder if he went through such agonies when he left me for Neve? But I can't worry about that now. What's done is done and nothing we can do will turn back the clock. I take a deep breath. 'I'm going back to Nepal.'

He looks at me blankly.

'I'm going back,' I repeat when he says nothing.

'What for?'

'I've arranged a teaching post.'

'But you're a magazine editor,' he says.

'Not anymore,' I point out. 'I resigned today.'

Jake studies his fingers, developing a sudden fascination for his nails. Eventually he says, 'Are you going out there to be with him?'

'Partly,' I admit. And I want to be with Dean. I sincerely hope that we have a future together, but that's not the full story.

'I phoned the clinic this afternoon,' Jake confesses. 'I want us to have another go at IVF. They're willing for us to continue with the programme.'

'I can't do that.'

'But you wanted a child more than anything,' he says. 'And now I do too. We've still got savings. We can blow it all on treatment.'

'I don't want a baby at any cost,' I reply. 'I think the price we've already paid is way too high.'

Jake hangs his head.

'What I wanted before was a baby for me. For what a child could do for me. Now I feel differently.' I give a shrug that doesn't help my inadequate explanation for my sudden change of heart. 'I'm no longer hung up on producing a replica of myself. It's not the end of the world if I can never have a child. I've had enough of hormones and injections, Jake. If it happens, I want it to happen naturally.' My period started this morning. I was actually late, but I hadn't even noticed. And that is just not me. Or not the old me. Somewhere, suddenly I've stopped counting the hours and the days. And when I saw the bright red, tell-tale speck in the loo, I didn't have any of my usual feelings of failure. I didn't want to end my life. It was a period. A healthy, natural cycle that sets me aside as a woman. I can honestly say that I'm not going to lose any sleep over this ever again. It just proves that an awful lot can happen in the course of twenty-eight days. How could Jake ever understand this? I look at his stricken face and wonder if he ever will. I push on, regardless. 'In the meantime,' I continue, 'I've found other ways that I hope will bring me fulfilment.' I think of the smiling faces of the delightful village children and I know that I have a lot to offer them and that they have a lot to offer me. 'What I don't want to do is go through my life never feeling as if I've made a difference.'

'I don't want to go through my life without you,' Jake says flatly.

'We can't always have what we want, Jake.' My insides are like acid at the thought of hurting him. Why is it easier to have your own heart broken than to break someone else's? It would be so much easier if I could simply learn to love Jake again, if my feelings for Dean would dissolve without trace, like sugar in tea. But it's just not going to happen.

Jake forces a brave smile. 'Aren't you going to ask me how my day was?'

'Of course.'

'I got a great new job,' Jake says. 'More responsibility. More pay.'

Less attractive colleagues? I wonder.

'I thought it would change everything. That this was the new beginning I'd prayed for.'

'Jake…'

'You can have anything you want, Lyssa—a flashy car, exotic holidays. An engagement ring. We can move to a bigger house. You can even give up work if you want to. Anything.'

I think of the man who can offer me nothing but his heart.

I reach out and touch Jake's hand. 'Jake—' How can I cause this pain to another human being? 'The only thing I want from you is friendship.'

Jake pulls away. 'Don't ask me to be your friend, Lyssa.' He stands up and tugs off his frilly apron, which he throws to the floor as he leaves. 'I love you too much to ever just like you.'

Chapter seventy-nine

'I wish I'd taken up smoking,' Edie says. 'I could do with a fag right now.'

I don't point out that she hasn't been 'without child' long enough to contemplate being a smoker. Instead, I indicate and skirt round an old granny doing two miles an hour in a brand-new Micra. I'm driving up Holywell Hill in my still-dented car and, as an afterthought, we've just been to the local petrol station to pick up a bunch of over-priced, gaudy flowers in the hope that they'll go some way towards placating my mother.

I'm seeing my home town with new eyes—now that I'm about to leave. Better late than never, I suppose. It's neat and tidy and inoffensive in every way. It has served me well for many years. It has a lot going for it, not least that you can make enough off your property in a few years to retire on. I think of the loving care that the Nepali women lavish on their mudbrick homes and would speculate that they don't view them purely for their future investment potential. And there's lots of culture here—it was a major Roman town, for heaven's sake. There are bits of Roman ruins sticking up all over the place. It's just that it doesn't feel very Roman. We have a watered-down version of culture—nice to have it in the background, but not so that it infringes on our daily lives. Don't get me wrong, it's nice, but not in any remote sense exotic. But will I miss it? I think not.

'Why do you think we've been summoned?' my sister asks anxiously.

'No idea.' We stop at the traffic lights. My sibling and I have been invited to Sunday lunch at our mother's house. Edie was instructed to come alone, minus husband and any grandchildren. This is not a good sign. It means our mother has something serious to say. We are very grateful that these family pow-wows don't happen very often. When they do, they involve eating Mum's indigestible food in stony silence and conclude with either myself or Edie getting a good telling-off about some minor—and usually imagined—misdemeanour. We can only hope the flowers will be enough.

'She'll go bonkers when I tell her I'm going to have another baby.' Edie fidgets with the fringes of her handbag.

We are taking this opportunity to make sure she has something to tell us off about. Edie, as she has mentioned, has yet to come clean about her forthcoming joyous event. And I've yet to tell her that I'm planning to do a moonlight flit to Nepal.

'It's only just hit me that I'm really pregnant again, Lyssa.' My sister shakes her head. 'I can't believe it. I'm going to end up as one of those women they feature in the middle spread of the *Express* with twelve ghastly looking children in tow. It'll be one of those articles about how many loaves of bread and pints of milk we get through in a week and how many long hours I spend ironing.'

Not enough is my usual reckoning.

'And there'll be a picture of us all smiling,' she continues. 'Except Lee, who'll be looking harried, and all the readers will think "Poor bastard".'

'She'll go even more bonkers when I tell her I'm going to teach underprivileged children halfway round the world.'

'Lyssa, why? Why? Why? Why?' My sister mimics our parent's haughtiest tones. 'What have the underprivileged ever done to deserve this?'

I giggle my agreement. Charity begins and *stays* very much at home with our mother.

'Mind you,' Edie says, reverting to her own voice, 'I'm at a bit of a loss to understand it myself.'

'You would if you saw the place,' I assure her.

'And the people,' she adds with a wink. I think we both know which particular one of the people she's referring to. 'I hope he's damn well worth it.'

I smile contentedly. 'I think so.'

'What am I going to do without you?'

'Kelly's old enough to babysit now.'

My sister punches my gearstick arm. 'That's not all I need you for.'

'Of course it is,' I protest. 'You've got Lee for everything else.'

'But you've always been around, Lyssa,' my sister huffs. 'Besides, look what happened last time Kelly babysat for us.' She examines her belly.

We pull up outside Mum's house and I notice the net curtain twitch—too late to make a getaway now. Our mum lives in a nice part of town in a small, semi-detached house that she keeps as neat as a pin. This is not because she enjoys housework but because you can never be sure who might drop in unannounced. It was never a very homey home, as we weren't allowed to do anything that would make it untidy. My mother is still resolutely attached to 1970s décor. She is the only person I know who thinks swirly brown and orange carpet is 'all the rage'. I believe this is where I get my love of all things fussy. The net curtain falls back into place.

'I saw Pip the other day,' I tell Edie before we get out of the car. 'I forgot to mention that you blame him for your latest happy event.'

My sister stares out of the window. 'How is he?' Edie says.

'Fine. In love,' I say. She spins her head towards me so fast that I think her neck's going to break.

'In love?' she queries. 'He told you that?'

'Yes.' I frown at her. 'Unrequited, I'm afraid. He's fallen for the same woman as his best friend. I don't think she knows how he feels.'

'Oh, you are a plum!' Edie snorts.

'What?'

'It's you. Pip's in love with you.'

'Is he?' I'm more than a little surprised. 'He never said.'

'It sounds like he dropped enough hints!'

'Oh shit,' I say. 'I laughed at him.'

'Nice one, sis.'

'He could have been a bit more obvious.'

'Could he? Apart from ripping all your clothes off and jumping on top of you, I'm not sure how.'

'I'll ring him,' I promise. 'I'll do a really grovelly apology.'

'Come on, then,' Edie says. 'Let's face the music.'

'Got the flowers?'

Edie grabs them from the back seat. We get out of the car and head up the path to Mum's front door.

'I don't think you've told me all that went on at your lunch date,' I say, several cogs and levers whirring in my brain. 'I seem to remember you being very vague about it.'

Edie looks at me askance and I see a spark of guilt in her eye.

With perfect timing, Mum opens the door. 'Darlings!' she says as if she weren't expecting us. 'How lovely to see you!'

'Hello, Mum,' Edie says, avoiding my questioning gaze and holding out the conciliatory bunch of flowers. 'Great to see you too.'

My sister's interrogation will have to wait.

Chapter eighty

The table is set with crisp, white Irish linen and pure white delicate porcelain. It looks fabulous. The silver is out in full force. So is the Stuart crystal. There's a delicate arrangement of white carnations and green frondy bits. My mother could set the table for a state banquet and not be found wanting. She has, however, turned lumpy mashed potatoes into an art form. Her skill at presentation surpasses her culinary expertise. With a graceful smile and an elegant sleight of hand, she puts a bowl of grey, humped puree down in the middle of the dining-room table and I have to admit there's a certain surreal sculptural quality to it. It wouldn't look entirely out of place in a Salvador Dalí exhibition. Edible, they will not be. Given the fact that her cooking could have had a chance to improve over the years, I can sometimes understand the reason why my father left us. I can only hope she was better in the bedroom—otherwise he will have my utmost sympathy.

'This is so lovely,' my mother says, clasping her hands to her delicate bosom. 'Having both of my big girls here together.'

Edie and I smile sickly smiles.

'And I know that a roast dinner is your favourite.'

Edie and I both hate roast dinner—particularly my mother's

version of it. The hostess trolley is steaming quietly in the corner of the room, which is never a good sign. It means the carrots will have been in it since some time yesterday. My mother likes to make her preparations well in advance. She is not familiar with the term *al dente*. Cabbage? Minimum two hours at a rolling boil. If you were sporting ill-fitting dentures, you would be safe eating in my mother's home. Unless, of course, you touched the meat. Mum puts down a block of something black.

'We all like our meat well done, don't we?' she says, flourishing a carving knife. 'Well done' in my mother's eyes means that she has reduced it to a lump of charcoal.

'Yes,' we chorus.

Edie and I exchange glances, but neither of us can identify it. And you can never ask my mother outright what it might be. I did once, and she didn't speak to me for over a month. Its accompaniments will give us the only clue to its origins. Pork—apple sauce will appear. Lamb—mint sauce. Beef—horseradish. Chicken—rather wet Pepperidge Farm stuffing. If my mother ever deviates from this routine, we'll be lost. She fusses about putting the oblong glass dishes from the hostess trolley onto heat-proof mats on the table and then produces a delicate crystal boat containing a livid green slurry of mint sauce. Edie and I exchange relieved sighs.

'Booze,' Edie mouths to me. 'I need booze.'

'You're pregnant,' I mouth back when my mother has turned away.

'You're driving!' she silently spits in return.

'I've bought some Blue Nun,' Cecilia says. I'm sure she can read minds. 'It's a lovely drop of wine. Nice and sweet. I'm glad it's back on the shelves. It was very popular in the seventies.'

So was Gary Glitter, and look how he turned out. Cecilia sits down and we all help ourselves to lunch. Edie and I take the smallest portions we can manage while still appearing polite.

'Cheers,' Edie says and knocks back her Blue Nun in one go. We both reluctantly start to eat, but my mother doesn't join us. Instead, she picks at her food with her fork.

Edie and I eyeball each other nervously.

Cecilia puts down her fork, clinking it against her plate as if she's calling us to order. She coughs delicately into her napkin and lowers her eyes. 'I have something I want to discuss with you,' she says.

The lumpy mash sticks in my throat. Normally she waits until after the apple crumble, so this must be desperately important if she can't wait to spit it out. Edie and I wait expectantly—each of us hoping that it's going to be the other one who's for the high jump.

'I'm getting married,' my mother announces without further preamble.

The lumpy mash goes down the wrong hole and I cough loudly, grabbing at my wine to glug while Edie bangs me on the back.

'I thought it would come as a surprise,' our unruffled parent says.

Surprise? I couldn't be more surprised if she'd told me that Boy George had decided to change sides and get married. 'Married?' I splutter. 'Married?'

My mother smiles and exudes an air of gentility.

'Who to?' I manage to spit out. 'Who to?'

'A very nice gentleman,' my mother says with a twinkle in her eye that I've never *ever* seen before. My mother hates men. All of them.

'Regis Philbin,' my sister mouths. 'I told you!'

'His name is John and he's a retired architect.' Our mother pats her hair. 'He's a lay preacher at the church and a magistrate. Very respected,' she says in hushed tones. 'He has a top-of-the-range Volvo and a weekend bungalow in Suffolk.'

My mother has hit the jackpot. The first man she's set her sights on in twenty-odd years and she's come up with three cherries.

'Wow!' I say.

'Fuck me!' Edie mouths.

'I heard that, Edith.' My mother bats not one eyelid. 'You're not too old to have your mouth washed out with soap.'

'Congratulations.' I raise my glass to her. 'When's the big day?'

'Soon,' she says. 'And I hope you won't be disappointed, but we're flying to Antigua to get married on the beach. Just the two of us.' She gives herself a cosy little hug. 'John is very romantic like that.'

Even better! No chance of being pressed into service as overgrown bridesmaids.

'Well,' I say. 'This calls for a toast.' Edie slugs some more Blue Nun into her glass and we all chink them together. 'To marriage!'

'To marriage!'

I'm glad that I no longer have to explain to her that I'm moving from *My Baby* to *My Divorce* or I *would* get a dressing-down re the sanctity of marriage.

My sister and I get up and give her a hug. 'I'm really pleased, Mum,' I say. And I am; she's been alone for far too long. From a purely selfish point of view, it also means that I no longer have to worry as much about leaving her. I just hope she doesn't offer to cook for Regis—John—before the wedding.

'Dinner's getting cold,' my mother says, as if she's not the one who caused the hiatus.

'Well,' I say, digging Edie sharply in the ribs. 'We both have little announcements too.'

'You first,' Edie says.

Thanks. I take a deep breath. 'I'm going back to Nepal.'

'For a holiday?'

'Permanently.' I hope. My mother recoils slightly. 'You see, I've met someone too.'

'What does he do for a living?'

Ah, the important things first! I'm not sure Dean has quite the same credentials as my mother's catch. 'He's a conservationist and trekking guide.'

My mother looks very worried. I can't really elaborate on this. Mum, he digs latrines, plants cabbages and earns less than thirty dollars a month—but, hey, he can do some extraordinarily athletic things in a very small tent.

'He's great,' I say.

'And does he love you?' There's a question.

'Yes. I think he does.'

'It's a very long way to go for "think", Lyssa.'

'I've got a teaching post out there,' I say. 'That's just as important to me.' How can I explain that I need to do this? I need to get away. I need to be in a place where I'm not frightened to look over my shoulder, where I'm not just living to pay my mortgage, where I can be surrounded by children every day, children who might just need me.

My mother looks horrified. 'You're not going to be living in a mud hut in the middle of nowhere, are you?'

'No. No. No.'

Edie nudges me.

'Yes,' I say. 'Actually, I am.' I can feel myself smiling and it spreads right inside.

'When am I going to see you?' my mother says, anguish creasing her brow. 'How will I visit you?'

'Get on a plane. It isn't Outer Mongolia.' I pause. 'Well, it nearly is.'

My mother turns her attention to my sister. 'And you're remarkably quiet, Edie.'

'I'm pregnant,' my sister blurts out.

Cecilia puts her hand to her forehand. 'I saw you holding hands with that flowery man in the restaurant,' she says. 'I trust you've nothing else you want to say to me?'

'No,' Edie says, looking shame-faced.

I glance at Edie, but she won't meet my eyes. My mother is excluding me too.

My mother dabs at her mouth and then folds her napkin, placing it on the table with a practised move. 'Then I'll say nothing more about it either.'

Edie looks suitably relieved. Wait until I get hold of her.

'Well,' my mother says. 'Seven grandchildren.'

'Seven is a very lucky number in some cultures,' I pipe up with false good cheer.

'Not in ours,' my mother says, as crisp as her linen.

Edie's head sinks lower.

Our troublesome parent reels slightly as she gets up from the table. 'Though I do think a little toast is in order. I'll get some sherry.' It'll be the same bottle she's had in the cupboard since last Christmas.

My sister goes to finish her Blue Nun, but my mother snatches it away from her. 'That's the last of your alcohol for a while,' she says. 'Elderflower cordial for you, young lady.'

Edie grimaces. Cecilia leaves the room.

'Is that as close as I'm going to get to "congratulations"?'

'Looks like it.' I stare at my sister. 'Flowery man?'

'Pip,' she says.

'Holding hands?'

'The holding hands bit was purely incidental.'

'I'm glad to hear it.'

My sibling meets my stare and ups it to a challenge. 'I was actually asking him to have an affair with me.'

'Right,' I say, feeling my breath catch. I've known Edie for long enough to judge that she's not joking. 'And is he going to?'

'No,' my sister continues. 'He said he wouldn't touch me with a bargepole and that he was in love with you.'

'Oh.' I need more Blue Nun too. 'He said that?'

Edie purses her lips. 'Something along those lines.'

'Good.' Or do I mean bad?

I wish my mother would hurry up with that sherry. I sink back into my chair, mind whirring. 'It's been a bit of a day for shocks, hasn't it?'

'Yes,' Edie agrees.

I'm not sure what else to say.

Chapter eighty-one

That's about it then, really. I've booked my ticket on the cheapo, cheapo airlines and am due to fly off to my new life later this afternoon. Ooo. How scary is that? I left *My Baby* with a modicum of fuss and a cheque for two and a half thousand pounds, which has more than funded my placement. I think they were glad to give me the money to get rid of me once and for all. Monica and Charlotte shed a few tears and promised to email me, but maybe they'll grow tired of it when I can't provide them with a steady stream of gossip.

It's a bright, sunny winter's day, pretending with all its heart that it's spring, and I feel like whistling. My trusty rucksack has been pressed into service again, so much sooner than it ever expected. I imagine it was looking forward to a long, languishing retirement in the back of my understairs cupboard—it just goes to show that you should always expect the unexpected. And I feel this is a good time to be leaving. My sister is going to be well and truly preoccupied with preparations for her new arrival, and I don't feel guilty about abandoning my mother now that she's turned over a new leaf and is no longer a man-hater but is getting hitched to a well-heeled Regis Philbin lookalike. It's all happened so quickly that I haven't really had time to sit and contemplate my actions—which is just as well, as I could get a severe case of cold feet otherwise.

All my clothes are laid out on the bed as I try to decide which few articles from my current life I can't live without. Surprisingly few of them really. There's an uncertain knock at the door and Jake puts his head round.

'Hi.' I see him take in the jumble. He shuffles into my room and lurks awkwardly by the door. 'So you're really going?'

'Yes.' Jake and I have been studiously avoiding contact with each other for the last few days.

'And there's nothing I can do to change your mind?'

'No,' I say softly.

'Thought not.' He gives me a weary smile. 'Can I at least take you to the airport?'

I shake my head. 'I'd rather go on my own,' I say. 'I've got a few things to do on the way.'

'I've drawn out half of our savings from the bank.' Jake holds out a wad of money. 'This is yours. I thought you might need it.'

'Thanks.' I'm not sure that I will need it. Where I'm going there's nothing to spend money on, but I do value the gesture. My meals will be provided for me and I get a weekly allowance for personal expenditure from the charity—which amounts to about five pounds. I've persuaded Monica that she might want to run a couple of articles about pregnancy in different parts of the world in the hope that I can write them to supplement my meagre income or to put some money away for a rainy day.

Unspoken words hang silently between us. 'What do you want to do about the house?' he asks.

'Can you afford to stay here alone?'

'Yes,' he says. 'The new job comes with a great salary package.' Jake tries to sound upbeat. 'We would have been able to have anything we wanted. Well...nearly anything.'

We avoid looking at each other.

'I might sell it and move somewhere bigger,' he says with a flash of bravado that doesn't quite ring true.

'There's no need to do anything hasty.' I'm a fine one to talk. 'I don't need my share of the money from the house yet,' I say. I have the offer of lodgings with my job if I need them. I've explained my situation to the voluntary organisation I'll be attached to and, in theory, they're trying to place me near Dean's village, but I'll have to wait and see. In practice I've agreed to be sent anywhere, as there are teacher shortages all over the Himalayas. I could be nestling in the foothills of Everest this time next week. And I wonder what Neve would think about that. 'Let's just see how it goes.'

'Well, it will go up in value if nothing else,' Jake says, reverting to the British way of viewing their homes as commodities. 'And if you need to come back...want to come back,' he mumbles, 'you've always got a place here.'

'I appreciate that.' And then to get onto less dodgy ground, 'When do you start your new job?'

'Next week.' He sounds brighter. 'I'm looking forward to it. It'll take my mind off...things.'

'I hope it goes well,' I say. 'I'm sure you'll be a big success.'

'I'd rather you were staying here to share it with me.'

'Well...'

'Look—' Jake picks at his fingernails, 'if this doesn't work out...for whatever reason...then I'll be waiting.' His eyes fill with tears. 'I'll be waiting.'

I go to him and hug him, kissing him gently. 'Don't wait for me,' I say.

'They say that if you love someone you should set them free, and if they really love you they'll come back to you.'

'I don't think I'll be coming back.'

Jake puts his finger to my lips to hush me. 'I can live in hope.' He breaks down and cries in my arms. 'I'm sorry,' he says.

'Me too.'

'This guy's a very lucky bloke.' Jake sniffs away his tears. His voice is cracking with emotion. 'I was too,' he says. 'I just wish I'd had the sense to realise it earlier.'

He holds me tightly and I wonder if either of us will ever be able to let go.

Chapter eighty-two

I'm not sure how much more emotion I can stand. My mother, Edie and Daisy are crying. We are all squashed into Edie's kitchen.

'But *why* are you going away?' Daisy is inconsolable.

'I'm going to teach children who need me.'

'*We* need you!' With a dramatic gesture, she wipes her runny nose on her hand and rubs it on my sleeve. I guess this is something that I may have to get used to in my new role as a teacher of small, snotty beings. My oldest niece, Kelly, is out. She chose to miss saying goodbye to me as she'd had a better offer of a date with the local teen heart-throb and, despite Edie's protestations and remonstrations, Kelly decided her favourite aunt could wait whereas Daniel Evans might not. Such is the fickle world of teenagers. My two nephews were completely unconcerned about my imminent departure and barely took their attention from the television and the antics of *SpongeBob SquarePants* to acknowledge the announcement. Anna very rarely shows any emotion, but quietly retreated to the sanctuary of her room, and Archie is too young to care about anything other than where his next meal is coming from. It's strange when you consider yourself at the centre of someone's universe and yet you can spin out of their galaxy without it causing much more than a blip on the radar of their lives.

My mother, however, is going to make sure that I suffer. Her white linen handkerchief is being pressed into good service. She is sitting at the kitchen table, sobbing delicately. John, the retired architect, my mother's paramour, is lingering on the fringes of our conversation, not quite included in the family strife yet. He has one hand on my mother's shoulder and another wrapped round a mug of Edie's builder's tea—so I can see that she's not standing on ceremony with him. John has kind eyes and flecks of steel grey in his hair. He looks like more than a match for my mother.

'I hope *this man* realises exactly what you're giving up for him,' my mother says crisply.

'Of course he does.' But he doesn't, primarily because I haven't yet told him. I just thought I'd turn up and see how it goes. Is that reckless? It feels like it.

'I think it's a wonderful idea,' John says bravely—which earns him a glare from my mother. 'Do something meaningful while you're young. I'm sure it will be marvellous.' He pats my mother's shoulder. 'Mrs Devereux's daughter, Colette, was a well-respected lawyer, and she gave it all up to work at a women's refuge in Egypt.'

My mother beams, her tears suddenly arrested. Her hand goes to her pearls. 'Really?' Mrs Devereux runs the local Women's Institute and is 'high up' in the church hierarchy. John winks at me. I love this man already. He has just provided my mother with a whole new world of kudos. Anything Mrs Devereux's daughter can do, hers can do better! I can see it whirring in my mother's brain—helping needy children must surely carry more clout than helping needy adults.

Lee is leaning against the fridge in his kitchen nursing a bottle of beer instead of his usual hammer. 'Who's Edie going to ring when she's in a panic about her morning sickness or some other girly nonsense?' my brother-in-law asks.

'She's had six kids already,' I point out. 'She knows a hell of a lot more about these things than me. All I've had is the theory from a weekly letters page. I'm sure she'll manage.'

My sister has taken to tying a jumper round her waist to hide her bump. Not that she has one—she still looks like a stick insect—but I know from past experience that it won't be long before her feet disappear from view. She comes and wraps herself around me. 'I'll miss you,' she cries.

'I'll miss you too,' I whisper into her hair.

'You won't be around when my bump's born,' she complains.

I hate to say that the more children she has, the less of an event it becomes for me. And I haven't had the customary pangs of longing that have accompanied all of Edie's other pregnancies. Maybe it will do us both good for me not to be so closely involved in this one. Or, in a few months' time, I might regret not being around—but either way, we'll have to live with it. I'm sure that in different ways we'll both have more than enough to occupy us.

I glance at my watch. 'I'd better be going.'

Edie, my mother and Daisy burst into fresh bouts of weeping and it's all I can do to drag myself out of the kitchen.

My lovely brother-in-law comes to my rescue. 'Bye, sis,' he says, kissing me warmly as he squeezes me.

My voice is about to give up on me. 'Look after her,' I say. 'Tell her you love her every day.'

'I will.'

Daisy takes the pink, sparkly scrunchy from her ponytail and hands it to me. 'Take thith to remember me by, Aunty Lytha,' she says solemnly.

I give her a big hug. 'I will.' I pull back my hair and slip on the scrunchy.

My mother forces herself to her feet. She takes me in her arms and holds me tightly. 'Be careful,' she says.

'I hope the wedding goes well.' I choke back my tears. 'Get Edie to email me some photos.'

She holds me away from her and studies my face as if trying to commit it to memory. 'I never thought you would do anything like this.'

I try to shrug lightheartedly. 'Me neither.'

I hug her for the last time before moving towards the door. 'Bye.'

Edie follows me and throws her arms around me again. 'He'd better be good to you,' she warns, 'or he'll have me to answer to.'

'I'll tell him that.'

Edie lowers her voice. 'Did you speak to Pip yet?'

'I'm going there on my way to the airport.'

'Give him my love,' Edie says.

'No,' I answer. 'Save your love for your husband.'

'Point taken.' Edie smiles ruefully. 'Who's going to keep me on the straight and narrow when you're gone?'

I pat where her bump will soon be. 'That will keep you out of mischief for a while,' I note. 'Besides, I can always nag by email.'

'Make sure that you do,' she says and we both burst into tears again.

Chapter eighty-three

So much for my noble ideas of casting off my old life—despite my best efforts, most of it seems to have sneaked into my back-pack, which now weighs a ton.

I get off the tube and plod my way to Pip's house. I'm glad to see his motorbike chained to the railings outside on the pavement. Hopefully, it means he's at home.

After knocking at the door, I wait with mounting trepidation. This is the first time Pip and I have met after Edie's revelations, and it seems to put a different slant on our relationship. I don't know why it should, but it does, so there.

Pip opens the door. He's bare-chested and wearing just sweats and I can feel the heat glowing on my face. His hair is all messed up and he tries to smooth it down. He looks fairly taken aback and I don't think his surprise is confined to the gargantuan size of my rucksack.

'Hi,' Pip says with a broad, but very confused smile. 'Travelling light?'

'I'm on my way to the airport.'

'Oh.' His face falls. 'Then you'd better come in.'

I struggle through the door with my unwieldy encumbrance and then busy myself trying to shrug it off my shoulders.

'This is Lena,' Pip says.

In wrestling with my distracting load, I'd failed to notice the extraordinarily beautiful and dishevelled-looking girl draped in the corner of Pip's sofa. It's December and she's wearing a skimpy camisole and very short shorts. She's also eating something white and creamy rather pornographically.

'Oh,' I say. 'Hi.'

Lena nods and waves her spoon at me. If I'd arrived a few minutes ago I might well have caught them at it.

I lower my voice. 'I should have phoned first.' Now I'm the one who's confused. 'I didn't mean to disturb you.'

'You didn't,' Pip says.

'I'll go if this is a bad time.'

'It isn't,' he insists. Then the penny drops. 'Well, it is if you want to talk to Simon.' He glances across at the pretty young thing. 'Lena is Simon's girlfriend.'

We both grin cheesily at Lena, who smiles back vacantly.

'Come into the kitchen.' Pip takes my arm and steers me in the right direction.

I lower my voice even further and leaning towards Pip, I murmur, 'I thought Simon was gay.'

'So did I.'

'Ooo.'

'Lyssa,' Pip says with a sigh, 'the ways of the world constantly amaze me.'

'I thought she was your...well...'

'I know,' he says with a bemused shake of his head. 'You might have credited me with better taste.'

We both exchange a furtive look.

'Have you got time for coffee?' he says, turning away from me.

I slide into one of the seats, remembering the last time I was here drinking coffee in less pleasant, but equally strange circumstances.

'No,' I say. 'I've literally popped in to say goodbye.'

'That sounds very final.'

'I'm going back to Nepal.'

He rocks on his heels slightly before recovering his composure. 'I'm pleased for you,' he says.

Jake has told me about his legendary poker face. Keep it all in, give nothing away. 'Are you?'

'Ah,' he says. 'So my blundering "confession" has finally clicked. I wondered how long it would take.'

'I had no idea. . . .'

'Well, at least it proves I'm not the only one who's slow on the uptake.'

'Edie told me about your lunch,' I say. 'The edited version.'

'How edited?'

'I know that she threw herself at you and that you kindly declined.'

Pip laughs. 'It was a bit more subtle than that.'

'Was it?' I say. 'That's not like my sister.'

'Well, we had a nice lunch, anyway.'

'She's got a nice souvenir to remember it by too.'

Pip looks puzzled.

'She's pregnant,' I tell him.

'Wow!'

'Yes. She blames you completely,' I add. 'I think she took your advice about having a wild night out far too literally.'

'Oh no!' He puts his head in his hands. 'I must give her a call.'

'Maybe it's best not to.'

'Maybe not,' he agrees. 'But give her my regards. She's a great woman.' He studies his feet. 'But not quite as great as her big sister.'

I don't know what to say.

'I guess Edie spilled the beans?'

'Yes,' I say weakly. 'It makes a change from her burning them.'

'And there was me thinking you'd got the razor-sharp brain of a super sleuth.'

We both laugh. 'No,' I say. 'When it comes to love, I seem to be extremely dim-witted.'

'I have to ask this.' Pip rakes his hair. 'Would it have made any difference if you'd known how I felt any earlier?'

'I don't know,' I admit. 'If I hadn't met Dean...' I tail off pathetically.

'One man too late.' Pip looks pained. 'I'm not sure if that makes me feel better or worse. Particularly when it was me who suggested you do something radical. I didn't think you'd go heading off to Nepal.' He gives a short laugh. 'I seem to have a knack of making inappropriate suggestions to women, which they then stupidly act on.'

'I guess there are complications with Jake too,' I suggest.

'Ah, Jake.' Pip sighs. 'Didn't the late great Elvis Presley sing about it—"The Girl of My Best Friend"? It must be a common phenomenon.' Pip gives me a wry look. 'Trust me to succumb to it. I wanted to make sure that you had every chance to go back to Jake if you wanted to. I now get the feeling that in doing so, I shot off my own bloody foot.'

'I think you're a really great bloke,' I say.

'With an appalling sense of timing.' Neither of us can deny that.

I try to offer some consolation. 'All my friends think you're irresistible.' And my sister, apparently.

'But not you?'

'I've never really thought about you...like that,' I flounder.

'I think that speaks volumes.'

I don't really know what else I can say. 'I could give you some phone numbers,' I offer.

Pip laughs. 'I'd rather make a bollocks of my own love-life, if you don't mind.'

'You've been fantastic. If things had been different...'

'Who knows?' He shrugs, throwing his hands in air.

'I want us to stay friends. Good friends.'

'Hey,' Pip says. 'If that's what I have to settle for, then so be it.'

I stand up and fuss with my preparations to leave.

'What do I do now? I don't know whether to shake your hand or grab you and ravish you while I have the chance,' he admits.

'Somewhere in between, I think.' I lick my lip nervously.

'Just don't do that licky-lip thing,' he warns, 'or I might not be responsible for my own actions.'

We study each other across the expanse of his kitchen, both of us wondering what might have been. Pip comes to me and, taking both of my hands in his, he kisses me tenderly. 'If you ever need anything,' he says, 'make sure that you call me.'

I tear myself away from him.

'Have a blast,' Pip says. 'And tell that man he's a lucky bastard.'

And that makes my heart do an unhealthy lurch. Because the only person on the planet who doesn't yet know of my impending long-term visit to Nepal is Dean.

Chapter eighty-four

I'm too stunned—and too puffed out—to speak. I'm finally here and my brain is struggling to catch up with my body. I've already walked for over three hours, but each bend is taking me closer to Dean. The idea was to surprise him, but I'm getting more and more worried that like Shirley Valentine—when she jacked in everything and turned up back in Greece only to see her lover schmoozing another woman—that the surprise will be on me. Supposing in the intervening few weeks, he's shacked up with one of the villagers or found himself another equally accommodating trekker? Or what if something's happened and he's hot-footed it back to California? Or what if when he sees me again he changes his mind?

But for me things haven't changed. My feelings for Dean remain the same. I'm all of a wobble and my senses have gone into overload mode. And, if anything, the scenery is more fantastic and more overblown than I've remembered it. The snow-tipped mountains are higher and more impressive, the sky reflects the rich blue hue of the Himalayan poppies, the white clouds froth like the foam on the Mardi Khola River. As I weave my way through the rice paddies to Dean's village, I can feel the joy of it seeping into my bones again.

I spent the first night in Kathmandu, which was supposed to help me recover from my jet lag, but I'm too ecstatic and wired to have jet lag. What's the opposite of jet lag? Because that's what I've got. My body is one big adrenaline surge. They could run the entire electricity grid in Kathmandu off me. I couldn't believe that I was so close to Dean and yet still so far. The people at the headquarters of Teacher Placements in Nepal were fab when I presented myself to them all washed and scrubbed and looking suitably teacherish the next morning and, miracle upon miracle, have found me a placement which is in a village right near to Dean. A measly hour's walk away! Which in Nepalese terms is a hop, skip and a very small jump.

I have a week before I start my training and I hope that will give me plenty of time to get reacquainted with the object of my desire. Then I'll spend six weeks in Kathmandu doing teacher training at a local orphanage. How difficult will that be? All those gorgeous, smiling faces appealing to me with their saucer eyes. I know before I even start that I'll want to take half of the kids home with me. I'm also doing a crash course in speaking Nepalese, which is great as my current knowledge extends no further than *'Namaste.'* After that I take up my permanent placement. I can't wait! I just hope someone else—who shall remain nameless—is half as excited as I am.

If my knees weren't aching so much from walking, then I'm sure they'd be knocking. The closer I get to Dean, the more I'm worried that this was a really bad idea. Maybe I should have emailed or sent him a telegram or something to say that I was planning to descend on him. As it is, I'm woefully unannounced and beginning to regret it.

I stop at the top of a hill, panting to get my breath back and looking down on the grassy sweep that serves as a road into the village. A few more minutes and I'll be there. This is not a good moment to be wracked by doubts. The village is quiet, peaceful and serene. The most exuberant movement comes from the billowy white clouds skipping across the sky high above the mountains. A few chickens cluck and pick their way across the grass, the marigolds from the Festival of the Brothers are still strung out between the houses, slightly faded but no less beautiful, a handful of children are playing a game that looks like chequers with pebbles outside the thatched hut of the only café.

I take my courage in both hands and set off towards Dean's house. I've come too far to be able to cope with rejection now. As I approach the last slope towards the village, the familiar cry of *'Gora! Gora!'* comes from the children. Foreigner! Foreigner! And I wonder how much longer they will be shouting that to me now that this beautiful part of the world is to be my home.

They crowd round me, tugging at my hands, joyfully shouting, *'Namaste!'* and pulling me down the street. And it's nice to know that some of them recognise me from my visit to the school and the festival celebrations—but then I guess they don't get that many blondes who pass this way twice. I try to head towards Dean's house, but the children are insistent and pull me in the other direction.

I can hear the haw-haw call of the threshers working the oxen in the fields as the last of the golden harvest is being gathered. A group of villagers is helping to pile the threshed millet into slender towering stacks and on top of one of the mounds is an unmistakable figure. He stands out a mile amid the small, dark Nepali men. His tee-shirt is stained with sweat, face frowning with concentration as he works hard hauling the bales of straw to the top of the haystack.

The children, still shouting and laughing, pull me faster and faster until we're running down the hill, full tilt towards the field. My heart is racing faster than I am. The men stop and look up at the noise. Dean puts down his bale of straw and straightens up, shading his eyes against the piercing sun.

'Gora! Gora!' the children cry again.

And suddenly there's a look of recognition on Dean's face and he's scrambling down the haystack as fast as his legs can take him. 'Lyssa!'

He runs across the field, clearing the low wall surrounding it in one mighty bound.

'Dean!' A big, unwieldy lump of emotion blocks my throat.

My lover doesn't slow down at all as he catches me and sweeps me into his arms, twirling me round and round until the sky and the fields blur into one and I'm deliriously dizzy. Gently, he puts me down and takes my face in his hands.

'Do you know how much I've missed you?' he says.

'I missed you too.'

We attract quite a crowd as the villagers, all thoughts of work forgotten, are flocking from the surrounding fields to form an inquisitive circle around us, familiar smiling faces whom I recognise from the festival.

'I knew you'd come back,' he says.

'I'm here to stay.' I can hardly speak. 'If you want me to.'

'If you stay, you'll have to marry me,' he warns seriously. 'It's the correct protocol.'

I grin at him. 'I think I can live with that.'

'So you'll marry me?'

Tears flow down my cheeks. 'Yes.'

Dean shouts out with joy. 'I have dreamed of you saying that!'

He kisses me full on the lips and, at this moment, I don't care whether it's the correct protocol to show such overt affection in public or not because I'm drowning in the sheer bliss of it. And I don't think the villagers care either as a cheer goes up and familiar strains of Nepali songs start up as they dance round us and shower us with marigold petals.

Dean slides his arm round my waist. 'It looks as if we may be having an impromptu festival, the future Mrs Macaulay.'

'That's fine by me,' I say, cuddling into him. We gaze out at the snow-capped mountains and the breeze lifts my hair. I feel my soul settle. 'Because I really think that we've got something to celebrate.'

What if you could have it both ways?

New from the author of *Milkrun*
Sarah Mlynowski

Me vs. Me

Gabby Wolf has a tough choice in front of her. Will she choose married life in Phoenix, or a career in Manhattan? If only she could have it all. Maybe her wish is about to come true.

On sale August 2006.

Available wherever paperbacks are sold.

www.RedDressInk.com

RDI588TR

It all begins with Paris…

21 Steps to Happiness

F. G. Gerson

Written by a fashion insider, this novel brings you behind the seams, and delivers the dish on life on (and off) the Paris runway.

On sale wherever trade paperbacks are sold.

www.RedDressInk.com

RDI583TR

Are you getting it at least once a month?

Here's how: Try RED DRESS INK books on for size & receive two FREE gifts!

The Jinx
by Jennifer Sturman

Loves Me, Loves Me Not
by Libby Malin

YES! **Send my two FREE books.** There's no risk and no purchase required—ever!

Please send me my two FREE Red Dress Ink® novels. After receiving my free books, if I don't wish to receive any more, I can return the shipping statement marked "cancel". If I don't cancel, I will receive 1 brand-new novel every month and be billed just $10.99 per book in the U.S. or $13.56 per book in Canada, a savings of 15% off the cover price (plus 50¢ shipping and handling per book).* I understand that accepting the free books places me under no obligation to buy any books. I can always return a shipment and cancel at any time. Even if I never buy another Red Dress Ink novel, the two free books are mine to keep forever.

161 HDN EFZY 361 HDN EFUZ

Name (PLEASE PRINT)

Address Apt. #

City State/Prov. Zip/Postal Code

Not valid to current Red Dress Ink subscribers.

Want to try another series? Call 1-800-873-8635 or visit www.morefreebooks.com.

In the U.S. mail to: The Reader Service, 3010 Walden Ave., P.O. Box 1867, Buffalo, NY 14240-1867
In Canada mail to: The Reader Service, P.O. Box 609, Fort Erie, ON L2A 5X3

*Terms and prices subject to change without notice. Sales tax applicable in N.Y. Canadian residents will be charged applicable provincial taxes and GST. All orders subject to approval. Offer limited to one per household. Credit or debit balances in a customer's account(s) may be offset by any other outstanding balance owed by or to the customer. Please allow 4 to 6 weeks for delivery. ® and ™ are trademarks owned and used by the trademark owner and/or its licensee.

RED DRESS INK™

© 2004 Harlequin Enterprises Ltd.

RDI06TR